*These busine...*
*claim their w...*
*lad...*

# TAMING THE TYCOON?

**Three bestselling authors deliver three glamorous, contemporary stories that stretch after office hours!**

We're proud to present

MILLS & BOON

# Spotlight

*a chance to buy collections of bestselling novels
by favourite authors every month – they're
back by popular demand!*

# TAMING THE TYCOON

The Tycoon's Temptation
**KATHERINE GARBERA**

Tempting the Tycoon
**CINDY GERARD**

Having the Tycoon's Baby
**ANNA DePALO**

MILLS & BOON®
*Pure reading pleasure*™

*This collection is first published in Great Britain 2008.
Harlequin Mills & Boon Limited,
Eton House, 18-24 Paradise Road, Richmond, Surrey TW9 1SR*

TAMING THE TYCOON © Harlequin Books S.A. 2008

The publisher acknowledges the copyright holders of the
individual works, which have already been published in the UK
in single, separate volumes as follows:

*The Tycoon's Temptation* © Katherine Garbera 2002
*Tempting the Tycoon* © Cindy Gerard 2003
*Having the Tycoon's Baby* © Anna DePalo 2003

*ISBN: 978 0 263 86111 2*

064-1008

*Printed and bound in Spain
by Litografia Rosés S.A., Barcelona*

# The Tycoon's Temptation

## KATHERINE GARBERA

## KATHERINE GARBERA

Is a transplanted Florida native who is learning to live in Illinois. She's happily married to the man she met in Fantasyland and spends her days writing, reading and playing with her kids. She is a past recipient of the Georgia Romance Writers Maggie Award.

Women friends are important to me,
and I wanted to take this moment to say
thanks to some of the incredible women
who have touched my life.

Nancy Thompson, Francesca Galarraga and
Mary Louise Wells: Thanks for being my
cheering section, crying shoulder and
laughing buddies – in short, my friends. Without
you ladies, I don't think I'd be sane!

Linda Beardsley, Donna Sutermesiter and
Charlotte Smith: Thanks for always
believing in me.

Jude Bradbury and Susan Hartnett:
Thanks for giving me a strong example to follow.
Thanks somehow seems inadequate, but
it will have to do!

And, too, two little ladies
who influence me by the example of their joy in
life, Courtney Garbera and Katie Beardsley.

ACKNOWLEDGEMENT:

A special thank you to Metsy Hingle, who
shared her knowledge of New Orleans with
me and also some books on her beautiful city.
Any mistakes are my own.

# One

"**M**r. Dexter will see you now."

Lily Stone gathered her day planner and followed the secretary through the walnut paneled door. New Orleans was hot in the middle of August, and she wished she were outside baking in the sun instead of standing in this nicely air-conditioned room.

She'd wasted at least two days trying to meet with Dexter, and she was determined to stay in his office this afternoon until he met with her.

Her heels sank into the thick carpeting as she walked into the office of the CEO of Dexter Resort & Spa, an international hotel company. The entire room was posh and sleek, decorated with chrome-and-glass furniture and the kind of big desk meant to intimidate whoever sat in the guest chair.

It worked.

Her attaché case felt as if it were made of lead instead of leather. It bumped awkwardly against her leg as she approached the large desk. She'd been successfully running her family's business since she was twenty, but she suddenly felt as if this was her first big client. She wore her best suit, a black-and-red affair that her assistant, Mae, said made her look sharp and professional.

Preston Dexter stood to greet her. He held her hand for the required three pumps and then slid away. His palm had been warm against hers, and his long, neatly manicured fingers had made her hand look small and fragile. Just the way she felt.

He smelled of expensive cologne but also of something essentially male. Not unlike her brothers. The thought helped her relax. It didn't matter that this man could buy her house and business with his pocket change. He was just a guy like Dash and Beau.

Except there was something indefinable about him that made him different from Dash and Beau. She stared at his gray eyes for a moment. There was an element of cold calculation in his eyes. An element of world-weary cynicism that her brothers didn't have.

"Ms. Stone, please have a seat. I'm sorry to have kept you waiting."

She doubted he was really sorry. Probably he regretted that she'd spent the afternoon sitting in his lobby, but she knew they were going to have a problem if they didn't talk now. He'd sent back three of her

her, yet he couldn't help but feel a little bit captivated himself. "No."

"Why not?" She asked before he could redirect the conversation.

He tried to think of one person he knew who might call him by a pet name. No one came to mind. He wasn't the type of man who inspired those around him to call him by a sobriquet. Never had been; he'd always been so serious, and intent on making his life a bigger success than his father's. "I'm just not a casual sort of guy around the office."

He stood and picked up his briefcase. Lily shoved her day planner into her attaché and stood, as well. Preston congratulated himself on having brought a close to that line of questioning.

"What about your close friends?" she asked, as they exited his office.

She was losing some of her charm, he thought. He preferred women who looked pretty and said little. She forced him to examine something he didn't really want to—there was a big emptiness in his personal life. Always had been.

"Brit calls me Preston. And I don't have any others who aren't also business associates." Even Brit was a business associate. Preston was a silent partner in the Seashore Mansion.

"That's odd."

"Not really. My work is my life." And he'd learned early on that most people wanted something in exchange for friendship with him—usually money, business advice or social connections.

She pondered that for a minute, worrying her lower lip. Her lips' natural color was a pale pink that reminded him of the roses his mother had always ordered for the breakfast room. Would they taste as soft as those rose petals had felt?

"My business is important to me, too, yet I still have friends away from it," Lily said.

She was charmingly naive to compare her small business to his international corporation. He liked that she didn't fully comprehend the power he wielded in the hospitality industry.

He didn't want to talk about his personal life or the lack of close acquaintances. Instead he wanted to move their conversation back to her. Why had she raised two younger brothers?

"Well, our lifestyles must be different."

She laughed. "I'll say."

He didn't want to like her because he desired her and he knew that emotional entanglements were better left as business transactions.

"I've never met anyone like you."

"Is that good or bad?" she asked.

He realized that seducing Lily would be good for him, because she had the kind of charming innocence that everyone needed to remind them of a better way of life. He knew he was going to seduce her, because for the first time in a long while he felt alive. He looked forward to the challenge of taming the feisty woman.

"I don't know."

The elevator arrived, and they traveled down to the lobby in silence. Joshua, one of his young security men had brought the Jag up and waited for Lily's keys. "We're going to the Van Benthuysen-Elms Mansion on St. Charles."

"Yes, sir."

Lily was busy digging her keys out of her bag. She handed them to Joshua, and he walked away.

"Okay, I'm ready to go," she said.

Preston deftly grasped her elbow and escorted her outside to his waiting car. Even though she was sassy and confident, she might still fall neatly into his hands. It had been a long time since anyone had challenged him on any level. Longer still since a woman had intrigued him on so many.

# Two

Lily knew she must have been temporarily insane to agree to ride anywhere with this man. His car had leather seats, a tracking computer that made adjustments to their travel plan, to avoid traffic, and Vivaldi in surround sound. His touch had traveled through her body like lightning through the night sky. A stark, brief illumination and then nothing but the rumble of aftershocks.

She didn't usually react to men she'd just met this quickly. He invigorated her. He also enervated her, making her skin feel too sensitive, her blood race through her veins and her senses sing.

He'd been impatient with her, and she knew he'd meant to brush her off after the first five minutes or so because she'd dealt before with busy executives. They always wanted top quality, yet they didn't necessarily want to invest the time needed to get it.

But an indefinable thing had passed between them. She felt a connection to this man because, despite what she'd told him, her work was her life, as well.

She felt his eyes on her legs as she tried to smooth her skirt down. Never again was she buying a suit without trying it on. His gaze on her legs brought back the insecurities of girlhood.

It was ridiculous, considering she was a mature woman of twenty-five. She ran a successful antique decorating business and had been operating it on her own since her grandmother had retired to Florida a year ago with her longtime love, Humberto.

She couldn't think when he was watching her. All she could think was that his car cost more than Dash and Beau's college tuition together.

"This is some car."

"I know. I had a hand in the design."

"Really?" she asked. Aside from decorating, the only thing she'd ever designed had been the advertisement she'd run in the phone book, and that had been somewhat limited.

"Yes, I gave them a list of items I wanted included."

He sounded like her brothers had when they'd gotten the exact gift they wanted on Christmas morning. She smiled to herself. What was it about men and cars? "I didn't know you could do that. Do American car makers offer that service?''

''I think most of them will if the price is right. Anything's possible if you're willing to pay for it.''

''I take it you are.''

''Haven't you found that things you want the most have the highest price?'' he asked. He glanced over at her as he cruised to a stop for a red light. She studied the intriguing lines around his eyes. He must spend a lot of time outdoors, she realized.

''No, I haven't.''

''Name one thing worthwhile that isn't costly,'' he said.

She hesitated. Once the conversation went down this avenue, there was no going back to being casual business acquaintances. Something in his gray eyes compelled her to speak from the heart. ''Love.''

The light turned green, and he accelerated, leaving the neighboring car in the dust. ''Love is a child's fantasy. Name something real.''

She couldn't believe his attitude. Without love she'd have nothing in her life. Her brothers' and grandmother's affection grounded her. ''Love is real.''

''Sure it is. And so is the Easter Bunny and Santa Claus.''

''Love is more than the holiday traditions, and it encompasses them, as well. It's the warm feeling that comes from knowing you're not alone in the world.''

''Affection.''

''It's deeper than affection.''

"I'll take your word for it."

"Why don't you believe in love?" she asked.

"Because it can't be bought."

She was silent. There was something about Preston that touched her heart. He made her want to fight battles for him, even though he was the kind of man who'd fight and win his own. He made her want to coddle him and shower him with caring, because there was a big cold dark part of his soul visible in those frozen eyes.

As much as she wanted to mother him, she'd been aware of him as a man. She shivered, remembering the narrowing of his eyes and the practiced warmth of his smile.

And there was something prepared about his charm, she realized. Something that wasn't quite genuine. Almost as if he'd learned how to manipulate women a long time ago and no longer had to think about what he was doing.

"Haven't you ever been in love?"

"No. But I've tried lust a time or two. What about you?"

"No to both of them. But I'm sure that my one true love is out there."

"What makes you so sure?"

His voice was dark and deep, sending shivers of awareness through her. She wondered if the attraction she felt toward him was to blame for her reactions. Or maybe it was the fact that for the first time in seven years she was free. She didn't have to be home by nine

to make sure her brothers had completed their home-
work and were getting ready for bed. She didn't have
to hurry back because Grandmother needed to be reminded to take her medication. She didn't have to answer to anyone save herself, and that scared her.

"I'm sure because my parents found each other."

"Maybe their relationship was a fluke."

"Then why do so many people spend their lives trying to capture that feeling?"

"Because they've been brainwashed into believing
in something that doesn't exist. Each generation passes
on the brainwashing so they don't seem foolish."

"Preston."

He raised one eyebrow. "Prove me wrong."

"How?"

He pulled into the parking lot of the mansion, and
the valet attendant came to park the car. Lily didn't
want to stop their conversation but knew she'd have
to. No matter how fascinating she found their discussion, he was still her client and she needed to remember
that.

She was aware that her views weren't necessarily the
views of her peers, but she'd always believed there was
a man out there waiting for her. A man who'd want to
live in New Orleans with her and help her run the business that had been in her family for three generations.
When the bellman opened the door for her, she exited
the car and waited for Preston.

But as she watched Preston pass his keys to the attendant and walk toward her, she forgot all of that.

Because even though he didn't believe in love, Preston Dexter made her pulse race, her skin tingle and her mouth long for the feel of his.

He pulled her into a small enclave outside of the hotel. "Still want to prove that love exists?"

"Yes."

"You find one example of someone who married for love and only for love and I'll give you your heart's desire."

She wondered if he was willing to pay the price she wanted, because her heart's desire might be this dark man with his cynical world view and fallen-angel eyes.

Preston Dexter seemed like an adventure waiting to happen. The male knowledge of intimacy in his eyes sparked an answering need deep within her femininity and promised more excitement than she'd had in her entire lifetime, and that scared her.

But she hadn't spent a lifetime keeping her family business a success and raising two unruly hellions for nothing. "You're on."

Preston asked the hostess to allow them to visit several of the rooms in the mansion. And though she warned it was against policy, she allowed them to tour the house. Preston gave Lily a list of things he liked and pieces he'd love to see her find for White Willow House. They lingered in one of the drawing rooms. The elegant settee was too small for a modern man but just right for the sweet lady who had perched on it to make her notes.

As well as he knew that Lily would be unable to find a couple who'd married for love alone, he kind of wished she would, because he wanted to give her her heart's desire.

"This place is lovely," Lily said.

"Not as lovely as you," he said. He sincerely meant the words. He'd mastered the art of compliments a long time ago and he'd forgotten how to be genuine, but Lily reminded him. She was charmingly naive about things like love and reality but she knew her stuff when it came to antiques and their worth. She'd spoken easily of the Italian sandstone mantels and the imported tapestries.

"Don't say compliments you don't mean. I'm not one of your society girls who'll believe them," she said.

"I never say anything I don't mean."

She walked toward him like an angel in an erotic dream. Her hips swaying in rhythm with the tapping of her heels on the hardwood floor. His pulse picked up the beat, pounding in time to her movement. She moved like sin itself. And though he was a sinner and easily tempted, he knew she'd entice a saint.

The heat of the day lingered in the house but was nothing compared to the fire Lily started in Preston's body. He didn't know where it started, only that it spread to every part of his being like a wild blaze out of control.

Every time she walked into a room he started to harden, and for once he wasn't certain of his self-mastery. She made a mockery of the possession he'd always had over his reactions. He knew why it didn't bother him: he liked the feeling. There was something forbidden about her.

"Don't flirt with me, Preston. I still believe in happily ever after, and once I find that married couple I'm going to make you believe in it, too."

He wished she could, but he knew himself too well. He had learned hard lessons early on. "We'll see, angel."

She bit her bottom lip, and he ached to take it between his teeth and suckle the sweet fruit of her mouth. He wanted to ravish her mouth and learn her taste so completely that he'd always know it. Though she'd gone from sweet to sassy in her conversation, her lips promised all sass and spunk with the honeyed warmth of woman.

She was innocence, where he was jaded realism. She was sweet light, where he was dark shadow. She was the warm feeling of home, where he was the cold luxury of an empty hotel room.

His body hardened in a sudden rush, and he knew there was no way Lily Stone would remain simply a decorator in his life. She was going to play a part in his personal life, too. His skin tightened and his groin hardened in a rush. He didn't question his success because seduction had always been something he excelled at.

Her eyes widened as they met his, and he knew he'd lost ground on the seduction front because right now he felt elemental and knew that shone on his face. He wanted her with the gut-deep longing that was shockingly new to him. He knew about lust and desire but never had he felt it this intensely.

"Isn't it almost time for your meeting?" she asked, her voice husky with arousal.

He wondered what she'd do if he leaned down and kissed her. Thrust his tongue deep in her mouth the way he wanted to enter her body. It was a ridiculous reaction from a man so coldly controlled and smoothly sophisticated, yet she'd started a chain reaction in him.

"Yes," he said, grasping her arm above the elbow to escort her downstairs. Her flesh was soft under his hand, and she smelled like fresh-cut flowers with the dew still on them.

He walked Lily to her truck even though he knew he'd be late to his meeting. She hadn't said a word since they'd left the mansion.

She looked up at him as she opened the door to her vehicle. Desire danced in her eyes, and she leaned a little closer to him. Double or nothing, he thought.

"Will you have dinner with me tomorrow night?" he asked.

"Why?"

"I want to get to know you better."

"How much better?"

"On this date or in general?"

"In general," she said.

"Then, I want to know you as intimately as a man can know a woman."

"And afterward?"

"What afterward?"

"When you've gleaned all of my intimate secrets, then what?"

"Then life will point us in another direction."

"Separate ones?"

"Yes."

"I see."

"Lily, I'm not a settling-down kind of guy."

"I know."

"That doesn't mean you and I can't enjoy this attraction."

She didn't say anything.

"Why worry about the future? Let's take this one moment at a time. I'm only asking you to eat with me." Even though he knew he was planning to do more than eat. He was planning to seduce this sassy woman into his bed so that he could experience her fire and verve with every part of his body.

"One moment at a time," she said.

"Exactly."

"Okay, dinner, but at my place. Dress casually."

Preston nodded and waited until she climbed inside the cab of the old truck. She looked out of place in her vehicle, but it had been lovingly restored. It made him realize that she was the kind of woman who cherished the past. He'd been running from it all of his life.

She rolled down the window and handed him a business card. "My home address is on the back, come by around seven."

Preston watched her drive away and didn't like the feeling. His mind raced ahead as he plotted a way to have her without giving up himself.

When Lily had called Preston to say she couldn't keep their dinner plans, Preston's first instinct was to spend the night working as he usually did. But he finished early on the job site. He was one of those work-aholic hands-on bosses. Jay had told him he worked too hard and to enjoy some of the sin in the Crescent City. Though she'd done nothing to encourage it, the image of Lily appeared in his head.

He had his secretary call Christian's Restaurant on Iberville and had swung by to pick up dinner. He told himself it was just good business to stop and see how the work was progressing on his resort, but he wanted to see Lily again. Wanted to prove to himself that she wasn't as sassy and sexy as he remembered. Wanted to prove to himself that she was nothing more than a subcontractor.

He pulled into the parking lot behind Sentimental Journey. Her shop had Old World elegance and New Orleans charm. Priceless antiques sat next to Mardi Gras masks and beads. It reminded him a little of the lady who owned and operated the place.

He sat in his eighty-five-thousand-dollar car listening to Mozart and doubting his actions. He'd always steered a true course to his destination, and this was an unplanned side trip. One that made no sense to the bottom line.

He thought about leaving, but that felt cowardly to him. He was a man's man. A man of action. Not someone who turned tail and ran. He could handle this situation and this woman.

He exited his Jaguar and pocketed the keys. The spicy Cajun food smelled aromatic. He figured she'd let him in for the food, if for nothing else.

He knocked on the screen door at the back. Harry Connick, Jr., played softly in the background. Lily glanced up and froze. He'd caught her off guard. Something he would wager not many people did.

"I brought dinner." Great. He sounded like some lame guy from a computer-dating service.

"I...uh...thanks."

"Can I come in?"

"Sure. Let me finish with this varnish, and I'll get the door."

He watched her through the mesh screen, feeling the way he had as a boy when he'd scored an unexpected soccer goal against an especially fierce rival team. The only thing he could imagine that would equal the sensation would be to kiss her. To feel her energy and passion up close and personal.

# Three

_____

"Thanks for bringing dinner," Lily said, as she opened the door for him.

"No trouble."

Her workroom was cluttered with antiques, most of them in a sad state of disrepair. "There's a table upstairs where Mae and I usually eat lunch."

"Lead on."

Lily was aware of how faded and worn her jean overalls were as she preceded Preston up the stairs. Though she knew it was probably only her imagination, she felt his gaze on her backside as she climbed the stairs.

The attic was large and spacious, sometimes serving as a guest room for her family when they all visited for Mardi Gras. There was an old butcher-block table that Lily had found at an estate sale three years ago and some ladder-back chairs she'd bought from a wholesaler last winter.

The kitchenette had a small refrigerator and microwave, and there was a tester bed pushed against one wall, covered with the first quilt Lily had ever made. Two wide windows let in the early-evening sunlight, and a big paddle fan kept the hot air circulating.

"Sorry there's no air-conditioning up here."

Preston removed his suit jacket and tie and rolled up his sleeves. There was a sprinkling of dark hair on his arms and at his neck. Lily wanted to touch it and see if it was as springy as it looked.

She took the dinner bags from Preston and began to set the table with mismatched plates. Preston took a bottle of French wine from one of the bags.

"Do you have a corkscrew?"

"In that basket by the microwave."

"I picked this up last summer at the vineyard in France," he said.

"I've always wanted to do one of those wine-tasting tours in Napa Valley."

"You should. Napa is beautiful."

"Maybe someday."

Lily and Preston took their seats, and the mournful sound of a saxophone from the street drifted through the open windows. Lily closed her eyes, enjoying the music and the scent of the food Preston had brought.

"I really needed a break. Thanks for doing this."

"I didn't mind. I'd been looking forward to seeing you again."

"Too bad you didn't meet me sooner. Then I wouldn't have been postponed on your calendar twice."

He smiled ruefully. "I am a busy man."

"When it suits you to be," she said.

"True."

Preston wasn't the type of man to bring a pizza and beer, Lily thought as she bit into the shrimp Marigny he'd brought from one of the city's most expensive restaurants. The food was delicious, and Lily waited until Preston was halfway through his meal before bringing up the challenge he'd issued her the night before.

"I think I found a couple who married only for love."

"Really?"

"My friend Kelly. I believe you mentioned you know her husband, Brit."

"What makes you believe they married for love?"

"Kelly wouldn't marry a man she didn't love."

"Brit would marry a woman he didn't love."

"You're kidding."

"No. He married her to arrange financing for the mansion. Her family has the connections he needed."

Lily knew what he'd said was true. Kelly was the daughter of one of the wealthiest men in America, but she was also a dreamer. She and Kelly had spent many a night talking about the white knights that would ride up and rescue them.

"But they love each other now."

"Who's to say what's in another man's heart. He does seem to care deeply for her."

"I know it's more than caring."

"How do you know that, Lily?"

"Because he has a picture of her on his desk."

"That proves nothing. I know adulterous men who keep their wives' pictures on their desks."

"There was something in his eyes and in his voice when Kelly was in a room with us."

"Passion."

"Love," she countered.

"I'm not convinced," he said, abruptly.

"I guess I'll keep looking."

"Futilely."

"I'm going to prove you wrong."

The rest of the meal passed in silence. She cleaned the plates while Preston poured the last of the wine into their glasses and sat down on the sofa in front of the window. Lily put on an old Dizzy Gillespie record and joined him to watch the sun set over the city. The night sounds accompanied the sounds of the jazz trumpet.

"How did you end up raising your brothers?"

"My parents died when I was eighteen. My grandmother couldn't handle the boys, so that left me," Lily said. It still hurt to think of her parents gone. She missed them more than she'd ever imagined she could.

"How old were the boys?" he asked.

Lily settled back against the cushions of the old sofa and slid toward Preston. His body heat engulfed her. Knowing she was too close for comfort, she started to move away. She placed her hand on Preston's thigh to scoot forward.

His sharp intake of breath made her look up at him. He watched her with narrowed eyes. Lily longed to be the kind of woman who would say something witty, but she wasn't.

Her pulse beat furiously from her closeness to Preston. Maybe it was the wine. She rarely drank. She only knew her skin felt too tight, and the heat of the evening seemed cool against her skin.

"Sorry," she said. Where had this achy feeling come from?

"No problem, angel," he said, picking up her hand, brushing his lips against the back of it.

Shivers rushed through her, making her squirm. Her blood seemed to run heavier, pooling at the center of her body. Her nipples tightened under her T-shirt and denim overalls.

What had he asked her? Something about the boys ages?

"Beau was fifteen and Dash thirteen."

She had to keep her impulses under control, because she wanted to give into the forbidden sensuality his eyes promised, but couldn't. Preston Dexter wasn't a man who'd settle down. More than anything in the world, Lily wanted a husband to share her life and to give her babies.

She stood and paced to the window, unable to sit by Preston any longer. She wanted to give in to her wild impulses and fling her leg over his lap, straddle his hips and pull his mouth to hers for a deep kiss. But he wasn't the man for her, and her soul warned that heartache would follow.

"What are you afraid of, Lily?"

She glanced at the dark man sitting on her sofa. The man who'd experienced more of life than she even knew existed. A world outside of her beloved antiques and the past that she liked to bring to life.

"You."

"Not me. I represent nothing for you to fear."

She could have hedged. Her gut instinct urged her to, but the raw need in his eyes compelled her to speak honestly. "You make me want to be bold and daring when I never have been."

He smiled slightly, just the tiny curve of his firm mouth. She watched him closely, wishing she were a different kind of woman. The kind who'd really be able to handle the sophistication of Preston.

"Then isn't it time you started living?"

She knew what he wanted her to say, what her body wanted her to say, but her mind wanted self-preservation. "I need more than a summer fling."

He stood and walked to her—a man out of place in this environment but sure of himself in the world. "So do I."

He slid his hands into her hair and tilted her face toward his. The soft exhalation of his breath brushed across her mouth. Her lips tingled. She wanted to taste him and see if that strong sensual mouth would live up to her fantasies.

"Isn't it time you started living life for yourself, Lily?" he asked, and slowly lowered his head.

Unable to believe he had her in his arms, Preston barely brushed his lips against her eyelids and her cheeks. She was sweet and tempting, making a mockery of the control he'd always exercised over his libido.

Gently, because she seemed innocent, he traced her full lower lip, as he'd wanted to since he'd seen her nibble on it nervously in his office. She tasted of the expensive French wine they'd drunk with their meal, bold and rich, but also of the spicy Cajun spices, promising an embrace that would exceed his fantasies.

"Are you going to kiss me?" she asked, breathless. Her breasts brushed his chest lightly with each breath she took. He wanted to crush her to him. To feel the feminine mounds pressed against his chest. To rip away the layers of cloth that separated them and be together the way nature intended for man and woman to be.

"Do you want me to?" he countered. Tracing his tongue around her bow-shaped mouth. He loved the fact that she'd worried her lipstick off again. He was able to taste the very essence of Lily instead of some manufacturer's illusion of what a woman should be.

"Yes," she said on a sigh, her hands closing gently around his shoulders and pulling him closer.

He waited to see if she'd attack his mouth the way most of his dates did, but she didn't. She hesitated, her eyes half-closed and her breath held. He felt the tension vibrate through her.

He bent to her ear and brushed the softest kiss he could right below her lobe. She smelled faintly of flowers and the earthy scent of woman. There was something real about Lily, almost too real. He realized he didn't want her to watch him kiss her.

"Close your eyes," he said.

"Okay." She closed them. He let his gaze trace over her features. They were soft and ladylike. She was so feminine she made him feel like a big brute. The lessons he'd learned from faceless women in the past deserted him, and he could only react with instinct. He had to have her. Had to assert his will over her even if just in this small way.

He took her lower lip between his teeth and suckled there for a moment. The need to know all of her was a dangerous fire in his blood. The plump flesh tasted sweeter than he'd expected. She moaned, and her hands moved restlessly from his shoulders down his back.

He thrust his tongue into her mouth just the tiniest bit, teasing her with the flavor of him. She returned the foray with a tentative thrust of her own. His appetite whetted, he took her mouth deeply, her opened lips inviting him to do so. She held him tight as if afraid of where the embrace was leading.

Preston gave up thinking and reacted. His body ached to feel her softness beneath his. His mind supplied images of what she'd look like naked on that damned tester bed with the twilight spilling in through the windows and the seductive sounds of the saxophone and jazz trumpet filling the air.

She was every temptation he'd ever known. He wanted to act on those desires, but there was also something very sweet and trusting in the way she held him. As if she wasn't sure where things would lead next and he knew that she wasn't very experienced.

He'd suspected it yesterday when she'd kept tugging at her skirt, trying to conceal those long sexy legs. One of which was sliding between his own. He slid his hands down her back, cupping her behind in his hands. Her cheeks were firm and generous as he sank his fingers into her and pulled her closer to his aching flesh.

She rubbed against him without any true rhythm, just the demands of desire coursing through her veins. He had to stop now or her innocence wouldn't matter. They'd be twisting on that old mattress in the deepening night as his instincts urged.

He pulled back, brushing her wet, full lips with a lingering kiss and cradling her close to his aching body. He held her until his pulse stopped racing and his blood no longer rushed in his ears.

"That was one hell of a kiss, Lily."

She twisted in his arms, looking up at him with deep blue eyes that asked for honesty. "Why did you stop?"

"It was either stop now, or stop later on the bed after I'd buried myself deep within you."

"Oh."

"Don't worry, sweet Lily, you're safe with me."

"What if I don't want to be?"

"Don't tempt me, angel, because I'm hanging on to my control by a thread."

"I'm sorry. You're right. I said I didn't want a summer fling."

"You deserve more than that from me, and I don't know if I have it to give."

"How about if I prove that love exists in *your* life instead of in someone else's."

"Do you think you can?"

"I know I can."

"And if you don't."

"Then we'll both have had something rare and beautiful that we wouldn't have experienced otherwise."

"What is that?"

"Each other."

"You think I'm special?" he asked. No one ever had. He'd always been one of many spoiled rich prep-school boys who'd been given too much too soon.

She smiled and her eyes lit like a child being given a treat. "Yes, I do."

He thought she was special, too, but wouldn't tell her. Lily was the kind of girl who cared too deeply, and he was beginning to realize that if she couldn't teach him to love, then he'd teach her to doubt in love.

He didn't want to destroy the part of her that still believed in fairy tales.

Lily knew after that soul-shattering kiss that she'd taken a hell of a gamble, but she couldn't help herself. She felt as if Preston had reached past the barriers she'd used to protect herself all these years. For once she was totally in the present instead of reliving the past as she repaired a walnut, gateleg, William and Mary table. She knew she should focus on her work but all she could remember was his kiss.

He'd seduced her mouth slowly, taking control of her senses and making her willpower seem like a distant dream instead of something she'd clung to while raising her brothers. She'd never been intimate with a man. Never desired to do so, because most of the men she'd dated didn't want the responsibility of raising two boys even if they were almost grown.

Lily had been testing the boundaries of her newfound freedom. She'd dated two men since Beau had left for school last fall, but had found that she wasn't a woman for casual relationships. All these years she'd thought it was the boys keeping her from committing herself to a man, but she'd soon realized it was her own dreams.

All her life she'd been the mother hen. Taking care of those who needed caring, and she'd never met a man with more need than Preston Dexter. He'd stayed in her shop to keep her company and help her finish her

work on a wrought-iron bedstead that would soon be
gracing a lovely Creole cottage just off Bourbon Street.

She'd found the piece in a salvage yard outside the
city earlier in the week, and the new owners of the
cottage had paid double her fee for a rush delivery.
Greedily she'd agreed to do the work, but now she was
questioning whether it was worth it.

Nearly 10 p.m. and she was still dusty and dirty. It
beat returning to her lonely, silent apartment. She
hadn't realized how isolated she'd become from her
friends in the years she'd been raising Dash and Beau.
They'd all either moved on or married and now she
spent most evenings at home reading or working late
in her shop. On the plus side, Preston was still here
with her, proving to her that he wanted more than her
body.

Part of her wondered if that was his seduction plan.
Was she flattering herself to think he had a plan relat-
ing to her? Did he want to lull her into believing that
he cared for her before taking what he desired and leaving her behind? She shook her head. Obviously she was
more tired than she'd thought. She wasn't cynical and
she wasn't planning to be used. She wasn't Mona
Stone's daughter for nothing. And if there was one area
in her life where her mom had control it was over her
men.

She glanced up and found Preston staring at her. She
knew that she'd been looking at him with all the longing of a child looking through a candy shop window.
She cleared her throat and spoke before he could.

"Look at this piece. Can't you just imagine the things it's seen."

Though he'd stayed, he seemed cold and arrogant. Much the same as the distant English noblemen in the gothic novels she loved to read. Would his home be dark and forbidding? It would match his looks and attitude.

"Oh, yes, angel," he said with a distinctive drawl.

Sex again. Growing up in the city that seemed to reek of sin, and not just once a year at Mardi Gras, should have inured her to the things he suggested with his silky tone and bedroom eyes, but it didn't. She'd always been a good Catholic girl.

"Not *those* things."

"What then?" he asked. Preston was polishing a brass wind-chime chandelier that she had to ship to a mansion in Atlanta on Monday.

"You know the life it's seen. Maybe a baby was born between these head- and footboards."

The only time she had a glimpse of his real personality was when he flirted with her. And she was so helplessly inept at it that he made her feel awkward. He winked at her. "I'm sure at least one was conceived."

His words made her hot. She'd been imagining them in that tester bed upstairs: his hard lean body over hers; the sounds of New Orleans pouring through the window with the scents of the Mississippi and the Gulf in the air; the warm breeze caressing their skin as they bonded together.

But she wanted more than sex from any man in her life. She'd never made love to a man, because she believed that love existed and Mr. Right was waiting out there for her. Preston made her doubt herself, and she didn't like that.

"Is sex all you think about?" she asked. Because when he was around it was all she thought about. She forgot about her dreams of getting married, wearing white and having a couple of babies with a nice guy who'd be content to buy a Creole cottage with a white picket fence and raise kids in her hometown.

"Lately it is."

With Preston working beside her on the steamy August night it was easy to believe the desire coursing through her body was something other than just lust. Since it was the one thing he understood, she answered honestly. "Me, too."

"Dammit, Lily, it wouldn't hurt you to lie once in a while."

She looked away. She'd never guarded her words. She'd always spoken straight from the gut and more often than not it had brought more trouble than a ship full of pirates intent on pillaging.

Tucking her polishing cloth into the back pocket of her overalls, she stood. She didn't trust herself around this man. He called to the dangerous part of her that had always longed for adventure but had never been brave enough to set foot outside of Orleans Parish. "Let's call it a night."

He crossed to her and stopped so close she could

count the individual eyelashes surrounding his gray eyes. "I didn't mean that the way it sounded. Your words go straight through me."

For the first time she understood there was more to Preston than he wanted the world to see. She'd suspected it when he'd hatched the love dare, but his words just now confirmed it. Could she break through the barriers he used to protect himself without getting hurt? Did she want to?

He stood so closely that if she leaned forward the tiniest bit, she'd brush his body. She teetered toward him before she realized what she'd done and retreated a half step. "I don't understand this attraction to you, Preston."

He said nothing. She knew he was a man accustomed to dating and bedding women. She'd seen his picture in the society pages since he'd moved to New Orleans in the early summer, but she wasn't used to this type of man. It's just business, she told herself. "I know we'd both be better off apart."

"I don't think I would be," he said.

"Why not?"

"I've been alone too long."

"Me, too," she said softly.

He brushed a butterfly-soft kiss against her forehead. "Don't let me hurt you."

I won't, she thought. But inside she didn't know if she'd be able to protect herself from him. There were emotions he brought seething to the surface of her soul that she'd never grappled with before and honestly didn't know how to control.

# Four

Two days later Lily still wasn't sure what to do about Preston and the attraction she felt for him. She'd invited Preston to accompany her to an antique importer just outside of town. It was a steamy New Orleans day, typical of late summer, and she knew riding in her '59 Chevy truck without air-conditioning would be hot and uncomfortable.

Even though it was ten minutes before they were scheduled to leave, when he was interested in meeting with someone, Preston was always very punctual. And as he slid out of the car, she acknowledged he was always very attractive.

She'd pored over books and the Internet trying to find romantic couples to use to convince him love existed. She didn't know which of them would hold out longer. Her or Preston. He had a secret ally in her traitorous body. She'd woken up in a sweat last night, dreaming of him moving over her in the bed. How was she going to prove love when she was obsessed with sex?

She had her doubts. Love was hard work and in the end she knew that it required effort and belief on the part of both partners in a relationship. Some things were worth the risk, she thought, but her hands continued to sweat and her body tingled.

Preston wasn't a man who'd learn to love easily, but she'd decided she wasn't going to let him fly out of her life as easily as he'd drifted into it. Actually, she thought it hadn't been all that easy. She scooted closer to the workroom window so that she could watch Preston. He stopped to talk to Leroy, her deliveryman.

The deep sounds of his voice drifted with the warm breeze through the open window. Lily closed her eyes and let both wash over her. There was something about a man with a deep voice—

"Va-va-voom!" Mae said from behind her.

"Mae," Lily chided, hoping none of her lustful thoughts were revealed on her face.

"Is he yours?" she asked. Mae wasn't in the market for a man, having married her high school sweetheart last year.

No, she thought, but I want him to be. "Maybe."

"Be careful, Lily. He's the World Series, and you've been having trouble in the minors."

Lily chuckled. "You don't even know what that means. Why do you try to use sports analogies?"

"You know what I mean. I've dated that kind, and they are only good for one thing."

"Sex?" she asked without thinking.

Mae arched her a look that told Lily she'd revealed more than she'd intended to. "No, Lily, heartache."

"Advice received."

"But not accepted."

"Not yet."

"Just be careful, honey."

Mae left quietly. Lily continued to watch through the window. Maybe Mae was right. He was out of her league. She knew, heck, he knew it, too. But she wanted to know the Preston who'd told her he was tired of being lonely. Because that man wasn't rich as Midas and needed something that plain Lily Stone could give him.

He stepped into her cluttered workroom as if he owned the place. Moving with confidence through dirty, broken pieces of the past. She'd told him to dress casually, but he looked ready to step onto a yacht. Didn't the man own a pair of jeans? And did he always have to look so arrogant.

"Hello, angel."

His gaze lingered on her mouth but he kept five inches of space between them. Fire swept through her body and the tingle in her skin increased. She wanted to clutch at his shoulders and pull him closer to her for a welcoming kiss, to feel his tongue sweep deep inside leaving no part of her untouched and making her long for another taste of him. But their relationship wasn't at that comfortable level yet. He wasn't her man. No matter how much she wanted him to be.

Though he was strong and sure of himself, he wooed her carefully because he wanted her and knew she was unsure. Her nipples tightened, and she leaned closer to him, brushing against his chest.

He groaned deep in his throat. "Want to play?"

More than she wanted her next breath, but she wasn't sure she was ready to pay the piper at the end of this dance. She stepped back. No matter what her body said, her mind wasn't ready to give in to Preston. "Not today."

"Angel, you're killing me," he said, but winked at her.

"You're in a good mood."

He nodded, absently picking up a sterling goblet and twirling it in one hand. "I just signed a deal for some property in Barbados."

"Congratulations," she said, and meant it. But part of her realized he'd be leaving some day. Even if she could convince him forever existed, he wasn't planning to stay.

"Come on, if we're not there when they open at eleven, all the good stuff will be gone."

"Then by all means, let's hurry." He smacked her on the derriere as he walked past her.

"Pres, I don't trust you in this mood."

"Neither do I," he said.

"That's not very reassuring."

"I know. Still going to prove to me love exists?"

"Yes. As a matter-of-fact, I'm planning a lovers-through-time thing to show you the different ways that love has been expressed."

"What a treat."

"You do sarcasm well."

"It's a gift."

"I hope you lose it."

They bantered back and forth until they reached her truck. She waited for him to get in the cab. As he climbed into her painfully neat but worn vehicle, she tried to ignore that he didn't fit in her world, but the image stuck in her mind as she drove away.

Preston let the warm Louisiana breezes waft over him through the open window. The hot setting sun lulled him into a feeling of almost contentment. He'd spent the day in an import yard going through dirty antiques and loading them in the back of Lily's pickup.

Though the work had been hard, he'd found it fulfilling in a way he'd never imagined blue-collar work to be. He'd really enjoyed himself and made a mental note to find some way of thanking Lily for giving him this experience.

Lily concentrated on her driving, and he had to admit she wasn't extremely skilled. She kept to the right hand lane and drove with care, but frequently looked at him, making eye contact as she drove. Swerving toward the center and back again. The bed of her pickup was piled high with furniture and covered with a tarp. He'd offered to drive for her but had received a quelling glance in return.

No one ever dared to stand up to him, but she did. It was as if she didn't care about his position or power. And maybe she didn't.

There was something very real about Lily and at the same time something ethereal. She moved with quick decisive actions, but when she touched her beloved antiques there was languidness to her movements, as if she really touched the past.

That bothered him because he'd been running from the past for most of his life and she seemed to wallow in it. To surround herself with bits and pieces of it instead of focusing on the future.

A rush of adrenaline pumped through his body. A big part of it was desire for Lily and her luscious body, but another part was the thrill of riding in the car with her. The wind in his hair and the sound of Dixieland jazz in the air.

Lily was dressed in faded denim jeans that should have been illegal. They'd been washed too many times and clung to her legs and backside like a lover. She'd discarded a man's work shirt earlier, leaving her clad only in a tight little T-shirt that accentuated the firm mounds of her breasts. All he'd been able to concentrate on while she'd been looking over antiques was whether her nipples would be brown or pink.

Would they respond to his mouth the way they had

to the cool air-conditioning in the manager's office at the import yard? Would she let him suckle her?

"Did you really have a Louis XIV settee in your childhood home?"

Preston shifted on the seat to relieve the tension in his crotch. "Yes. My nanny and I used to sit on it to read bedtime stories."

"You had a nanny?" she asked.

"Yes. She raised me until I was eight."

"What was she like?"

Preston thought about it. Greta Parcell had been all that was warm and kind. Loving in a way his mother never had been. In fact, he'd thought Greta was his mother until she left abruptly. "She was a paid servant, Lily. What do you think she was like?"

"I'm sure she was very motherly."

"She was."

"My grandmother used to employ Dora to help around the house, and she's practically part of the family now. Do you still keep in touch with your nanny?"

"No, she took another position when I was eight and I've never heard from her again." Preston still remembered how he begged her to stay. But in the end his father had been right. Money was a powerful motivator, more powerful than any of the emotions despite what people might say they'd do anything for money.

"Did your mother take over raising you then?"

Preston glanced out the window at Lake Pontchartrain. Leisure boaters and fishermen vied for space on the water. He didn't want to dwell on his mother. He wondered if he could coax Lily onto his yacht tonight. Take her out under the stars, let the rocking of the boat seduce her as he wooed her carefully into his arms.

"No," he said quietly.

He put his fingers over Lily's lips before she could ask another question. He didn't want to talk about his family any more or answer any of her questions. He wanted to steer her back onto safer ground. "How are you going to prove that true love exists in my life?"

"By showing you the love that is already there."

"You're going to have to dig deep to find any in my life."

"I don't think so," she said, quietly. She stared at him for a minute until a honking horn drew her attention back to the road. Waving apologetically out the window while Preston observed her in silence.

He wanted Lily like he'd wanted no other woman. But he didn't want to hurt that rose-colored view of the world she had. She was a shrewd businesswoman, he'd seen the evidence with his own eyes as she'd bargained at the import yard but a part of her had remained innocent about life.

"I thought you mentioned lovers in history."

"I did. My theory here is that love is kind of sneaky. Are you ready?"

"As ever."

"Do you know the tale of Tristan and Isolde? It's a Celtic tale from the twelfth century."

"I'm not familiar with it. But then, I've never really been interested in the past," he said.

"Well, it's a good thing I am. You're going to love this tale of passion and devotion that withstands all trials."

"I can't wait."

Preston rested his head against the backrest and watched Lily drive and talk. Sometimes swerving into the other lane as she became more involved in her story. Her large sunglasses covered her eyes but when she came to the ending where they both died and two trees with their branches entwined sprung up from their graves, tears spilled down her face.

"How's that for true love?"

He realized then what a fragile flower Lily was. She wasn't the tough gal who negotiated with the butcher-faced man at the import yard. She was a closet romantic who probably waited for her fairy-tale prince to come and sweep her away to his castle.

But Preston had never been too good at happily-ever-after. Not once had anything lasted long enough for him to look beyond the surface of what his money had purchased.

"Preston?"

"Great tale. But it's not real life."

"I know. I'm priming the pump and getting you thinking about epic love. You'll find it yourself in life once you learn what to look for."

"You're sure of that?"

"No, but I'm hoping."

He was hoping, too, because he liked the spark that

Lily brought to his life and he wanted to keep it for a while longer. He liked the challenge she represented.

Lily hated social situations that required her to know which fork to use. She knew them, but her nerves usually guaranteed she'd drop something before the night was over. Though Preston had said that a night in his home wasn't cause for nerves, she was agitated just the same.

He'd been watching her the way a lion watches its prey. Gauging her reactions to him and carefully keeping his distance all day at the import yard so his invitation to dinner had caught her off guard. She'd almost said no. But he'd leaned closer, the scent of his cologne surrounded her and she'd been unable to say no.

Her only alternative was a lonely night at home watching public television. So now she stood in the foyer of his condo and wished she'd chosen television. Soft music played in the background, and candles provided the only light.

"Let me take your bag," Preston said, leading her into the living room. A bank of windows looked down on the French Quarter. The evening stars were bright, and she knew from experience that the night air would be filled with chattering tourists, hawkers and jazz music. But tonight she and Preston were ensconced in air-conditioned splendor.

She rubbed her bare arms and looked idly around the room. It was decorated with cutting-edge furniture all chrome and glass. Sleek leather sofas and plush velvet pillows. An avant-garde painting hung on one wall and a bank of mirrors lined another. Lily thought she looked out of place in the room.

She glanced quickly away. She'd always imagined how the rich and famous lived but this didn't seem too great to her. The plush carpeting invited her to kick off her shoes and run her toes through the pile, but she knew Preston would never do such a thing.

''Wine?''

She nodded. Preston's shirt was open at the collar and she glimpsed the hair curling at his neck. She trembled as she reached for the wineglass.

He motioned for her to be seated on one of the leather sofas. Miles Davis's ''Summer Night'' played in the background. The warm, smooth trumpet melody highlighted the loneliness of the room and the man who lived there.

Lily perched on the edge of the seat afraid to move, lest she spill her merlot. For the first time since she'd met him she had nothing to say. She acknowledged she was out of her depth with him and realized that put her at a disadvantage.

Though he sat next to her, they were separated like the French and Spanish inhabitants of early New Orleans. A respectable five inches separated them, but the heat of his body reached her in waves. He smelled of expensive cologne and a scent that was uniquely Preston. She leaned closer to him before she realized what she was doing.

Like a debutante in search of the elusive gold bean

in a King Cake, she wanted him. The King Cake was baked only during Mardi Gras and whoever got the bean received their wish. For once she wanted to be like the city she'd grown up in: the city had been built of saints and sinners, but she was tired of being the good girl.

The revelation startled her, and Lily deliberately scooted away from Preston. Trying for a hint of normalcy, she said, "Your place is very nice."

"It mirrors my penthouse in Manhattan. I like to feel at home wherever I go."

She had a glimpse of the man behind the corporate success and generations of wealth. It revealed to her the craving she doubted he was even aware of—the craving for home. Suddenly she knew she wasn't going to just have to prove to him love existed, she was going to have to show him that family and friends were the key to nurturing love.

"Why did you ask me here tonight?" she asked before taking a sip of her wine. She knew that he was uncomfortable with her attempts to show him love in the world. But she was determined that Preston would learn to love.

"So that I could seduce you," he said in a deep voice.

She sputtered, choking on her wine. His words sent tiny contractions throughout her body. Tightening her breasts against the lacy cups of her bra and making her feminine place moist. If only seduction were that simple, she thought, but the consequences would have long-reaching effects.

"Relax, little red, I'm not the big bad wolf ready to pounce." He took her goblet from her and set it on the beveled-glass coffee table.

"This place makes me uncomfortable," she said. His gray eyes watched her carefully, and she wondered if he felt that same nervous-tingly-anticipating emotion she did.

He settled his arm against the back of the couch, his hand resting innocently on her shoulder. "Really? I thought I did."

Lily's pulse picked up, and she barely understood what Preston was saying. Her breasts felt full as his finger moved idly back and forth on her bare upper arm. Prickles shot from her shoulder throughout her body.

"Angel, do I make you nervous?"

"Yes, but I'm getting used to you in my world. Just seeing you in your own is different." She had trouble holding on to the thread of the conversation. She wanted to slip closer to him on the sofa and feel his masculine body pressed against her softer one. She wanted to pull him closer for the kiss he hadn't claimed when she arrived. She wanted something she'd never wanted from a man before and that scared her.

"Don't start treating me with the respect my position usually commands. I won't know how to deal with you."

She smiled wryly. Here was the Preston she'd come

to know. She had a feeling he was just coming to know this side of himself, as well. There was a lot of himself that Preston walled off from the world. This Preston made her want to hold him closer and show him the world she'd come to know.

"Don't worry. I'm sure you can keep up."

"No doubt."

He still rubbed at her shoulder and if they didn't get up soon, she'd be moving closer to him. She scooted a few inches away from his touch.

"What's the matter, angel?" he asked, his eyes harder than diamonds. She shivered a little as she realized another facet of this amazing man.

Honesty had always been one of her credos even when it left her in an uncomfortable position. "I'm not ready to make love to you tonight, Preston. But I think you could make me believe I am."

He cursed under his breath and picked up his wine-glass, draining it in one swallow. "I know that."

"Why did you really invite me here?" she asked for the second time.

He looked at her, and Lily thought it was to make sure she could handle the truth of his words. She tried to look brave and gave him a weak smile.

"Because I want you and you want me. It's time we really learned about each other."

"Why?" She couldn't for the life of her figure out why he'd want to know more about her, because the man who lived in this apartment was used to successful seduction.

"Because sooner or later I'm going to have you, and I don't want you to regret it."

She thought about that for a minute. "I'd never regret anything I did with you."

He reached out to touch her cheek gently. "I hope not, angel. I hope not."

# Five

Preston knew he'd almost lost Lily earlier in the living room, but here on the balcony, with the remains of a five-star dinner on the table between them, things were different. Maybe it was because the city she loved was spread beneath them. A thriving sea of humanity with all its glories and faults.

They'd talked about books they liked, and he wasn't surprised to learn Lily preferred fiction that had a happy ending. She was well versed in ancient mythology and had regaled him with love stories from classic Greece. He didn't believe that learning about the toils some lovers went through to stay together was going to change his mind about modern love, but he appreciated the time she was putting into the project.

"Do you really think love is worth all that?" he asked after she told the tale of Odysseus, which he'd heard before.

"You're missing the point, deliberately I think. Love is the reward you get after overcoming the tough times in life."

"Interesting. Have you been rewarded?" Preston knew he'd never been rewarded. He'd often taken pleasure in people and in possessions but he'd never known anything lasting from them. Even the car he drove would be replaced, probably next year.

"I wouldn't be here with you if I had. I do have the love of my brothers and grandmother, though."

"What of your parents?" he asked.

"You know that story. But they loved me when they were alive. Didn't yours?"

"No."

He knew she wanted to know more, but he wasn't going to bare all for her. He didn't talk about his family with anyone. Not even his closest acquaintances knew his true feelings about them. And he would never reveal them. He had been raised to be polite, to buy what he wanted and take what he could. Never look back, he remembered his father saying as they watched his mother leave them for what would be the final time to go to one of her many younger lovers.

"Do you want to talk about it?" she asked, her small hand resting lightly on his own.

He shook his head. "Not tonight."

"We're never going to get to know each other if we don't talk about what's made us who we are, Preston."

"Hard work and ambition have shaped me," he said, bluntly. He wanted her but didn't want her prying. He wanted to probe her depths, to find the secrets of her soul but at the same time he wanted to stay safe within his own world.

"Me, too," she said with a small smile.

"Tell me what it's like to own your small business."

"It's hard work. Grandmother wanted my parents to take over, but they were archeologists and traveled all over the world on digs. They always left us behind, and Grandmother said she wasn't losing another generation to the world, so she raised me to love the past and her shop."

"Do you like what you do?"

"I wouldn't do anything else."

He realized she meant that and longed to feel the same about something in his life. His job didn't give him the sense of satisfaction that was radiating from Lily.

"What about you?" she asked. "What's shaped you?"

"My dad had a sudden heart attack when I was in my last year of college. He died instantly."

Her fingers tightened on his and he was tempted to squeeze back but didn't. He wanted to find the safe neutral ground with her. Sex and the present but not the past, he warned himself.

"Anyway, Dexter Resorts was in some trouble. The

board of directors wanted to sell off the different properties. I convinced them to give me a year to turn things around.''

"And you did it," she said.

"Damn straight."

"Because you didn't want to lose what your father had worked so hard for?"

His father had been a bit of a playboy, spending more money than the resort chain could ever have made. So following in his dad's footsteps had never been a goal. In fact, he'd never analyzed too closely just why he'd had to save Dexter Resorts.

"What do you do for fun?" she asked, leaning across the table. He wondered if the wine had made her a little tipsy.

"Work. You?" he asked, finishing off his own glass of merlot.

She batted her eyelashes at him and smiled like the temptress she was when she relaxed and dropped her guard. Heat shot straight to his groin, and he had a hard time concentrating on her words. "I play a mean game of basketball."

He eyed her frame. Soft and sexy, Lily was everything that was feminine and ladylike. Also she barely topped five-three in heels. "Sure you do, angel."

The temptress disappeared, and the hoyden who'd challenged him to believe in love reappeared. "I could beat you anyday."

This was the lady he knew would go up in flames

in his arms. The adventuresome woman who Lily tried to keep under wraps. "Prove it."

"Okay, let's go. We can play at my shop. I have a hoop in the alley." She stood up, hands on her hips. Challenging and ready for a fight.

Preston grabbed her hand and tugged her closer to his chair. Her sundress was made of some sort of flimsy material and the light from inside his apartment illuminated her body. She was so tempting. One tug and she'd be in his lap. "Not tonight. Tomorrow afternoon."

"Great. I look forward to it. I've always wanted to see a man eat crow." Her eyes sparkled, and suddenly resisting her wasn't something he could do.

"Really?" he asked, pulling her closer to him. She leaned down so that they were face-to-face. Her breath brushed over his mouth, and he closed his eyes so that he wouldn't be able to see the sweet innocence in hers.

"Yes," she said breathlessly.

Her chest rose and fell rapidly, and her nipples were beaded against the flimsy bodice of her dress. His hands shook with the need to touch her more intimately.

"Want to make it a little more interesting?" he asked, hanging on by a thread.

"With a wager?" she whispered. Her gaze on his mouth. He brushed his mouth gently over hers. Back and forth, teasing them with barely a glimpse of each other.

"Oh, yeah," he said.

"Name your price," she said, licking her lips.

You in my bed, he thought. But that was the surest way to drive her out of his apartment and his life. "An evening together, winner's choice."

Her free hand came up to cup his face, and for a moment he forgot about seduction. Forgot about spending the evening in that big king-size bed just a few feet away. Forgot that she wanted from him the one thing he'd always feared.

"I'll make you see that love does exist," she promised.

"I'll make love to you until you forget about girlish notions of love," he returned, turning his face in her palm and biting the flesh.

"Should we shake on it?"

"Hell, no," he said, pulling her down on his lap and taking the kiss he'd been dying to claim all evening.

Lily knew that she could beat Preston in a game of one-on-one. She'd been playing basketball everyday of her life. Her father had gone to school on a basketball scholarship, and whenever he'd come home he'd always taken her to the courts to play.

Dash had been All-State in high school, and Beau had played in college, and she could beat both of them when she concentrated on her game. But then, she didn't think of them as men. She'd never noticed anyone on the court apart from her game strategy, but she noticed Preston.

Actually it went beyond noticing. She told herself

that it was due to the fact that she'd never seen him in anything other than business clothing, but she didn't know if that was true. His athletic shorts and tank top were new, but fit him like a second skin. He moved across the court with grace and ease, and she knew she'd have to concentrate to beat him.

But she couldn't help notice the rippling of muscles as he made a free throw or the power in his legs as he dribbled down the court. He leaped in the air and made a throw that would have done a pro proud.

The now-familiar excitement started pumping through her veins. Dammit. This was the one time she really wanted to win, and he was distracting her with his body. She glared at him, wanting to believe he knew what he was doing to her but feared he didn't. He hadn't even kissed her when he'd arrived. A first since he'd told her he wanted her in his bed.

She had to get her mind on the game. There was more at stake here than she wanted to admit, but she knew she had to win. He passed the ball to her, and she practiced dribbling down the court and took her shot. It hit the backboard and bounced out of bounds.

"Nice try, angel," Preston said with a wink.

"Never let the competition see your strengths," she said. Damn, she never missed from the free-throw line. Breathe, she reminded herself, and don't think about his body.

"What are you showing me?"

"Nothing. I'm letting you build false confidence."

"Oh, yeah?"

"Yeah," she said, wishing it was true.

"Ready to start?" he asked.

"Whenever you are, pretty boy."

"Was that an insult?"

"Did you take it as one?"

He eyed her carefully and tossed her the basketball. "Ladies first."

They played fast and furious, as if the outcome were more important than they'd both been telling each other it was. Lily had never met a man who'd treated her as an equal on the court the way Preston did. She had to admit he was a better player than she'd given him credit for being, but he wasn't better than her.

Also, he wasn't above using any means at his disposal to win. When he blocked her as she went to score the winning point, his hand brushed her breast. The ball bounced out off the rim and Lily stood trembling, afraid to move.

"You missed," he said, his voice husky with exertion and sexual tension.

"That's cheating," she said, trying to ignore the ache in her nipples. At least she was wearing a sports bra. Maybe he wouldn't notice.

"Purely accidental," he said, but his gaze lingered on her chest. She had the impulse to cross her arms over her breasts but didn't give in to it. Instead she thrust her shoulders back, watching as he swallowed visibly and looked away.

Did she affect him as deeply as he did her? Lily decided to try a little experiment. She blocked him as he tried to take a shot and this time used all the tools in her feminine arsenal. This was man against woman, she realized.

Turning, she used the back of her body to block him and then as he coiled to jump she thrust her hips back toward him, brushing against his groin. She took a step forward; planning to excuse herself for the below-the-belt touch, but Preston was quicker than she'd expected.

Letting the ball roll off the court and grabbing her waist, he pulled her closer to him. His ragged breath brushed against her neck, making gooseflesh spread throughout her body.

"Is this how you want to play?" he asked, dropping small biting kisses along her neck.

Lily couldn't even think. It seemed she did have some effect on him and his control. She knew he wanted to keep her in the role of a woman he was seducing, but she wasn't going to let him. Because last night at his place she'd realized that Preston needed everything she had to give him. He needed more than her body and her company. He needed someone to show him how to love with his soul.

She wanted him but feared the wild impulses racing through her body. He made her react and damn the consequences. But she knew that the sinner always had to repent. Her instincts screamed for her to take what he was offering, to know what it was like to really be a woman. But her heart warned she'd get hurt. And she wasn't ready to risk her heart.

She was already energized from going toe-to-toe with him on the court. She wanted to win the game there, but she'd rather win on the personal level. She'd rather have him at her mercy here, man to woman than player to player.

She shifted back against him, enjoying the feel of his hard body behind her softer one. Enjoying the pressure of his body against her. Enjoying the fact that he could make her feel as if each of her senses was on overload.

Preston groaned, his hands coming up to cup her breasts. She felt like a tease, because she knew that she wasn't going to let him make love to her until she believed he could love her.

"Are you forfeiting?" She forced herself to ask.

A silence, broken only by their breathing, filled the air. The sounds of cars passing on the road and pedestrians on the street provided distant background music. The city pulsed around them and through them. And though they weren't visible to any of the passersby Lily suddenly felt embarrassed by what she'd done. By what she'd allowed to happen.

"I'm sorry," she said in a rush.

"Don't be."

"I'm not a tease," she said. Say it again, maybe you'll believe it.

"Lily, angel, I started this."

"No, you didn't. I'd been lusting after you since you showed up."

He smiled one of his sweet smiles that made her

know there was a wonderful lonely man inside of him waiting to get out. "That's good to know."

"I'm…"

"Overreacting," he said. He hugged her close, and the wild desire that was pulsing through her was oddly quieted by the strength in his arms.

"I think we'd better call this game a draw."

"Why?"

"Because I'm in no condition to finish."

She glanced down at the distended front of his shorts. It didn't give her a rush of power or a feeling of victory over him. It made her feel a little ashamed that she'd tried to cheat to win. She never had before.

"I think you would've won," she said, stepping back from him.

"Lily, there's no shame in what you did."

"I've been trying to tell you that lust without love is something you could find with anyone."

"I already know that."

"Than why did I just treat you like some boy toy?"

"Because love really is a myth, and attraction is a powerful impetus."

"I've always told myself that I was waiting for love, waiting for my Prince Charming to come along and awaken me but suddenly I'm alive and filled with desire and…"

"There's no Prince Charming," he said, and turned to walk away.

Lily watched him go, knowing she'd wounded him

but unsure how to fix it. Because in her heart she believed he could be her Prince Charming.

Preston stayed away from Lily and the White Willow House for two weeks. He'd flown to New York and partied with his socialite friends. But the lifestyle left him cold, and though Lily had hurt him with her words, he acknowledged they were the truth.

Now, standing in the refinished atrium of White Willow House, Preston realized he'd been running away because he felt like he'd come home. As though he'd found the one place he belonged and it wasn't his familiar environment.

Lily started when she saw him. Preston didn't fool himself that it was surprise coursing through her. He knew from the way she'd played basketball to win that it was anger controlling her now. He may have gained ground on convincing her love didn't exist, but he was pretty sure he'd lost leagues on the seduction front.

Part of him knew it was for the best. She was too good for him. He'd realized how fragile she could be that night in his home. He didn't want to be a big hulking masculine beast, tearing at the safe haven of her world, but he knew that he was.

She turned away as he approached and walked across the marble floor with a stride that would have done a marine proud.

"Lily."

She stopped but didn't turn around. The faded denim overalls she wore should have made her look out of place in the plush hotel lobby surrounded by her antiques. But she seemed more at home among the pieces she'd picked and refurbished than he felt.

He'd lost her. He felt it deep in his gut where he'd felt Greta's betrayal when he'd been eight and unsure of the world. It ticked him off because he was old enough to know better.

"It seems I've won our bet," he said silkily. Needing to reach through the barriers she'd erected around herself to keep him out.

She glanced over her shoulder, her blue eyes cold instead of warm and welcoming. Even that first afternoon in his office she'd at least had the gleam of challenge in her eyes—today nothing. She was still sexy as hell with her short hair mussed and clinging to her face and neck. He longed to taste her skin there. To linger as he hadn't trusted himself to on the basketball court.

"Which one?" she asked.

"The love one. It seems even you have decided it's not worth the risk. Good thing I'm not waiting at home for you in a house filled with infidels."

She pivoted on her heel and marched over toward him. Her chest rose and fell, and her lips narrowed. She should have looked like a prim schoolmarm, but no teacher had ever affected him the way Lily did. Straight to the groin with enough heat to power the electrical needs of New York for a month.

"How dare you?" she asked, jabbing him in the chest with her index finger.

"I dare anything I please," he said with all the arrogance he'd learned from his parents. But he didn't know how to handle this situation. He'd never been near anything that vaguely resembled this woman or her approach to life. She wasn't staying by his side because of his money. Why, then?

"You're the one who ran away," she said.

She always went for the jugular, and while he could admire her style, he admitted that it hurt. Especially since the innate vulnerability in her face always stopped him from reciprocating. He was sure someday someone was going to disillusion her, but he didn't want it to be him. "I was on a business trip."

"Is that what they're calling it these days?" she said. There was more than anger in her body, and as he searched her eyes, he thought he saw hurt, as well.

"What exactly are you implying, Lily?" he asked, because although he'd partied every night, he'd been in town for a business meeting that couldn't be rescheduled.

"I read the papers like everyone else, Preston. Did you think because we're in the South that your escapades wouldn't reach us? You're a big-time businessman, and New Orleans likes nothing better than debauchery."

Must have been a slow day for news if he'd made the papers. Usually only acquisitions and mergers brought him press coverage. "Hell, angel, this keeps getting better and better. You say debauchery like it's a disease."

"Isn't it?" she asked, most of the anger gone from her voice, leaving only that hurt he didn't want to see. How was he going to mend this?

He considered how much he needed to touch her. When they were together and touching, things were right between them. He didn't fool himself that a mere brush of his hand down her arm would right this perceived wrong, but he needed to do something to erase the damage in her eyes. "To some."

"To me?" she asked.

He took her hand in his. It was so much smaller than his was. He circled her palm with his forefinger. "Not to you. You have a soul for adventure."

"Then why do I prefer the home life?"

Preston wasn't sure he knew her well enough to answer, but from the beginning he'd felt she was hiding from something. "You're afraid of yourself."

She wrinkled her nose at him. "How did you turn this back to me? I'm not the one who was in the papers with a gorgeous blonde."

"Was I?" he asked, wishing he'd thought to find the photographer and pay the man to keep his film unexposed. But it was too late; the damage had been done.

"Don't play games with me. I believed you were serious when you said we wouldn't be better off apart. Did you have a change of heart?"

She wanted more than he felt comfortable giving, but he knew he would need to show her some of himself if he wanted her to stay. And suddenly he knew that he did. It was more than the desire hardening his body every time he looked at her. He wasn't sure what, but he needed to be with her. To enjoy her smiles and laughter. To seduce her into his bed and life so that he could bathe in her sunshine for at least a little while.

"I needed to get away, and this business trip had been scheduled. I'm within an inch of taking you, angel. It's not every day that I take the pure and noble route. Believe me I won't do it again."

"I thought you at least cared for me."

I do, he thought, but didn't say anything out loud. "Lily, fate tends to demand a price for that kind of deep emotion."

"I can't imagine going through life without caring."

"You should try it."

"Why?"

"It's pain free."

She closed the gap between them. Cupping his cheek in her palm. She brushed her thumb across his bottom lip. "Oh, Preston."

He didn't say anything else to her, because he knew he'd come close to losing her and he didn't want to lose her yet. He didn't want to admit that she mattered to him in the least, but he knew he'd miss her smile if he never saw it again.

# Six

The loud Zydeco music swirled around them like the sounds of Mardi Gras, fun, frivolous but masking something deeper. It was the lyrics that were anything but light and funny. The bride, her cousin Marti, and her new husband, Brad, danced with all the fervor that they felt. There was an exciting sort of sexual tension in the air as bodies brushed together and swung apart.

"Champagne?" Preston asked.

She nodded and accepted the flute from him. It was really sparkling wine, but she doubted any of her family or friends realized. She knew that Preston would. He was easily the best-dressed man there, but he was relaxed and charming, making her realize how easily he flitted through the throngs of people without them realizing they were only seeing a mirage—not the real man.

"How did you like the ceremony?" she asked trying to think of anything but how good he looked dressed in black and white.

"A little long but very nice."

The high Catholic Mass had lasted for an hour, and Lily had been aware of others shifting in their seats around them, but Preston had been focused on the ceremony. She'd always loved the rituals of her church and had been glad to see that Preston appreciated them, too.

"Brad and Marti married for love," Lily said, sipping her drink.

"They do seem to be infected with the love bug," he said dryly.

"Ha! So you admit it exists." She felt giddy. Probably from being around those closest to her. Probably from the champagne. Probably from sitting so close to Preston, having his cologne tempt her senses and his wit tempt her mind.

"Hell, angel, I admit that many people believe love exists. That doesn't mean it's real." He scooted his chair closer to her, draping his arm over her shoulders. The weight was pleasant on the back of her neck. His fingers kept beat to the music against her shoulder. It was a light brush of his finger against her skin and made warmth spread throughout her body, pooling at her center. She shifted in the chair and hoped he wouldn't notice.

But those clear gray eyes missed nothing. He raised one eyebrow and bent to kiss her below her ear. She shivered and shifted again. She wanted to pull him to her and kiss him as she had that night in his apartment. She wanted to feel his strong hard body against hers.

He distracted her and made her forget she wanted something from him that he doubted he could ever feel. "How can I prove that to you?"

He glanced away from her. His touch stopped, and she felt him pull into himself, searching for an answer. She knew that what she'd done when she'd blindly challenged him would open them to a world of pain if she failed. She was asking a man who'd forgotten how to hope to try again. If she failed, Lily realized, they'd both be affected. She'd been worrying about herself. Trying to figure out how she'd protect herself from needing him too much, but Preston had been opening up to her. Letting her see the things he needed.

"How do you make love stay?" he asked. She knew he really wanted to know.

She didn't have an answer for him, knew he didn't expect one from her, but felt the silence weigh heavy between them. The only way she could prove love would stay would be to fall in love with him herself and stay with him all their lives. But who could live with unrequited love?

"Want to dance?" he asked.

Her mind in turmoil, she wanted to say no. To demand he give her a good reason why he doubted the bride and groom would stay together. But the music changed and a slow and sensual Miles Davis tune came on. She couldn't resist Preston or Miles Davis.

She nodded and stood. He took her arm to lead her to the dance floor. His fingers brushed on the inside, teasing her with their light touch. Her sleeveless sundress was light and flirty, a gauzy fabric that made her feel like a princess.

Her heels gave a few added inches but Preston still topped her. He pulled her into his arms. His lake-gray eyes weren't cold now. In fact, she saw fire reflected in their depths and wanted…wanted things she knew better than to ask for.

She rested her head against his shoulder to escape his probing gaze. He saw too much. Made her see herself in a new light, and she wasn't ready to look that closely at herself. Wasn't ready to acknowledge that something had to be missing for her to have caved so easily to Preston's advances. She'd stayed celibate a long time, but suddenly she wished she hadn't.

Because the man rubbing her back and cradling her against his body was special to her…more than she was to him, and Lily knew she wouldn't let her first time be with someone to whom she meant little or nothing. For her, firsts were celebrations.

His lips rested against her temple as they danced, and he talked quietly to her. Telling her how exciting it was to hold her in his arms, seducing her slowly with his words and body. She closed her eyes and let her senses revel in Preston Dexter—a man who no longer seemed like a cold man in pursuit of seduction. When the song ended, and they returned to their seats, he still felt unsteady.

Preston reluctantly joined Lily on the dance floor for a more rousing number. Cousins and friends surrounded her, and she threw her head back laughing as they danced around her. He felt the familiar tension pool in his lower body and didn't fight his reaction.

He'd been hard since he'd taken Lily in his arms on the dance floor an hour earlier. Though he'd always enjoyed the game of seduction and teasing, he was ready to have her in his bed. But he wasn't ready for her to be out of his life.

As she twirled past him in the arms of one of her beefy cousins, their eyes met and something magical passed between them. Preston stopped in the middle of the floor aware that everyone else still teemed around him. The world narrowed to only him and Lily. Seducing Lily had always been his goal, his objective, but he'd found himself losing sight of that.

Suddenly he realized that Lily was seducing him with her smiles and laughter, with the joy she found in everyday life that he never knew existed. He cut in and took her in his arms, dancing to the loud wild music as if he'd been born to it. He forgot about love and lust and let the music sweep both him and Lily away.

He let it play over him like his first illegal sip of whisky when he'd been fourteen. It was hard going down but the rush that came after thrilled him to his toes, and he knew he'd have to have another hit.

When the music stopped his ears were ringing. Lily was smiling up at him. The room was hot and close with the press of bodies, and he tugged on her hand, leading her outside. A naked bulb illuminated a rough path down to the waterfront.

Lily took his hand and led him down it. The moon was bright and full lighting their way. The music from the hall started again, fainter as they moved away. The smell of overripe vegetation and fresh water filled the air. The small canal flowed steadily toward the sea, and a wooden dock emerged from the shadows as they approached the bank.

"I haven't danced like that in ages," Lily said.

She seemed like an enchanted being from another world. One who would inhabit the earth for only this one night. If he didn't capture her, hang on to her, she'd be gone forever.

"I never have," he admitted.

"You must have natural rhythm." She glanced up at him from under her lashes. It was a flirty look and it intensified the tightness in his lower body.

He hugged her to him. She smelled of her exertions and of the floral perfume she wore every day. The scent reminded him of the exotic orchids the gardener had cultivated in his childhood home.

"Ah, Preston, I missed you when you were gone."

I missed you, too. "I'm back now."

Her entire body quivered with excitement, probably from the wedding and the dancing. Preston wanted to feel that same energy coursing through him. He wanted to feel it coursing from her into him as he joined their bodies together.

Nothing else would suffice.

"Wasn't it romantic?"

"The wedding?"

"No, their first kiss. I've always dreamed of that kiss."

He realized that Lily might have had a little too much to drink because she would never reveal that much of herself to him. Her natural resistance was lowered, and he knew that he could, if he played his cards right, finally be successful in tempting her into his bed.

"What kind of kiss is that?"

"I don't know. Magical, I guess."

"How are my kisses?"

She smiled at him, sweetly seductive, and laid her head on his shoulder. "Yours are steamy and hot, promising forbidden pleasures."

"I'm ready to deliver on them."

"I know."

He brushed his lips softly against hers. He wanted to taste some of the magic that Lily thought came from true love. Preston was beginning to realize it came from true goodness. There was something special about the way he felt for Lily, and that bothered him.

She should be like every other woman in his life. She shouldn't make him hard with just a glance. She shouldn't make him laugh over the silly things that happened during the day. She shouldn't be lying so trustingly in his arms, because he knew once he kissed her he wouldn't be able to stop.

"Hey, they're getting ready to cut the cake," someone called from the doorway.

Preston pulled back, aware that he was riding the razor's edge. He wouldn't take her in his arms again and not make love to her.

He put his hand on her back and directed her toward the hall. The music grew louder, and he heard laughter from the open windows. "Thanks."

"No problem."

"Are you okay, Preston?"

"We need to talk tonight."

"Okay," she said, and she walked away. He took his time following her. Making sure he didn't get back in the hall until after the dancing had started up again. He didn't want to see what Lily wanted in life. Didn't want to acknowledge what he knew deep in his soul— that she deserved her Prince Charming. She deserved her wedding and her groom, and he wasn't the man for either of those roles.

Lily leaned dreamily against the plush leather seat as Preston piloted the car through the late-evening traffic. It grew increasingly heavy as they neared the city. New Orleans never slept, and for once Lily didn't want to, either.

Her body still pulsed in time to the Cajun music from the reception. Her mind still dwelled on the fantasy of herself as bride and her groom none other than her sophisticated companion tonight. She hummed a nameless tune.

She slipped a CD she'd given him into the player. A Lena Horne disc of love songs. The sweet and sometimes bittersweet lyrics brushed over her aroused senses like moonlight on the ocean. She turned to her side, watching Preston in the flickering light provided by the passing streetlamps. He looked alone and aloof.

She wanted to penetrate the aura of loneliness that surrounded him, but how could she. How could she? She wasn't sure of anything any longer, especially love. Never had she backed down from anything in her life. Never had she had so much at stake, and for the soul of her she couldn't be sure of winning.

"What are you thinking?" he asked, his voice a husky rasp.

"Can I drive your car?" she asked, not wanting to open up her soul to him tonight. On the dance floor he'd felt like Prince Charming and she'd known exactly how Cinderella felt but now she wasn't so sure.

"Not tonight," he said, with a wry chuckle.

"No, not tonight," she agreed. She still had a pleasant buzz from the reception and the alcohol she'd consumed.

"Are these new CDs helping you to believe in love?" she asked.

He glanced at her as he coasted to a halt for a red light. "I wish they were."

"Don't you feel seduced by the promise of love?"

"Not especially."

"What would it take to seduce you, Preston?"

She watched him closely. She wanted him: his hard body and supple strength; his cold gray eyes sweeping over her feminine body; his warm touch spreading over her and bringing to life longings that only he could fill.

He pulled into her drive and turned off the engine. Her house, draped in darkness, should have been forbidding, but it looked the way it always did—a safe haven. She'd never ventured from her safe neighborhood. Part of her had longed to when she was younger, but as an adult she knew she never would.

The CD continued to play. Lena sang "At Long Last Love." This song broke her heart. Lily didn't want to listen to it because sometimes she felt as if this might be her. Searching fruitlessly for something ephemeral that she'd never find.

"Invite me in and I'll tell you," Preston said.

Tell me what? she thought. Then she remembered. He'd tell her what it took to seduce him. She had bought a book of quotes the other day and planned to inundate him with words on the subject but not tonight. To bring love to his life she knew she'd have to risk herself, and suddenly the risk seemed worth the pain that might come.

"Come in?" she asked, teasing him with a look from under her lashes. She knew then that she wanted to be seduced. That she wanted him to deliver on the forbidden treasures his kisses and eyes promised. Tonight, at least, that seemed enough.

"Yes, angel."

He came around and helped her out of the car. His hand was solid and sure at her elbow. Heat spread up the inside of her bare flesh, tightening her breast and bringing her nipples to an aching point.

The moonlight played over his chiseled features. There was nothing soft about Preston, and in the shadows he lost the facade of civilization that he wore, day in and day out.

She swallowed. This man, who was more at home in darkness than in light, was the one who'd challenged her to teach him to love and didn't believe she could achieve it.

She led him into her house. The light she'd left on in the parlor spilled onto the hardwood floor in the hallway. She hesitated when she entered the room and saw the books she'd left perched on the end table. Books about love and its celebration. She led Preston to the love seat farthest from the books. Maybe he wouldn't notice.

Good manners demanded she offer him a drink, but she knew if she left the room he'd find those books, and she wasn't ready to discuss love tonight. Not tonight, because it might spoil the mood that permeated through her like the champagne had at the wedding. The intimate setting of Preston's plush car and the mellow music had made her want to live in the bubble of intimacy, even if it wasn't real.

"Let's talk seduction," she said, sliding closer to him on the love seat. He'd left his jacket in the car, and his body heat drew her closer. Her thin dress was adequate for the temperature outside, but inside it suddenly didn't seem enough. She put her hand on his thigh and teased herself with the image of his naked leg beneath her pink-tipped fingernails.

"I don't think an expert like you needs to discuss anything," he said with a pointed glance at her hand on his thigh.

She was in a mood to tease him. The way he'd been when she'd dined at his apartment. She slid one finger up the inside of his thigh. "Expert?"

He covered her hand with his own. "Of course. Don't push me too far, Lily."

"I'm sorry." She slid her hand out from under his, feeling more and more like someone she didn't know.

"What do you want from me?" he asked.

She didn't know. Part of her wanted to believe he could be that man she'd been waiting for all of her life, but another part didn't want to leave herself open to the vulnerability that would bring. "I'm the novice here. I'm the one searching for love."

"But you're seducing me into believing that myth, as well."

"It's only seduction if it's against your best wishes."

"It is," he said with a finality that should have made her leap from the couch and kick him out of her house. But she sensed the fear under the words. Someone had taught Preston that loving was weak and brought only pain. It was up to her to show him the real value in it. Was Preston vulnerable, too?

"What would it take to seduce you, Preston Dexter?"

"Tonight?"

She nodded.

"A bit of that magic you mentioned earlier."

She blinked against the emotion swamping her. "Come here."

He leaned closer. She pulled him into her arms and into an embrace that brought them body to body, that let her touch her lips to his. She tried to bring the magic that had been surrounding her all her life to him.

Preston took control of the kiss with a harsh groan. His grip on her shoulders tightened, and his mouth slanted on hers. His tongue penetrated deeply, as if trying to learn the taste of her completely. He tasted of the coffee he'd had before they left the reception and of something undefinable that was only Preston.

She thrust her tongue into his mouth, trying to assuage a thirst that had sprung from nowhere and wouldn't be stopped. She didn't know where the line between seducer and seduced had ended but suddenly that didn't matter. She only knew that having Preston in her arms was where he belonged. He always seemed so cold and lonely, except when she tempted him into her arms.

# Seven

**P**reston had never craved anything as much as he craved Lily's body under his. He wanted to sheath his throbbing erection in her warm, welcoming body. To see if she'd deliver on the promises her eyes had been making all night.

He'd been wrong to make any sort of dare with her. Success lay in the familiar. He bent to nibble on her neck as she leaned back against the cushions of the sofa. There was something vulnerable about the curve of a woman's neck, and Lily's seemed more so. Though he wanted to stop and caress it with his fingertips, to touch her as he would something fragile, he didn't.

He smoothed his mouth to her ear and whispered

dark promises to her. She shifted restlessly on the couch. Her eyes half-lidded as her hands grasped at his shoulders and tried to pull him closer. But he knew the only type of closeness that would satisfy them both was naked flesh to naked flesh.

He couldn't give her magic, but he could give her passion. It was the one area of his life where he'd always excelled. He'd never had any trouble mastering his body and his reactions to women. At an early age he'd learned the game of seduction.

Lily's hands found his head, and she pulled his mouth to hers. She wasn't grasping in her desire but welcoming. She wanted him and wanted him to want her. *As if he didn't.*

It felt he'd wanted her forever. Blood pounded through his veins like the rush he got when driving his Jag wide open on a deserted highway with no care given to speed limits or safety. He never let himself dwell too long on the man he was then because that man didn't know how to survive in the real world.

Lily brushed her lips to his, barely touching them. Back and forth until he thought he would completely lose control. He held her head still in his grasp, needing to be inside at least her mouth. But he felt the challenge she'd thrown down as clearly as if she'd waved a red flag in front of his face. That kiss of hers had been a provocation. And he called on the skills he'd honed on faceless women from his past to entice her now.

He bent to her, but she slid back from the kiss and nibbled instead on his lower lip. The world narrowed, and only one person existed. The exhalation of her breath seemed loud in the silent room. His thundering heartbeat steadily drowned out the sound. He had to have her.

He sucked her upper lip into his mouth and Lily moaned. ''Oh, Pres...''

He remembered how shy and tentative she'd been the first time he'd embraced her. She'd grown bolder, and Preston reveled in her reactions to him. The one time men and women were most honest with each other was in a physically intimate situation.

He took possession of her mouth, molding it to his own, thrusting his tongue past the barrier of her teeth as he caressed his way down her body with his hands. She rubbed her tongue against his, and he shifted on the couch, bringing Lily onto his lap.

Her full breasts rose and fell with each breath she took. The light from the lamp cast a soft glow in the room, but Preston wished it were brighter. He wanted to see the body he was caressing. He wanted to know if her breasts were pink tipped, as he imagined, if her hair were red everywhere and if she'd let him stare at her until they both felt as if they'd go up in flames.

He teased her with a circling touch around her breast, confirming what he'd suspected earlier—she wasn't wearing a bra. Just the tiniest light caress, knowing she wanted—needed—more from him.

But he wanted this to last forever. Suddenly it was important that she experience satisfaction. He needed to watch her blossom in his arms. And she was doing so, beautifully.

Her nipple hardened under his stroking finger and he had to taste it. He tugged her forward. Her hands kneaded his shoulders and then she scraped her fingernails down his back, following the line of his spine.

With a firm touch between her shoulderblades Preston brought her chest in alignment with his mouth. He suckled her through the layer of her thin dress. She moaned and her hands clutched at his head. Preston sucked harder, trying to pull a response from her that would match the one pulsing through his body.

Her legs straddled his hips, and through the thin layer of her dress he felt her feminine warmth. His fingers tingled to touch her. To feel her honey spilling on his fingers. He wanted to open his fly and feel that warmth on his engorged flesh but knew better. He didn't want this to end yet.

He was so hard, he could scarcely breathe. Yet he couldn't pull away from the temptation of her body. He turned his attention to her other breast. Lily's hands roamed over his back searchingly.

He wanted her long fingers on his flesh but didn't have the patience to remove his shirt. Her hips rocked against his groin. Sliding his hands up under her dress, he took the taut globes of her butt in his hands, fondling her through her lace panties. She gasped and rocked harder against him.

"Preston?" her high questioning sound drew his attention.

"It's okay, angel."

She was on the knife's edge and he realized that she'd never been there before. How innocent was she? His body didn't care, but his conscience nagged. He slid his palm around to cup her feminine heat. She was as warm and tempting as he'd imagined but there was more. He found the center of her excitement and teased it gently with his finger until she couldn't stay still. She brought her mouth to his and as he slid his tongue deep into her recesses, he entered her body with first one finger and then, stretching her gently, added another.

Her body was warm and tight, sheathing his fingers like a warm glove. He almost lost it right then, imagining her tight warmth on his erection. He thrust deeper into her body and watched her arch in response. He knew he couldn't stop now. Wouldn't be able to stop until he was hilt deep, surrounded by her tight heat and the warmth that came only from Lily.

"Oh, Preston, what's happening?"

"Just ride it out, angel."

She did—beautifully so. Arching against him, holding her body tight until tiny contractions tightened her even more around his fingers. Before falling against his shoulder, her uneven breathing filling the silent room.

Preston was rock hard and wanted nothing more than to slip into her body. But he realized there were consequences to this that he'd never thought of before. Consequences that hadn't ever existed in his world until now. "Lily, are you a virgin?"

She snuggled closer to him, burying her face against his chest. "Yes."

The White Willow House was slowly returning to the splendor it had enjoyed in its pre-Civil War era. Some of the antiques she'd ordered from France and Spain had started arriving. She'd hired a local artisan to craft replicas for each of the guest rooms. Lily knew she'd done her best work yet.

She'd neglected some of her other clients to concentrate on the Dexter Resorts project. And she'd been working long days to make up for it. Which was just as well, because in the two weeks since she'd confessed to being a virgin, Preston had left her alone.

Part of her, the Catholic girl who'd gone to confession once a week, was glad. But in her heart she wanted to experience Preston as only a woman could. He made the world seem brighter and life more…exciting and interesting.

She wondered if he thought he might catch it from her. Always willing to go to the wall to win, she hadn't let his busy schedule detract from her campaign to convince him love existed. Last night she'd sent him two e-mails and a fax with some quotes she'd unearthed.

He hadn't responded. But he'd sent a thank-you note for the basket of romantic CDs and DVDs that she'd had delivered on Monday. Twilight cast long shadows on the hardwood floors of the suite she'd just added a candelabra to. She imagined how it must have been to live in the days of candlelight. When everything was a little softer.

She imagined a Mozart waltz floating upstairs from the ballroom through the open window and bowed to an imaginary partner, then waltzed around the room.

Someone cleared his throat and she turned guiltily toward the open door. Preston stood in the shadows like a vampire afraid of the light of day. Embarrassed, she put her hand to her throat and looked around for her planner. He looked tired, she thought. As if he was running from something that was gaining on him.

She longed to open her arms and offer him the solace of her body, but she was afraid she'd be left a shell of a woman when he moved on. She wanted him to realize what a precious gift they had been given because she'd come to know that Preston was her soul mate. He looked to the future while she fixed the past. Together they both brought things to each other that neither could live without.

"Don't stop on my account." His voice brushed over her senses. That deep husky sound that brought back the last time she heard it. On her love seat two weeks ago. Two long weeks ago. Her heartbeat had doubled and blood rushed to the center of her body.

"It was a private show." She gathered her stuff and walked toward him. He blocked the doorway with his body. She realized how tall he was for the first time. Maybe it was because she was wearing Keds instead of her work boots.

He raised one eyebrow. "I'm very discriminating."

That he was. Plus he played his cards so close to his chest no one had any idea what he was thinking. "I know."

"So dance for me."

She was tempted because she knew it would give him pleasure, and Preston seemed to have too little of that in his life. But he had to learn that she wasn't an oddity in his life. She wasn't a new toy that could be taken out and played with when he was bored. She was a real woman and deserved to be treated as such by him. "Preston, I'm not one of your flunkies. You can't avoid me for two weeks, then expect me to do whatever you ask."

"I've been busy."

"You're the boss. You could rearrange your schedule." But she knew he wouldn't. She'd realized when he'd disappeared the last time that when emotions started to affect him, Preston backed away and regrouped, coming back stronger and more resolute in the confidence that love didn't exist.

"I don't think of you as one of my flunkies."

"What do you think of me?" she asked, realizing she might not like the answer.

"The woman who's going to teach me to love."

It may have been a little thing, but for the first time he hadn't said to convince him love existed. He'd said to teach him to love. Appealing to his mind was a tack that might convince him. Because beyond the monetary, she'd discovered that Preston liked things he could take apart and figure out how they worked. Like that expensive car of his. He knew it inside and out.

"Did you like the Balzac quote?"

"Which one was it?"

"'Love is to the mortal nature what the sun is to the earth.'" It was one of her favorites, and she'd spent a lot of time finding just the right quote for him.

"Not particularly. The sun is eating through more of the ozone layer each year and bringing us closer to death."

Sometimes he tried her patience. "The sun warms us in winter and gives us food in spring and summer."

"You believe love provides that?"

"It provides the foundation for a happy life."

"It also has that rare side effect of tearing someone's life to shreds."

She shook her head. "For every one person burned by love there are ten more who rejoice in it."

"Some people live their entire lives without love."

"Because they are afraid of it."

"Are you calling me a coward?"

"No, I wasn't thinking of you at all." But she had been. He frustrated her sometimes, and her good nature only lasted so long.

"I think you were. You didn't really wound me," he said, but his eyes told another story. She forgot that Preston was good at hiding his real emotions, and she had lashed out when she shouldn't have. She'd known from the beginning that he'd be a tough nut to crack.

"I haven't given up on you yet," she said.

"You will."

His quiet confidence unnerved her, and she walked out of the room afraid to say anything else. But her heart was weary and her body was aching. Her instincts told her that if she was alone with him again, his belief in love might not matter to her body.

"How's your wife, Jay?" Lily asked. They were sitting in one of the three gazebos that were behind White Willow House. It overlooked a man-made lake that Preston planned to stock with bass and offer water-skiing and fishing trips to his guests.

Lily had brought lunch back for the crew from town when she'd arrived with another truckload of antiques. The weekend had passed with lots of attempts on Lily's part to involve him in her life, but Preston had remained resolute.

She was so open and friendly that he wasn't surprised she knew about Rohr's wife. Nor did it surprise him that she'd taken the time to bring po' boy sandwiches for the crew. That was the kind of thing that Lily did.

Because she cared, he realized.

"Well, we're in the homestretch. Thanks for those books you recommended," Jay Rohr said. Jay was one of the most competent of Dexter's vice presidents. He'd been with Preston from the beginning and though only two years older, Jay had been a mentor to Preston those first few years when he had more gumption than know-how.

KATHERINE GARBERA                          103

"Homestretch of what, Rohr?" Preston asked. He
vaguely recalled Rohr's wife, a brown-haired woman
who was as tall as Jay. They'd married a year and a
half ago. Rohr hadn't taken a vacation since his marriage.

Lily stared pointedly at him. The dappled sun made
her red hair shine. "June's pregnancy."

Preston realized that Lily knew his people better than
he did. It had never bothered him before and wouldn't
now if he hadn't realized that Lily had found him lack-
ing. He didn't care what type of life his employees had
away from the office. "Is that why you requested she
accompany you down here?"

"Yes. June asked me to be active in the birthing."

"How?" Preston asked. There was only so much a
man could do.

"I asked the same thing. She wants me to be coach-
ing her. I can't explain it, but it makes her feel better
to see me every night."

Preston had no idea what else to say. None of his
friends had kids or even wanted them. But as Lily
picked up the conversation turning it away from Rohr's
upcoming fatherhood, he realized that the thought of
Lily pregnant wasn't an unwelcome one. Dammit, of
course it was, he reminded himself.

But his mind lingered on the image of her swollen
with his seed. Her hands cradling her belly while his
child rested, safe within her womb.

"Preston?" Lily said, drawing his attention.

"What?" He didn't want to be a father. He wanted

Lily in his bed for the normal male reasons. Lust, desire and, well, affection. But he didn't want a future with her or any other woman.

"Jay married his wife for love," she said, with a smile that shot straight to his groin. He'd been walking around aroused for weeks and knew he was reaching the point where he'd have to take Lily to bed or leave entirely. He didn't trust himself in this mood. His control was shaky and his emotions were in turmoil.

"You don't say," Preston said, dryly. He knew for a fact that Rohr loved his job more than any woman—even a wife.

"No, he does."

"Only love, Rohr?" Jay straightened his tie and stood up.

"No, sir."

"Oh, really, Jay," Lily said as if she were heartbroken to hear the news.

"Sorry, Lily. June married me to escape her family. There were pressuring her to join the family law firm, and she wanted to be a housewife. So she made me an offer I couldn't refuse."

Preston bet the offer involved sex but hoped Jay knew enough not to say that to Lily. She had some strange notions about men and women but he didn't want her disillusioned. That was the reason he'd returned every night to his cold, dark apartment, his body tormented by the memories of her in his arms.

"Do you love her now?" she asked.

"More than life itself."

Preston felt a little sorry for Rohr and doubted the man knew what to say when Lily was questioning him the way a marine corps drill sergeant would a new recruit.

"I better be getting back to the office. I have a conference call in forty-five minutes with the Italians on that marble you wanted."

Jay left, and Preston watched Lily tidy up her lunch bag and then pat her hair as if afraid a lock was out of place.

"Just because Jay didn't marry for love doesn't mean he wasn't in love with her."

"I think he was in lust with her."

"Really. Do you think men focus on lust because it's safer?"

"I don't know. I do know that most of the men I know who are married are always vague about how they ended up in that state."

"Do you think they were brainwashed, Pres?"

"No, I just think they wouldn't have chosen to be there."

"They weren't forced to marry."

"Who says a woman didn't use emotional blackmail or maybe the enticement of a child."

"Would that be enough for you? A child?"

"Hell, no. I'd be a lousy father but some men want to pass on their names."

"You don't?"

"I want the Dexter name to stand for first-class resort hotels. I'm not too concerned about a Preston, Jr., running around.''

"Children are the future."

"I live in the present," he said.

"Sooner or later we all have to look forward."

"I do, just not personally."

"Why not?"

"What will be will be."

Lily didn't say anything else, but he knew his life purpose differed greatly from hers. "If you decide to be with me in a relationship, Lily, it will be for now. For as long as we both are happy together."

"Do I make you happy, Pres?"

He stared out across the lake and saw not the leisure boaters who'd bring him revenue but Lily and a small family picnicking on a sailboat.

"Preston?"

"Yes," he said, standing up and walking away from both the woman and the image.

# Eight

**W**atching Preston walk away, Lily knew that she wasn't going to convince him love existed without loving him completely. He needed to experience it and learn to recognize it. Her feelings for him had been steadily increasing since the night they'd almost made love, and for once in her life she was ready to gamble. Ready for the adventure that seemed always on a distant horizon. But habits were hard to break, and she admitted to herself that she was afraid of getting hurt.

"Preston?"

He stopped outside the gazebo. Lily leaned over one of the walls so that she was closer to him. "Don't run away."

He pivoted on his heel, facing her with the pent-up

fury of a god who'd been defied. She'd been playing with fire without even realizing it. He was a dangerous man, but because she'd cared for him, she'd never noticed.

"Lily, I'm damned tired of you accusing me of being a coward."

"I'm not."

"It sure sounds that way. I'm a man people are afraid of."

"I understand," she said, and for the first time she really did. If she was confused by what was happening between them, Preston would be doubly so. Lily had always believed in happy endings. He thought anyone who did was a few bricks short of a load.

"When I walk away from you, angel, it's so that I won't ruin your rose-colored vision of the world."

That hurt. "I've seen plenty of reality."

"Then where is the realism that comes with it?" He stalked closer to her. The white wood barrier of the gazebo was a scant one. She wanted to shrink away from him but at the same time was drawn closer.

"I don't have to be cynical to have experienced pain."

"No, but you should be practical enough to avoid the same situation."

"What are you talking about?" she asked.

"The truth you keep harping on."

"What truth?" She feared his answer. Preston's cold gray eyes were harder than the glaciers of the North Atlantic.

"That you haven't been embracing love but hiding from it."

Lily was stunned and silent. Was that true? She'd been busy the past few years. She'd never hidden from love, because she wanted to experience the beauty her parents had.

"You've used your brothers for an excuse to keep men at bay for the past few years, and now you're using devotion as a reason to keep me away."

"I'm not." But Lily doubted herself for the first time. There was some truth to what he'd said. She'd never let anyone close to her after her parents' deaths. But she wanted Preston closer to her. She'd done everything she knew to get him to be her man, and he'd walked away.

"Then why do you keep tying us both up in knots? Why do you fight the one thing that would convince me you feel some sort of affection for me?"

"What thing?" she asked, fearing the answer.

"Intimacy."

"I don't fear it any more than you do."

"No, you just hide from it or run from it because you can't control it, Lily."

She had no answer for him. It was true she feared what Preston made her feel. Feared how out of his league she really was. Feared that she might never meet anyone again who would ever make her feel as alive as he did.

"I'm just—"

"Trying not to get hurt."

"Is that what *you've* been doing? Is that why you always walk away when I get too close?"

"Yes."

The sincerity in his voice struck straight through to her heart. Preston knew what she felt because he felt some of it, too. He walked away again, and this time she didn't stop him.

Her emotions ricocheted through her like an out-of-control electrical wire. She wanted Preston with a passion that had to be experienced to be believed. But she liked him, too. The little idiosyncrasies that made him human. The things that the society pages never covered. Like his obsession with his car and his thirst for winning. The way he could make her see a side of life that she'd always trivialized.

Maybe it was time for another quote. She'd had greater success with them than with any of the real couples she'd introduced him to. Reaching into her purse, she pulled out the small book she'd been using as her main source. Thumbing through the pages she stood stock-still as she realized the answer was in her hands. Staring her in the eye as it were. A quote by Hannah More: "Love never reasons, but profusely gives, like a thoughtless prodigal, it's all, and trembles then lest it has done so little."

She closed her eyes and repeated the quote to herself. It felt like the answer but she wasn't sure that it was. She had to give to Preston to make him realize that love existed. *Give to Preston....*

She gathered up the remains of their lunch and

walked slowly back to the main house. She had no idea how to convince Preston. But she knew protestations of love weren't going to get it done. It was going to take more than she'd ever given a man before. She wondered if being a virgin was going to hamper her efforts at breaking through the wall that Preston used to protect himself from the world.

Part of his problems lay in the past. She'd have to be blind not to notice the way he focused only in the now. She didn't want to fix his life. She just wanted to find a way for them both to be happy. Find a place where they'd both be comfortable. She wasn't ready to give her body and not her heart.

Seduction was the key, she realized. She'd have to plan carefully. She'd use everything at her disposal to convince him to love her. Frankly she was afraid to move forward, but she wasn't one to back down from a challenge and Preston was right: it was time to face *intimacy*.

Preston stared out the floor-to-ceiling windows that lined the general manager's office at White Willow House. He'd claimed the office as his own while the project was still in the production phase. The sun sank below the horizon and darkness fell. In the distance the Crescent City lights beckoned, promising revelry to all who entered its streets.

He hadn't been this tense since Dexter Resorts had gone public his second year at the helm. The White Willow House was progressing on schedule, but his life

was careening out of control. Everything he'd ever
taken for granted now seemed different. For the first
time ever he wanted to talk to someone, but he didn't
know whom to turn to.

He'd insulated himself from those around him so
thoroughly that he'd never noticed the silence before.
Never noticed the polite chitchat that masqueraded as
conversation. New Orleans pulsed around him with a
life force of its own. For once he wasn't out enjoying
the nightlife and the endless round of women it offered
a man in his position.

The office door creaked open.

"You're here late," said Lily.

He watched her reflection in the plate-glass window.
She looked pale and withdrawn. He'd almost sent her
a dozen roses as an apology for his words yesterday
afternoon, but if he apologized she'd realize how much
she was coming to mean to him. And he couldn't let
that happen. He wouldn't depend on anyone for anything.

He'd never been tempted to. Not since he was eight
and his world had been shifted irreversibly. He'd done
a good job at keeping his distance from many people.
How had one small woman slipped through?

"You look so lonely tonight," Lily said. He heard
her footsteps and watched in the glass as she came
closer to him. The light from the room shone through
her thin cotton dress revealing her curvy female body.

He didn't know if it was emotion he was battling or
his conscience. Because he knew that he wanted her

even if she was a virgin. He wanted to peel away the layers she kept between herself and the world and find the real Lily, the one he'd hurt yesterday. Then he wanted to put her back together again.

"Preston?" She brushed her hand down his sleeve, stopping at his palm. Her long cool fingers gently caressing.

He grunted. Words were beyond him. He wanted her with the same soul-searching devotion that a preacher had to save sinners' eternal lives. At that moment he shook with the need to pull her into his arms. To feel her mouth under his and tangle his tongue with hers. To press her soft body to his harder one until there were no lines left where he ended and she began.

"I'm sorry I let things go too far the other day," she said. He knew he should say something, but he couldn't concentrate. Her scent assailed him. Flowers and *Lily*. She smelled distinctly like woman. Not something that could be manufactured and bottled but an essence that spoke straight to his hormones and sent his testosterone level skyrocketing.

Blood rushed through him, hardening his groin. He wanted to move his legs, to shift his position, but she was too close. If he moved, he'd take her. Sweep her up over his shoulder and not stop until they reached his desk. He'd push that flimsy skirt to her waist and rip her panties out of his way. Then he'd slide home. *Yes, home.* He needed to be inside her and feel her wrapped all around him. Clinging to him as he moved with fierce thrusts until she exploded for him again.

"Preston, I've been thinking about something."

He had no idea what she was talking about, only knew that he had to move away from her. Had to put some distance between them or he'd give in to his instincts. Yet his feet felt rooted to the ground.

"Preston, what is wrong with you?" she asked, cupping his face in her palm.

"Don't touch me," he ground out. It had been too long since he'd had a woman. Too long since he'd wanted any woman except Lily, and frankly he didn't want to wait another night. But she deserved better than him for her first experience in the sensual arts. She deserved a man who could love her. A man who'd take that trip down the aisle with her.

"Sorry." She took a half step away from him. Her eyes met his in the glass window, and she flinched. A telltale sheen of tears glittered in her eyes.

He knew he was hurting her again. Why did that keep happening? He was trying so hard to protect her from the beast he knew lurked beneath the sophisticated man he presented to the world. Why did she keep coming back to him with her soft touches and kind words?

"Lily, this has to stop."

"I don't understand. You challenged me to make you believe in love."

"I want you in my bed. That was the reason for the challenge."

"I wasn't saying no after the wedding reception."

"Well, you should have been."

"Why? Because I'm a virgin."

He glanced at her, no longer trusting the distorted image in the glass. "Yes."

"I think I'm big enough to make my own decisions." He let his gaze sweep over her body, and it inflamed the fire already running through his veins. She was his dream woman, he realized. Nice-size breasts, long slender legs and that short, sassy red hair that framed her angelic features.

"Sure you are, but I'm the one who'll have to deal with the consequences when you believe that you've traded your body for love."

"I know better than that. I'm the one who's been trying for weeks to convince you love is real."

"Don't trust me, Lily."

"Why not?"

"I want you too badly now to play fair. So here's your warning, angel. Leave now or stay and pay the consequences."

"What consequences?"

"Gamble with that sweet body of yours."

She paled but didn't walk away. He admired her spirit but wanted to warn her to not let every damned thing she felt show on her face. He should walk away. He should return to Manhattan and let Rohr finish this project or head to Barbados so that Lily wouldn't tempt him.

She stood poised, ready like a rabbit to run from a predator. He knew one wrong word would send her flying from him. And he knew that he should be saying that wrong word and sending her away.

*One right word would make her stay.*

He had no right, but he wanted what others took for granted. He wanted what he'd seen her give to her customers, friends and family. He wanted to bask in her light and wallow in her purity. He wanted…Lily.

"Lily, please."

"Please, what?"

"Stay with me."

She bit her lip and looked around the rather sparse office. The desk that he'd imagined taking her on was a sleek mahogany that would have tempted a more experienced woman. The floors were cold hard marble, and the only chair, a big leather executive model.

"Here?" she asked. She was game but scared.

Because he wasn't going to be her forever man, Preston knew he had to make Lily's first time special. Not some hurried coupling in his office.

"No, not here. And not tonight. Spend this weekend with me on my yacht. We'll go out on the Gulf. Just the two of us."

She took a deep breath. He hoped she didn't change her mind or he'd have to resort to that damned desk.

"Okay."

Relief coursed through him, and he wanted to pull her into his arms, but he'd wait until they could really be alone to make love to Lily.

Preston hadn't spoken to her for two days. He'd sent flowers, champagne and a negligee that would've made an experienced woman blush. Lily, though excited about her weekend with Preston, was ready to back out. Suddenly she didn't know if loving him would be enough. And how she would protect herself if it turned out he couldn't love her.

She'd phoned her brothers and grandmother and told them she'd be out of town for the weekend. They'd been surprised that she was going anywhere but hadn't asked whom she was going with. As if they'd believe she was spending the weekend on a yacht with a man. She was living it and hardly believed it.

Mae had offered her practical advice—don't let him know how much you care. But Lily didn't know how to lie like that. Didn't know how to protect herself from the one thing she wanted most in the world. Preston Dexter.

A sleek, black limousine pulled up in front of her house. Lily nervously wondered if he expected her to make love in the back seat with him. She'd heard stories of people doing those kinds of things. But she'd never once imagined it.

Oh, God, she thought, I can't do this.

Preston had been right. She was afraid of intimacy. Afraid that she'd lose again the way she had when her parents died and her world had been shattered. She'd built a safe haven for herself where nothing but predictability ruled.

Preston emerged from the car, dark glasses covering his eyes, his Armani suit fitting his frame perfectly. He moved up the walk like a man who ruled the world, and Lily realized he ruled her heart. He hesitated on the walkway. Turned as if he was going to get back in the limo and leave.

Seeing Preston's indecision forced her to open the door. She wanted Preston in her life. She wanted him enough to take risks.

"Pres?"

He strode to her with the smooth determination she'd always known him to possess. If she hadn't seen him from her window she wouldn't have suspected he'd hesitated. She wanted to ask him what he'd been waiting for, but he didn't give her a chance.

"Ready to go, angel?"

"Yes," she said, but her answer sounded weak to her ears. She knew that one of the reasons Preston had been drawn to her from the beginning was that she'd met him as an equal. She had to do so now. She wasn't normally a cowering type and didn't plan to start now.

"Yes, I am," she said again. This time, though, the words were for her. She was going to win their challenge, because neither of them would be satisfied with anything less. Her heart's desire now seemed twined to Preston, and her future seemed less exciting without him in it.

"Where's your suitcase?" he asked.

"In the hall. Having never been on an illicit weekend before I wasn't sure what to pack. I picked up a magazine that advertised 'What to Wear to Tempt Your Man.'"

"Then we won't need your suitcase. Because nothing is exactly what you should be wearing."

She blushed. She knew they'd have to be naked, and she wanted to see Preston's body and to feel him moving over her. But she was uncomfortable in her own skin. It had been different after Marti and Brad's wedding, because there had been magic in the air, but today, standing in the front yard of the house she'd lived in all her life, she felt a little too ordinary for Preston.

"You can seduce me without even trying, angel," he said, his voice a husky rasp. He brushed one finger along her chin and then cupped her head and brought her closer for a kiss. He rubbed his lips briefly over hers and pulled back before she'd had a chance to reciprocate.

"You, too," she said, with a shy smile.

"So what'd you pack?" he asked, picking up her suitcases.

"A swimsuit."

"Well, there goes my fantasy. That must be one big suit."

"Maybe one or two other little things."

"The negligee?"

"You'll have to wait and see."

"I've been fantasizing about that damned lingerie since I saw it in the catalog."

"I might not look as glamorous as the model did. You know I think they airbrush their bodies—"

Preston's finger over her lips stopped the flow of words that her nervous system kept feeding her.

"I know that you won't look like they did."

She swallowed against the disappointment. Of course reality dictated that she wasn't going to be able to compete with an underwear model, but she would have liked to cling to the illusion that he found her sexy despite the fact that she was a rather ordinary girl-next-door type.

"You're going to put her to shame."

She glanced up at him and saw herself reflected in the dark lenses of his glasses. Without thinking, she removed his glasses. Sincerity and some other emotion, something she couldn't define but that warmed her to her toes shone there.

She knew then that she was meant to be Preston's woman. That he made her stronger than she could be on her own. And she had the power to do the same to him. But he wasn't looking for the future, and when Lily looked at him, stared deep into his beautiful gray eyes, she saw them growing old together.

# Nine

**P**reston had never had a woman on the yacht before. He used it mainly for business deals. In fact, it felt odd to have only Lily with him on the yacht. When he entertained, he had a crew of five who catered to the whims of his business associates. Since they were only cruising out in the Gulf, Preston dismissed the staff and asked only the captain and chef to remain onboard the *Gold Digger*. His father had named the yacht after his third wife had left him.

He carried Lily's suitcases into the master stateroom and felt her following closely behind. She was nervous, and he wanted her so badly. He was tempted to pull her into his arms and soothe her with kisses. But the bed was only five steps away. And the floor covered with thick rich carpets imported from Persia. If he started kissing her they'd spend the weekend docked instead of out on the sea. And he wanted more than that with Lily.

He glanced over his shoulder and found Lily with her shoes off and eyes closed. Her red-painted toenails burrowed into the thick carpet, and a small smile graced her face. She had a toe ring on her left foot, and Preston couldn't stop staring at it.

"Pres, this is great. How long have you had the yacht?"

All he could think about was that damned toe ring. He wanted to suckle her little toes. He wanted to feel the ring scraping along his calf as he made love to her.

"It was my dad's."

"I like it a lot. Is that a print?" she asked, pointing to the Gauguin oil above the bed.

"No. It's a bear to keep in good condition, but it really makes the room." Or so the decorator had told him.

"Who named the yacht?"

"Dear old Dad."

"I was afraid you'd named it." The way she watched him made him feel better than he was. Like he'd done something to deserve her trust and respect. He knew he hadn't.

"Nah, he did."

She walked closer to him and sat down on the bed. Preston's instincts screamed at him to push her back and settle himself over her. To take her lips in long, drugging kisses until they were away from the coast and out at sea.

"There's got to be a story behind it." She smiled at him, and his pulse increased. She went through his system faster than hundred-proof whisky. Her body was pressed against his and he felt each inhalation of breath through her body.

"Well, my dad had a lousy track record with women, and after his third divorce he bought this boat and named it *Gold Digger* to remind himself that all women were after only one thing."

She stared pensively away from him, and Preston realized how that would sound to her. The story had always seemed kind of funny to him as he'd been growing up. Even his mother had chuckled when she'd heard the name. But then, his mother was wealthy in her own right and hadn't married his father for money.

"Well, now I know where you got your theory on relationships."

"Lily, it doesn't mean anything. It's a joke." He tried to pull her closer. Brought his arms around her but she shifted subtly away from him.

"Yeah, I know. I guess I just don't get it."

She stood and started to walk away. He grabbed her wrist.

"Where are you going?"

"Um... I think I'll go up on deck while we leave the harbor. I've always loved the sea breezes."

She kept talking until she'd disappeared up the gangway. Damn. He'd hurt her again. Part of him realized that it might have been intentional. He knew that Lily wasn't after his money, but he wanted to hear her say it.

He left the cabin, found the captain and asked him to weigh anchor. He didn't want to lose Lily but didn't know how to undo the hurt he'd unwittingly inflicted. Ordinarily he wouldn't bother worry about it, but this was Lily and she mattered more to him than he wanted to acknowledge.

He grabbed a bottle of Dom from the galley and the fresh-cut strawberries he'd ordered left in there. The trappings of seduction. He hadn't thought he'd need them but now knew he did.

He found her on the aft deck sitting on one of the sun chairs. Large glasses covered her face and her hair whipped around her head. She lifted her face to the sun and took a deep breath as if she were trying to deal with some deep, tearing emotion. Had he done this to her?

He set the berries and champagne on the deck table and sat at her feet. Where he knew he belonged. Startled, she jerked upright and turned her face away.

"Angel, don't give up on me yet."

"I can't fight this, Preston."

"I'm not asking you to."

"No, you're not, but someday you're going to look at me and wonder if I'm staying with you because of your money."

"I won't," he said, but knew the words were a lie. No one had ever stayed except for money.

"Yes, you will. And you know it, don't you?"

"Maybe. It doesn't mean anything. I'll change the name of the damned boat."

"Can you change how you were raised?"

"No. Can you?"

"I don't want to. I don't believe everyone in the world who has less money than I do can be bought."

"I don't believe it, either. Not anymore." He still couldn't see her eyes and wasn't sure she trusted him. But it was the best he could do. Life had taught him some harsh lessons. And though Lily tied him in knots sexually, he wasn't sure he trusted what he felt for her.

He reached for the bottle of champagne and the long-stemmed flutes he brought with him. "I didn't ask you to spend this weekend fighting with me."

He handed the glasses to Lily. She hesitated, then, sighing, took them.

"And I didn't agree to come just to argue with you."

"Why did you agree?"

"For reasons you wouldn't believe."

"Don't be coy."

"I'm not. I never realized how hard winning that challenge was going to be until this moment."

He said nothing.

"I can't make you love," she said softly. He knew he should fill the void, give her something she needed from him, but he honestly didn't know how. Lily wanted something from him that he knew didn't exist. Now she knew it, too.

* * *

Preston suggested they go for a swim when they stopped in the early evening. There was no land in sight, only endless sea in every direction. Lily felt as if she and Preston were the only two people in the world. After their tense conversation she'd been afraid he'd pressure her into bed. In fact, she wasn't sure when they'd make love. She still wanted him with a fierce desire that sent her pulse racing whenever she looked at him, but she was leery of him emotionally.

Her battle to teach him to love kept encountering defenses that she'd never known existed. Like hidden land mines going off in peacetime, she thought.

Uncomfortable showing a lot of skin, she normally wore a very conservative one-piece suit, but Mae had taken her shopping, insisting she needed something flashier. So here she was donning a tiny two-piece affair that made her feel like... A glance in the mirror stopped that thought. Her body was revealed but she didn't look as bad as she'd imagined she would. In fact, the color brought out what was left of her tan, and the cut made her legs look longer than they really were.

For a moment she felt as if she belonged on this well-appointed yacht and with the wealthy man who owned it. The man who thought that naming a boat *Gold Digger* was a pretty funny joke. Despite what he'd said, she felt he'd been sending her a message. And she knew there was no way she'd ever have enough money for him to believe that his didn't matter to her.

She pushed that thought away. This might be the

only chance she had with Preston. The only way to convince him love really existed. She'd prepared a few little notes and gifts for him. Really small things, but he was important to her and she didn't give herself lightly. She needed to know he understood that.

She taped a note to his bathroom mirror and one on his pillow. They were more love quotes. One by Mandino about treasuring love above gold and wealth that she hoped would reach his heart. And one by Longfellow about love never being bought. She liked it because it reminded her that love was giving and she wanted to give to Preston.

She grabbed her cover-up, slid her feet into her sandals and headed up on deck. Preston stood at the back of the boat, leaning over the rail. The breeze ruffled his dark hair, and he seemed an island unto himself. She paused for a moment.

His lean, muscled body must draw women to him as much as his money, she thought. He wore a pair of trim black swimming trunks and despite the casual pose he seemed tense.

She hurried to him, her shoes clip-clopping on the deck. For a minute she felt like the awkward girl she'd always been in social situations, but then she felt the heat of Preston's gaze and slowed her stride. He made her feel like a woman, and as she moved she was aware of the sway of her hips, the way the fabric of her cover-up slid open and closed over her chest as she moved.

He straightened and walked toward her. As usual,

confidence was in every motion he made. "Ready for that swim?"

"Yes," she said, slipping her cover-up down her shoulders and tossing it on a chair.

A long, low whistle broke the silence. She glanced over her shoulder at him.

"Do you like it?" she asked.

"Hell, yeah."

He pulled her close to him in a fierce hug. His mouth took hers as he pressed his erection against her. Oh, he more than liked the suit. A surge of female power rushed through her, and she realized she had been given a gift, this ability to affect Preston.

He pulled back abruptly. "Let's go for that swim before I forget the plans I've made for your first time."

Plans. That must include more of the trappings of romance. They'd eaten their strawberries and drunk champagne on the deck. Preston had fed them to her the way she imagined Roman demigods feeding their goddesses on Mount Olympus.

The romance of their relationship seemed important to him. "Are you okay with this being my first time?" she asked.

He raised one eyebrow in question.

"I mean, I know it makes you uncomfortable." She didn't want to have another solo orgasm. She wanted to experience all of Preston.

"As you pointed out, you are a big girl."

"Why do we have to wait?" she asked, ready to make love to him now. Even on the deck of this boat.

"Because you deserve soft candlelight and flowers—a romantic fantasy."

"What about you? What do you deserve?"

"Less than you are giving me," he said.

"I don't need the trappings of love," she said.

"No, you need the real thing."

"Don't you?" she asked. It was the first time he'd come even close to admitting love might exist.

"I need you, Lily," he said, tossing his sunglasses on her cover-up. He stepped down on the attached dock and dove cleanly into the water. He surfaced a few feet away but didn't say anything else.

*He needed her.*

What had it cost him to admit it? She knew he'd deny the sentiment behind those words if she pressed him on it. But he did care for her.

Lily dove in after him and let him tease her into playing games that were fun but light, when what she really wanted was to hold him close to her and assure him that he deserved everything she had to give.


"Close your eyes," Preston said. Lily, who'd been an enchanting temptress all night, did as she'd been asked. Unable to resist the creamy length of her back for another moment, Preston bent and dropped a kiss on the center of her spine. He was ready to explode.

Dinner had been a nice affair, but he couldn't remember what they'd eaten. Lily had smiled across the table from him all evening, making him feel as if he did indeed deserve her love.

Knowing that Lily had never made love to another man, he'd wanted to give her something special today. But all of the teasing touches and innocent activities had whipped him to frenzy. His control was hanging by a thread. Could he hold on?

"Pres?" she asked. Everyone else addressed him formally. Always had. He wasn't sure how she'd given him a nickname, but it made him feel special…part of her circle of intimates. He wanted that, but at the same time feared it. This gift Lily was giving him had strings she didn't even realize it had. But he didn't dwell on that tonight.

His bed lay on the other side of that teak door, and he longed to have Lily under him. "Right here, angel."

"Can I open my eyes?"

"Not yet."

He opened the door to the master stateroom and led her inside. "Take off your shoes."

"Just my shoes."

"Any other articles of clothing you want to remove are fine with me."

She laughed. But she sounded nervous. Scrupulously she kept her eyes closed as she stepped out of her high-heeled sandals. She teetered for a moment, and Preston stepped forward to support her.

"Thanks," she said, her voice soft.

Preston led her forward. The carpet had been sprinkled with rose petals. He'd kicked off his own shoes. The petals were soft but not as soft as Lily's skin.

"This feels nice," she said.

"Open your eyes."

The room had been made to look like a romantic lover's dream. Candles lit every surface, flowers were laid in between and her negligee had been placed on the bed.

"Oh, Preston."

He loved hearing his name on her lips. He pulled her back in his arms, unable to wait another second to touch her. She sighed and put one hand on his back, the other behind his head.

"Thank you for doing all of this."

"I know the romantic fantasy is important to you."

"How?"

He brushed his lips against hers. He didn't want to talk. She tasted like sin itself—sweet, hot and tempting. And like the sinner he was, he took her mouth in long, drugging kisses, convinced he could stop after one. But he couldn't.

She writhed against him. He slid his hands down her back. He took her bottom in his hands and brought her closer to his aching erection. He'd been hard for so long. He didn't think he could slow down.

She pushed his dinner jacket off his shoulders, and he let it drop to the floor. "If we don't slow down now…"

"I don't want to, Pres, make love to me."

"Yes," he said, lifting her in his arms and carrying her to the bed.

He settled her in the center and undressed himself quickly. Lily's breath caught as she looked at him naked for the first time. She looked a little hesitant when she saw the size of him.

"Trust me," he said.

"I do," she said.

"Will you take off your dress?" he asked. He was afraid to touch her. She slid her dress down her body and kicked it to the end of the bed. She lay in the center of his bed, where he'd wanted her for the longest time, clothed only in the skimpiest pair of red lace panties he'd ever seen and that toe ring.

The color inflamed him. He fell to the bed, his hands caressing her pale body, his mouth suckling her breast and his erection rubbing softly at her humid warmth through the layer of lace.

She moaned and grasped his shoulders. Her nails bit into his skin, but he scarcely noticed the sting. Levering himself up on his elbows, he slid his mouth down her body. She tasted as sweet as he'd known she would. Not just of the innocence she projected but of something more. Something that he'd never tasted before. Something so hard to identify that he gave up.

Her pretty round breasts begged for his attention. He caressed her nipples with his fingers, and they hardened under his touch. He couldn't wait any longer. Bending to her slim body, he suckled her.

She moaned again. A deep, husky sound that brought him even closer to the edge. He trailed his lips to her other breast and sucked her nipple deep into his mouth. She writhed on the bed and held his head to her body.

Arching up under him. He slid one arm behind her to hold her to him.

"Preston…"

He'd die hearing the sound of his name on her lips. He couldn't wait any longer. He lowered her to the bed and slid his hand down over her smooth, slightly curved stomach to the nest of red curls hidden beneath red lace. Never had anything enflamed him more.

She was warm and wet to his touch. Impatiently he shoved her panties down her legs. She kicked free of them. Preston reached for the condoms he'd put on the nightstand before dinner.

He sheathed himself, glancing up to find Lily staring at him. He wondered what she was thinking. She smiled at him. That sweet, innocent grin that made him want to protect her from the world and from himself. But not tonight. Not while fierce desire pumped through his veins and testosterone robbed him of the ability to be rational.

"Spread your legs, angel."

She blushed and separated her thighs by the smallest inch.

"Don't you want me?"

"More than I'd believed I could."

"Then make me feel welcome."

She opened her arms and her legs. "Come here, Preston."

He did. He slid into her tight body carefully because he didn't want to cause her pain. But she was so incredibly tight. He waited tensely for her to relax around him, then thrust slowly, gathering momentum only as she started to move with him. That toe ring of hers scraped along his thigh, bringing him closer to the edge. Then he heard her breath catch and felt her body tighten around him, and she was calling his name the way she had that night on his sofa.

His consciousness dimmed and he thrust heavily until release washed over him in waves. He held her close in the dim candlelight, rolling to his back and keeping her pressed to him, their bodies still joined. He held her tightly and hoped she didn't feel the desperation pouring through him. Hoped she didn't realize how deeply into his skin she'd crawled. Hoped he wouldn't hurt her too much when he pushed her away, because he knew if he didn't she would leave on her own, and he'd only just realized how much that would hurt.

# Ten

Lily had never experienced anything like what she'd shared with Preston. He was quiet but held her fiercely to him, and it worried her that he hadn't said anything. Was he trying to pretend she was just another woman? Like that blond society woman she'd seen him pictured with in New York.

Her soul insisted that the emotions she felt for him were too strong not to be reciprocated, but her mind wasn't as easy to convince.

He'd challenged her to convince him to love, promised her her heart's desire, and she'd only just realized those two were intertwined. That she would never have one without the other.

Preston shifted her to his side and left the bed for a

minute to dispose of his condom. Her thighs ached a little from accommodating him but she found she wanted him again. The fierce ache started at her center and spread outward.

"You okay?" he asked as he settled back into bed and tugged her close again.

"Yes. It was wonderful for me."

"Me, too," he said, his words special to her because he so rarely revealed what he was feeling.

"Did you get my notes earlier?" she asked, unsure of herself for the first time with him. From the moment they'd met he'd made her uneasy, but not like this. She'd always been sure of herself—that she could handle the situation and being in bed with him. Her body still dewy from his possession made her…uncertain. She remembered that love was giving.

"The one on the pillow?"

"Yes."

"You think love lasts longer than gold?"

"You know I do."

"That didn't convince me."

"There are so many poor people who are happy and love each other," she said.

"The fact that they have someone to share their pitiful existence probably creates that feeling of affection."

"Preston."

"Lily."

She knew that he was a tough, cynical man, but sometimes he made her want to scream. This love dare was taking everything she had to give, and Preston wasn't even close to acknowledging real love might exist in the world much less in his life.

"Let's forget about love for tonight and concentrate on each other. I've wanted you for so long."

"Me, too," she said, softly.

Preston pulled her closer to him. Silence built between them as he rubbed her back from neck to backside. She squirmed closer to him. He smiled down at her, that wicked seducer's grin, and she pinched his side.

"Stop teasing me."

He caressed her again, this time a deeper touch that furrowed between her legs to her feminine flesh, still sensitive from his earlier possession.

"I'm teasing myself," he said.

"Well then, I might do some of the same." Preston needed a lover who was bold. Someone who wouldn't cower and be afraid of him. She could be that woman. She was that woman.

"I'd welcome it."

She walked her fingers along the line of dark hair that tapered over his chest and stomach. It was springy and warm and smelled faintly musky. She leaned closer, wanting to taste him. She'd been so passive when they'd made love. She'd been unsure of what she was feeling and afraid to explore. But now, in the dim glow of the flickering candles, she wanted to know Preston.

"Can I kiss you?"

He nodded.

Leaning forward she dropped a soft kiss on his hard stomach. He sucked in his breath, and she used the edge of her teeth to trace the line her fingers had just followed. His manhood stirred. She tilted her head and glanced up his body at him.

"You like that?" she asked.

"Just a little."

"Want some more?"

"Only what you're comfortable with."

"You make me feel very sensual, Pres."

He watched her. His gray eyes hard as diamonds, but she thought she saw a sparkle there that hadn't been present before. "Show me."

She bit her lip. This was what she'd wanted. "I will."

She'd show him more than physical attraction, more than what they'd experienced earlier—she'd show him love. She caressed his chest. His pecs were hard and flexed when he moved his hands to lift her over him.

His erection pressed urgently against her thigh, and she felt control slipping further and further from her grasp.

"No more touching, Pres."

"You've got to be kidding, angel."

"I'm not. This time I'm calling the shots."

"You're in the driver's seat."

"Yeah, but it's a remote control car."

He laughed and she felt it everywhere they touched.

He hugged her close and kissed her hard on the lips. It took her a moment to realize he wasn't touching her.

She started at his head, traced the shape of his ear and bit on the lobe. His neck smelled of the expensive cologne he wore, and she burrowed nearer to him. She touched her tongue to the pulse she could see beating in his neck and watched his Adam's apple bob as the center of her body brushed over his erection.

She did it again and this time he tensed and sucked in his breath. She couldn't wait much longer to feel him inside her again. To feel him filling her where she'd always been empty. To feel she'd come home when she'd been journeying for so long.

"Can we make love again?" she asked.

He grunted.

She grabbed a condom from the box by the bed and slid down, resting on his thighs. She tore open the package and covered him with it. He gritted his teeth, his breath hissing out. "Come here, angel."

"I'm still in charge."

"I know."

She slid over his body and decided being in charge wasn't what she wanted. She didn't think she could impale herself on him. Wasn't sure how to proceed, and that disappointed her. She wanted to be Preston's equal, but—

"Lily?"

She nodded. He positioned her over his erection and thrust upward while driving her hips down. It seemed as though he went deeper than before. Her head fell back and she moaned. She rode him harder until she felt that unique feeling begin again deep inside her. Preston's hips moved faster and as her body tightened and lights swirled behind her eyelids he called her name and ground his hips against hers.

She'd never felt anything half as real as what she'd shared with Preston and knew he'd have to acknowledge that love had begun to grow between them.

The tickling of feminine fingers walking along his spine brought Preston out of sleep. He'd been enjoying a vision of himself on an island with just one other person, no phones, no faxes, no demanding meetings. Only two naked bodies on sugar-fine sand with a warm tropical breeze blowing over them with the waves nearby.

''Wake up, sleepyhead,'' Lily said in his ear. Her soft voice brushed over senses already aroused. Gentle biting kisses dotted his neck. Heat shot to his groin, and he started to reach for her but stopped. Lily would be sore this morning.

He knew that they shouldn't make love this morning. She hadn't protested when he'd rolled her beneath him in the early morning hours and taken her again, but he knew that accepting him had been painful for her at first before passion swept through her and brought her to completion.

He had never been a woman's first lover before. But it had felt right to be Lily's. There was an odd possessiveness running through him as if he had branded her

in some way that made her his for all time. It was
ridiculous, of course. He was a man who always moved
on, but for the first time the thought of other men
touching what had been his was unacceptable. He had
to find a way to bind her to him. Sex was great for
creating intimacy, but this morning he'd have to find
another way.

"You're not one of those cheerful morning people
are you?"

"Only when the morning is this glorious."

He smiled. Lily enchanted him in a way that made
him want to believe in love, or at least tell her he did,
but he never lied. He'd been on the receiving end of
one too many "good-natured" white lies to ever do
that to anyone.

"I'm almost tempted to open my eyes."

"What would lure you, Pres?"

You, he thought, but didn't say it out loud. Instead
he rolled to his side and captured the fingers that had
been caressing him. Her eyes were deep and serious,
filled with the emotions she hadn't learned to hide, and
it made him ache for her. She believed in love, and
he'd bet his newest hotel she believed herself in love
with him.

The unacknowledged part of his soul hungered for
affection from her. Wanted to hear some avowal of her
feelings for him, but the other part, the weary man
who'd been left time and again, knew they wouldn't
come. Not without a price tag.

He'd pay the price for Lily and not regret the money.

Though he'd be disappointed if she asked him for jewels or real estate, at least he'd be able to deal with her. Instead she came to him with her sweet innocence and sultry passion. Setting his body on fire and making his soul long for something his mind had proof didn't exist.

Time to get out of the bedroom and back to the real world. Back to a place where he could think on his feet and find some workable answers. In bed with Lily he was enticed into believing the fantasy—that love existed for him. "I'd get out of bed for breakfast."

She snaked her hand down under the covers to his stomach. He remembered her mouth on that same spot last night. Maybe they wouldn't be getting out of bed today. There were many ways to make love.

"I knew Grandmother was right when she said the way to a man's heart was through his stomach."

Though he knew she'd been teasing, her words put a damper on his ardor. *His heart.* The muscle had been beating strongly for years but she wanted to reach his other heart. The seat of his soul where all of his vulnerabilities lay.

He wasn't happy about admitting even to himself that part existed. He wasn't about to let Lily find it. He wasn't about to parade out all of his foibles even for Lily. "Is that what you are trying to reach?"

She glanced away, a pink blush spreading up her cheeks. His erection stirred beneath the sheets; he was too damned old to be ruled by his groin.

"I'll settle for whatever I can get from you, Preston."

"What if all I offer is passion?" he demanded. He'd been foolish to think that sleeping with Lily would be the answer to the questions plaguing him. Though he now knew how exquisitely they fitted together he still had no idea how to relate to her.

She bit her lip. "I'll take it but I want more."

"I don't have *more*."

"I don't know where we stand now."

He didn't, either. But he was the experienced one, and for once he thought he might have the upper hand with Lily. "We're having an affair."

"For how long?"

"However long it lasts."

"And if that isn't enough."

"It will be," he said.

She left the bed, picking up his shirt from the floor and slipping it on. She looked lost and alone. He regretted his honesty but wouldn't take back the words. She'd get bored with him. There was a big empty hole inside of him that couldn't be filled, and though he was content with that emptiness, he knew from the past that women weren't.

He watched her go into the bathroom, listened to the sounds of her shower, knew he had to get up. He entered the bathroom and gathered his shaving gear, preparing to use one of the other staterooms.

But he'd been alone all of his life and would be alone again, he knew. For a few more weeks or months, whatever time Lily had to spend with him, he wanted to wallow in the sunlight she'd brought to his life. He couldn't do that on his own. He couldn't do that in another stateroom. He could only do that with her.

He entered the shower. Lily's eyes widened as he stepped inside, and for a moment he was afraid she wouldn't come into his arms, but as he spread them wide she didn't hesitate. He held her with a desperation he hoped she wouldn't notice and then loved her as if she was the only woman on the planet, and for a while he believed she was.

Lily tried to hurry through the cleaning of an eighteenth-century chandelier but she knew that a quality job took time. She should have finished the chandelier two weeks ago, but she'd been spending every free minute with Preston. Although his schedule was much more demanding than hers, she knew she couldn't keep giving unconditionally.

A glance at the clock told her it was time to wrap up for the night. It was November 1, All Saints' Day, and she'd visited her parents' gravesites that morning to deck the tombs with flowers. Tonight she'd convinced Preston to visit one of the candlelight vigils held in one of the older cemeteries in the city.

Already night was beginning to fall and the sounds from the French Quarter beckoned. She grabbed one of Dash's jackets and headed outside to wait for Preston. November had a chill that made her long for the humidity of September.

Last night for Halloween she'd asked Pres to dress as a vampire and help her hand out candy to the local kids at the school gym, knowing this would be a first for him. He'd agreed without any hesitation and had donated electronic toys for each of the seven hundred children who'd preregistered. Preston had made her agree to play Lady Godiva alone for him in her house after they'd returned home. Remembering his passion made her smile.

There was more to the arrogant person Preston wanted the world to see. Slowly he was letting his guard down, and each new layer he revealed made her love him more. She was working on the love dare and felt as if she was getting close to a breakthrough. He no longer seemed so distant and often prompted her for the quote of the day.

He'd even surprised her by spending an evening on her front porch wrapped in her arms while he read her poetry from Lord Byron. His warm, dark voice swirled through her mind. With a few nudges Preston could be a very romantic person.

He pulled up in his fancy car and called to her from the open window.

"Lily, you ready?"

She walked to the car and got in. The sounds of the Dave Matthews Band filled the air. She loved the jazz band and had given Preston one of their CDs. He'd gone out and bought every CD the band had made and tried to give them to her. Uncomfortable accepting presents, especially from him, she'd returned them.

Slowly all of them were ending up at her house or in her possession by default.

"Have you heard this one? It's another live album."

"It's good."

"I'm sure we won't be able to listen to the whole thing tonight. Metarie Cemetery is only a short drive across the city. You can take it home with you to-night."

"I'm not taking the CD, but I'll take you."

"Not unless I take you first."

He leaned over for a quick, thorough kiss that left her feeling branded. He glanced over his shoulder and pulled out onto the street and headed for the cemetery. All Saints' Day was celebrated in unique fashion in the Crescent City. She'd been going to the evening cele-brations since she was a little girl and still cried when she remembered the first of November, the year her parents' died.

"Looking forward to tonight?" she asked, as he fi-nally found a place to park the car.

"I have to admit it creeps me out."

"A little?"

"A lot," he said with a laugh.

A group of people passed them with flowers in their hands. Preston tugged her close to his side, slinging his arm around her shoulder.

She'd brought chrysanthemums earlier to her par-ents' sites. And she wondered if Preston had anyone to remember. He spoke of his father as if the man were dead, but she really knew nothing of his family.

They'd entered the cemetery, which used to be a racetrack way back in the late 1800s before being converted to a graveyard. Slowly they walked hand in hand through the candlelit plots, pausing to read inscriptions and listening to the conversations of those keeping vigil.

"I've always used this time of year to remember people I've lost, regardless of whether they're buried in New Orleans or not."

"Who are you remembering this year?" he asked quietly.

"My friends Pam and Carol." She still saw their smiling faces and remembered the good times with them. It was kind of cleansing to share her memories of them with Preston. She talked about them for a few minutes, knowing they would have liked Preston.

"Who are you remembering?" she asked.

"This is your tradition not mine."

"Have you lost anyone close to you?" she asked. She knew he was uncomfortable with the topic, but she wanted to know more of his past. Never had she met anyone who ignored it the way he did.

"I don't think I have."

"What about your parents? Your dad's dead, isn't he?"

"Yes. My mother is, too. But we were never close."

She started to ask another question but he placed his fingers over her lips so softly. She looked into those gray-lake eyes of his and for once they didn't seem frozen. "Have I told you how lovely you are tonight?"

She shook her head, letting him change the topic she so desperately wanted to pursue. She knew the key to teaching him to love was in the past but she'd yet to find it.

"Well, you are exquisite."

"Oh, Preston, you say the silliest things."

"I don't."

But he did. She was an average, ordinary girl—the girl next door—and he always made her feel like a fairy princess. Even tonight, surrounded by the crowds at Metarie, she felt like the only woman in the world beautiful enough for him. She was ready to go home with him. To reaffirm the bond that she knew was growing between them. To make love with the man who'd taken over her heart.

"I have one more thing to show you, then let's go home."

"Let's hurry."

She led him to a rather plain-looking tomb. The flickering candlelight made it hard to see the inscription, but Lily had tucked a small flashlight into her jacket pocket before leaving her shop.

The words were simple. A large tomb that held the bodies of...

Two Lovers United on Earth, Together for Eternity.

"What do you think?" she said, sniffing a little at the injustice of a couple dying when they were only twenty and twenty-two.

"That you are one in a million."

Lily knew then that a real chink had opened in Preston's armor. Loving him was bringing him closer to her, and she wouldn't stop until he could see what she'd only just realized. They were a couple for all time. With that magical love that would outlast time.

# Eleven

Preston had made two trips to the office, even though it was Thanksgiving. When he returned the second time, he found himself surrounded by Lily's family.

Mae, her assistant, and Jim, Mae's husband, had arrived with a store-bought pie and a bottle of domestic wine. Her neighbors, the Conroys, a golden anniversary couple, had arrived next. Preston had found himself seated on the couch next to Mr. Conroy, listening to tales of his courtship of Annabelle and how he'd convinced her to marry him.

Lily's family was a little intimidating. They were all so protective of her that he felt uncomfortable. Like the cold seducer he'd started out being. He couldn't explain to them what he didn't understand, but he knew that Lily meant more to him than only nights of pleasure.

He felt like a heartless Casanova who'd coaxed their little lamb out into the cold, dark world and taken advantage of her. Even though he knew Lily had come to him of her own free will.

Business was the one thing he could count on. The closer Lily got to him the faster he wanted to retreat. She'd refused to let him sleep over last night with her brothers at home. She didn't want to give them the wrong impression.

He didn't have the heart to tell her that they weren't fooling anyone. Dash and Beau knew he was more to their sister than a business associate. Her grandmother, a young-looking sixty-eight-year-old, had waved her arms around him and read his aura.

She'd stared into his eyes and muttered something in a language he couldn't recognize.

"You've got potential," she said before walking away.

It had been a bit of a weird experience, and Preston would take on both of the brothers with one arm tied behind his back before he allowed Lily's crazy grandmother to corner him again.

"Pres, would you give me a hand in the kitchen, carving the turkey?"

He followed her down the short hallway, aware of Dash glaring daggers in his back the entire way. "You're not doing me any favors by alienating your brother."

"Don't be silly. Dash likes you."

"He'd like to see me staked out in the sun."

"I told him we were friends."

"Men aren't fooled by that old line."

"But they can be fooled into believing love exists."

"Lily…"

"I know. I'll leave it be. There's the bird. Do you know how to carve it? I saved a page from a magazine with the proper instructions."

"I've never done it before."

"Do you always eat out on the holidays?"

"Sometimes. But when I'm home, my cook takes care of this."

"Oh, should I go get Dash?" she asked. He knew she'd be disappointed if he said yes. And he didn't want to disappoint Lily.

"No, I'll do it."

It felt strange but also right to be carving the turkey. An image danced through his mind's eye of Lily and him and a brood of kids filling the kitchen. He blinked. He wasn't a family man, dammit.

He finished cutting the bird per the instructions. Lily slid up behind him and gave him a kiss on the cheek. He wanted more. He wished her family and friends were somewhere else so that he could take Lily here, in the kitchen, with the savory smells filling the air.

"Good job," she said.

He bent and took her mouth in the kiss he'd been craving since he'd been banished last night. "I can do better."

"Pres, we have a houseful of people."

"They wouldn't miss me."

"I think Humberto would."

Preston had talked briefly with Lily's grandmother's husband. He was an interesting man who'd been an investment banker for thirty years.

"Your brothers wouldn't," he said wryly. There was something unnerving about the two intense young men who'd been tag-teaming him. Asking discreetly about his intentions and promising retribution if he made Lily cry. It had made him realize that he didn't want to ever make her cry.

"I'm sorry."

"Don't be. You're their pretty sister, and they're worried about you."

She blushed at the compliment and stood on her tip-toes to brush a kiss against his jaw. Desire tingled to life, and his pulse beat heavier.

"It's because they love me."

"Not today, Lily. Please don't start on *love* today." Especially not while he held her in his arms. She felt small and vulnerable, though he knew she took strength from having those she cared about around her.

"Why not?"

Preston felt his pager vibrate at his waist. Saved by the bell, he thought. He let go of Lily to read his alpha page.

"What's up?" she asked.

"I just got paged," he said, reaching for his cell phone. *Thank God.* He'd had enough of hearing about happily ever after and how he'd better treat Lily right. He needed a break. But Lily was staring up at him with those beautiful blue eyes of hers, and he knew he wouldn't leave if she asked him to stay.

"On Thanksgiving? That's ridiculous."

"The resort industry is busy on holidays." Which was true.

"Is there a problem at one of your domestic resorts?"

He shook his head. "I like to have the general managers to call me every two hours with updates. I'll just go out to my car and make the calls."

"Preston, you're not leaving again."

"Why not?" he asked. He knew what a caged animal felt like, because he was trapped and walls were closing in.

"It's Thanksgiving. You don't have to return calls."

"Lily, I have to—"

"Please, Preston."

She'd never really asked him for anything before and he knew he couldn't tell her no. He nodded because he felt raw and aching, realizing for the first time what had been missing all of his life. He knew that there was no way he could make it last. Knew there was no price he could pay to convince Lily to leave this all behind and travel with him throughout the world.

Lily wrapped her arms around him and held him tightly. His own arms hung limply by his sides. Fear swamped him, and he was afraid to touch her. Afraid to reach out because she might disappear. Afraid to trust in the dream he'd only just realized he'd been searching for all his life.

He was startled to understand that he wouldn't mind staying here. That he would gladly give up the hotels and traveling, the excitement of being a mover and shaker in the hotel industry, if he could be guaranteed a lifetime with Lily.

But he also knew he wouldn't take the chance. Wouldn't risk what he knew couldn't come true. What Lily had never understood was that he knew life held no happy endings for spoiled rich boys who'd grown into cold men.

The thousand-year-old oaks that lined the driveway to White Willow House were creepy in the dark, Lily thought as she drove past them. The big circular drive that would welcome guests in just a few days was empty. Her old Chevy chugged to a halt in front of the Doric columns.

She'd miss this place once the job was completed. She wondered if Preston would still be in her life. A big part of her believed she'd made some progress in convincing him love existed, but another part knew he was a man who lived in the eternal present and always looked forward. He'd made a few vague references to his next resort in Barbados.

As sure as she'd been that she could convince him to love, it was hard to admit defeat. And most of the times it didn't feel as if she was losing the bet, losing the chance of a lifetime she'd been given. But other times her affection for him seemed doomed. Maybe it was the big oaks and weeping willows on the shoreline of his man-made lake that were influencing her feelings.

The landscape at White Willow House harkened back to the days of arranged marriages and illicit trysts between quadroons and upper-crust gentlemen. Though not a true Creole, she felt like one in her blood, and she wondered if her commoner status affected Preston's ability to love her.

A security guard rapped on her window, startling Lily into movement. Enough of these thoughts.

"You okay, Ms. Stone?"

"Yes, Jeff. I could use a hand with the writing desk and George I chair in the back of the truck."

"I'll help. I'm afraid most everyone has gone home for the night."

"I think we can handle it. I'm stronger than I look."

That's right, she thought. She was stronger than she looked. Strong enough to make even the hardest heart crack open and believe in love.

With Jeff's help she got the George I writing bureau to the owner's suite and situated. Jeff left her alone in the suite of rooms she'd created for Preston's personal use. The resort would have its grand opening on New Year's Eve only ten days from now. Tickets had been sold out for weeks and Preston had asked Lily to spend the night in the suite she'd created just for him.

In the weeks since Thanksgiving they'd grown closer and she knew he'd begun to need her the way she needed him. Loving Pres was hard. But worth the effort. He was coming to appreciate the little things in life and had stopped trying to buy her affections.

Still something was missing. She longed for the man she only barely glimpsed when they were alone in bed in the dark of night. The man who cradled her close to his body and whispered his plans for the future. The man who'd visited a graveyard at night and stood beside a century-old plot and held her like he was never going to let go. The man who'd been her first lover, and she had a feeling, would be her last. The man who'd conquered her body and soul.

"What are you still doing here?" Preston asked from the doorway.

"Working." Fatigue lined his face, and he moved stiffly into the room. As if he'd been sitting down all day. He worked too hard. Always trying to increase his revenue and outdo his competition.

"Are you ready to knock off?" he asked, rubbing the back of his neck with one hand.

"Sit down on the settee."

"Why?" He moved with ease through the room, and she congratulated herself on making him comfortable in the past. Something he'd never been before.

"I'm going to give you a neck rub."

"I'd rather have a naked skin massage."

"Not in your contract, bud."

"I'm willing to renegotiate."

"I'm listening." She wanted to renegotiate, as well. Wanted to be more to him than a lover. Maybe he was ready to admit that they could make a life together. A life as husband and wife.

"How does an all-expense paid trip to Barbados sound?"

"A vacation?"

"More like an extended stay. I've finalized the property deal and I'm ready to begin work. What do you think?"

"It sounds complicated." She'd love to travel to an island paradise with him, but she couldn't live there with him for the months it would take to open a resort.

"Only if you make it," he said, taking her hands and pulling her around to his lap.

She let herself rest against him, inhaling the clean, crisp scent of his cologne. It was easy to be lulled into believing that she and Preston were meant to be, when she sat close to him in the dark. But in her heart she knew that she couldn't travel with him as his mistress. Honestly, she wouldn't even follow him around the world as his wife.

Her life was in New Orleans with her shop on St. Charles Street and anything else would leave her feeling like a shell of a woman. She needed her family and her antiques and...Preston.

"Barbados is only complicated if you let it be."

"I can't go with you, Preston."

He was silent for a minute. Only the sounds of their breathing filled the air. She was afraid of what he'd say next. Of what his actions would be. Both of them needed something the other couldn't provide, and they were reaching the point where one of them would have to compromise. Lily didn't know if she could.

"Why are you here so late?"

"My boss is a slave driver."

"I'll have the man's job."

"You already do."

"Seriously, I was having a great fantasy of you in bed and me sneaking in and waking you up."

"What would this waking up involve?"

"Every nerve in your body."

"Ooo, I'm sorry I'm going to miss it."

"You won't. You'll just be lucid when we get started."

She smiled to herself. She'd given him a key to her house last week and he'd yet to use it. More than likely if she'd gone home he'd have woken her with the doorbell.

"I can't wait," she said, her heart heavy.

"You don't have to," he said. Picking her up in his arms, he carried her into the darkened bedroom and laid her on the bed.

Lily never seemed more out of reach to him than when she talked about love. He reinforced the bond he'd created between them by making love to her. Tonight he'd felt her slipping away. Knew that a woman like Lily wouldn't be content to travel around the world as his mistress, but he had nothing else to offer her.

She'd eschewed the things that women in the past had clung to. Even the trinkets that advertisers promised would please women didn't please Lily. She liked roses and chocolates and fancy dinners, but he knew she preferred quiet nights spent together in her home.

The navy-blue coverlet was plush. He wanted to see Lily's skin against it. He'd purchased it with her in mind.

The spill of light from the other room illuminated the bed but also provided cover for him. He was torn between wanting to see every nuance of Lily's face and body as he made love to her and not wanting her to see what he couldn't hide any longer. He needed her with a quiet desperation that was making him doubt his beliefs.

And she was slipping away. He had to keep her tied to him. Had to find something to keep her close if only for the next few days, until he left Louisiana. She watched him with feminine awareness and something else. Something deeper. He figured she'd been telling herself that she was in love with him and when he looked into those deep-blue eyes, he almost believed she was.

He stripped off his clothing with impatient movements. Wanting to bond with Lily in the most elemental and satisfying way. Longing to feel her tender flesh under his. To be held tight in her embrace.

Naked, he approached the bed. Lily had kicked her shoes off and began disrobing as if sensing his urgency. The primal animal that lurked beneath the surface of his sophistication had been released. He had to bond with her. Had to mate with her. Had to make her his.

"I can't wait," he said. His voice guttural to his own ears.

Lily didn't flinch away. Only opened her arms and welcomed him.

"Come to me," she said, her voice that of the sirens.

He took her mouth in a deep, drugging kiss. Her taste assuaged a thirst he wasn't conscious of having until she entered his life. He let his mouth leave hers and found the pulse at the base of her neck. Her life force flowed through his lips into his body.

He couldn't wait another minute to touch her. All of her.

He pushed her skirt to her waist and her panties down her legs. He palmed her breasts through the layer of her bra and shirt. Her nipples hardened and he needed to taste her. Not through a barrier of cloth but mouth to flesh.

"Open your blouse."

She followed his command. Her fingers working quickly on the buttons that lined the front of that white shirt. The one she wore when she had a meeting. The one she thought made her look professional but only made him want to peel it away.

Once her pretty breasts were bare, he bent and suckled her gently, knowing the kind of touch she liked. She writhed under him, and he took her nipple deeper in his mouth, scraping his teeth along her aroused flesh.

She was always so responsive. She made him feel like the only man in the world.

"I need you now, Preston."

The words sliced through him, fueling the desire already careening out of control in his veins. He couldn't wait a minute longer, had to make her his own. Sliding his hands up her thighs, he caressed the hidden secrets of her body. She was warm and wet.

He stretched her carefully open with two fingers and positioned himself at the portal of her body.

"Hurry, Pres."

He lifted her hips and slid home. She tightened around him and he plunged faster and deeper taking her into his soul. He reached between their bodies and stroked the center of her desire until she made that high keening sound that signaled her climax. Preston grabbed her hips and plunged one last time. The release spread throughout his body, and he let himself rest cradled in her arms.

Knowing he'd found the home he'd always searched for. Knowing he'd found a woman to match him on every level. Knowing he'd finally met the one woman who couldn't be bought.

# Twelve

Lily had looked forward to the evening of the grand opening. She felt like Cinderella finally going to the ball. It had taken her two weeks of shopping, but she'd finally found a dress as magical as she hoped the evening would be. It was only a simple sheath, but it was made of a light-green, almost see-through, chiffon and covered in sequins and beads. She'd splurged and spent time in the tanning salon to make sure her back was tanned so that the deep vee in her dress wasn't wasted.

She'd had a pedicure and manicure and felt feminine from the top of her coifed hair to the tip of her painted toenails. Standing in front of the mirror in only her underpants and high heels she thought that later on Preston would enjoy what was underneath the sexy dress as much as the dress. She spritzed perfume on her body and then wiggled into her dress.

Her hair fell around her face in sassy curls and she applied just a little blue highlight to her eyelids. She wanted everything to be perfect tonight because she was going to present Preston with the perfect couple. The one he denied existed. A man and woman who were together for one reason and one reason alone—love.

She'd had her doubts that Preston would believe in love, but after Christmas morning when he'd held her tight and told her he never wanted to let go—the first time he'd ever come close to confessing what he was feeling—she'd known he loved her. He didn't have any practice saying the words or identifying the emotion but once he realized how perfect they were together, he'd understand.

She'd softened him up by writing another love quote in a card decorated with a picture of Bourbon Street in the rain. She wanted him to see it tonight before she confessed her love. She'd added candles around the room. And put her favorite Miles Davis CD in the player. Next to the quote she laid a specially wrapped gift she'd made for Preston.

He had everything money could buy so she'd thought long and hard to find something that he couldn't buy for himself. She'd decided on a collage on a red heart of their time together. A picture of the two of them at her cousin Marti's wedding was situated in the center, and around it she'd added the matchbook cover from Van Benthuysen-Elms Mansion where he'd first asked her about love. A post card from Rockefeller Center and a shell she'd collected when they'd spent their weekend together on his yacht. She'd added a bunch of other little mementos, but those held center stage.

She wanted Preston to see the love she'd showered on him. To realize how important they were together and how deeply their lives had become entwined.

Someone knocked on the bedroom door of the suite she'd decorated for Preston. She knew it had to be him. She took one last glance at herself in the mirror before crossing to let him in.

"Hello, angel."

Preston was born to wear a tuxedo. He made her feel underdressed in her flashy eveningwear. It had something to do with the ease in which he moved. However, the intensity in his gaze assured her he didn't find her apparel offensive.

"Turn around," he ordered.

She pivoted slowly, feeling every inch a woman and proud of her female body. And when she felt the brush of his lips against her neck, she melted back against him. Only with Preston did she feel this complete.

"Gorgeous. Want to skip the party and stay here?"

"No. I spent a lot of money on this dress."

"It's a shame none of it went toward fabric."

"Ha."

He continued to watch her with an intensity she

found unnerving. Was the dress not right? "It's okay, isn't it?"

"What?"

"My dress."

"If it were any more okay, I'd spend the evening fighting off every man at the party, to keep them from trying to steal you away from me."

She smiled at him. Her heart melting. "No one could steal me from you."

A darkness entered his eyes. She knew he didn't believe that any emotion could last. Even lust ended. Success and the flush of victory were short-term. How could love last? she knew he was asking himself.

"I would fight to the death for you, Preston."

"Let's hope it doesn't come to that. We're not dressed for battle."

He turned them so they were reflected in the mirror. He was strong and solid behind her. The man of her dreams, the one she'd hadn't realized she'd been searching for until she found him.

"I feel like I'm a fairy princess."

"Tonight you are."

"What happens at midnight?" she asked, unable to help herself.

"The prince will fulfill your every desire."

"You already do."

"Well, tonight I have something important to ask you," he said, and led her out of the room.

Preston had decided to formalize his request for Lily to come and live with him in Barbados. He knew she'd never settle for a marriage to someone who couldn't love her. He'd tried to convince himself that lying about love would be okay, but it hadn't worked. Relationships based on falsehoods never survived. Even he knew that.

But he was convinced he could persuade her to become his companion. To call Lily a mistress would be a slur on her character and on what she meant to him. He watched her charm her way through the crowded ballroom as the clock came closer to midnight. Instead of jealousy a certain sense of pride flooded him.

She was the perfect balance to his personality even in a social setting. She was charming and friendly and knew details about the people who surrounded him that Preston had never bothered to learn.

He'd never noticed the distance he kept between himself and others until Lily had entered his life. He waved at some friends but didn't stop to chat. He wanted to spirit Lily away from the ball.

Even though he'd scheduled the gala to take place on New Year's Eve, he didn't want to be in the middle of the crowds at the beginning of the New Year. He wanted Lily to himself so he could ask her to spend the next year traveling and working with him. They could renew their agreement every year at midnight. He kind of fancied the idea, especially when Lily had made her reference to fairy tales.

He'd even had a diamond-slipper charm made for Lily to wear once she'd agreed. It was a trifle, but she wasn't the type who expected expensive jewels, clothes and cars.

He pushed his way through the throng of men surrounding her. She smiled when she saw him and reached for his hand as he approached. She never broke her attention to the man speaking, but she'd let Preston know she'd been aware of him.

He claimed her for a slow dance. Needing to feel her close to him. Closer than this public place would allow. He wanted to carry her from this place but he couldn't leave yet.

"Everything going smoothly?" she asked, her fingers toyed with the hair at the back of his neck. Heat surged through his body. He hardened in a rush as if he'd never known the paradise of taking Lily into his arms and loving her deep in the night.

He forced himself to answer her question. "Yes. Several of my colleagues have complimented the decor. I gave them your business address."

"Thanks. I did do a good job here."

She flushed. He'd noticed that she could accept a challenge with finesse but a compliment always knocked her off guard. And while he'd take any advantage he could get with this feisty woman, she should be more confident of herself and her skills.

"You're too modest."

"No one likes a braggart."

"It's not ego when you acknowledge the hard work involved."

"I don't see you strutting around the room."

"Would you like to?"

"Oh, yes. But only if we're alone."

"You think I should strut."

"Yes, I do."

An uncomfortable emotion flooded him, and he changed the subject. He didn't mind wanting Lily with a desire that made him want her by his side, but he couldn't admit to caring for her.

"This resort is going to be the crown jewel in the Dexter Resort Hotel chain."

"It will always be special to me."

He cleared his throat and looked away. He was uncomfortable for Lily when she let her heart show. He figured she thought she was in love with him. He knew she couldn't be. He'd given her nothing of value. A few trips and some trinkets, but she genuinely cared about him.

"Well my dress blended very well with this crowd."

"You were concerned about your dress?"

"A little, but I've had more offers than you'd care to know."

"Any of them indecent?"

"More than a few."

"Should I call anyone out?"

"No."

He would do it, he realized, for Lily. She stirred his blood in a primal way that made him react at the gut level. "Are you ready to leave?"

"Your party isn't over yet."

"Ours is just beginning."

He kissed her. She moaned deep in her throat and clutched at his shoulders. That primal scream echoed in his body, urging him to pull her close. To never let go of her until he was hilt deep inside her welcoming warmth and home.

*Home.*

He hadn't realized he'd been searching for it, but there it was. She offered him something no one else could. The chance to be who he really was without the pressure of worrying about the image.

A discreet cough interrupted them. Rohr stood a few steps away with his very pregnant wife. ''Excuse me, sir.''

He left Lily talking with Mrs. Rohr while he and Jay discussed a minor problem the kitchen was having. By the time he'd put out that emergency and found Lily they had five minutes until midnight.

''Come on,'' he said, none of his usual flair.

''Where are we going?''

''I told you I want to have our own party.''

''Cinderella got to stay at the ball until the ninth stroke of midnight.''

''I'll give you at least nine strokes at midnight.''

She blushed but patted his backside. ''I'll take you up on that.''

He hurried her through the lobby and into the elevator, impatiently waiting until they reached the penthouse floor. He swept her up in his arms and carried her down the hallway. For the first time in his life he almost believed he'd found something that could last.

*Someone who'd stay with him forever.* And though he would never admit it, that scared him to the bottom of his soul.

The moon spilled in through the skylights, painting the room in shadows. The candles on the dresser that Preston had lit earlier had died down. Her body, though, was still flushed from Preston's lovemaking. Overcome with emotion, Lily brushed a kiss on his well-shaped mouth. Preston pulled her closer, sucking her bottom lip between his teeth and nibbling on her flesh.

She wanted him again. But she longed to have their relationship settled. She broke their kiss, and Preston kept her close to him in the intimate cocoon of their bed.

''What did you want to discuss with me?'' she asked him when her breathing settled.

''I have an offer for you. Wait here.'' He padded naked through the room to his closet. She loved the way he looked naked. His hard body moved with ease and grace.

When he removed a small box from his coat, she grabbed her present, too. The one she'd made for him from her heart. He had a gift for her, she thought.

She turned on the nightstand lamp, wanting to be able to see his face when she realized he was in love with her. And she knew that it would probably shock him. He'd been resistant to emotions since they met but he'd changed since the night they'd visited the graveyard.

"I have something for you, too."

He sat next to her on the bed. He stared at her chest. Her nipples tightened. If they were going to talk, it had to be fast. She tugged the sheet up to cover her breasts.

"Talk fast, Lily."

She nodded. "This is harder than I thought it would be."

"You don't have to say anything."

"I do. You see, Preston, while I've been searching for true love and convincing you it existed... What I mean to say is I've found the perfect couple."

"Who are they?"

"Us."

"Us?"

"We're perfect for each other."

"Lily, listen, we're good in many ways, but that doesn't make what we have love."

"How would you know what love is?"

"I know what it isn't."

"Then why are we together?"

"Lust, money."

"I don't want your money."

"What do you want?"

"Your love. I love you. Those aren't words that I say lightly but I need you in my life."

"Lily, I'd like you to be part of my life. Things don't have to change."

"What do you mean?"

"I have a gift for you that will cheer you up."

She doubted it, but took the small jewelry box from him. Inside was a beautiful diamond pendant in the shape of Cinderella's slipper. It took her breath away and proved to her how well they knew each other. She felt like the struggling girl to his wealthy prince.

"I'd like you to be my companion for the next year."

His words made no sense to her. She suddenly realized that Preston wasn't thinking of happily ever after. "Companion?"

"Yes, travel with me and be my partner."

Oh, God. Her heart shattered in a million pieces while he continued speaking. Telling her the places they'd go. Barbados, again.

Preston saw a future for them that involved her running from the past, too. And she wasn't willing to do it. Wasn't willing to chuck a lifetime worth of memories for a man who thought that lust and money were the key ingredients to a successful relationship.

On shaking legs, she stood. Preston stopped talking, and she felt his gaze on her as she gathered her clothes. She was embarrassed by her nudity and hurried to put on her jeans and shirt. The damned buttons were crooked but she couldn't fix them now. She tossed her lovely dress into her garment bag and started putting her other things in there.

"Lily, where are you going?"

"I'm leaving."

"I don't have time for games. I have to be in Barbados on Monday."

Anger left her speechless for a moment. She was less important to him than his schedule.

"How can you be so stubborn? The truth is all around us."

He stood, but she couldn't look at him. Couldn't see the man who'd taught her the beauty of physical love and the pain of the emotional. "The truth is there is no perfect couple or perfect love."

"I know love isn't perfect. All I know is that I'm in love with you."

He put his arms around her. Cradled her in his warmth, rubbing her back and speaking gently in her ear. Tears burned the back of her eyes. She blinked frantically trying to stall them. "Calm down. Please don't leave like this."

She loved him, but not enough to give up her life and become what he hated. And she knew she would. He'd start giving her gifts instead of his time and because she'd spend her time alone waiting for him to return to her she'd take them. She pictured herself alone in a hotel room in a foreign country while Pres was off working.

"I can't stay. I've been telling myself that you can love. You see, I've loved you for a long time, and I know that love hurts. But you won't even admit you can be hurt by it."

"That's because—"

"Don't say it doesn't exist. You have to take a risk for love to come to you." She stalked away from him.

"The truth is, Lily, I know all about so-called love. I've heard those words before, and every time I wasn't willing to pay to keep that person around, love disappeared."

"I'm different."

"Prove it."

Ah, a ray of hope, she thought. "Open my gift."

He opened the card and read the quote inside. He didn't touch the wrapping on her heart. "I knew it."

His soft words should have elated her, but the expression on his face told her that he'd missed the point.

"'Love is a rain of diamonds in the mind,'" he said, softly.

"Did you understand why I left it?" she asked.

"Yes. I'm sorry but I don't have a shower of diamonds for you. If you open the box, we can consider this a deposit."

Lily searched the room for her purse. There was no way Preston was ever going to understand. He couldn't love her because he only understood one thing: money and the power it held over humanity. She blinked again trying to hold back her tears.

"Well, it looks like you've won our bet," she said.

"This wasn't about a bet."

"No, it wasn't. But it was a gamble all the same."

"Stop talking like you just lost big in Vegas. I'll shower you with diamonds."

"I'd rather be showered with your love."

He said nothing. She sniffled and knew that blinking wasn't going to stop the tears from falling. "Goodbye Preston."

She ran from the room as if the demons of hell were chasing her. But she knew they weren't. Her demon was all too real and more painful, because she knew that he didn't have to be a demon but chose to.

# Thirteen

---

**P**reston picked up the jewelry box that Lily had discarded in her mad dash from the room. He called down to security and asked one of the guards to follow Lily home. To make sure she made it back to her place safely.

Uncomfortable with the feeling that he was alone again, he crossed the suite to the bar and poured himself a stiff drink. The alcohol bit as it went down, but he didn't flinch. Unnamed emotions roiled through him as he caught his own reflection in the mirror across the room. He looked like a man who'd lost everything.

He threw the glass against the wall and listened to it shatter. The suite felt too small and confining. Memories of Lily were everywhere. He saw her as she'd been just a few nights ago, standing at the window and looking at the darkened lawn. He saw her in her workshop refinishing the settee that now graced one of the walls.

He remembered her face when she'd offered him a massage because he was tired and he'd seduced her into his bed once again. Knowing that he couldn't give her what she needed, he'd offered her only what he had.

*And it wasn't enough.*

He called the airport and had them ready his jet. He needed to get out of New Orleans. Away from the slow-beating rhythm of the South and the memories of Lily. She'd taught him to care again and then left him.

He walked into the bedroom to dress and caught sight of Lily's gift to him. He'd never opened it. Never looked at it to see what it was she'd given him. He'd been so focused on making her stay with him.

He would open it later. He packed his clothes and glanced around the suite one last time. Something glittered in the corner of the room. *Lily's shoe.* That pretty silver high-heeled shoe that she'd worn last night. The shoe that had made her feel like a princess and him like her fairy-tale prince.

When had the prince turned into a pumpkin? When had the clock struck twelve for them?

He placed her shoe in his briefcase next to the wrapped gift. He told himself it was so that he'd have something to remember her by, but he knew he'd never forget Lily.

He called downstairs to have his car brought around and walked out of the suite that had become more of a home to him than he'd ever had before. More of a home than he'd ever expected to have. He never looked back and didn't now as he walked away from the resort. But he wanted to. He wanted to glance over his shoulder and see in his mind's eye Lily standing in the doorway.

But he didn't.

It was chilly in the early-morning hours. The road was clear of traffic as late-night revelers slept off last night's celebrations. Preston tried to make sense of Lily's departure.

He still couldn't understand what she wanted from him. He'd promised her a life of excitement and riches for at least a year.

Maybe she wanted more than a year, he thought. Maybe she didn't care about the money. In retrospect it seemed as if he might have overreacted to her quote about diamonds. Normally if a woman walked out on him he wouldn't care, but he'd already acknowledged to himself that Lily was anything but normal in his life. He picked up his cell phone and dialed her home number.

It rang eight times.

"Hello."

Lily's voice sounded as if she was still crying. A strange pain assailed him, but he didn't examine it. *Angel, I never meant to hurt you.*

She sniffled but said nothing else. He hung up the

phone. Lily wasn't a woman who'd live with a man without the hope of family and lifelong commitment. He had no right to her sweetness and he knew it.

The silence in the car was deafening, and his own thoughts were making him crazy. He turned on the CD player and the sounds of Miles Davis filled the car. Lily had it cued to her favorite song, "I Thought about You."

He'd give himself tonight for the memories and then he was moving on. Lily Stone was a part of the past, and Preston Dexter never, never looked back.

New Orleans was gearing up for Mardi Gras, but Lily didn't feel like celebrating. She'd signed the contract to refurnish and redecorate an older mansion that a friend of Preston's had purchased. It had hurt to hear his name, but she was trying to move on. Falling out of love wasn't easy. In fact, it was really hard. Her brothers were planning a visit for Mardi Gras the first week in February and Lily knew she had to get over Preston before then.

She had to start sleeping again. She had to find a way to forget about the two of them on her love seat almost making love. She had to find a way to forget he'd ever shared her bed and then shared her kitchen with those soulful eyes of his that made her want to show him the world because for all his wealth Preston couldn't see it.

The cellular phone rang and she answered it. Nothing but silence on the other end.

"Hello?"

"Lily, its Jay Rohr. We're processing the final payment to you today and I wanted to thank you again for the wonderful job you did with White Willow House."

"Thanks for the opportunity, Jay. I learned a lot from the project." More than he'd ever know, she thought.

"Are you at your office, Lily?"

"No, I'm on my way home. Why?"

"I wanted to fax you the final change order for signature."

"Oh, I can swing by and get it."

"It can wait until morning if you're on your way home now," Jay said.

"I am."

She asked about his wife and their new baby, a girl they'd named Angela, and then she concluded the call. She wanted a baby of her own. She'd spent the day in the import yard, and she was tired. She'd found a piece that she knew Preston would love but had not purchased it because she was going to get over him.

Pulling into her driveway, she sat for a moment looking at the small Creole cottage that been her home all her life. She remembered her mom and dad dropping them off to stay with her grandmother while they went off to explore cultures of hunter-gatherer tribes around the globe. She remembered leaving in the black limo the day they'd buried her parents. Playing tag football on the front lawn with her brothers.

But as she looked at the house now, she realized that

hanging on to possessions wasn't going to bring those people back to her. She'd stayed put for so long, craving normalcy and routine and only now realized that she'd been letting life pass her by.

Preston had given her someone to love, but she'd never been brave enough to love him more than her home. More than this old house and Crescent City. She opened her door slowly. She wasn't going to get over Preston because they were meant to be together, and if she had to follow him around the world to prove she loved him for him and not his money she was going to do it.

"She's on her way home," Jay Rohr said.

"Thanks, Jay. I owe you one," Preston said, disconnecting the call.

It had taken him three weeks to open the gift from Lily. He'd been sure that it was a steel watch or gold pen. Some sort of trinket that was worth a lot of money. His heart had stopped when he'd uncovered the photo heart she'd given him.

He'd stood in the empty living room of his penthouse apartment. The one with no photos of his family or links to his past and realized that love had been staring him in the face all along. That love had been what had kept him in New Orleans long after he needed to stay there.

That love had been why he'd hidden behind long-ago learned behaviors instead of remembering what

Lily had shown him. That love was giving. How many times had he heard that and not understood.

Finally he did, and he only hoped it wasn't too late. He'd been waiting on her porch for almost four hours and it was getting late. He'd had Jay call her cell phone on some pretense of business, but he wanted Lily back where she belonged. Back in the place he'd foolishly kicked her out of. Because he knew now he couldn't live without Lily. Oh, he'd survive but his quality of life would be below poverty level.

He'd missed the slow rhythm of New Orleans, Lily's jazz music and her crawfish pie. He'd missed the simple evenings they'd spent together in her family home.

But most of all he'd missed Lily. He'd delegated the Barbados resort to one of his junior vice presidents when he understood that his heart was in New Orleans. The organ he didn't think he'd had before a sweet, sexy redhead had dared him to believe in love.

How was he going to convince her that he'd changed his mind? A car pulled into the driveway, and Lily sat behind the wheel for a minute before stepping out of the car.

She looked more beautiful to him than anything he'd ever seen before. His hands started shaking and his palms grew sweaty. Oh, God, he didn't know if he could do this. What if she had given up on him?

He stepped from the shadows of her porch. ''Lily?''

She froze.

For once he had no words. No glib comment or challenging dare. He had only his heart and he knew he wore it on his sleeve.

Carefully she crossed to him. The stadium jacket she wore was too big, and she seemed to have lost weight since he'd seen her last. He hoped to God she wasn't sick.

When she was an arm's length away, Preston pulled her close for a hug. Her curves fitted his body in all the remembered places. Damn, she felt good.

"I know you deserve better than me, Lily, but I can't let you go. And I want to get married and raise children with you and spend the rest of our days challenging each other."

"Why, Preston?"

"Don't you know?"

"I need the words."

He took a deep breath. "I love you, Lily."

She stared into his eyes. The only other time he'd ever uttered those words he'd lost the most important person in his life. Suddenly tears ran down her face and she hugged him to her tightly.

"I thought I lost you," she said.

"I thought you did, too."

"You're sure about this?" she asked.

"Yes, I am."

"When do we leave for Barbados?"

"We're not going. I don't have to oversee the opening of each new resort. I will have to go to the grand opening celebrations but I don't have to be so hands-on."

"Won't you miss it? I don't want you to regret being with me."

"I suspect that you'll keep me busy."

"Where will we live?"

"I'd like to divide our time between New Orleans and New York."

"That would work. I can take on fewer decorating jobs and just do refinishing work."

"We can talk about the details later," he said. "I have something for you."

He pulled her shoe from his pocket and got down on one knee. He took her left hand in his and brushed a kiss across her knuckles. "Lily Stone, will you marry me?"

Lily crouched down and kissed him. "You bet."

Preston stood and scooped her up in his arms, carrying her into the house to seal their love with lovemaking that put to rest the doubts of the past.

\*     \*     \*     \*     \*

# Tempting
# the Tycoon

# CINDY GERARD

## *CINDY GERARD*

Two RITA® Award nominations are among the many highlights of this bestselling writer's career. As one reviewer put it, "Cindy Gerard provides everything romance readers want in a love story – passion, gut-wrenching emotion, intriguing characters and a captivating plot. This storyteller extraordinaire delivers all of this and more!"

Cindy and her husband, Tom, live in the Midwest on a small farm with horses, cats and two very spoiled dogs. When she's not writing, she enjoys reading, travelling and spending time at their cabin unwinding with family and friends. Cindy loves to hear from her readers and invites you to visit her website at www.cindygerard.com.

This book is dedicated to my intrepid Florida
connections, Susan and Jim Connell.
I love you guys!

And to Glenna –
What can I say? You're always there for me.

# One

Well, *this* wasn't supposed to happen. She was *not* supposed to be affected. Not like this anyway. Not by a man like him.

Brows pinched in concern, Rachael Matthews fought to ignore the arc of pure and instant attraction that zipped through her blood like a bullet the moment she looked into Nate McGrory's eyes. Wielding her maid-of-honor bouquet like a makeshift shield, she clung to cool reserve and forced herself to hold the best man's gaze as he met her at the center aisle of the church wearing a crooked and way too confident grin.

He was, after all, just a man. Just a man in a Pierce Brosnan/Antonio Bandares sort of way.

All right. She'd give herself a little latitude. What woman wouldn't have a strong reaction? Just look at him.

His flashing brown eyes matched the color of the perfectly styled hair he wore rakishly long and combed straight back from a stunning, masculine face. Contoured, suntanned cheeks dimpled with saint or sinner charm. His straight blade of a nose, wide brow and strong jaw were classically and unapologetically male. A crescent-shaped scar cut into his left eyebrow, just beyond the arc toward his temple—his one concession to imperfection. It should have messed up his incredible face. Instead, it lent a suggestion of vulnerability that was completely at odds with an overall air of confidence that practically purred, *Since you asked, yeah, I am master of my domain—but not to worry—I rule with a kind and gentle hand. And oh, by the way—I like my women hot.*

Okay. That snapped things back into perspective. Arrogance. The man oozed it, a fact that finally nudged Rachael back to her senses with a barely suppressed snort. Oh, yeah. She knew his type. Too well. High-gloss, high-maintenance and way more trouble than they were worth.

When she offered little more than a clipped nod, he widened his killer smile with a look relaying increased interest, along with a clear message. *We meet at last. Let's get these two married and then we definitely need to get to know each other.*

For Karen's sake and for the sake of the two-hundred-odd guests filling the pews and waiting with anticipatory smiles for the main feature—the bride and groom—Rachael made sure her return smile was polite, but about 98.6 degrees cooler than his. A careful lift of her brow did a little speaking, too, though, spelling it out for him, she hoped, *Yeah, sure, whatever.*

He laughed at her.

Oh, not out loud, but with those speaking eyes again—the ones that leveled an unmistakable challenge. *Lady, if I make my mind up to have you, you don't stand a chance on God's green earth of resisting.*

To arrogance, she added egomania.

Well, he might be arrogant, but she, evidently, was an airhead to let herself be affected by him this way. Forget it. This—whatever *this* was, flashing between her and this man she had never officially met—was *not* going to happen. Not only didn't she have the time, she didn't have the patience. Or really, let's face it, she didn't have the inclination. Life was good just the way it was.

Maybe the pressure of planning her best friend's wedding had finally gotten to her. She'd mapped out this day step by meticulous step for Karen. It's what she did. Planning weddings was her career—and for the past several years it had also been her life. But this was Karen—her best friend—so Rachael was that much more invested in the outcome. She wanted everything to be perfect, had done everything in her power to make sure it was. The flowers, the music, the reception later at the Royal Palms Hotel where she operated Brides Unlimited—she'd personally seen to every last detail.

So far, it *was* perfect. And Karen looked beautiful. Thoughts about the glow on her face broke through Rachael's tension and tapped hard on what was left of her romantic streak. The one that, despite several attempts to drown it in a sea of turbulent, shipwrecked relationships, had decided to bob stubbornly to the surface for one final gasp before sinking to be lost forever to the deep just because she'd finally met Nate McGrory.

She started a little when he offered his arm, but recovered and, squaring her shoulders, took it. She could do this. No big deal. It was just the shock of finally seeing him in the flesh after all of Karen's hype that had gotten her going.

"Rachael, I'm telling you," Karen had insisted on one of the rare days, given their busy schedules, when they'd had a chance to get together for a little shopping and catching up last month, "just wait until you meet him."

They'd been lunching at a table on the brick sidewalk at Pescatore, a little pocket of West Palm Beach charm nestled on the corner of Clematis and Narcissus. Fountains flowed in the background, birds sang, exotic Florida flowers bloomed in a riot of intoxicating fragrance and color.

Karen had been blooming, too. They'd just bought her bridal veil—finally—and Karen was extolling the princely virtues of Sam's college fraternity brother, Nate McGrory, a hotshot millionaire lawyer from Miami who would fly in for the wedding at the eleventh hour on his private jet.

"I mean it," Karen had continued emphatically. "If I wasn't so in love with Sam, I'd be boogying on that dance floor myself. Got to be that blend of Irish-Latino blood running through his veins. Rach—I am not exaggerating when I tell you that this guy is not only charming and loaded, he's heart-stopping, to-die-for gorgeous.''

''So are hibiscus blooms and they last for…what? A day?'' Rachael had lifted her glass of merlot, waggling it in warning. ''I'm really not interested.''

''But he's so perfect,'' Karen insisted.

''Sweetie, I don't care if he's Ben Affleck, Donald Trump and red-hot Latin lover all rolled into one tidy little testosterone-wrapped package. Karen, please. Get married. Have a great life, but stop trying to couple me up with someone. I've got everything I need to make me happy. Good friends and a great job.''

Why couldn't her friends accept that her life really was fine exactly the way it was? She was productive, successful and self-contained—even if she sometimes fought a niggling notion that there was something more, something out there that eluded her. Something she should be entitled to and didn't have.

Shaking off her thoughts, she tuned back into the minister then cut an uneasy glance toward Nate McGrory.

Grudgingly, Rachael admitted that Karen had delivered on her hype. Mr. Perfect was, indeed, perfect in a black, cutaway tux that made his shoulders look as wide as the intracoastal waterway. Standing at parade rest at Sam's side—very tall, darkly, dangerously handsome—he listened intently as the minister went about his business of joining Karen and Sam as man and wife.

And, she realized with a muffled groan, she'd just spent the bulk of the wedding ceremony ogling him.

Let's blame it on the shoes, shall we? Since she

hadn't wanted to look like a munchkin—she was five-three stacked against Karen and Kim's willowy five-eight and five-nine respectively—she'd opted for four-inch heels. Couple the altitude issue with the pointed-toe factor and the darn shoes must have cut off the blood flow to her brain—pooled it somewhere in the vicinity of her libido, which she'd put in mothballs a couple of years ago and which did not do her thinking for her.

"…I now pronounce you man and wife."

The minister's words brought Rachael back to the reason they were all here.

"Ladies and gentlemen…it is with great pleasure that I present to you Mr. and Mrs. Samuel Lathrop."

Appreciative applause echoed through the church, bounced softly off the stained-glass windows, caromed up then down from the vaulted ceiling and cavernous outer walls as the newlyweds sealed their vows with a kiss that was chaste enough to satisfy the clergy but enthusiastic enough to win a chuckle or two from the congregation. And a knowing wink from the best man, aimed directly at her.

Throwing all of her enthusiasm into Karen and Sam's happiness, she pretended not to notice. And then she pretended she had this puzzling reaction to Nate McGrory under control. A tough trick considering her knees had just turned to mush.

She forced a bright smile that she hoped expressed how truly thrilled she was for Karen and Sam. Then she gritted her teeth as Mr. Wonderful laughed again, sort of a *Fight it if you can, babe, laugh, but I'm gonna getcha.*

She met his eyes as she took his arm and, following the bride and groom down the aisle, delivered her own message. *In your dreams, billionaire boy.*

# Two

"**I** want to be loved like that," Kim Clancy murmured with a wistful sigh as she sat back in her chair at a table flanking the Isle of Paradise Ballroom on the Royal Palms' sixth floor.

Sitting beside Kim, Rachael toyed with the trailing pewter and burgundy ribbons of her bridesmaid's bouquet. All around them, couples danced and laughed—most notably, the starry-eyed bride and groom.

While the pink of the crepe bridesmaids' dresses was a soft complement to Kim's rosy complexion and jet-black hair, Rachael was afraid she hadn't fared as well. In her opinion, green-eyed redheads and hollyhock pink were about as compatible as snowboarding and Jamaica—no matter that the hot glances she'd been dodging all night from Nate McGrory said he more than liked the way she was packaged.

Setting aside her bouquet to systematically shred a paper cocktail napkin with Karen's and Sam's names and wedding date embossed in elaborate gold script, Rachael dragged her thoughts away from the unsettling attention she'd been getting from the best man for the bulk of the evening. She angled Kim a bland look. "I don't want to burst your bubble, Kimmie, but love like that only happens in movies, songs and romance novels."

Okay—and maybe sometimes in real life, she admitted to herself. It just didn't happen in *her* life. Cupping her chin in her palm, she sighed deeply as Karen and Sam waltzed by, eyes only for each other, Karen's antique satin and lace wedding dress swirling around them like a misty cloud.

"I can't believe you aren't happy for Karen."

"Oh, honey, you know I'm happy for her," Rachael assured Kim, who was obviously a little perturbed by Rachael's jaundiced perspective. "Sam's a great guy, but so help me, if he ever hurts her—"

"For heaven's sake. He's not gonna hurt her."

"We'll see."

Kim shook her head. Delicate pink baby roses and wispy sprigs of baby's breath surrounding Kim's upswept black curls fluttered with the motion, reminding Rachael that her hair, too, was wreathed in flowers. On Kimmie they looked elegant. Rachael was pretty sure, however, that despite all attempts to gather her own straight shoulder-length bob up onto her head and encircle it with blossoms, she looked more as if she'd fallen into a patch of wilted weeds than like a wood nymph adorned with wildflowers—which was how the proudly beaming hairdresser had described the result of his labors.

"Don't your shoulders get tired," Kim asked, "what with the weight of that cynicism bearing down on you all the time?"

Rachael lifted a flute of flat, lukewarm champagne. "I don't make the rules. I just observe them."

"You're gonna fall in love for real some day. I, for one, can't wait to watch it happen."

Rachael sipped, swallowed, then shook her head. The motion sent a tendril of red hair in a downward slide. She felt it on her bare nape and attempted to tuck it back up into her circlet of flowers. "Read the book. Saw the movie. No need to play the part, so don't hold your breath on my account because it's never gonna happen."

"Never's a long time, Rach," Kim said softly.

Rachael knew about long times. It had been a long time, for instance, since she'd felt she could count on anyone but herself. She was fine with that. She was independent and proud of it—plus the mere thought of committing to one person, depending on one person—well, it just wasn't something she felt comfortable with.

Kimmie and Karen both accused her of having "issues" with trust. This was not news. She admitted it. They were right. But she didn't necessarily see anything wrong with being careful. Or with being single and content with it.

She forced a smile for Kim, who was always and forever an optimist. Rachael forgave her for it because she loved her like a sister. And because she understood that Kim had no reason not to believe in love and romance and family-ever-after. Rachael, on the other hand, knew a little too much about that great American fallacy. She thought fleetingly about her mother and wondered how she'd had the strength to carry on given all she'd been through.

"Just give me good old-fashioned lust," she said, breaking away from her thoughts. "At least it's honest."

"Yeah, right." Kim snorted. "Like you'd ever go for that kind of arrangement."

Okay. So Kim knew her well. Rachael didn't do casual sex. Every once in a while, though, she wished she could be one of those women who could take the sex without the commitment she needed to make it worth the effort. It seemed to work just fine for the guys.

"You never know," Rachael said with false bravado, "maybe I'll turn over a new leaf. Go for the gusto without the grief."

"A new leaf, huh? Better make it a fig leaf, 'cause it looks like you just might get a chance to put the new you front and center."

When Rachael shot her a curious look, Kim nodded in the direction of the man dodging couples on the dance floor and heading toward them. "Hunk alert at six o'clock. Hubba-hubba-holy-cow-what-a-man. If you don't want him, put in a word for me, would you?"

Rachael felt her shoulders stiffen. She'd felt Nate McGrory's hot gaze on her all night—in the reception line after the ceremony, in the limo on the way here and at the bride's table during dinner. He hadn't slacked off since the band had played their first chords three hours ago. Except for the traditional dance when the best man and maid of honor were expected to dance together, she'd managed to keep herself occupied with details surrounding the reception and him at a distance.

"Ladies," he said, by way of greeting, his killer smile locked and loaded.

Rachael tried to look bored, all the while thinking of how he'd smelled—like musk and spice and something exotically sexy—when they'd danced that one, seemingly endless dance. She tried not to remember the heat of his broad hand spread wide across her back, or how protected and small she'd felt when his chin had brushed the top of her head and his warm breath had stirred the flowers in her hair and made her flush warm all over. She tried—really, she tried—not to remember the feel of his thighs brushing hers, her breasts pressed against the broad chest beneath his tuxedo jacket.

"You're both looking very…pink tonight," he observed dryly as he sat down in the empty chair beside Rachael.

Rachael toyed with the mints on the plate beside her untouched wedding cake and hoped the little bump, bump, bump of her heart against the left cup of her merry widow didn't bump her right out of her dress.

"Why yes, we are," she said with false brightness, "and it's only because Karen would walk over hot coals for us that we agreed to wearing these—"

"Very pink dresses?" he supplied with a cheeky grin she chose not to return.

"Close enough."

His smile mellowed into something intimate and way too friendly as he propped an elbow lazily on the table and leaned directly into her field of vision. Rachael stubbornly held his gaze in a game attempt to let him know he didn't affect her. She thought she'd managed a pretty good job of it, too—until he poked an index finger into the frosting on her untouched cake, studied it idly, then brought it to his mouth.

She swallowed, her mouth dust-dry, as he sucked it slowly off his finger.

"Good."

The single word, uttered in his deep voice, rubbed along her senses like lush velvet. Heat flooded every freckle from her breast to her hairline. She jerked her gaze away.

Good God.

"So, how's it going, Nate?" This from Kim, who was kicking Rachael under the table in a bid, no doubt, for her to lose the frown and a show a little interest.

"Not so good," he said, and Rachael was peripherally aware of his gaze drifting along her flushed face to the curve of her jaw, slowly working its way lower, to her bare shoulder and along the low-cut line of her dress. "This is one of my favorite songs," he said with just enough pout in his voice to make it sound even sexier, "and here I am—no one to dance with."

Hyperaware of the direction his gaze had taken, Rachael toyed with the stem of her champagne flute and paid undue attention to the small stack of shredded napkin piled in front of her.

"Give a guy a break?" he asked with the sultry charm of a prince—or a sultan. "Dance with me?"

She was about to utter a polite but firm no thank-you, when she looked up and realized he'd extended his invitation to Kim.

She snapped her mouth shut, carefully bit back her surprise and gave an uncertain and confused Kim a nod of encouragement. "Go ahead. Dance your socks off."

With a puzzled look, Kim followed the best man's lead onto the dance floor then floated into his open arms.

Well, Rachael thought as she watched them meld into the crowd. That was a relief. A huge relief that he'd finally gotten the hint and backed off. And she didn't feel confused, or rejected, or let down that it was Kim he'd come for, not her. She didn't feel any of those things.

Not even when they danced the next three dances, their dark heads together, laughing, talking, absorbed with each other and oblivious to anyone else in the room. Totally oblivious to her when she rose and left the ballroom unobserved to double-check on the hundreds of white balloons and baskets of heart-shaped confetti that were to be released at midnight, just before the happy couple left for their honeymoon.

It didn't bother her—not even a little bit.

From the dance floor, Nate watched over Kim's shoulder as Rachael Matthews sneaked out of the ballroom like a thief taking a hike with the family jewels. He wasn't sure why he was so intrigued by the little green-eyed redhead. Hell. For the better part of the day she'd regarded him the way she would a piece of meat that had been left out in the sun too long.

He grinned and shook his head. He was used to excessive reactions from women. Avoidance wasn't one of them. He wasn't conceited but he wasn't blind, either. He wasn't oblivious to his looks—not his fault or his doing that he came from a great gene pool. Also not his doing that the lure of his family fortune and his unsolicited reputation as one of Florida's most eligible bachelors netted him his fair share of female attention. And yeah, to a degree, he liked that attention—would even admit he'd used his looks and his financial and social position to his advantage from time to time.

Not that any of it would get him anywhere with Rachael. Her reaction continued to both amuse and stymie him. Since he hadn't known her long enough to offend her, he had to figure it was the lady herself who had the problem—and he'd decided he'd like nothing better than playing the role of problem solver.

"Okay, you can cut the pretense now."

Nate swung his gaze down to the pretty woman in his arms. "Excuse me?"

Kim Clancy smiled sweetly. "She's gone. Rachael," she said, nodding to the double doors where Nate had last seen her. "She's gone, so you can get down to the nitty-gritty. What do you want to know about her?"

One corner of his mouth tipped up. Busted. "Am I that transparent?"

"Clear as plastic wrap," she said with that same cheerful smile.

"I'm sorry. Do you mind?"

Kim met his eyes with frank candor. "What I would mind is for Rachael to get hurt. She's not a player, Nate. Beneath the brass and barbwire, she's fragile.

"So," she continued, her gaze assessing as the slow dance came to an end, "if all you have in mind is a hit-and-run, as her friend, I'd appreciate it if you find another moving target."

He wasn't sure what he had in mind, but target practice wasn't among the options concerning this woman who inspired such loyalty from another woman.

"How about we go somewhere and talk," he said, his hand at the small of her back as he guided Kim off the dance floor.

"About Rachael?"

"What can I say? I think I've got it bad." He grinned at her less-than-sympathetic look. "Be a pal. Tell me something about her that will make it all go away."

# Three

$\overline{\qquad\qquad}$

The Monday after Karen's wedding was one of those Mondays Rachael both relished and dreaded. She'd hit the ground running when she'd walked through the ornate revolving doors of the Royal Palms Hotel at seven-fifteen. Now it was close to lunchtime and she hadn't had time to draw a deep breath yet.

She'd barely walked up the stairs—she much preferred them to the elevator—and entered her third-floor office with the breathtaking view of the beach and the Atlantic when Sylvie Baxter started firing questions at her like bullets. Did she remember she had a meeting with the head of a new printing company who wants to pitch his work at 8:30? Was the tasting for the Jenner wedding reception still on for this afternoon or had she dreamed it had been re-scheduled? Did Rachael know that Alejandro, the

sous chef for the fourth-floor restaurant, had run off
with the manager's wife? Don't forget to call the San-
bourns, oh, and Mrs. Buckley is on line one.

Rachael had talked the hotel management into expanding Brides Unlimited—Royal Palms' upscale
bridal service—to a full-service wedding operation
three years ago. After business had increased by a full
twenty percent the first year under her management,
she'd asked for and been granted permission to hire
an assistant. Sylvie, a sixty-something widow, was
Rachael's best "perk" yet.

Sylvie'd been on the job for eighteen months now;
Rachael couldn't imagine running things without her.
And she couldn't imagine herself doing anything else.
This job was the single most important thing in her
life. It was what she banked on. It was what she be-
lieved in.

And her hard work was really paying off. Business
just kept getting better. Projections forecasted an additional fifteen-percent rise in clientele for the quarter—possibly thirty-five percent for the year—and it
was only March. The year was young.

This day, however, was getting old fast—mostly
due to her current phone conversation.

Rachael sat at her desk, her hands steepled in front
of her as Mrs. Haden Buckley the third's nasal voice
grated through her headset. Gweneth Buckley was a
royal pain in the hiney. She also represented her biggest account to date and possibly Brides Unlimited's
ticket into the crème de la crème of Palm Beach high
society. If Mrs. Buckley liked what Rachael did with
her daughter's wedding, word would spread not only
among Palm Beach old guard, but among the nouveau

riche. Business would grow. And for that reason, Rachael tried to ignore the fact that it was almost eleven-thirty and this was Gweneth's fourth contact of the day requesting changes in the wedding plans.

Rachael adjusted her headset, checked her watch and wondered if she'd have to break her lunch date with Kim. She hadn't seen or spoken with her since Karen's wedding Saturday and some small part of her wanted to hear how she'd made out with Mr. Wonderful. Not that she had any interest in Nate McGrory, but she *was* interested in Kim. Kimmie was romantic and naive and Rachael wanted to hear if he'd given her the total bum's rush before he returned to Miami and his law practice—and the legion of women who followed in his wake like a jetstream if the article she'd stumbled across in *Florida Today* was to be believed.

"Yes, Mrs. Buckley," she agreed pleasantly, "we'll be happy to substitute the Grand Marnier crème brûulée for the mignardises. A fine choice for dessert." At this point she really didn't care if Mrs. Buckley's guests ate the torched custard or the chocolate-dipped fruits, truffles, European cookies and biscotti. She just wanted a firm decision to send to the pastry chef.

"I'm sorry, what?" she asked when she realized she'd zoned out. "Oh, yes. Yes, I've been able to negotiate a contract with Butterflies, Inc., that will meet your budget." As if the Palm Beach Buckleys needed to work with a budget, she thought silently.

She drew a deep breath, then carefully dived in. "Mrs. Buckley, all of your choices have been brilliant—including these adjustments. I understand how perfect you want everything to be. The wedding will be spectacular. Your daughter will look stunning. The guests will be raving about the food for months. We'll be at a point soon, however, where I'll need to send confirmation notices to all the vendors on any last-minute alterations.''

Ten minutes later, she'd finally managed to get off the phone. She was just lifting her headset from her ears when Sylvie rapped a knuckle on her door then poked her head inside.

''Your lunch date's here,'' Sylvie said with a coy grin.

Puzzled by Sylvie's dancing eyes, Rachael eyed her with suspicion. It wasn't like having lunch with Kim was a special occasion. They had a standing Monday date. ''And?''

''And…I thought the light on line one was never going to go out.''

''Mrs. Buckley,'' Rachael said by way of explanation.

''Say no more. Well…um, I'll just…let you go to lunch then,'' Sylvie said brightly.

Rachael didn't have time to contemplate the waggle of Sylvie's eyebrows as she popped her head back out the door.

''Leave it open,'' Rachael called as she rose and tucked her hair behind her ear. ''I'm right behind you.''

She slipped into her royal-blue blazer with the Royal Palms Hotel crest on the breast pocket and straightened her matching skirt. Her head was down and she was digging around in her purse for her sunglasses when she rushed through the door.

"Hurry," she said without looking up. "Let's make a break for it before she calls with another cha—" she stopped midword and midstride, halfway out the outer office door when she saw who was waiting for her in the reception area.

It was *not* Kimmie.

With one hand on the doorjamb, Rachael turned back to Sylvie who cast a speculative glance between her and the man artlessly arranged in a casual slouch in a raspberry-upholstered and chrome chair. A smile as wide as Palm Beach stretched across the face Rachael was mortified to admit she'd dreamed about the past two nights.

Nate McGrory's pricey taupe silk polo shirt hugged his broad shoulders and tapered to his lean hips and long legs covered in tailored black trousers. Casual chic, very masculine—sexy personified. It was a style he wore even better than he had the cutaway tux. Possibly the softly curling chest hair peeking from the open placket at his throat and the deeply tanned and nicely muscled biceps had something to do with it. Possibly she needed to close her mouth before she started drooling. And absolutely she needed to pull herself together.

She shot Sylvie an accusing glare. "Where's Kimmie?"

Sylvie tucked a pencil into her short, stylishly coiffed salt-and-pepper hair and, with a nod, deferred to Nate.

"Regrettably detained," Nate explained as he unfolded all six-plus totally buff feet from the chair. "I volunteered to fill in. Hope it's okay."

She closed her eyes. Let out a breath.

"You know," she said, and forced a brittle smile, "that's very nice of you—really—but I just remembered. I have another appointment outside the office right about now."

His grin only widened. "Then I'll drive you." He shrugged, a man on an unmistakable mission. "We can pick up something to eat on the way. Wouldn't want you to miss your lunch."

His eyes were very dark. His smile was very warm—so were her cheeks and other places she didn't want to think about. And her adolescent physical reactions to him were really starting to tick her off.

"Sylvie—could you check my calendar, please? I may have misspoken. I think my appointment is here at the hotel, after all. In five minutes, right?" she added, meaning, *Go with this and lie for me or you will live to regret it.*

Sylvie blinked and affected a smile as innocent as a baby's. "Nope. All I've got down for you is lunch with Kim."

*You will die tomorrow,* Rachael assured Sylvie with a look that had no affect on her whatsoever—except to broaden her smug grin.

Behind her, Nate laughed. The sound rumbled through her senses, and to her disgust, jacked up the speed of her heartbeat. "Come on, Ms. Congeniality. Looks like you're stuck with me. Might just as well give it up and make the best of it. You have no way of knowing this, but it's been rumored that I'm a fun date," he added with one of those slashing grins she remembered from the wedding—and from her dreams.

She blinked and clung to her defenses with a slippery grasp. "This is not a date."

"If it makes it easier for you to deal with," he said amiably and touched his hand to the small of her back, "then you just put whatever spin on it you want. Me, I kind of like the idea of it being a—"

"Not a date," she repeated in a clipped tone that she hoped didn't sound as desperate as she suddenly felt.

She shot Sylvie—who was looking far too amused—a dark look. She was enjoying this, damn her. Okay. Enough was enough. This little scenario could play out forever, but she had no intention of being Sylvie's or Nate McGrory's afternoon entertainment as she fumbled around for feeble excuses to get out of going to lunch with him. It was also not a hill, she decided, on which she chose to die. She could do this. She could go to lunch with the man, convince him he was wasting his time and he'd back off. End of story.

"I'll be back by twelve-thirty," she told Sylvie, and, feeling a nearly compulsive need to move away from the warm pressure of his hand at the small of her back, she marched ahead of him out the door.

It wasn't that his touch repulsed her. Just the opposite. That slight but proprietary and wholly male gesture, the barest pressure of his fingertips at the small of her back, had far from repelled her. It had made her shiver—and not because the air conditioning was turned down to iceberg to accommodate Sylvie's hot flashes. No, his touch had nothing to do with making her cold and everything to do with making her feel hot. And edgy. And exposed. And all of that made her feel vulnerable. And that, she decided, was the real kicker and the reason he was throwing her so off guard.

Vulnerable was something she didn't have any inclination to be. Especially not around this man—because this man, she finally admitted, just might have what it took to break down her defenses. This man—with his incredible smile and loyal legion of friends who thought he was the best thing since the microchip—had gotten to her the first time she'd looked into his eyes despite her best attempts to ignore him.

Okay. What, exactly, are you doing here? Nate asked himself as he drove west down Royal Palm Way. Beside him, a very silent Rachael Matthews stared straight ahead, her hands folded primly on her lap.

She sat so stiffly and formally she could have been wearing a police uniform instead of the royal-blue skirt and blazer that were the trademark and standard attire for the Royal Palms Hotel staff. The white blouse and neat red tie knotted securely at her throat were intended to express a chic but professional presence. And, absolutely, they did. Except…the way the short snug skirt and tailored jacket hugged Rachael Matthews's curvy little body undermined the business statement.

She was every inch the luscious little morsel who had looked so pretty in pink at Sam's wedding. In fact, he hadn't been able to get the picture of her wrapped in clingy crepe out of his head. Now he was wondering what kind of underwear the prim and proper Ms. Matthews wore beneath her formfitting uniform. Lace, he was guessing. Something frothy and feminine and sheer and maybe just a little naughty. Something about her shouted sensuality, regardless of how professional she looked.

Lust—a good healthy punch of it—had knocked him for a loop the moment he'd set eyes on her. It still had a hold of him, or he probably wouldn't be here now, beating his head against the brick wall she'd laid with thick mortar and a big trowel, fantasizing about her underwear. The lady had clearly given him the ice-cube shoulder at the wedding Saturday night. She was not interested then—in capital letters. She was not interested now—with exclamation points.

Her reaction didn't negate the fact that he *was* interested—very—not only in the package, but in the person inside it. So what, exactly, did he see in her, since so far she'd snubbed him? Or was that the crux of it? It was embarrassing that most women tripped over themselves getting to him. Not her. To her, he was very resistible. Call him crazy, but he liked that about her.

He tapped a thumb on the steering wheel and braked for a red light. Was that it? Was it the challenge of breaking down her cool reserve? She wasn't reserved with her friends. He'd observed her for the better part of the reception Saturday night. Her touching toast to Karen brought tears to the eyes of most of the women in the room and had a few guys—him among them—clearing the lumps from their throats. How could a woman who obviously had such great capacity to love have sworn off men, as Kim had told him? And how was it that a woman who planned other women's happily-ever-afters didn't see one for herself? There was something sadly ironic in that.

He'd been hoping a heart-to-heart with Kim would cool his jets, but she'd reaffirmed what Sam had already told him. Rachael was a hard-working, make-it-on-her-own kind of girl. Unlucky in love, Kim had said. The look on Rachael's face when she'd accidentally caught Karen's bouquet at the reception had been sheer panic and had spoken volumes. She'd tossed it to Kim like a hot potato.

Had somebody burned her? It would seem that way, but even Kim, who had warmed to the role of matchmaker as the night had worn on, wouldn't give up the details, which only went to show the kind of loyalty Rachael inspired.

He shook his head, knowing he might be fighting a losing battle. Evidently, there was something about Rachael that brought out latent masochistic tendencies, because here he was, strapping on a bull's-eye for a round of target practice and she was just itching to shoot him down. He'd actually hung around in Palm Beach for an extra day for this chance at seeing her again and she'd made it clear—again—that she'd rather spend five minutes in a snake pit than an hour chatting and chewing with him.

He cut her a sideways glance. Grinned in spite of himself. The sun cut across her profile as they breezed down the busy street. She was so pretty.

He checked his rearview mirror and changed lanes. *Pretty* was a simple word for such an intriguing package, but in all honesty, it was the one that fit her best. She wasn't gorgeous, not in the goddess sense, although her huge, wide-set eyes—as green as colored glass and just as bright—sparkled with intelligence and independent pride and were more mesmerizing than any eyes he'd seen gracing a cover of *Vogue*. She wasn't what most people would consider beautiful, although the silky sweep of copper-red hair—that looked so much more natural today falling loose and straight around her shoulders than wrestled into a wreath of flowers—had a stunning effect and made a man itch to feel it sifting through his fingers.

Her mouth was too wide, her lips too full to be considered classically perfect. Her nose was short and sweet and cute. Just like she was. He grinned and figured there'd be death to the man who was stupid enough to call anything about her *cute* to her face. Or *sweet*.

No. Ms. Rachael Matthews did not regard herself as cute. Sophisticated, yes. Professional, absolutely. Dynamic, for a fact. She was all that.

And pretty.

And he was smitten.

Helluva deal.

"I have to be back in forty-five minutes," she informed him stiffly when Royal Palm Way became Okeechobee Boulevard and they continued across the bridge over Lake Worth and into West Palm.

"Slave driver for a boss?" he asked conversationally.

"A very full day."

"Then it's a good thing you're getting out and away from it for a little while. It'll give you an edge for the afternoon."

No response. Not that he'd expected one. He did

get a reaction, however, when he pulled in to a fast-food drive-through line.

She actually smiled, although he could tell she didn't want to.

"So, who have you been talking to?" she asked, her voice just a little less edgy and a little more relaxed.

"Sorry. I never reveal my sources. But I take it they were right? While you look like a caviar-and-truffles kind of girl, deep down you're a closet fast-food junkie."

In answer, she merely tilted her head. "I'll have a number four, please."

He smiled and turned to the squawk box. "Two number fours—and super-size 'em, okay?"

When he turned back to her, she was looking out the passenger window. He didn't have to see her face to know she was still smiling.

Score one for the good guy, he thought smugly and pulled ahead to the pay window.

Things were looking up.

"So, is it just me, or is it lawyers in general you regard as toxic waste?"

He'd driven back across the bridge into Palm Beach and parked at a metered spot along Ocean Boulevard. Rachael had left her jacket in his rented black SUV in deference to the warm March sun. They sat side by side on a bench behind the seawall, facing the ocean, eating a lunch that was sure to send her into a carbo-coma later this afternoon. But not now. Now, all of her senses were revved to warp speed. This man—this man pulled reactions out of her she'd told herself she wasn't going to submit to until she was darn good and ready. Which she wasn't. Not yet. Maybe not ever. She was too busy. Building her career. Proving she didn't need anyone but herself to make her life complete.

She hadn't understood her reaction to him the first time she'd met him. She still didn't understand it. He was too brash, too bold and too confident and way too full of himself. And just like the first moment they'd met, she was far too aware of the unexplained zip of sexual heat arcing between them. And it was just sexual. She didn't know him well enough for there to be anything else. Even this unexplained tug she felt toward him was sexual. Probably.

Damn Karen for making him out to be God's gift and suggesting he might be hers for the taking.

Several yards below them, down the wooden steps and beyond the wrack-strewn sand, a stiff easterly wind had riled the Atlantic into pummeling swells. The lifeguard board posted undertow and man o' war warnings. Oiled bodies lounged or lay here and there on jewel-colored towels, soaking up the Florida sun. Children played in the sand at the base of the rugged rock walls of the jetties while surfers poured into wet suits, straddled their boards and paddled past the lesser waves, waiting for the ultimate ride. Further out, the gleaming white hulls of pricey yachts and the occasional cruise ship dotted the horizon.

Behind them, sidewalk and road traffic buzzed by, adding another level of noise to the surf and the wind and the screech of swooping gulls. And yet, Rachael's world was reduced to the moment and the man who sat beside her, eating his lunch with gusto, apparently oblivious to her discomfort. She didn't want to react to him, but she was filled with that same hyperawareness she'd experienced at the wedding—awareness of his utterly male presence, of his dark eyes dancing over her face, of the way he smelled, like citrus and salt and masculinity.

He'd asked her a question. *Is it just me, or is it lawyers in general you regard as toxic waste?*

Oh, how about—you throw me completely for a loop and I don't know why. Sure. Like she was going to admit that.

Instead of coming clean, she asked a question of her own. "What, exactly, happened to Kim today?"

He popped a French fry into his mouth, chewed, then swallowed as he looked out to sea. She watched, fascinated, in spite of herself, by the way the muscles in his jaw worked, intrigued by the little scar in his brow and the mobile lips that were so quick to smile, so clever and ready to tease.

"Well, I called to ask her if she thought I could talk you into going to lunch with me and she very graciously suggested I substitute for her."

The easy way he said it stirred her anger. "Kimmie's special," she said, meeting those glittering brown eyes. "She's not someone to play with then throw away."

He looked taken aback, then raised a hand. "Hey— I *like* Kim. She's great."

"Then why did you put the moves on her then turn around and try to make time with me?"

He tilted his head, shook it, then nodded as if understanding had dawned. "You're talking about the reception."

"You looked pretty tight."

"I was pumping her for information about you—which, I might add, she was more than willing to give up."

Oh, she thought. Oh. So *that's* what they'd been about. She didn't want to be pleased by the thought. And she didn't want to be charmed by him. Yet, she was dangerously close to both reactions. "You could have asked me."

"And you would have answered?" He snorted and tossed back another fry. "I don't think so. You ran like a rabbit every time I got within a city block of you."

"I didn't run. I avoided. There's a difference. Most men would take it as a sign I wasn't interested."

He grinned, crooked and disarming, and brushed salt from his fingers. "I'm not most men. And you *are* interested."

No, he wasn't most men, she thought morosely and averted her gaze to the ocean. And she wished he was wrong. She wished she wasn't interested. She didn't have time to be interested. She couldn't afford to be interested.

"I'd like to get to know you, Rachael," he said quietly. "Would that be such a bad thing?"

Like his smile, this sudden sincerity was disarming. She shook her head, determined to stay the course. "Look, Nate—"

He cut her off with the touch of his hand to her cheek. She turned her head slowly and swallowed when he brushed a stray strand of windswept hair away from the corner of her mouth. "What are you afraid of?"

She stood abruptly, balled up the lunch she'd hardly touched, and tossed it in a nearby trash can. She wasn't afraid. Not exactly. She was simply wise. She knew how to protect herself and every instinct she trusted told her she needed to protect herself from him. "Let's just say this isn't a good time for me right now and leave it at that, okay?"

He was quiet for a moment and then she heard him rise. "So when would be a good time?"

When his shadow fell across hers on the sidewalk, she walked the few feet to the seawall and away from him. She stared out at the breakers rolling in, felt the sea salt and wind in her hair. When she sensed him beside her again, she looked up and over her shoulder.

The sun played across the sculpted angles and planes of his strong face as he tugged off his sunglasses then reached down and tugged hers off, too. She quelled the urge to reach up and run her fingers along the scar splitting his eyebrow.

Heartbreak. He was heartbreak waiting to happen and she was too smart to let herself in for the pain he could dole out.

"How long has it been since you were involved with someone?" he asked, settling a hip onto the seawall. With his back to the ocean, he crossed his arms over his chest and watched her face.

"How long?" he persisted softly, his expression so interested and so sincere, she was mortified that she wanted to tell him.

Long enough to know I don't have it in me to open up and give a relationship what it needs. Long enough to know I'm not cut out for couplehood.

She decided the short version was the best. "Long enough."

"Sounds like the perfect time to try again, don't you think?" His voice was very deep, brimming with the suggestion that he thought it was time to explore the possibility with him.

It took everything in her to shake her head. "No. I don't think so."

When his expression pressed for more than that, she relented.

"Look…you're getting way ahead of yourself here, okay?" She felt on the defensive suddenly and, damn him, his earnest look compelled her to say more than she wanted to say. "In the first place, you're moving way too fast. In the second place, I'm not interested. And in case those two didn't do it for you, I don't do well with relationships."

She paused, disturbed to hear the huskiness in her voice, then felt her cheeks flush with embarrassment at her choice of words. *Relationships*. Well, that ought to scare him off. Men like Nate McGrory didn't do relationships. They did flings, affairs, one-night stands. No doubt just breathing the word had him thinking about packing up his toys and, like those who had preceded him, heading for a new playground.

And yet, when she looked up to see if he was searching for the nearest exit, his gaze was intent on her face.

"Why is that?" His voice was so soft she had to strain to hear him above the rush of the wind and the call of the gulls and the traffic breezing by behind them.

"W-why is what?" She'd totally lost the thread of conversation, captivated by the fervency of his gaze.

"Why don't you do well at relationships?"

Nerves had her pushing out a humorless laugh and letting down her guard. Because relationships required something she didn't have in her to give. They required opening up to someone, laying yourself bare. And that just wasn't going to happen. "The usual reasons—too many, too varied and too boring to relate."

"Try me."

She dragged a hand through her hair, drew a bracing breath. "Look, Nate," she said, gathering her composure and turning to fully face him, "this is all very flattering. You're a really gorgeous guy—I'm sure you're very nice, but I'm just not up for any kind of—entanglement," she finally finished, deciding the word covered a plethora of possibilities.

His eyes were very dark as he pushed away from the seawall and cupped her shoulders in his big hands. "All I'm asking is that you think about it. Think about the possibility of an...entanglement," he said with a kind and gently teasing grin.

"And while you're at it," he whispered, watching her face as he lowered his mouth to hers, "think about this."

# Four

———

**R**achael should have seen it coming. She should have sensed, when Nate's strong hands gripped her shoulders and he started pulling her toward him, that he was going to kiss her. And maybe she did. Maybe she did see it coming, and maybe she could have stopped it.

But she didn't. Instead, she stood there, letting the worst possible thing that could happen to her draw her unerringly toward him.

His dark eyes, framed by thick, long lashes, searched her face, offering her the opportunity to pull away as he lowered his head to hers. He would have. He would have backed off if she'd given him the slightest indication. Yet all she could find it in herself to do was stand there and hang on for the ride.

The first touch of his mouth was electric. Softly,

sensuously electric. A mere brush of lips to lips. Not a tentative touch…more of an introduction, a promise, a gentle hello that reawakened the woman's need she'd told herself was not essential in her life. But, oh. She'd been wrong. She'd missed this. She'd missed this illicit little rush of yearning, this sweet quickening of a heartbeat he managed to alter more than any other man had.

His breath fell soft on her cheek as his nose brushed hers in a playful caress, while his mouth continued a tender assault on her defenses.

She heard a sigh, realized it was hers when his lips curved into a smile against her mouth just before he drew her deeply, decisively into his embrace and into a kiss the likes of which she'd never in her life experienced.

Delicious longing, humming passion infused her senses, easing her beyond any protest she might have lodged, spiraling her into an isolated cocoon of sensations too lush to categorize, too consuming to fight.

She wasn't aware of any conscious decision on her part to slip her arms around his waist and lean into him. She was aware only of heat. His. Hers. And of the broad musculature of his chest pressed against her breasts, the lean hardness of his hips meeting hers, the unmistakable and growing ridge of his erection nestled against her tummy.

Before she could react to the shock of it and pull away, he smiled against her mouth again, groaned a husky, "Sorry…that just sort of happens when I'm around you," and eased her into another drugging kiss.

*Intoxicating* was the perfect word for what he was

doing to her. She enjoyed the occasional glass of wine but didn't now and never had indulged in chemical stimulation. Yet drugged was exactly how she felt. Why else would she let down her defenses this way? Why else would she let him play with her mouth...nipping...nudging...testing with the tip of his tongue then shooting sparks through her body in a dizzying rush before he took her mouth again?

Oblivious to her surroundings, she melted into the kiss that was all silky heat and skillful seduction. He opened his mouth wide over hers, coaxed her with gentle but insistent pressure to open up, to let him in, let him taste, let herself feel the wonder of his total possession.

And still, he was never demanding. His tongue played in her mouth, learning her taste, exploring her textures, tempting, teasing, inviting her to do some exploring of her own. She couldn't resist. She followed his tongue as he withdrew, beckoning her to linger along the seam of his lips before delving inside and indulging in the illicit excitement of the experience.

With a deep groan, he changed the angle of his mouth and lifted her, setting her onto the seawall, then made a place for himself between her thighs. Time, place, proximity—they were all lost to her as he made love to her mouth and pressed the now very strong evidence of his physical reaction into the cleft between her legs. His hands spanned her hips, holding the part of her that pulsed with need tight against him.

It was the catcalls that finally penetrated her fog of pleasure. The sound of a skateboard and a trailing, "Hey dude, way to go, man," that finally forced her to open her eyes and snag a tenuous hold on her senses.

She broke the kiss, blinked up into eyes that were slumberous and dark and by all indications, deeply pleased by the turn of events.

He loosened his grip on her hips, slid his hands in a lazy caress to the small of her back and kneaded softly. "Well." He pressed his forehead to hers and smiled into her eyes. "Well, well, well."

She looked like a little bird as she blinked up at him, Nate thought. An adorable, thoroughly kissable, totally rattled little bird. He hadn't meant for it to go this far. He'd only meant to kiss her. Just kiss her. Just initiate a little physical dialogue to open her eyes to possibilities and break the tension that had been building between them.

He hadn't meant to turn it into a marathon session that he'd wanted to go on forever—or until he had her naked somewhere where they could take it to the next level. He hadn't meant to lose himself in her taste or the feel of her breasts pressed against his chest and his erection nestled into the sweet heat between her thighs.

He hadn't meant to do a lot of things. But he hadn't burned this hot this fast since—hell…he didn't know when a woman had flipped his switch this way.

Well, now he knew that one blistering hot kiss from Rachael Matthews—who, he reminded himself smugly, had done a little igniting of her own—was not going to be the sum total of their physical relationship.

Now seemed as good a time as any to make sure she knew it, too. He dove back for another kiss. The quick pressure of her hand on his chest between them stopped him.

"What?" he asked, only a vague interest in what kind of protest she was going to lodge crossing his mind. He didn't really care how much she protested verbally. She'd just shown him how she felt. She wanted this as much as he did. They didn't have to analyze why it was so spontaneous and intense between them. They just had to go with it.

"I don't *do* this," she blurted out, and this time she brought up her other hand to join the one making a half-hearted attempt to push him away. "I don't go around kissing men I hardly know. And I don't make a habit of making a spectacle of myself on a public sidewalk."

He would have felt guilty if he hadn't been so pleased by her rattled admission. And the unflappable Ms. Matthews was definitely rattled. He was doubly pleased that she'd as much as admitted it wasn't just any guy who tripped her trigger. It was him.

"For not *doing* it," he said, feeling another smile slip into place, "you *do* it remarkably well."

"Let me go," she enunciated carefully but without much heat.

In spite of his reluctance, he felt himself smiling again and did as she asked. Besides this fairly constant state of arousal he experienced when he was around her, he found himself doing that a lot. Smiling. Again, he wasn't sure why. Something about her. Something unexpectedly appealing, incredibly sexy and softly vulnerable no matter how businesslike and stern a facade she'd built to hide her true feelings.

It intrigued the hell out of him, this interest he felt

in her. It wasn't just sexual—although, good night, Isadora, the woman messed with his control. It was more. He liked her...hadn't felt this drawn to a woman since Tia.

The thought of Tia gave him pause. He'd been purposefully keeping her out of the equation. Until now. He loved Tia. Always would. The unfortunate fact that he could never have her, kept him from acting on that love.

In the meantime, he was a man. His love for Tia didn't stop him from enjoying other women. It *did* stop him from committing to long-term relationships. No. He didn't walk that road. It wouldn't be fair. Not to the woman. Not to him.

So why were you making noises a little while ago about wanting to get to know her better? Why aren't you taking your cues from Rachael and ending this with "Well, it wasn't meant to be, nice knowing you, see you around sometime?"

Damned if he knew why.

Just like he didn't know why the thought of stripping her out of that prim and proper Royal Palms uniform and seeing her in nothing but that pretty, pale skin, had him instantly hard again and trying to figure out a way to make his little fantasy a reality. Or, at least, a way to make this moment last until he could work this puzzle out.

"Let me take you to dinner tonight," he said abruptly.

"No."

He laughed at her immediate and decisive reaction then reached for her hands, holding them loosely in his. "You didn't even think about it."

"I don't have to think about it. Look. You caught me off guard there, okay?" She pulled her hands free. Hiking herself down off the seawall, she tugged down her skirt and readjusted her blouse. "But that..." she paused searching for the words.

He decided to provide them for her. "That incredible, mind-bending, sexy-as-hell kiss that you enjoyed every bit as much as I did?" he said, reaching for her tie and helping her straighten it.

"Whatever." She batted his hands away as her face flushed red. "It was a mistake. I don't even know you." She held out her hand for her sunglasses then turned and walked toward the rented SUV.

"I was born Nathan Alejandro McGrory, second son of Gloria Sanchez McGrory and Ryan Nathaniel McGrory in Miami thirty-two years ago come July," he said, deciding he'd worry about the whys and the consequences later and followed her. "My brother's name is Antonio Nicholas McGrory. His wife's name is Tia. They've been married five years and have two beautiful children, Marco and Meredith."

When she glared at him over the roof of the SUV, he just grinned and unlocked the doors with the remote.

"I graduated from Ohio State, went to law school at Harvard. Joined the family shipping firm and worked as corporate council until five years ago when I established my own law firm—still in Miami. I have all my own teeth, I jog five miles a day and am as healthy as a horse. And if you can overlook the fact that I still sleep with my teddy bear, Ted, I'm a pretty regular guy."

Gotcha, he thought as a whisper of a grin tipped up one corner of her mouth.

"Now what else would you like to know?"

"I'd like to know," she said, rearranging her face back into a stern scowl as he pulled out into traffic, "what it's going to take to convince you I'm not interested."

He cast her a sideways glance as he headed for the Royal Palms, just three blocks down the street. "A reaction a hell of a lot cooler than the one I got when I kissed you."

Silence, as thick as syrup, filled the SUV as he pulled into the Royal Palms circular driveway and stopped under the portico.

"Goodbye, Mr. McGrory," she said and let herself out. "Thank you for lunch."

"I'll call you," he yelled as she jogged up the grand outer staircase toward the four sets of gleaming gold-and-plate-glass revolving doors.

"Don't bother," she tossed over her shoulder.

"No bother," he said to himself as she disappeared into the opulent hotel. He sat there for a long moment before he finally put the SUV in gear. And damn, if he wasn't grinning again. "No bother at all."

"Well?" Sylvie stood just inside the doorway to Rachael's office, drawing out the word in an attempt to interject any number of leading questions. The one she finally settled on was, "How was lunch?"

Rachael tossed her purse into her lower left desk drawer and dropped into her chair. She had to sit. Her knees were too weak to hold her another minute.

Oh, Lord. He'd scared her. Scared her good. He'd

gotten to her, and somehow she had to figure out a way to get herself back under control.

Angry with herself for letting things get out of hand between them, and with Sylvie for encouraging him, she propped her elbows on her desk, folded her hands in front of her and shot Sylvie an evil smile. "See if I cover for you the next time Edward from accounting comes looking for you. You remember Edward of the terminal dandruff and phlegmy cough? Edward of the little comb-over thingy he does with his ten oily strands of hair? Ever notice the way his eyes bug out when he hears your name?

"Oh, yeah, *Ms.* Sylvie." Rachael leaned back in her chair, linked her fingers together over her midriff and relished the horrified look on Sylvie's face. "Not only will I *not* cover for you, I will lead him to the end of the earth to find you. I will extol your virtues—or lack thereof—while we search, in such graphic detail the man will be drooling on his bowtie by the time we find you. And," she added, holding up a finger when Sylvie tried to cut her off, "I will, with great pleasure, relate to him how hot you are for his body—pudgy little paunch and all."

"All right. All right," Sylvie sputtered. "I get it. You're ticked. How was I supposed to know you'd lost your mind completely? How was I supposed to know you wouldn't want to go out with the most luscious hunk of mankind this woman has ever set eyes on?"

"Oh, I don't know," Rachael returned with mock confusion. "How *would* you have known? Maybe from hints the size of Mack trucks I was dropping about a fake appointment?"

Sylvie waved away her scowl with a sweep of a beautifully manicured hand. Her nails were crimson red today—with little white stars and stripes on the tips. "So sue me. I thought you were having a brain cramp. I mean, what woman in their right mind would not want to go out with that man?"

"This woman," Rachael insisted and told herself if she repeated it often enough, she'd begin to believe it.

"Which begs the obvious question—did you have a stroke or something?" Sylvie rose, leaned across the desk and touched her palm to Rachael's brow. "A fever, maybe?"

Rachael let out a deep breath and finally gave up a grudging smile. Sylvie meant well. "He's not my type, okay?"

Sylvie laughed. "Oh, sweetie. He is every woman's type."

"Yeah, well, I don't have time for every woman's type."

"You would, if you hadn't married yourself twenty-four seven to this job."

"I love this job," Rachael protested, pulling out her Palm Pilot and double-checking her afternoon appointments with the intention of grounding herself in her work.

"To the exclusion of having a life?" Sylvie asked, serious now as she met Rachael's eyes with kind concern.

"Why is it so hard for everyone to accept that I like my life exactly the way it is?"

"You are wasting away here, Rachael. You're

young. You're beautiful. You need to have someone special in your life.''

"I am not wasting away. I feed off this job. And Nate McGrory is not looking for someone special. He's looking for a fast, hot fling.''

"So...what's wrong with fast and hot just to get your juices going before they all dry up from lack of use? Let him rev your motor for a while. You don't have to fall in love with him. You just have to enjoy him.''

Sylvie's comments gave her pause. "This from a woman who was married for thirty-five years to the love of her life. *You* could do that? You could go for the sex and forget the rest?''

"We weren't talking about me. Buck and I—we were soul mates. We were like mallards. We mated for life. I have no interest in short, meaningless encounters.''

"And you honestly think I do?''

"No,'' Sylvie said soberly. "I don't. But who knows—maybe it would turn into something more. I saw the way he looked at you. He was really interested.''

"He was really interested in a conquest. It's not going to be me. Now—are we finished with this conversation or do I need to bring Edward back into the fray?''

Sylvie rose. "Okay, okay. Your life. Your call. The Davises are due in about five minutes,'' she added, letting the subject of Nate McGrory drop. "The file's on your desk.''

"Thanks,'' Rachael said and watched Sylvie walk toward the door. "Hey...I'm sorry I was taking my bad mood out on you. Thanks. Thanks for caring. It means a lot.''

''You always draw the line at caring,'' Sylvie groused, her voice trailing behind her as she left Rachael's office. ''I never get to meddle. I think I'd be really good at it.''

Rachael grinned and shook her head. ''Trust me on this—you *are* good at it.''

Sylvie was efficient, fun-loving and just a little on the quirky side. Rachael loved her. She could always count on Sylvie to get the job done, to make her laugh, and to take the time to ask, ''Are you all right?'' when she saw something in Rachael's eyes alerting her that no, she wasn't all right. On those rare occasions when Rachael actually let down her defenses enough to confide in her, Sylvie would take the time to listen and then gently ask her how long it had been since she'd talked with her mother.

Her gaze landed involuntarily on the framed family portrait sitting on her bookshelf—the family portrait she should have been a part of, but she had begged off, making excuses at the last minute, and told them to go ahead and have it taken without her.

She walked across her office, picked it up, rubbed her thumb across the smiling faces of her blond stepsisters. Allison and Carrie had been twelve and thirteen at the time the picture was taken four years ago. They were sweetly smiling, pretty in the yellow and pink sundresses she'd bought them for Christmas. Behind them, her hands resting with maternal love on their shoulders, Rachael's mother smiled her loving-wife-and-mother smile, while beside her, John, Rachael's stepfather, draped his arm over her mother's shoulders. The portrait of the perfect American family. Happy. Healthy. Complete.

She set the photograph back in its place. After all these years, it still surprised her to realize she wished she could be a part of that picture even though she was the one who had sabotaged it, as well as any meaningful relationship with her family. She shoved back the longing for something she purposefully denied herself then felt a pinch of relief when her phone rang. "Yes, Sylvie."

"You're mom's on line two."

Rachael's heart skipped a little beat. "Hi, Mom," she said brightly when she punched the button.

"Hey, kiddo. How's it going?"

"Good. Busy."

"Exactly why I called. I want to make sure you didn't forget about dinner Thursday."

Rachael groaned. She *had* forgotten. Sort of. "Oh, Mom. I'm sorry." She sank down on the corner of her desk as guilt flooded her. "I'm sorry," she repeated, reacting to her mom's disappointed silence. "I scheduled a late appointment—it's one I can't afford to miss. Can we reschedule?" she asked quickly, hoping to undo some of the damage.

"This *was* a reschedule," her mom reminded her. "I don't know, honey…sometimes I think you do this on purpose."

"You know that's not true." At least Rachael didn't think it was. "How about I call next week and we'll set something up?"

Her mother sighed heavily. "Sure, honey. Whatever works for you."

"I'll call, okay?"

"Okay."

Only they both knew she probably wouldn't call. She'd intend to…but she just wouldn't get around to it. Echoing her mother's goodbye, she pressed the end button on the receiver. Then she stared at the phone clutched loosely in her hand, wishing she could get past all the things that kept her from letting her mom be a part of her life.

"You canceled dinner again, didn't you?" Sylvie asked from her open doorway.

Rachael forced a smile and set the receiver in its cradle. Over a bottle of wine one night, she and Sylvie had had a little chat. At Sylvie's gentle probing, Rachael had told her about her childhood. Sylvie had nailed it in one.

"So you figure that since your dad was abusive to you and your mother, and since your mother eventually found someone who made her life complete, that *you* must have been the problem."

Well, yeah. Sylvie's astute assessment had pretty well summed up her inability to make any relationship work. Rachael knew it was a self-defense mechanism to push people away. She even understood, in a convoluted sort of way, why she did it. Could even justify that she was determined to have something a lot more stable in her life than love. Love was something elusive—something she'd never been able to count on, even from those people who professed they felt it for her.

Knowing *why* she pushed people away, however, didn't necessarily equate with figuring out how to do something about it without hurting them. So she generally avoided dealing with it at all. Now was no exception.

"I didn't cancel dinner. I just postponed. We'll reschedule soon."

Sylvie bit her tongue and nodded. "The Davises are here."

"Great," Rachael said, ignoring Sylvie's doubtful look. She forced a bright smile. "Give me a minute then send them in."

She needed a minute. A minute to remind herself that she was twenty-nine years old—not nine and clinging to her mother and wondering why her daddy hated her as they raced to the closest battered women's shelter to get away from another one of his blind, fist-swinging rages.

How many times had they run in the middle of the night—a dozen? twenty?—before her mother had finally gathered the courage to file for divorce and relocate from Ohio to Florida to get away from Calvin Matthews? It had been just the two of them then. Two against the world, her mother used to say as she kissed Rachael good night.

And then her mom had met John Cooper. He was the antithesis of Calvin Matthews. John was kind. He didn't drink. He treated her mother like a queen. He patted Rachael's head with absent affection. Everything was going to be wonderful. Everything was going to be great. And it was—until two years later, the year Rachael turned twelve and that first pretty little pink baby was born.

Like everyone else, Rachael loved Allison to distraction. "Don't hover," her mom used to scold.

"Don't always be loving on her. She needs some room. So do I."

As it turned out, they all needed a lot of room from Rachael, who wanted so much to be a part of this beautiful new family that she annoyed them with her smothering attention.

It was gradual, the way they shut her out over the years. She was certain her mother wasn't even aware of what she and John had done to her—of how much it had hurt her always to feel that she was on the outside looking in. As if she was a part of her mother's past that reminded her of bad times. Even after her mother had confided several years ago that she'd suffered a deep depression after the girls were born, and even though intellectually Rachael had seen how that depression had affected her mom's treatment of her, she still felt the loss. She still pushed people away before they could push her.

A shrink would have a field day with her and a couch. Only she didn't need a shrink to tell her she had issues with commitment. Issues with trust. So what? She was doing just fine.

Sylvie thought Rachael should get involved with Nate McGrory? Not a chance. As she'd told him, she didn't do relationships, or more accurately, she ruined relationships by making sure no one ever got close enough to her to matter.

And that, she reminded herself, was why her position at the hotel suited her. She could calmly and with cool reserve plan weddings for people who walked in and then right back out of her life. They weren't looking for long term with her. They were looking for spectacular, short-term results. She gave them both. And she didn't get involved.

That was enough. She made it be enough.

The flowers started arriving from Nate the next day.

The note accompanying the roses on Tuesday said: Did I mention that big dogs and little children love me?

The note with the lilies on Wednesday read: Say the word and Ted is history.

"Ted?" Sylvie asked with a quirk of her brow.

"His teddy bear," Rachael supplied, fighting a grin and not liking herself much for giving in to it.

"You're not going to give me more than that are you?"

"Nope," she said, feeling smug, and went back to work.

"Oh, God, you're gonna love this one," Sylvie said the next day, laughing as she brought the latest exotic bouquet into Rachael's office and set it on her desk.

"I don't remember telling you that you could read my personal messages," Rachael groused as she snatched the card from Sylvie's outstretched hand. Her manufactured scowl faded when she read the card. She shook her head, rolled her eyes and finally grinned.

Me strong—like bull.

"Got to give the man credit. He's nothing if not persistent. And dogs and kids love him," Sylvie added with a grin. "And he's strong—like bull."

"Har har."

But it was Friday's offering that really dented her

defenses. No flowers this time. Just a hot and tasty value meal from her favorite drive-in and a note that read: There's a lot more where this came from.

"Are you just melting over there?" Sylvie asked as she reached into the sack and dug out a cheese fry.

Oh yeah. She was melting. "No. I'm not melting. I'm annoyed."

"My turn," Sylvie said. "Har har."

"Okay. So it's flattering. But I'm still annoyed. And I'm really not interested."

Sylvie shook her head. "The man is willing to give up his teddy bear for you," she reminded Rachael with a waggle of her brows. "Trust me on this— that's not a sacrifice to be taken lightly."

"I have two words for you," Rachael said sweetly, folding her hands together on the top of her desk. "Comb-over."

Sylvie hissed, made a cat's claw, then marched out of the room.

Rachael grinned. And smelled the flowers. And ate a fry. And told herself he could send all the flora and junk food he wanted. She wasn't going to get involved with him. With him in Miami and her in West Palm, she figured it was pretty much a sure bet she'd seen the last of him anyway.

# Five

So much for sure bets, Rachael thought two weeks later. Not only had she *not* seen the last of Nate McGrory, she was seeing way too much of him—literally—as he sat a little to the right and way too close behind her watching Karen and Sam open gifts at their post-honeymoon party.

"From the looks of things, I'd say the honeymoon was a huge success," Nate whispered in her ear.

He was so close she could feel the warmth of his breath feather across her bare shoulder. His voice was hushed, as if he didn't want to take the focus away from the newlyweds—or as if he wanted to cocoon the two of them in an intimate little conversation.

Rachael reminded herself she didn't want to be intimate with Nate McGrory—conversationally or horizontally—so she did her darnedest not to react to the

way he looked and smelled and smiled and the way
he somehow managed to keep pressing his bare thigh
against her leg. Or the way he'd lean over, just so, so
that his broad chest grazed her bare shoulder. Or he'd
arrange it so his fingers brushed hers as he passed her
a glass of mimosa, or his breath would tickle the fine
hair at her nape where she'd swept it up into a hap-
hazard knot in deference to the heat.

More than once already this afternoon she was glad
she'd worn her plain yellow cotton tank top and white
capris instead of shorts to the casual gathering. More
than once she'd wished she could make herself ignore
him as she smiled across the great room at Sam and
Karen. Just back from their honeymoon, they were
glowing, tanned and rested and so completely in love
it hurt, just a little, to watch them.

Along with Sam and Karen's immediate family, all
members of the bridal party who could make it were
gathered in the newlyweds' new home in Jupiter, just
north of West Palm, while the happy couple opened
their wedding gifts. They'd decided to make a party
of it. At least thirty people were in attendance at the
get-together that would wrap up with a backyard
cookout then a game of volleyball, if the net set up
near the pool was a clue. Rachael had been told to
bring her swimsuit. She'd also been told Nate wasn't
going make it.

So much for what she'd been told.

Rachael hadn't seen him since that day he'd shang-
haied her into lunch then kissed her silly on the seawall. But he'd made sure she'd thought about him
every day during the weeks since. And as often as
she told herself to ignore him, she hadn't been able

to get herself to reject the deliveries or throw the flowers in the trash, or toss the sinfully delicious burgers and fries. He hadn't called her though. She'd mulled that fact over with relief tinged just a little too heavily with regret and told herself to snap out of it.

Now he was here. And she couldn't get herself to stop thinking that he was even more dazzling and gorgeous than she'd remembered. And close. Lord, he was close.

His nylon shorts were short and black; his tank top was white. Both were stunning contrasts to the deep, natural tan of his skin. Both revealed an impressive amount of well-toned muscle and a soft pelt of dark chest hair. A tingling sensation streaked through her tummy at the thought of touching her fingers there— just there at the base of his throat—to experience its softness and the heat of the skin beneath.

"You smell great, by the way. Have I mentioned that?"

"Twice," she said grumpily and wished there wasn't something about his dogged persistence that made her want to get a little soft and mushy inside. People didn't go the extra mile for her. Men especially didn't. Her cold shoulder usually did the trick. But not with him.

He'd been lobbing little compliments her way all afternoon, making sure she couldn't ignore him if she tried.

She cast him a sideways glance, saw the heat in his laughing eyes and, tipping her mimosa to her lips, quickly looked away. Why did he have to seem so sweet in spite of his blatant flirting? And why did he have to look so good? He should look like a BuBu, sitting there with his legs spread wide, his elbows propped on his thighs, a delicate wineglass clasped loosely in his large hand. A Miami Dolphins baseball cap sat backwards on his head. His dark hair peeked out beneath the cap's bill in the back, touching his shoulders, looking silky soft and artfully styled instead of shaggy and unkempt.

She closed her eyes, mentally shook her head. He could have sat beside anyone, she thought as she edged a little to the left and away from him on the overstuffed hassock. Yet he had made a point of sitting by her—on a footstool that barely accommodated one, let alone two people.

"Can you play volleyball in those shoes?" he whispered, dropping his chin onto her bare shoulder and looking up at her from beneath a web of thick, dark lashes. She'd kill for lashes that thick. On most men they'd have looked effeminate. Since she'd already established he wasn't most men, it was a given that on him they looked darkly dangerous.

She jerked forward, breaking the contact. His look, his touch—both were too familiar and too loaded with sexual intent…and with the promise of fun and a silly kind of sweetness that she simply did not want to fall prey to.

She made a show of studying her three-inch platform sandals. "I can play volleyball in cowboy boots," she informed him silkily, "and still outplay you."

She wasn't sure what made her say it—she'd break her ankle if she didn't ditch the shoes before they started playing. Maybe it was the too, too easy way he had of turning her awareness meter up to overload.

Maybe it was the fact that he was so sure of himself—
and so determined to ignore every hint she'd dropped
that she wasn't interested and for him to just back off.

Maybe, it was because she was lying. She *was* interested, didn't want to be and he knew it.

"Oh-ho, baby." Unconcealed amusement shot
sparks through eyes the deep, rich brown of cappuc-
cino. "I think I detected a definite challenge in that
statement."

"No challenge," she said slowly, "just stating a
fact."

"Don't know how to break this to you, darlin'"
he whispered so the others couldn't hear him, "but
you're a little vertically challenged for the game. I'm
pretty certain your head won't even reach the bottom
of the net."

"Well, *darlin'*," she drawled back, latching on to
any reason to let her dander rise above this compul-
sion to like him and above the humming sexual
awareness for which she'd yet to find a defense,
"what I lack in height, I make up for in speed and
just plain meanness."

He covered his face with his hand then grinned at
her from between spread fingers. "Somehow I knew
a little mean streak would factor into any game you
decided was worth playing. I, for one, can't wait to
find out just how mean you can get."

She was pretty sure he was no longer talking about
volleyball. And, darn it, she was having a hard time
not grinning back. This was not good.

She forced starch into her spine. "You'd better
hope we're on the same team, McGrory."

He winked. "Any time you want to team up, *Matthews,* I'm more than ready for the merger."

"Uncle Nate!" a little voice cried in excitement from across the room.

Rachael looked up, glad for the distraction as approximately sixty pounds of squealing freckles and blond pigtails sporting a Popsicle-stained smile ran across the room and hurled herself into Nate's arms.

"Emily," he proclaimed, lifting her onto his lap and into a huge bear hug. He planted a smacking kiss on her cheek. "How's my favorite chuckle-head?"

"I'm seven now," the little cherub proclaimed, pride in her voice as she looped her hands around Nate's neck and grinned into his eyes with unbridled adoration.

"Seven? Already?" he asked, sounding properly astounded.

"Uh-huh. Pretty soon I'll catch up with you and we can get married, 'member?"

Nate hugged her hard and laughed. "I'm saving myself just for you, doll."

This silly little bit of banter elevated Emily's smile from proud to pleased.

And melted Rachael's heart.

*No fair.* Nate McGrory had to be gorgeous and sexy and rich and charming—and let's not forget strong—like bull—but did he have to be sweet and gentle and indulgent with children, too? *Big dogs and little children loved him.* Rachael dropped her forehead to her hand and wondered if he helped little old ladies across the street.

"I'll be just as pretty as Karen won't I?" Emily asked, her eyes full of hope.

"Every bit, sweetie. Do you know my friend, Rachael?"

Perfect. Now he was going to draw her into the conversation with this adorable little imp and make her like him even more.

"Hi, Emily."

Emily smiled then looked her up and down. "Don't you think Uncle Nate is handsome?"

"Um...well—"

"Sure she does," Nate supplied, grinning over the top of Emily's tow head. "She's just a little shy about saying what she thinks. Isn't that right, Rachael?"

She forced a tight smile for Emily. "Yeah. Shy. That's me."

"He's not really my uncle," Emily explained. "He's Uncle Sam's friend so I call him Uncle Nate 'cause he's like one of the family. Hey—wanna go swimmin'?" she asked Nate, skipping on to bigger and better things with a mercurial shift of topics that left Rachael's head spinning.

"Sure," Nate said. "*Wanna* go with us?" he asked Rachael, the dare evident in his devil grin.

Just as she was about to launch into an emphatic no thanks, grateful for the opportunity to place some much-needed distance between herself and Mr. Perfectly Wonderful, Emily joined in on the arm-twisting.

"Come on Rachael. It'll be fun."

"Yeah," Nate said, covertly raking her body with a gaze as hot and smoky as his voice, "It'll be fun."

"Let's go get our suits on." Emily slipped off Nate's lap and latched on to Rachael's hand. "I've got a bikini—a red one. What have you got?"

What did she have? Nate's silent but obvious interest in Rachael's suit made it clear that what she had was trouble—with a capital *T* and that rhymed with *P* and that stood for pool—and not the kind Meredith Willson had in mind when he'd written his famous song from the *Music Man.*

"Hurry up, silly," Emily insisted, tugging her to her feet, "or Nate will beat us to the water."

"Last one in's got to pay with a kiss," Nate said, eyebrows waggling. His soft chuckle trailed behind her when Rachael practically dragged Emily toward the cabana at a dead run.

At ten that night, Rachael glanced across the front seat of her car to where Nate sat holding an ice bag on his right eye. She let out a deep breath, braked for a red light and flipped her left-turn signal.

She hadn't meant to bloody his lip. She even felt a little bad about the way his right eye was swollen. She'd only wanted to prove a point. Well, okay. She'd wanted to do more than that. As she'd faced him across the volleyball net after their swim, her team down five zip with the spike king, McGrory, scoring four of the points, she'd wanted to beat the pretty-boy smile right off his poster-boy face. She'd wanted to put him in his place and when his ego collapsed like the portable lawn chair she'd stowed in her trunk along with her empty salad bowl before heading home, she'd wanted to watch him slink away with his tail tucked so securely between his legs there'd be no chance he'd ever call her again.

So far, it was a dud of a plan.

Why? Well, it was mostly because aside from his

blatant interest in her, Rachael had seen a side of him tonight that Karen had been telling her about and that she hadn't wanted to believe. He'd let up on her the moment he'd slipped into the pool—all caramel-gold skin and hard, rippling muscle. He'd extracted a peck on the cheek from Emily who had made it a point to be the last one in. Then he'd pretty much left Rachael alone to drool in peace while he'd repeatedly lifted Emily up onto his shoulders so she could dive off, or coach her when she jumped off the diving board, or show her the nuances of the back stroke.

He'd been gentle, patient, and full of fun with the little girl—and a regular Boy Scout with her. He'd taken a long, hard, appreciative look at her in her modest black one-piece, honed in on what could only have been distress plastered across her face and must have decided he'd stroke out if he so much as came near her, water dripping from that glorious black hair and trailing down his very buff body. So, he'd kept his distance.

Just when she'd thought she could dislike him for using a little girl to get to her, he turned into a gentleman. Just her luck, Nate McGrory drew lines and didn't cross them. How did you defend against those kind of underhanded tactics? He really was more than he appeared to be. A genuine nice guy. A guy she could lose her head over…and *that* was the reason she couldn't let anything happen between them.

Was she the only person on the planet who saw disaster written all over this?

It didn't matter that he was as nice as everyone said he was—like Karen who marveled that unlike most filthy-rich men, he wasn't quirky, or cruel or self-absorbed. He was *normal*. From Rachael's experience, he was an anomaly among the rich and famous—and he wasn't supposed to be, darn it. He was supposed to be severely flawed in the character department and he had the nerve to be well-adjusted, kind, charming, patient, sexy and…yada yada yada.

And *that* brought her to the real reason she'd lost it on the volleyball court. It had been hit him or hug him and, well…she really did have a little mean streak in her. Unfortunately, it had come out with a vengeance and he'd paid the price. Gracefully, she might add—damn him.

"How's the eye?" she asked as guilt got the best of her. Just as it had gotten the upper hand when she'd grudgingly agreed that since she'd maimed him—his words—the very least she could do was give him a ride to his hotel since he wasn't in any shape to drive—again, his words and his assessment. She'd figured he could drive just fine. No one else had.

Fine, she thought grumpily. She'd knuckled under. She was giving him a ride.

Much of this was Kimmie's fault, she thought in disgust as she eased into the right lane. Kimmie's and Karen's and Sam's who had all been on her team. Kim had been bemoaning a broken nail for the better part of the first set. Sam and Karen spent more time fabricating reasons to run into each other and indulge in long hot kisses than keeping their heads on the game. Her natural competitive spirit had kicked into overdrive. *Somebody* had to do something to stop the one-man wrecking crew. Rachael had felt obligated to step up to the plate. Or, in this case, up to the net.

And had proceeded to drill the ball straight into his face.

"I'll live," he said and when she glanced at him, she saw that incorrigible smile curve his lips. "I'd rather talk about how you can make it up to me."

The suggestion in his tone left little doubt that his idea of making it up to him involved the two of them naked somewhere kissing more than boo-boos. After seeing him in his swim trunks today, she had less to imagine and more to anticipate in that area. "I said I was sorry."

"But was your heart in it?"

Oh, God. He was going to make her smile again if she wasn't careful. "My heart was in the spike I slammed into your face. But my good intentions were behind my apology if that's any consolation."

"Fair enough. Just so you understand that *my* good intentions must have lost out if my attorney hits you with a lawsuit."

Her head swiveled toward him. "You're kidding."

"Probably." He slumped deeper into the seat, his long legs cramped against the consol of her compact car. The muscles in his thighs were lax, his head lolled against the headrest as he pretended to consider. "I'm not sure yet. Maybe we could litigate this ourselves. Say…over a nice bottle of merlot and a candle-light dinner tomorrow night?"

The look on his face was both endearing and maddening. Darn him, he just wouldn't let up. "I don't get you, McGrory," she groused aloud. "Besides the fact that I'm clearly not interested, I don't run in your social or financial circles. We probably have nothing in common. So why are you bothering?"

"Why does the sun rise?" he returned, playfully mimicking her dramatic tone.

She rolled her eyes.

He laughed, but the sound was colored with frustration as he resettled the ice pack on his eye. "Okay. Try this. Instead of wondering why, why, why, let's go with why *not?* Why not just go with it and see where it leads? Why are you making this so difficult? Why can't you just give it up, go out with me and see if we enjoy each other's company as much as every red blood cell in my body is telling me we will?"

Well, he didn't much mince words did he? It didn't help that her blood cells were doing some talking, too. It was her job to lie for them. "I don't want to sleep with you."

He snorted. "Now tell me you're sorry you broke my face. I'll try to believe that, too."

"Okay. I *might* want to sleep with you," she finally confessed, then could have kicked herself when he sat up, threw an arm over the seat back, lowered the ice pack and shot her a victorious smile.

*Had she really said that?*

"Progress at last."

"But that's biology," she defended hastily. "Simple chemistry."

"Two of my favorite subjects."

She sighed deeply. "I don't do casual sex, Nate."

"Who said anything about casual?"

His voice was soft, sincere and too much to believe. So she didn't. "Isn't that what this is about?"

He was quiet for a moment before saying, "Don't you think you're selling us both short?"

She couldn't think of a single thing to say to that.

"How about I tell you what this is about," he continued as if he were actually giving it some serious thought. "It's about this attraction and this general feeling that if we walk away from each other without ever seeing what direction this takes, we're both going to be very, very sorry.

"Come on, Rachael. Don't you ever just free fall?" he asked when she remained stubbornly silent.

It was more than disconcerting to admit her silence was mainly because she was simply running out of arguments, or at least running out of strength to defend against his.

"Don't you ever just risk something and screw the consequences?"

Finally, an easy question. "No. Never," she said. It was the risk factor of the equation that finally got her back on track. She didn't do risk. She did safe and secure. She needed safe and secure. He was neither of those things.

"Then don't you think it's time you considered it?"

Rather than answer, she evaded. She seemed to do that a lot around him.

"I believe this is your hotel," she said, pulling up in front of the charming and pricey Brazilian Court. Very intentionally, she left her foot on the brake and the car in gear as a valet magically appeared and opened the passenger-side door. It took everything in her to stare straight ahead instead of meeting Nate's eyes.

"I don't suppose a last-ditch plea for mercy would

convince you to come up to my room and administer a little triage?''

Her snort said, Not on your life, although she had to wrap her fingers around the steering wheel and hang on tight.

"Didn't think so."

Silence filled her car then, as intrusive as a flood-light.

"If I give you my number, you won't call me, will you?'' he asked as if he already knew the answer.

She shook her head, resolute in the face of the genuine regret she heard in his voice.

This was it then. He finally understood. A disappointment she hadn't expected colored her words as well. "No. I won't call."

Another long moment passed before he finally got out of the car then ducked back down so he could see inside. "Then I'll call you."

She jerked her head toward him. "Nate—"

He stopped her protest with a shake of his head. "I'll call you, Rachael." Then he turned and, tossing the ice pack from hand to hand, walked into the hotel.

Rachael was fitting the key into the lock of her town house door when her phone rang fifteen minutes later.

"Just wanted you to know I make good on my promises,'' Nate said without preamble when she snatched up the receiver and breathed a breathless hello.

She sank down on her sofa, too aware of her pleasure at hearing his voice. For once, she didn't fight the involuntary reaction to smile. "A man of his word."

"I think I might have covered that in one of the cards I sent with the flowers."

Still smiling, she laid her head back against the sofa. "So you did."

"Did I mention I was persistent, too?"

She touched her fingers to her curving lips. "Among other things, I believe so, yes."

Silence settled like a silk scarf all light and shimmery and set all of her senses on simmer mode. She stared into the darkness of her living room, her heart pounding, afraid she was waiting for him to ask her out again, afraid she'd say yes if he did.

"Good night, Rachael."

"Good night," she whispered after the moment it took her to process the finality of his words—and to convince herself she wasn't disappointed that he'd given up. "Take care of that eye."

He chuckled. "I'll do that."

And then he hung up.

Rachael sat in the dark for several minutes, thinking about all those things she'd promised herself she wouldn't think about. Like how, under all that arrogance, she was beginning to believe that those who knew him best were right when they swore he was a kind and generous man. How he made her laugh, even when she didn't want to. How her entire body had come alive in a way that had elevated her to a new height of awareness the moment their eyes connected.

She thought of how long it had been since any man had drawn this strong a reaction from her. Of how long it had been since she'd let down her guard enough to want to react this way. And finally, she silently confessed to how badly she wanted to be with Nate McGrory.

With a low growl of frustration, she rose, threw her deadbolt and headed for the shower.

She was applying the cream rinse to her hair before she realized she'd been humming an old show tune under her breath.

If only she could wash that man out of her life as easily as she rinsed her shampoo out of her hair.

# Six

Sunday dinner at the McGrory Miami mansion was always part business, part family catch-up session and pure torture for Nate. Not that anyone would ever know. He always made sure they didn't.

In the corner of the lanai, under the shade of a coconut palm, Nate's father, Ryan, and his brother, Tony, huddled over the chessboard talking shipping business and baseball and grumbling good-naturedly at each other over their offensive and defensive strategies. Nate was several yards away in the yard, playing catch with little Marco, Tony and Tia's four-year-old while Meredith, their two-year-old, napped in the nursery.

Regardless of the full-time household staff at the elaborate estate his father laughingly referred to as Dublin West, his mother, Gloria, who Nate resembled physically, sharing her dark hair and complexion and eyes, insisted on preparing the family's Sunday dinner. With dinner over, she was in the kitchen putting the finishing touches on some sinfully sweet desert. Eventually, she'd carry it out to the lanai and insist they all eat it, regardless of the fact that they were still stuffed to the gills from a dinner that somehow managed to blend Cuban and Irish cuisine into a sumptuous feast.

"We don't see much of you anymore, Nate. The kids miss you. So does Tony. So do I."

Nate gathered himself, managed a smile then glanced over his shoulder and into the eyes of the woman he'd loved and lost to his brother. Tia. Beautiful, sensitive, gentle Tia. Seeing her at these Sunday gatherings always brought home the bittersweet reminder that he loved her. But since Tony was the one who'd been smart enough to admit it and then do something about it, that had left Nate in the cold. To date, he hadn't found a way to combat his love for her save stow it away.

"You know how it goes, sis. Too much work, too little time."

And it was just too hard to be around them together. No one knew that he loved her, of course. Nate had never professed his feelings; he'd never hurt Tony or Tia that way. They'd been friends forever, the three of them, and then one day, out of the blue, Tony announced he and Tia were getting married. Nate had been stunned—and a little confused. All he could think was, Man…how could I have been so blind? Not just to Tony and Tia's love for each other, but to his feelings for Tia.

It wasn't a conclusion he'd reached overnight, but after a while, when no woman ever measured up, he'd finally realized it was his love for Tia that kept him from committing to a relationship. Most of the women he saw didn't seem real next to her. They were pampered, plastic princesses; they wanted him for his wealth, his reputation, his social status.

It had finally come to him then, that he'd missed his opportunity for a soul mate. But, he'd carried on. He'd just gone about his business of enjoying life as best as he could. Some things, however, were just too tough. Like seeing Tia and Tony together on a daily basis. That's the reason he'd opted out of the family business shortly after they'd gotten married even though he'd told the old man he simply needed to be out on his own. That had been five years ago.

And then came Rachael Matthews…and she had him buzzed on something that had eluded him for a very long time. Fascination.

"What's this I hear about a new woman in your life?" Tia asked, rousing him from his musings.

Nate caught the ball when Marco tossed it then pasted on another brotherly smile. Tia's brown eyes were big and round, her full mouth smiling and curious. "Tony has a big mouth and you know I never kiss and tell."

Speaking of kisses, he'd spent a lot of time thinking about the hot kiss he'd shared with Rachael, even now he felt an answering heat pool low in his gut. Interesting. He'd never so much as kissed Tia. Never made any attempt to relay his feelings. Marriage was sacred. So was his brother's love. And while he'd come to believe there wasn't another woman out there for

him, he'd grown up in this lovingly blended Latino
and Irish family and he wanted very badly to believe
in the continued solvency of the institution of marriage.

Not that he thought it would ever happen for him.
Not now. And he hated that. Really hated it—more
so every day. Once he'd wanted home, hearth, kids—
the whole nine yards. He'd given up on that scenario
because the one woman he saw completing the picture
was out of reach.

So why did you mention Rachael to Tony, a little
voice in his head asked.

Darned if he knew. He saw a lot of women. Enjoyed the hell out of them as long as they understood
up front it was fun and games and nothing more. But
he never talked about them to his family.

Back to square one. Why Rachael? Most women
fawned over him. Rachael wouldn't give him the time
of day. It tickled the hell out of him that she wasn't
impressed by his money or his looks or his social
status. She was smart and feisty and dedicated and
driven—all things that had been said about him at one
time or another.

Bottom line, she intrigued him, but he'd never let
things get too serious between them. It wouldn't be
fair. Not to her. Not when his heart was lost to Tia.

You told her your interest wasn't casual, bozo.

Yeah. There was that. Was he resorting to lying
now to get a woman into bed with him? If so, why?
Was it the challenge? Or was he getting tired of fun
and games and looking, again, for something he'd
given up on having?

"Hello-o-o."

He jerked his head around. Curiosity tinged with amusement colored Tia's face.

"Where'd you go, Nate?"

He'd totally zoned out on her. "Sorry. I was concentrating on my main man here," he lied with a grin and tossed the ball to Marco. He laughed when the little boy made a dramatic dive to catch it, bobbled it, then belly-crawled across the grass to retrieve it.

"Come, come," Nate's mother called from the lanai. "Dessert is ready."

"That's our cue, boyo." Relieved for the opportunity to escape the one-on-one conversation with Tia, Nate scooped Marco up and onto his shoulders and dodging a pineapple palm, headed for the lanai.

Then he spent the rest of the afternoon wondering why he was working so hard to breach Rachael Matthews's—of the saucy green eyes and irresistible mouth—defenses.

Two weeks after Karen and Sam's party, Rachael had decided Nate McGrory had finally gotten the message. Oh, he'd called a few times but Sylvie had deflected him for her. And then the calls had stopped altogether. She hadn't seen so much as a daisy or smelled a rose with some silly note attached since. And that was good. That was…great, she told herself as she sat at her desk looking over an array of printed material on entrées and wine selections for the upcoming Jenson wedding reception.

"And it only took a blackened eye and a bloodied lip to do the job," she muttered under her breath.

A sound at her open door brought her head

up…and set her heart racing as she connected with the vivid cappuccino-brown of Nate McGrory's eyes.

While her heart did a back flip and shot heat to every extremity in her body, his only reaction was that one corner of his fabulous mouth kicked up in an endearingly boyish smile.

"The door was open," he offered by way of apology for interrupting her.

"I…um…"

His smile widened. "No life guard on duty today?"

"Excuse me?"

"Your assistant? She's not running interference today?"

"Oh." He was referring to Sylvie who had been reluctantly screening her calls—several of which had been from Nate. All of which Rachael had made up some excuse not to take until he'd finally stopped calling. "She must have…I don't know. She must be running an errand or something."

"My good luck."

She could only stare as he shoved his hands deep into his trouser pockets and leaned a shoulder against the doorframe.

When her phone rang, she couldn't help but think Saved by the bell.

She dealt with the call, all the while watching him while he prowled around the room, checking out her view, as well as the personal marks she'd put on her office.

"Your older sister?" he asked looking over his shoulder when she disconnected. He held the picture of her mother and stepfather and stepsisters in his hand.

Unable to stop herself, she walked around her desk and lifted the portrait from his hands. "Mother," she said stiffly.

She read the questions in his eyes, but set the photograph back on the shelf before he could voice them. He took the hint and let it go.

"So, how's it going, Rachael?"

It had been two weeks since she'd left him at the Brazilian Court with a promise that she wouldn't call. She'd thought of him every day—and night—since. Sitting close beside her on that tiny hassock. Tanned, wet skin in the pool. Rippling muscles spiking a volleyball. Irreverent grin and bedroom-brown eyes.

*That's* how it was going.

She walked back to her desk and sank into her chair before her knees buckled because he was standing here in the flesh with that delicious face and that amazing smile and extraordinary body.

*That's* how it was going.

And she thought of his gentleness with Emily and his friendship with a good man like Sam and the resigned disappointment in his eyes when she'd said, no, she wouldn't call.

*That's* how it was going.

"Busy," she said and left it at that.

"Ah. So that would explain why you couldn't take my calls."

She blinked, folded her hands together on top of her desk and ordered herself to tough it out. "If it makes you feel better to think so."

He laughed. "Don't you want to know what brings me to Palm Beach?"

She rose, gathered the literature together and

tapped it on her desk to straighten it. "My guess would be business, since there's nothing else here for you."

He stabbed an imaginary knife in his chest and sagged against the doorjamb. "You have a mean heart, Rachael Matthews."

She crossed the room, opened a cabinet and tucked the material neatly inside the Jenson file, praying he wouldn't see her hands shaking—or her heart beating beneath her blouse. "I thought we'd already established that."

"Why yes, my eye's fine. Thanks for asking," he said brightly and settled a hip on the corner of her desk.

She threw him what she hoped passed for a bland look as she returned to her desk and sat behind it.

"Okay, here's the deal," he began without preamble. "I've been thinking and this is the way I've got it figured. I've been too subtle with you."

She leaned back in her chair, regarded him with an incredulous stare. Then, because he was just so impossible, she laughed. "You don't have a subtle bone in your body."

"The flowers, the phone calls," he went on, ignoring her disbelieving look, "they just don't cut it with a woman like you. I need to be more decisive. I need to be more assertive."

"Nate," she began, but he cut her off.

"So I've made reservations at Mara Lago for tonight."

Had he said Mara Lago?

Rachael had *always* wanted to see Mara Lago, but like so many things in her life, the idea of ever setting

foot inside the palatial private club was beyond her.
Mara Lago was the famous Post mansion on South
Ocean Boulevard that Donald Trump had purchased
and transformed into an exclusive members-only
club. Only the obscenely rich could afford member-
ship. She catered to the obscenely rich; she did not
rub elbows with them.

She studied Nate McGrory's face, let her gaze slip
down to the white silk shirt that she recognized as
Armani, to the butter-soft loafers that were most
likely Gucci or Prada. They were designer names she
knew, styles she admired but could rarely afford.
She'd known he was rich but Mara Lago wasn't just
rich. It was mega rich and it elevated their differences
to heights too lofty to comprehend.

"Mara Lago?" she repeated, unable to mask the
wistfulness as his smile broadened in victory.

"Yep." He crossed his arms over his chest and
settled in to enjoy her discomfort. "I decided it was
time to roll out the big guns."

"So...I'm supposed to be impressed?"

"If that's what it takes to get you to say yes.

"Look," he added when she just stared at him, "I
figure it this way. Something or someone in the past
has hurt you and I'm paying the price. That doesn't
strike me as fair."

"Fair?" she repeated, blindsided by his assumption. Dumbstruck by his accuracy.

"Good. You agree."

"What did I agree to?"

"Seven o'clock, I'll send a limo."

And with that, he rose and walked out the door.

When Sylvie poked her head into Rachael's office

five minutes later, she was still staring into space and
floating in a fog, wondering what barge had just hit
her.

Rachael slid a glance toward her bedside clock and
groaned. Six fifty-five. The limo would be pulling up
in front of her town house any minute. For the hun-
dredth time, she considered changing her mind. She
hadn't told Nate she'd go, after all. But we were talking Mara Lago here. *Mara Lago.*

It wasn't that she had any wish to elevate her social
status by being seen with the elitist crowd who fre-
quented Mara Lago or any of the other exclusive
clubs for which Palm Beach was famous. She had no
illusions about who she was and where she belonged—which was definitely not in the hub of Palm
Beach society where women like Gweneth Buckley
called the shots and basically ran the show with their
formal balls and charity functions that kept the cash
flowing and the economy pumped.

No, she didn't want to be a part of that. But Mara
Lago held a mystical appeal to her. She'd read stories
about the Post empire, about the parties they'd
thrown, the grandeur of the estate and it had always
been her dream to just once…

Kimmie, she thought, eyes narrowed, as understanding dawned. Kim knew about her Mara Lago
fantasy and even though Rachael had made her promise not to talk to Nate about her, it was obvious she'd
spilled her guts. No doubt she and Nate had been
talking again and she'd relayed that little tidbit of
information. And, of course, he'd capitalized on it.

That did it. She'd been manipulated. And this night wasn't going to happen.

"But we're talking Mara Lago," she reminded herself with a groan, and, damn her weak-willed hide, she started reconsidering again. She'd already done her makeup and her hair, after all. And she was dressed for the occasion—or was she?

Because she often played MC or hostess for wedding receptions held at the Royal Palms, she was given a generous clothing allowance. The proof was in the discarded pile of cocktail dresses she'd slipped in and out of then tossed in a heap on her bed. She'd once thought of them as sophisticated and tasteful. Tonight, they simply seemed sedate. And boring. Not so, the dress she was currently wearing.

She glared at her reflection in the mirror, assessing the siren-red, sequined Spandex tube dress. It was so not her. Kimmie had talked her into buying it in a weak moment. She'd never had the nerve to wear it. It revealed way too much leg, way too much chest and sent a definitive statement to any man with half a clue: I wore this so you could peel it off me.

What was she thinking?

She was about to shimmy out of the skin-tight dress that only allowed for a thong underneath it when her buzzer rang.

Her heart fluttered. With a steadying breath, she stalked out to the foyer and pressed the call button— her mind changed *again*—and prepared to send what was undoubtedly Nate's limo driver on his way. "Yes."

"Ms. Matthews?"

"Yes."

"Mr. McGrory bid me to extend his wishes for a good evening and to inform you his car is at your disposal to take you to Mara Lago at your convenience."

"Thank you," she said and bit the proverbial bullet. "I'll be down in a few minutes."

She drew a deep breath, squared her shoulders and went in search of her silver heels. She was going to do this. She was going to let Nate have his way and meet him tonight.

But, she decided, a sudden burst of resolve rolling through her, she was going to make him pay for manipulating her this way. He wanted to play games? Fine. Let 'em begin. At this point, she didn't even care who won or what was at stake. She just wanted him to know she could hold her own and tonight she was going to prove it.

He wanted assertive? He was getting it. In spades. In her line of work, she'd finessed more business and massaged more decisions than anyone would ever imagine. It came with the territory. Give the customer what they wanted—only make sure you sold them on the idea of wanting it in the first place—and everybody went home happy.

Nate McGrory thought he wanted her? Well, he was going to get her—until she said enough was enough. She wasn't a siren by nature. She wasn't a tease. But she could manipulate with the best of them if she had to. And she'd had a bellyful of Nate McGrory's tactics. It was time to pull a few tricks out of her own bag.

Oh yeah, she thought, applying a shimmering crimson gloss to her lips, the red dress was the perfect choice after all.

She dabbed perfume—heavy on musk and blatantly sensual—behind her ears, between her breasts, on the pulse points at her wrists, then adjusted the top of her sequined dress downward to show a little more cleavage. Satisfied with the results, she snagged her little beaded bag from her dresser and headed for the door.

And what, exactly, do you think you're accomplishing with this little act, asked the devil on her shoulder.

Satisfaction, that's what. She hadn't started this, he had. She hadn't wanted it, but he'd pressed. Well, she was going to press back. If Nate McGrory wasn't drooling and reduced to monosyllabic mutterings by the time she was through with him tonight, she'd go out and join a nunnery.

By seven, Nate was afraid he'd blown it. Pushed Rachael too hard and driven her further away. Lord knew, she had a stubborn streak as long as the Florida coastline and he—well, he'd been heavy-handed and blatantly obnoxious, not to mention pretty damned presumptuous.

Eyes on the Moroccan-style gated drive guarding Mara Lago from the general public, he watched for the limo and reviewed his list of transgressions. First, he'd assumed she didn't have plans for tonight. Second, he'd counted on her shock at his unexpected appearance in her office to stall her resistance. And third, he'd relied heavily on Mara Lago as his ace in the hole. Bless Kim for the inside info.

"And thank you Lady Luck for sitting on my

shoulder tonight,'' he murmured in a sigh of relief as the hired limo eased through the gates and pulled up in front of the Mara Lago Club at approximately seven-ten.

He was feeling pretty good now, cocky as all get out as he shot his cuffs, smoothed the lapels on his tux and walked down the steps. He waited as the chauffeur rounded the limo and opened the rear passenger door.

And then he got a look at her—and damn near felt his tongue hit the ground.

''Well...hello,'' he said huskily as he took the hand she offered and steadied her as she stepped out of the stretch.

She looked *incredible*.

All creamy skin—lots of it—and slim toned limbs that looked a mile long in those silver stiletto heels that sent a jolt of electricity straight to his groin. She looked chic and elegant. Beyond pretty to gorgeous. And hot. The lady was definitely hot. Her sexy little tush was barely covered by her short, short dress. And her breasts—full and high and lush—all but spilled out of the red sequined bodice.

It wasn't as if he wasn't used to the company of blatantly sexy and obviously interested women, but on Rachael—the original power-suit and power-broker type—the deviation from the norm was...well...it brought out the animal in him.

And if he didn't get the beast leashed, he was going to tumble her right back into the limo and start working that miniscule little red number down her luscious curves in about another second. He was about to suggest just that when he caught her eye.

A victorious gleam—one he'd never seen before—sparkled in her mystic green eyes. And just that fast, he knew.

She was messing with him. Big-time.

Damn. He pulled her into his arms. Laughing through a groan, he tipped her face up to his with a curled index finger under her chin. "You cunning little witch. You're trying to kill me here, aren't you?"

She smiled serenely. "*Kill* might be a little excessive, not to mention illegal."

"Torture then?"

"That'll work."

He laughed again, then growled as he lowered his mouth to within an inch of hers. "How about we skip dinner and go directly to the nearest bed before I do something illegal right here in the driveway?"

She evaded his lips, regarded him with pity. "I hate to break it to you, sport, but you're not the main attraction here."

"Mara Lago," he deduced with a sage nod and knew he'd been taken to task by a master. "Hoist with my own petard."

"Oh, would you listen to that. He's not only well-heeled, he has a brain in that pretty little head." She patted his cheek and smiled as though her pet puppy had just performed a new trick. "What more could a girl ask for?"

Brushing a kiss across his lips, she pulled out of his embrace, her hands lingering on the lapels of his tux before she slowly turned and strolled toward the grand entrance doors.

"I'm a dead man," Nate muttered with a shake of his head as he watched the sassy sway of her hips.

"I'd say so, yes, sir," the chauffeur agreed from behind him.

Nate turned and threw him a grin. "But what a way to go, huh?"

"What a way indeed," the man said with a tip of his hand to his hat.

"Coming, Nathan?" the little vixen had the nerve to ask as she waited for him at the door.

"Oh, yes, ma'am," he said on a grimace. "One way or the other, with or without you, I'm definitely coming tonight."

"Tell me something," Nate said later as they stood barefoot in the sand while the rush of the surf sluiced around them and moonlight washed across her face, limning her delicate features in gold.

"You're wondering what I'm wearing beneath this dress, right?" She blinked up at him, all guileless eyes and shimmering red lips.

"Well, there is that," he agreed with a grin. He'd been wondering all night, in fact. He was pretty sure he had it figured out—there was little between her and him but a foot or two of moonlight and what the eye could see. Quickly steering his rogue thoughts away from dangerous territory, he took her hand and led her down the beach toward the jetty. "But actually, I was thinking of something else."

He'd peeled off his shoes and socks at the base of the wooden steps and left them there in the sand along with her strappy silver heels. Parked above and behind them on the street behind the seawall, the limo and driver waited in discreet silence.

Nate hadn't meant for them to end up on the beach

when they'd left Mara Lago. But he hadn't been ready to take her home. Just as he hadn't been ready to do what he'd decided he had to do when he took her there.

He'd have to leave her. It was the only way he could convince her he was in this a little deeper than he'd ever been in a relationship before—that this wasn't just a game of chase and conquest. He still hadn't figured out exactly what game he *was* playing—or even if it was a game anymore—but in the meantime, she was killing him by degrees in that glittering skin of a dress, with her irreverent little smiles and staged-to-be-wicked innuendos.

Oh yeah. She had his number. And she was giving back as good as he'd given her. With one exception. It had been apparent from the beginning that she'd set out to teach him a lesson tonight then leave him twisting in the wind.

It was time to eat some humble pie.

"Rachael…is there even a remote chance that we can start all over?"

She stopped walking when he did then looked up at him. "Start *what* all over?"

"Oh, how about everything?" He smiled, shook his head. "I've been a jerk."

She regarded him with an interest that showed he'd surprised her. "You finally picked up on that, did you?"

He grunted and let her soft smile take some of the sting out of her agreement. "Yeah, well, never let it be said I don't recognize some of my own tactics when I see them thrown back at me. I've learned my lesson."

She batted her eyes, all guileless innocence. "And what lesson might that be?"

"The one where I finally realize I've been coming on to you like a sailor hitting the beach after a year without shore leave. I've been in your face, obnoxious, intrusive—umm—don't hesitate to jump in here any time and stop me," he suggested with a little plea for mercy.

She thought about it then shook her head. "I don't think so. I'm enjoying this little bit of soul-searching far too much."

"Just like you enjoyed putting me in my place tonight."

"I did do that, didn't I?"

"Oh yeah. You've got me revved up, wrung out and singed to the bone—and you don't have any intention of letting me past your apartment door, do you?"

"Got it in one, *sailor.*"

He tipped his head back, grinned up at the sky, then down at her. He took her hands in his, watched the play of his thumbs as he rubbed them along her knuckles. "Let's try this. Hi," he said softly, "I'm Nate. Nate McGrory. I saw you at Karen and Sam's wedding. Haven't stopped thinking about you since. And I'd really, really like to get to know you."

Oh, damn, Rachael thought morosely as she looked into his eyes. Why the heck did he have to go and get sweet on her when she'd had him exactly where she'd wanted him? Why couldn't he just have continued playing this Sex-and-the-City game they'd been playing all night long so she could leave him at her door and congratulate herself for a job well done?

His eyes were so dark, so sincere, and truly apologetic. And it just…melted her.

Warning bells clanged in every corner of her brain. She told herself to run, not walk, back across the beach, up the steps, hail a cab and get as far away from this man as fast as she could. And yet she stood there.

With that one look, those few words, he'd managed to win the fight she'd been waging against succumbing to his wit, his charm, yes, even his arrogance and steamroller tactics.

She'd set out to show him tonight—with wicked smiles and teasing innuendos—that two could play this game, but that she could make her own rules. Rule number one: Bring him to his knees. Rule number two: Leave him frustrated and fixated and finally understanding she didn't have to play his game if she didn't want to. Rule number three: Tell him goodbye.

For three years she'd distanced herself from the pressure of this kind of involvement with her absorption in her work and with a steely resolve not to open herself up to the one thing she knew would always elude her. And yet she stood there. Just stood there, looking down at their joined hands, then up into his eyes.

"Hi," she whispered, and Lord help her, in one insane, irrational moment, blew every defense she'd worked so hard to erect and stepped headlong into certain heartbreak. "I'm Rachael. And I think maybe I'd like to get to know you, too."

# Seven

"**A**gain? Tonight?" Sylvie asked with an intrigued arch of her brow as she settled into a chair opposite Rachael's desk. She began working on her nails with an emery board. "That's what? Three times this week?"

"Twice," Rachael corrected her. "And I didn't know you were counting."

"Sweetie—I can count my heartbeats every time that man calls, or every time he and his killer smile slip inside the office."

Okay, Rachael thought. Things were getting out of control here. Two weeks had passed since Mara Lago and that night on the beach. She wasn't sure how Nate found the time to drop what he was doing to fly from Miami to West Palm to accommodate her schedule. The private jet helped. So did his money. Just as both helped to continually remind her that they were worlds apart in every way that counted.

"You're making too much of this. We're just…enjoying each other's company," Rachael assured Sylvie. And that was the sum total of what was happening between them. She'd insisted.

On the long walk on the beach that night, she'd stumbled over her better judgment when she'd agreed to get to know him better, but she'd righted herself again by the time he'd delivered her to her door.

"We have to have finite ground rules," she'd insisted as she fit her key into her lock, aware of his dark eyes watching her.

He'd turned her toward him, cupped her shoulders in his big hands. They'd felt warm and strong and she'd fought an almost irresistible urge to ask him to slide those capable hands down her arms, around her waist and pull her snug against him.

"Ground rules?" he'd asked with a puzzled quirk of his brow.

"I've already told you, Nate," she began with as much steely resolve as she could muster. "I don't do well with relationships. So let's not try to make this into one, okay? I want to make sure it's understood that when it runs its course and one of us is ready to call it quits, the other agrees to walk away. No harm. No foul. No bad goodbyes."

His eyes had darkened in both confusion and challenge. "What makes you so sure it's going to end in goodbye?"

That one had been easy to answer. "Because it always ends in goodbye."

He'd watched her face for a long time, measuring,

clearly wondering, but he hadn't argued and he hadn't asked why she was so sure. He'd only squeezed her shoulders and said, "Let's just take it slow and see where it goes, okay?"

"And what if it doesn't go where you want it to? What if I said I'm still not sure I'm going to sleep with you?"

She'd figured that question would put the skids on things. She'd held her breath in both anticipation and dread of his reply.

"Then I'd say I'll hang around until you make up your mind."

She'd blinked up into his eyes, realizing she had no clue what made this man tick. "I haven't even been nice to you. Why do you want to do this?"

"You're right. You haven't been nice," he added smiling that infuriating, wonderful, patient, penetrating smile. "Just imagine the possibilities when you finally decide I'm not such a bad guy after all."

She'd looked up at him, studied his face wondering, who is this man?

"You'll need to give me a sign, though."

His non sequitur threw her even more than the soft look in his eyes. "A sign?"

"When you make up your mind. To let me make love to you."

He'd surprised her yet again. He was supposed to push here. He was supposed to shove a little and say Hey—no sex, no deal. It had been an unspoken but assumed condition of any relationship she'd ever been in. But then, she reminded herself—this wasn't a re-lationship.

She couldn't help it. She'd stretched up to her tip-toes, touched her fingers to his strong jaw and kissed him. "Believe me," she'd said, forcing herself to pull away after a little sample of his mouth when what she'd wanted was a long, satisfying feast, "you'll be able to figure it out if and when I do.

"Good night, Nate," she'd whispered and slipped into her town house. "And thanks. For Mara Lago."

He'd shoved his hands into his pockets. "My pleasure."

He was still standing there, watching her with a probing frown when she'd closed the door.

"Houston...do we have a problem?"

Rachael dragged herself away from the memory of that night and tuned in to Sylvie's amused smile.

"No. We do not have a problem."

"So...it's going well then?"

"Don't make more of this than it is," she repeated, recognizing Sylvie's speculative look and knowing she was seeing things that were not meant to be. What was meant to be was that Rachael was destined to go it alone. She'd learned that lesson early on—from her father and her mother and then from her own inability to relate to the men in her life. She couldn't be what they needed her to be.

She had to remind herself of that very thing every time Nate picked her up to take her to dinner, or to a movie, or kayaking or just for a long drive. Don't make more of this than it is became her mantra as she worked constantly to remind herself just to enjoy the moments with this man.

Just because they liked the same music and the same movies and fast food and Mara Lago—fast food and Mara Lago, now there was a study in contrasts—

and just because he made her smile and had honored her wishes and not pressed her about a physical relationship in their non-relationship, it didn't mean anything.

The truth of the matter was—and she was ticked with herself because of it—she sort of wished he would push a little in that area...the one that had to do with a bed and him and her in it. Talk about not knowing what she wanted. He'd been the perfect gentleman. Hadn't done more than drop a chaste kiss on her cheek when he'd walked her to her apartment door each night.

It was what she wanted, right? No pressure. No messy complications.

When her phone rang, she was relieved for the distraction until Sylvie announced the caller.

''Mrs. Buckley,'' Sylvie said with a sympathetic smile and handed her the receiver.

Rachael suppressed a groan then listened and made notes as the Palm Beach matron made several more changes to her daughter's wedding plans.

She looked like a sea nymph, Nate thought, watching Rachael where she sat on the foredeck, her hands propped behind her for support, her fingers wrapped around the cleats of the little Sunfish he'd rented for the afternoon. Like some mystical creature spun from legends and myth and midnight dreams of a lonely seafarer's obsession with romance.

And he was, in a word, spellbound. Had been— just as he'd been looking at her in a different light— since that night on the beach when she'd agreed to let him start over with her.

*No regrets. No bad goodbyes.*

He'd thought about what she'd said often, wondered often, what had prompted her to say it—and to sound so certain she knew what she was talking about. But today, he was simply thinking about today and the way she looked.

Despite the drying power of the warm Florida sun, she was soaking wet from his last little stunt that he hoped to hell she'd never catch on to. The wind dragged her sodden hair back from her face. The sun and excitement had painted her cheeks a berry-pink. And the look of wonder on her face had had him grinning for the better part of the afternoon.

"This is so wonderful!" she shouted above the whip of the wind and the snap of the sail as they scooted across Lake Worth.

"Yeah, well, you weren't saying that five minutes ago when I landed you in the drink," he reminded her and had the pleasure of seeing her blush then laugh and look out across the lake as if she were seeing the world—or this part of it—for the first time.

She'd been a sport, though, once she'd realized they weren't going straight to Davy Jones's locker. He'd turtled the little sailboat twice since they'd hit the water a couple of hours ago. They'd flipped once by accident—if you could call his preoccupation with the look of her an accident. The second time, he'd done it on purpose.

He'd had so much fun treading water alongside her the first time as they'd clung to the capsized sailboat, his arms circling her to reassure her, their bare legs brushing against each other under water as they flut-

ter-kicked to stay afloat, he'd felt the need of an excuse to do it again.

And then of course, there had been that exquisite
opportunity to have a legitimate reason to cup her
sweet little tush in his palms after he'd righted the
craft and given her a helpful, but lingering push to
get her back aboard.

"You're a sick man, McGrory. Copping a feel like
a schoolboy," he muttered under his breath, but he
was grinning as he adjusted the sail and set an easterly
tack.

He felt a little like a schoolboy around her. A little
nervous even and it was one sharp kick in the keister
to admit it to himself. But he didn't want to blow it
with this woman. She was loosening up but she was
still a little skittish. Damn. He just kept going back
to his gut feeling that someone must have done a
number on her.

And she, intentionally or not, was doing a number
on him. He'd never been in such a chaste relationship
with a woman. Not that he saw sex as the be-all and
end-all, but with the chemistry zinging between them,
he was champing at the bit to take what they had to
the next level. He enjoyed the hell out of being with
her. She had an irreverent sense of humor, shared his
passion for movies and music and she was quickly
becoming enamored with some of his favorite sports.
Like snorkeling and kayaking and today—sailing.

"You've lived in Florida *how* long?" he asked,
still amazed at the sun-and-fun sports she'd never let
the closet adventurer inside her indulge in. "And
you've never been sailing until today?"

These were the kind of things that constantly

amazed him about her. Okay. So there was nothing amazing about the fact she'd been born in Ohio and moved with her single mom to Florida when she was just a little kid. What was amazing were the little bits and pieces of herself she parted with in those moments when she let her guard down enough to give them up. What was amazing was how little fun she'd allowed herself in her life—and how much information she still shielded from him.

A private person was Ms. Matthews, he thought, watching her lift a hand to her hair to drag an errant strand away from her mouth. His heart flat-lined, then picked up the beat again with a thudding ker-whump when she kept her arm raised, elbow to the sky, holding back her hair, effectively making her back arch and her sweet breasts thrust against the skyline and press against the cups of her black swimsuit. Her nipples poked against the thin, wet fabric like hard little diamonds.

He wanted to feel them poking against his tongue. He wanted to taste them. And then he wanted to taste the rest of her.

The woman was built like a centerfold. Small, delicate and stacked. Before today, he'd gotten lasting impressions of her drool-worthy body, but there was something about her today. She was relaxed and beautiful and the really amazing part of it all was that she was oblivious to how exotic and enticing she truly was. And about how hard he got just thinking about her coming apart beneath him.

The punch of lust he'd been fighting for the better part of the day—hell, who was he kidding? He'd been fighting it ever since he'd met her—hit him with the

wallop of a Patriot missile. A man could only take so
many pecks on the cheek at the end of an evening
before he started suffering from SRS—sperm-
retention syndrome.

And there was only one thing to do about it right
now. With the flick of a hand and the tug of a rope,
he flipped them into the water again.

"Whoops," he said, as he surfaced and saw her
treading water in front of him.

Laughing, she dragged wet hair away from her face
with one hand and clung to the side of the overturned
boat with the other.

"You are either *really* bad at this or *really* good,"
she said and surprised him when she reached out and
finger-combed his hair back and out of his eyes. "I
haven't decided which."

He took advantage of a rocking wave that tossed
him closer, until they were practically breast to chest
in the water. And then he took heart in the look in
her eyes and the lingering touch of her hand, drifting
to his shoulder now, to close the small distance between them.

"It does make a body wonder if I really know what
I'm doing, doesn't it?" he murmured, transfixed by
the spiky wetness of her lashes and the sudden and
unmistakable heat in her eyes.

"On second thought," she whispered as he
wrapped an arm around her waist and pulled her the
rest of the way toward him—until the cool resilience
of her thighs brushed against his under the surface
and the supple buoyancy of her breasts nestled against
his bare chest. "I think maybe you know exactly what
you're doing."

He searched her face, then dropped his gaze to her breasts, plumped and pressed against him. He swallowed. Hard. Met her eyes again as the water lapped around them and sunlight glinted like diamonds on the gentle chop. "Yes, ma'am. I believe I do."

And then he kissed her.

The way he'd been wanting to kiss her since that day he'd claimed her mouth on the seawall.

Open-mouthed, seeking tongue, unleashed need.

She was so wet, her lips so cool. But inside, beyond the water-chilled softness of her incredible lips, her mouth was hot. And open. And willing, as her tongue tangled with his and she told him without words that she was as needy and as thrilled by the contact as he was.

With a low growl, he let go of the boat and wrapped both arms around her. Tunneling one hand up and inside the high-cut leg of her suit, he cupped her bare bottom in his palm. When she slid her leg up and along his, hooking it around his hips, he pressed her against the monster erection nestled against her belly and ravished her mouth with a hunger that, if he'd had his wits about him, would have scared the ever-loving hell out of him.

He heard a gurgling, "Yikes," against his mouth just as their heads sank under the surface of the water.

It wasn't until she started pushing away and kicking that it registered he might manage to drown them out here yet if he didn't get his senses about him.

With a firm grip around her waist, he kicked to the surface. They broke water with gasping breaths.

"God. I'm sorry. You okay?" He held her against him, cupping her pale face in his palm.

"Umm...well...I guess that depends."

He tilted his head. "On?"

"On whether you're too waterlogged to swim that far." She notched her chin toward the far distance behind him.

His wet hair slapped against his forehead as he whipped his head around. The Sunfish had drifted a city block away while he'd been leading with his libido.

He scrubbed drops of water out of his eyes, faced her grimly. "I'm some fun date, huh?" he asked, bemoaning his stupidity.

"Yeah," she said softly, and, after a prolonged moment, smiled. "You're some fun date."

With her eyes on his, tentative, searching, she pushed away then started swimming toward the capsized boat.

He trod water for a long time, feeling every heartbeat, watching her long, strong strokes, wondering what that kiss had meant. Wondering what the look in her eyes had meant. Wondering if he knew—really knew—what he was getting into with this woman.

She did things to him. With a dewy look. With an innocent touch. With those shuttered green eyes. She held secrets behind those eyes and harbored a pain he wanted to make go away but suspected he might, one day, contribute to. And that notion made him angry. At himself. At whoever had hurt her.

What do you want from her? he asked himself as he started swimming after her. What do you *really* want?

The word *forever* echoed through his mind, like the

wail of a fog-shrouded lighthouse warning—distant, out of focus, out of bounds.

*Forever.*

Not possible. There was only one woman he'd ever thought of in those terms and she was forever out of his reach.

Later that day, after Nate had dropped her off at her town house, Rachael stood under the shower in her bathroom, washing sea salt and sunscreen and the scent of Nate McGrory from her skin.

Him and his teasing smiles and gentle patience when he'd tried to teach her the basics of sailing. He seemed infinitely patient, a fact that endeared him to her so much more than she wanted. Patience wasn't one of her best virtues, so his fascinated her.

So did his kisses, she thought with a deep breath and shivered under the steaming hot spray. Low in her belly, heat pooled, along with a deep aching need that grappled for control over her better judgment. She could still see him there on the Sunfish—his strong face tipped to the wind, his capable hands working the rudder and the sail. He'd been tanned and lean and muscled in all the right places—especially when he'd hoisted himself up and out of the water and back into the boat. His shoulders were so broad, his hair so black, his lashes long and spiky wet as she'd watched his face. As he'd lowered his head to kiss her.

She remembered every moment of the day they'd spent together on the water. In the water. Under the water. And prayed for the strength to keep herself out from under him.

It would be…wonderful between them. She knew that. His kisses had shown her exactly how wonderful. He was thorough with his mouth. He liked to take his time. Liked to seduce her by white-hot degrees with the playful swirl of his tongue, the subtle—and not so subtle—nudge of his hips, before he showed her what he really had on his mind.

And yet, he never pushed, didn't demand, she realized as she soaped her breasts and shuddered as the brush of her fingers over her nipples made them tighten, and pucker and long for the warm wetness of his mouth there.

The kiss they'd shared had been spontaneous. He hadn't maneuvered her into it this time as he had the first time on the seawall. It had just happened.

She tipped her face to the spray for a final rinse then twisted off the faucets and stepped onto cool white tile. Wiping steam off the vanity mirror with a towel, she studied her face. Despite the color the sun had painted on her cheeks, she looked pale, weak even.

"Weak-kneed," she grumbled as she dried off then grabbed the hair dryer. "And weak-willed," she muttered, shutting off the dryer and bracing her palms on the vanity. She lowered her head in defeat.

She was going to make love with him. The next time he came to see her, she was going to take the chance. And damn the consequences.

A spiral of longing licked through her, starting at her breasts and fanning out to her extremities like a liquid sunburst on a hot August morning.

She shook her head.

She'd never wanted, never needed, never hurt this

much for the touch of one man's hands. One man's mouth.

"Sex," she declared, straightening with a resolute set of her shoulders, "does not have to lead to anything but…more sex," she reasoned, warming to her argument—and to the thought of his mouth on her body.

Her nipples puckered again, tightened, just thinking about it.

She knew the score going in, didn't she? She knew they weren't talking about love. She knew that love wasn't something to count on even if they were.

"Well, don't you?" she snapped at her reflection and, snagging a bottle of lightly scented lotion, slathered it over her sun-warmed and arousal-flushed skin.

"Yes. I do," she assured herself and walked into her bedroom to slip into panties and bra. "I know that."

So what if she liked him. A lot. So what if he listened to her, asked her about herself as though he was interested—really interested—in what she'd done in her life, what she liked, what she thought? He'd lose interest soon enough when he got to know her. Or rather, when he realized he was never going to get to know her.

It had been a long time since she'd wanted to open herself up to a man. A long time since she'd thought she could trust a man that much. But she knew herself. She knew she'd freeze up and freeze him out. It's just the way she was. And she didn't know how to be any different. Not be any different and protect herself in the process.

She'd wanted to believe in love once. She'd wanted

to believe she'd find it. But long before Nate Mc-Grory had come into the picture, she'd accepted that it was never going to happen for her.

And if she had any false and fleeting illusions about it happening with Nate all she had to do was log on for a little reality check. Other than their single status, their close proximity in age, and, well, the fact that he seemed to enjoy her company as much as she enjoyed his, they did not have one single thing in common except chemistry.

He lived in Miami. He flew in private jets, for God's sake. Per the society magazines, he had women flocking around him like flies. And he liked his life that way.

Not wanting to be alone with her thoughts anymore, she grabbed her phone and dialed Kim's number.

"Hi," she said, when Kim answered. "Wanna go to a movie or something?"

"Sure," Kim said. "What do you want to see?"

Something to take her mind off Nate McGrory's slow hands and hot mouth.

"Anything but a chick flick," she said resolutely. The last thing she wanted to see was a movie where the girl got the guy in the end.

# Eight

His momma would be proud of him, Nate thought with a frustrated groan a week after their sailing adventure. He was back in West Palm, approximately twenty steps away from Rachael's bedroom, a few weeks into their nonrelationship, and it was still as pure as the driven snow. Actually, some snow right now might not be a bad idea. Right down the front of his pants. He could use something to cool himself down.

"I'm out of merlot but I've got a nice pinot noir," she called out from the kitchen where he heard cabinet doors open and close and the tinkle of wineglasses as she slid them from the rack.

"Sounds fine."

It was Friday. They were at her town house. He was sitting outside the open sliders at a glass-topped table on her lanai, absently thumbing through a Ludlum novel she'd left on a table beside the chaise, waiting for her to join him. After their afternoon on the sailboat last week, they'd made plans to attend an outdoor festival at City Place Plaza tonight. He'd flown in this morning for a business appointment and had finished up early.

After he'd checked into his hotel, showered and changed into a white knit polo shirt, tan shorts and sandals, he'd killed a little time on Worth Avenue. Then he couldn't stand it a minute longer. He'd taken a chance and dropped by early knowing she'd have just gotten home from work.

She'd been surprised when she'd answered his buzz a few minutes ago. It had shaken her composure a bit, seeing him standing there, unexpected. That was good. Ms. Matthews was entirely too controlled and too in control to suit him and he figured rattling her a bit was good for her. Maybe good for him, too.

He liked the look of her. She hadn't been home long. She'd ditched her blazer and tie but still wore her skirt and white blouse. The top two buttons were undone. That little concession to comfort shouldn't have made his pulse leap—neither should her bare feet—but they had. Couple those two seemingly austere elements with the little bit of white lace peeking from above the southern-most open button and he'd been pretty much buzzed on the thought of flicking open a couple more.

It said a lot about his state of mind—and his unraveling self-control.

"I don't suppose you've got anything to eat?"

It had come to that. He had to do something with

his hands or when she walked out here, he was going to drag her onto his lap, grind her sweet little hip against his erection and let her know just exactly how much he wanted her. A wineglass in one hand, food in the other and his mouth full ought to keep him busy and the footing on her terms, which were getting harder and harder—no pun intended—to keep.

"Did you miss lunch?" she asked from the kitchen.

If only it was that simple. "Just got the munchies." For her.

"Okay—I think I've got—"

He heard her refrigerator door open then close.

"Yes. I've got brie and crackers."

"That'll do it."

It would have to. The past weeks had been some of the most fun, most surprising—most sexually frustrating—of his life. Being with her and not having her was killing him. But, he had to admit, being with her without indulging in a physical relationship had also been enlightening. He'd learned things about her that he might not have if they'd spent the kind of quality time he'd have liked to in her bed.

For instance, he'd learned that little Miss Rachael was a very sentimental person. She teared up at spectacular sunsets, wouldn't visit a pet store because she couldn't bear to see all those poor little kittens and puppies needing homes. And then there was the other side of her—the one well-versed on both domestic and foreign affairs—they'd had some thought-provoking and heated debates. She volunteered what time she could spare at a women's shelter. That one had really gotten to him. It made him wonder about her childhood, and had him worrying about what she

might have lived through. Some day he would ask
her about it. In the meantime, he'd take what he could
get.

She was a voracious reader—everything from bi-
ographies to do-it-yourselves to cloak-and-dagger to
romance. She was a contradiction, in more ways than
one and for some reason, the romance section of her
bookshelf gave him hope.

Her eclectic decorating style reinforced his growing
conviction that at heart she was a sensualist. She
clearly loved bright colors and soft fabrics, airy open
space and modern art. Scented candles and sumptuous
desserts. Even out here, on the lanai, she'd surrounded
herself with hibiscus, bromeliad and any number of
brightly flowering plants that scented the late afternoon with exotic fragrances. Sensual, he thought
again—right down to her love of salsa music. He was
dying by degrees to see her let loose and give him a
private showing of that side of her.

She walked out onto the lanai then. Without a
word, she slid a plate of cheese and crackers in front
of him and set a glass of wine on the table.

The air seemed to crackle between them as she
accidentally bumped his shoulder.

"You're sure it's all right that I'm a little early?"
he asked, when she pulled quickly away. Had she felt
it, too? How could she not have felt it?

"No. No that's fine. I'll...I'll just jump in the
shower quick, if you don't mind waiting."

The huskiness in her voice skittered across his
senses like a live wire. So did the thought of her slipping out of her skirt and blouse—then standing beneath the hot fingers of the shower spray. Every mus-

cle in his body clenched at the image of her
soap-slicked breasts and rivulets of water sluicing between them, past her navel and lower.

He didn't look up. He didn't dare. He wasn't sure
he could keep his hands off of her if he did. "Fine.
Great. Take your time."

He downed a huge gulp of wine as he heard her
bare feet slap softly across the tile on her kitchen
floor. Then he stuffed some crackers into his mouth.

Something had to give. Soon. Or he was going to
burst a vein.

Rachael turned off the shower and with an unsteady
hand, hooked a towel and wrapped it around her, se-
curing it above her breasts. Her heart danced to a hard
rock beat—which was a little disconcerting considering she'd slipped a sultry Latin guitar track into the
CD player in her adjacent bedroom before hitting the
shower. Her legs felt weak as she stood in front of
the bathroom vanity mirror and thought about the man
waiting for her on her lanai.

Dark eyes, sleek muscles, barely veiled desire.

It was all there when she looked at him. He wanted
her.

And, oh, my—mistake or no mistake—did she ever
want him.

She might have made up her mind last week that
tonight was the night things were going to change
between them, but it didn't diminish the impact of the
step she was about to take. Or relieve her of her jit-
ters. She'd had the entire week to acclimate herself
to the idea and convince herself she could do this.
She could enjoy a physical relationship—there was

that word again—with this attractive, attentive man and when it ran its course, she could walk away from it without regrets.

She'd had it all planned. When he arrived tonight, she was going to meet him at the door wearing her red sequined Spandex number. He'd have taken one look, known what she had in mind and that would have been the end—or in this case the beginning—of that.

Only he'd shown up early, knocked her off her stride. Now she wasn't entirely sure how to proceed. He wasn't going to make the first move, that was for sure. He was a man of his word, Nathan McGrory. She'd said hands off until she gave him a sign and except for that blistering kiss in Lake Worth last week, he'd played by her rules.

Those stupid rules had only made her crazy with wanting him, achy with need. And suddenly, she was very decisive.

She toweled herself dry then slathered her legs and arms with lotion spun with essence of melon and strawberries and flowers and cream. She didn't bother to dry her hair but brushed it back from her face instead. With the determination of a woman on a mission, she dropped the towel and slipped into her short green silk kimono.

Pushing back all self-doubts, she shrugged off distant warnings that she was going to live to regret this. With one last look in the mirror, she stepped out of the fragrant, steam-clouded bathroom and into the last thing she needed…and the one thing she wanted as much as she'd once wanted someone to love.

* * *

Nate heard the bedroom door open and steeled himself. Rachael's scent floated ahead of her into the living room where he'd been prowling around like a restless cat for the past quarter hour. Whatever mind-altering female concoction she'd drenched herself in made him think of jasmine and fruit, fragrant, juicy fruit, and damn if the thought of licking mango juice from her breasts didn't materialize in vivid color in spite of his Herculean efforts to keep it at bay.

"You're a bigger man than this, McGrory," he muttered under his breath. Yeah, and growing bigger by the minute.

Ignoring his altering body parts, he sucked it up, shoved his hands in his pockets and feigned total absorption in the brush strokes and unique style the artist had rendered on the unframed canvas hanging above the credenza in her dining area. The oil painting was all slashing color and sweeping lines. Vivid. Bold. Sensual. Like Rachael.

He glanced at the bowl of fruit on the island counter that separated the open living area from the kitchen and thought about sex. Noticed the ice tongs in the dish drainer and thought about sex. Hell. He could understand the sensuality in oranges—but in silverware, for Pete's sake? He swung back around toward the living area then froze when the soft sound of her bare feet on the white Italian tile floor behind him stiffened his shoulders.

"Nate?"

He braced, wrapped his mind around the idea that they were about to spend another platonic evening sampling local cuisine at the open-air festival. They'd be surrounded by hundreds of people, cocooned in the safety of numbers in a very public place.

"All set?" he asked and as mentally prepared as he could get, turned to the sound of her voice...and felt the earth—or this little patch of it—cave away like a landslide beneath his feet.

She was not all set. She was *so* not all set. Not by a long shot. She wore a short green robe—and from his initial assessment, nothing else.

The long-sleeved robe was the cool, shimmering green of her eyes. Silk, he guessed. It hit her mid-thigh. It hit him dead center in his libido.

He swallowed, his gaze tracking up that expanse of smooth bare thigh to the wide sash she'd belted loosely at her waist. So loosely the lapels lay open in an enticing *V* that closed low and gaped slightly in the valley of her breasts.

Her breasts. He'd fantasized about her breasts like this. Unbound. Full. Shifting with a subtle and evocative little jiggle with every step she took toward him. Tight little nipples pressed shockingly against the fabric.

He swallowed, and turned as hard as stone.

"I...umm...need a little help," he heard her say through what sounded like an underwater tunnel.

He clenched his hands into fists inside his pockets and dragged his gaze away from her chest to her liquid-green eyes. Eyes he could drown in. A body he could lose himself in.

"Help?" he finally managed but it came out more plea than question.

"With this...if you wouldn't mind." She stopped by the island counter, extended an uncapped bottle of lotion. The scent of it and of her, fogged his already overloaded senses. "I can't reach my back."

"Help." Definitely a plea this time as he closed the distance between them. He latched on to the bottle with numb fingers then watched, in sensitized silence as she presented him her back.

He was still standing there, his brain synapses trying to snap back together when she shrugged the robe off her shoulders until it sagged in gentle folds to expose the creamy length of her bare back. Slim. Elegant. He swore he could count each vertebra. Wanted to. Using his tongue.

Clutching the robe together in front with one hand, she lifted her wet hair off her neck with the other and looked over her shoulder—her bare, silky shoulder—at him.

Waiting.

Expectantly.

"Nate?"

He swallowed a lump of longing as his eyes tracked the sleek lines to the small of her back where her slim hips, barely covered in green silk, flared gently.

She said his name again before he found it in him to croak out a rusty, "Yeah."

"In case I'm not making myself clear…that sign you said you needed? Well…you do understand that this is it, right?"

His heart slammed him a good one, right in the back of his sternum. He smiled then, and visibly relieved, she did the same.

"Yeah." He cleared the corrosion out of his throat and moved up close behind her. "As bricks go, it's a big one.'' As in, she'd just hit him over the head with a whopper.

He closed his eyes, breathed her in, then lowering his head, touched his mouth to her exposed nape. Lingered. ''You make me thick-headed, Rachael. You make me crazy.''

''Yeah…well, I'm feeling a little crazy, too.''

She was uncertain of this, he realized through the fog of sensual heat. And feelings so tender, so unexpectedly protective surged ahead of his desire.

''You're sure about this?'' he whispered against her skin, praying her answer was yes, knowing he was only so strong, fast getting intoxicated by the possibilities her invitation implied.

She sighed, a silky, surrendering sound and leaned into him when he slid a hand around her waist, squeezed gently. Setting the lotion on the counter beside them, he spread the fingers of his other hand wide across her firm abdomen and pulled her back against him.

''Yes, Nate. I'm sure.''

And in this moment, Rachael had never been so sure of anything in her life. She closed her eyes, confident of her decision. Surrendering to the delicious reality of Nate finally holding her in his arms, she glided into the moment like a skydiver in free fall.

''We're going to be so good together,'' he whispered against her skin, tracking a string of slow, biting kisses along the curve where neck met shoulder. She shivered and he buried his face in her damp hair.

''I've wanted this…'' he let his words trail off, and she could feel the effort it took for him to slow things when she'd have been pleased as punch if he'd back her up against the wall and take her hot and hard and fast. "I've wanted this for so long." His voice sounded strained, as thick with arousal as the erection she felt nestled against her bottom.

She made to turn in his arms, but he held her still.

"Oh no," he whispered. "Now that this is finally happening, I plan to take my sweet time with you. We're in no hurry here."

A nervous laugh slipped out. "Speak for yourself."

Her put-upon objection earned a low chuckle that rumbled against her neck as he nuzzled her there and made her shiver again.

"You think that after all this time, I'm not going to make this last? I'm going to make love to you slowly, okay? I'm going to wring out every possible response from your sweet little body and then…you know what I'm going to do then, Rachael?"

His breath was a sultry promise. His question a threat she couldn't wait to experience. She sucked in a harsh breath when he nipped the tendon along the side of her neck beneath her jaw then soothed the tiny sting with the wet slide of his tongue. "I'm…I'm afraid to ask."

His big hands spanned wide over her pelvis, pressing her tighter against him. "Be afraid, Rachael Matthews. Be very, very afraid…because when I'm done…I'm going to start all over again."

Her knees turned to pudding. One hand held her snug against him, holding her upright. The other skated slowly up her body, skimmed past her waist then up between her breasts. Fingers spread wide, he clasped her jaw and tipped her head up and back, forcing her to meet his gaze.

His dark eyes smoldered. His lashes dropped to brush his cheeks as he lowered his head and covered her mouth and seared her with a kiss that was all heat, raging and real.

He opened his mouth wide over hers, demanded she do the same, then ravished her mouth with a marauding tongue that plundered and withdrew then plundered again. He drew her with him into an inferno of desire that transcended thought, outdistanced simple need and sent a shock wave through her blood that burst through her body in spikes of molten pleasure.

With his fingers still bracketing her jaw, he lifted his head. Breathing heavily.

"Yikes," she managed with a shaky breath, then had to clutch the island counter to keep from collapsing like a rag doll when he released her.

"I think," he said, his voice husky as he reached for the lotion and poured some into his palm, "you said something about needing some help."

"I…umm…"

"Yeah," he murmured, the fire in his gaze matching hers. "Me, too. We'll get there. In good time. Lift your hair for me, Rachael."

She knew what he saw in her eyes when she met his over her shoulder—she felt shy suddenly, in over her head with this man who had, with one hungry, incredible kiss, melted every bone in her body—but she raised her left arm and did as he asked while clutching her robe together between her breasts.

Slowly, he spread the cool, scented cream from her nape to the sensitive spot between her shoulder blades, then using both hands, he worked the lotion up and over the round of her shoulders.

"Here?" he asked, spreading his fingers over her back then working them around her neck, where he stroked over her collarbone in outward and downward caresses, barely skimming the upper part of her breasts.

She rolled her head and sighed, aching for his clever hands to sweep lower. To touch her breasts. To pinch her nipples between his fingers then turn her and take her in his mouth. She'd never felt so sensitive or so malleable or sensual in her entire life. He could do anything to her, anything, and right now, her only response would be a helpless plea to do it all over again.

"So soft," he murmured as he worked his hands over her skin. Up again, over her shoulders, down her back then slowly upward. She loved the feel of his hands on her, loved the little quiver of anticipation eddying through her body when he worked his thumbs into the tight little knots on either side of her neck.

"Lift your arms for me, Rachael."

She closed her eyes and without a thought of denying him, raised her arms and looped them over his shoulders, loosely clasping her fingers behind his neck.

She didn't think about the fact that they were standing in broad daylight in her kitchen. She didn't think about the very real issue that for all practical purposes, she was totally exposed to him now and he was totally dressed. Her robe hung open, the belt giving up its tenuous link around her waist. The silk slid over her sensitized skin like cool water, making her shiver as he lowered his mouth to her jaw and covered her bare breasts with his hands.

A groan eased out, part relief, part anticipation, all aching need. Finally, finally he was touching her. His big palms cupped and caressed, gently kneaded, reverently shaped and lifted as he pressed her breasts together and fluttered his thumbs over her erect nipples.

She was on sensual overload, barely aware that he'd coaxed her arms down so she could slip off her robe before running his hands along her arms and repositioning them around his neck again.

"I love the smell of you," he whispered and all she could do was watch as he filled his palms with more lotion. "Love the feel of you," he murmured and pressed the center of each palm over her nipples.

She sucked in a breath at the shock of the cool lotion against her heated areolas. And then he was rubbing his hands all over her. Massaging lotion into her breasts, down across her rib cage, then up again, all the way up the length of her raised arms before returning to her quivering breasts.

"Feels good?"

"I...umm."

She felt his smile against her earlobe when he nipped her lightly. "I'll take that as a yes."

He rocked against her, his heat and hardness to her bare back and bare bottom, his hands constantly roaming, arousing, torturing her into gasping little sobs and plea-choked whimpers.

"Nate..."

"Shh…" His breath fanned her nape. "Just go with it. Just…yeah. Just let yourself fly."

One strong arm banded around her ribs, his large palm cupping her left breast, as his right hand forayed lower. She pressed her head back against his shoulder, licked suddenly dry lips as his fingers brushed her curls with lazy, teasing strokes at first until he had her whimpering with frustration. She covered his hand with hers, pressed it against her.

"Please," she whimpered. "Please, please, please."

# Nine

With her hand riding the back of his, he finally cupped her, gently parted her. He slid a finger over her wet heat...and then he did a little groaning, too, as he finessed her body with such utter attention to her pleasure, she thought she'd pass out from the glut of sensation.

"Nate...s...stop. I'm...I...I can't hold—"

"I don't want you to hold back." His breath fanned hot against her ear as he wedged a long thigh between her legs and opened her more fully to his touch. "You're beautiful like this. Let it come, Rach. Just let it come."

To make sure she did, he deepened his touch, working his fingers in and out of her, massaging the sensitive center of all sensation until she climaxed on a ragged sob. Heart pounding, breath clogged in her throat, she poured into his hand and rode with the exquisite rush that rolled on and on and on.

The force of it stole her breath, the intensity robbed her strength and just kept getting stronger. Just when she thought she couldn't stand it any longer, the high ripped through her and finally tumbled her into the steamy aftermath of the longest, strongest orgasm she'd ever experienced.

He held her in silence, letting her recover, letting her slide into the fuzzy glow of mindless completion.

"W-wow," she finally uttered as her head lolled back against his chest.

He pressed a kiss to her temple, tightened his arm around her waist. "You okay?"

She managed a shaky laugh, felt the sheen of perspiration coating her body cool by slow degrees. "I am beyond okay. And utterly selfish," she added with a shiver as he slowly withdrew his fingers from her ultra-sensitized flesh.

"Utterly beautiful." He turned her in his arms. She rested her hands on his chest as he clasped his hands loosely at the small of her back. "Hi." He bent his head to place the most tender of kisses on her mouth.

Not for the first time, she wondered who this man was that he could just give her the most selfless, most incredible sexual experiences of her life and then stand there as if he didn't have a care in the world when his own body had to be screaming for release.

"You," she said, pulling away, and heedless of her nakedness, took his hand and led him toward her bedroom, "come with me."

"Oh, I plan to, darlin'." The wicked grin in his voice kicked up one side of her mouth. "I have very definite plans to do just that. But I'm going to have to make a supply run first." A pained look crossed his face as he stopped her just inside her bedroom door. With a growl, he wrapped her in his arms for a long, hungry kiss.

When he lifted his head and she dragged herself out of another sensual haze, the import of his words finally hit her. "Supply run?"

"You took me off guard, Rachael." His big hands slid down her back, cupped her bare bottom and lifted, pressing her against his erection. "I didn't come prepared to protect you."

She stood up on tiptoe. Pressed a kiss to his mouth. "Good thing one of us planned ahead then, because I don't want you going anywhere."

Unwrapping herself from his arms, she walked around her bed, opened the bedside table and pulled out a box of condoms.

If he was put off by her forwardness, he hid it behind a grin that blossomed beneath the shirt he made quick work of tugging over his head. His sandals and shorts were next. And then his boxers.

She looked from his smiling face to his proud, jutting sex and managed a smile of her own. "Oh. My. Good thing I told them to supersize them."

And then she squealed when he dove over the bed and laughing, snagged her arm and neatly rolled her beneath him.

"About that taking-my-sweet-time thing?" Rising up on one elbow, he snagged a condom, ripped the packet open with his teeth and with fire in his eyes, sheathed himself. "Not gonna happen this time, okay?"

"More than okay." She knotted her hands in his hair, moaned when he pushed inside her in one deep, delicious thrust and wrapping her ankles around his hips hung on for the ride of her life.

How she managed to talk then was beyond her. He filled her completely as he pumped into her, driving her toward another sharp, shattering climax as she gasped each word in cadence to his fast, powerful strokes. "So. Much. More. Than. Okay."

They took it slow the next time. And the next. And it did Nate's heart a whole world of good to know he'd obliterated the proper Ms. Matthews's control each time. He didn't feel so bad himself.

Moonlight danced in through the windows in her bedroom, gilding the room and the woman lying spread-eagled on her stomach in the middle of rumpled sheets. He glanced absently at the clock on her nightstand. It was close to 3:00 a.m. The last time they'd made love had been less than an hour ago. And he wanted her again—even though he felt wasted on the sight and the feel of her and the sultry scent of melon and flowers and fabulous sex.

Incredible. He'd known it would be good between them. He'd never guessed it would be off-the-charts fantastic.

He watched her sleeping face in the subdued light. And felt humbled suddenly by the gift she'd given him. This had been a huge decision for her. And she'd given him more than her body. More than sex. Great sex, he reminded himself, not wanting to minimize the experience for even a heartbeat.

What humbled him was that she'd given him her

trust. If he'd learned one thing about Rachael Matthews in the past few weeks, it was that trust was not something she gave easily. And because she'd given it to him, it compelled him to want to give her something, too. Something that walked like, talked like and looked suspiciously like promises.

And it was those kinds of thoughts that had him wondering just what the hell was going on here. He wasn't in a position to make any promises. A thought of Tia flitted briefly through his mind—and then Rachael stirred. Made one of those soft, sexy kitten sounds that instantly turned him to stone. And he was done thinking for a while. Except about how he could give them both pleasure.

He rose to his knees behind her, straddling her hips and indulged himself with the feel of his hands on her back. Gently stroking, patiently arousing, he woke her with lingering caresses until she reached up with a limp hand and dragged a skein of tousled red hair away from the beautiful face pressed into her pillow.

"Nate?"

He bent over to press a kiss between her shoulder blades then lick his way down those sexy vertebrae to twin dimples at the small of her back. She wasn't the only sensualist in this bed tonight.

She shifted her hips restlessly, then let him lift her, until she was on her knees in front of him, her pretty little bottom so tempting, he bent down to take a taste of it.

"How can I need you again?" he whispered as he rolled on protection, fitting his heat to hers and guided himself to her silken opening. With a groan that transcended pleasure, he entered her, his fingers clutching her hips to draw her nearer as she clawed for purchase on the sheets and took him deep.

His mind was full of her. His body burned for her as he drove into her, set a rhythm as old as time, as natural and pure as breathing. Slowly, he eased them up and over an edge tempered by tenderness, fired by mutual need until they gave themselves over to the sensation and the wonder and the joy.

Exhausted and spent, he lowered her to her side and wrapped himself around her back. He filled a palm with her breast, buried his face in her hair and tried not to think about the emotions churning around in his chest.

Tried and failed even as he drifted closer to sleep. He cared about this woman. A lot. He respected her. Above all, he desired her. And that, Jack, was the only track this train ran on, he reminded himself. It was not the love train. He'd known that going in. He was in love with someone else and Rachael didn't do relationships.

He fell asleep to the rhythm of her breathing, to the gentle thrum of her heartbeat pulsing against his hand. And tried to ignore the hollow sense of emptiness he didn't want to deal with or explore.

It was as if the dam had broken, Rachael thought the next morning as she stood in the shower and felt the sting of last night's activities on her breasts and between her legs. Years of pent-up sexual energy had flooded through her. She'd done things, said things, begged for things she hadn't known she'd wanted or needed or desired. It had been a very long time for her—and in a couple of instances the first time. He was inventive, her multicultural lover.

She'd never been so uninhibited in a physical relationship. Granted, her experience was pretty limited, but still, some of the things they'd done! Her face flushed red as she stepped out of the shower and carefully dried all the tender spots on her body.

Was she sorry? No. Sore? Oh yeah. And it had been worth every moment. She'd suspended reality last night. She hadn't thought about always and forever, no matter how persistently they'd hammered away at her shields. She'd thought about the moment and the night and the man. And she'd made that be enough.

Determined not to have one of those uncomfortable first morning afters, she wrapped up in her robe and followed her nose to the kitchen.

Looking gorgeous and sleep-rumpled and as appealing as the fresh-brewed coffee he'd made, Nate looked up from the stove and grinned.

"Hey," he said softly, his eyes asking a thousand questions.

She ignored the small corner of her heart that melted at the look in his eyes, ignored the gnawing ache that warned her she might be getting in too deep. Easing gingerly onto a bar stool at the island counter, she accepted the mug of coffee he poured for her with a grateful nod.

"Hey, yourself." She nodded toward the stove. "And you cook, too?"

Looking very domestic and very sexy with a spatula in his hand and wearing nothing but his navy boxers hanging low on his lean hips, he walked to her side, touched a hand to her hair. "Hope you don't mind. I'm starved. Thought you might be, too."

"Let me think. Do I mind waking up to freshly brewed coffee and a manly-man cooking my breakfast? I think that falls in the no-brainer category."

He leaned down and kissed her. A gentle, morning-after-the-best-sex-of-her-life-hello of a kiss. His lips were softly swollen, as were hers; his breath carried the faint scent of her toothpaste and coffee and orange juice.

Heat filled her belly and she arched involuntarily toward the hand that tunneled inside her robe to cup her breast with such sweet reverence that tears stung her eyes.

"You okay?" Concern darkened his eyes as he pulled away.

She got a handle on her emotions, then tried not to flinch as she resettled herself on the bar stool. "Never better. You?"

In answer, he returned to his omelette and shot her a killer smile. Smug. Satisfied. Master-of-his-domain type of smile.

You're not going to break my heart, Nate McGrory, she reminded herself. She knew what she was doing.

"What does your weekend look like?" he asked oh-so-casually as he flipped the omelette then popped some bread in the toaster. "Are you working?"

Most weekends, she did do some sort of work related to Brides Unlimited. Sometimes she went in to the office; often she brought work home. Anticipating the possibility that Nate might end up sleeping over, however, she'd cleared her schedule—at least for today. "Actually, no. I'm not."

He gathered two plates from her cupboard, turned with them in his hands. "Spend it with me."

Her heart did a little jump start—just to remind her she was treading some dangerous ground here. Just to advise her that as choices went, agreeing to his request would not be a wise one. So why exactly did you clear your schedule?

"Please," he added, setting the plates aside and walking barefoot back to her side. He kissed her again with that firm, gentle mouth that had done things to her in the night that made her blush in the light of morning.

Brushing his lips back and forth across hers, he did some pretty effective, pretty sexy and pretty silly wheedling. "Pretty please?"

Those two words sent a current of sexual heat sizzling from her breast to her belly. Lord, he was beautiful. All golden skin, rippling muscles and inky black hair that hung over his brow à la an Irish-Latino Rhett Butler rake about to ravage the South—or in this case, the square foot of southern Florida on which she sat.

And he was hers for the weekend, if she wanted him. Talk about a no-brainer.

"Well. Since you asked so nicely."

He kissed her as a reward, leaving her a little dazed, then dished up their omelettes. Setting the plates and silverware on the island breakfast bar, he sat down across from her.

"What would you like to do?"

She lifted a forkful of egg, onion, green peppers and cheese into her mouth then groaned in appreciation. "Finish this," she finally replied and nibbled on the buttered toast he'd placed on the corner of her plate. "It's delicious."

"I mean, *after* breakfast. What would you like to do?"

When she shifted again, a little twinge reminded her of the rigors of last night's lovemaking. This time she couldn't stall the wince. "I think it's safe to say bicycling and horseback riding are out."

He laughed, then slanted her a sympathetic smile. "How about we start with a long, hot soak in your tub?"

Sympathy had laced with heat by the time she managed to meet his gaze. It was all she could do to keep her voice steady. "As appealing as that sounds, I think the *we* portion of the equation might undermine any soothing effect."

He smiled again. "Poor baby. Then how about I run you a bath and while you soak in it *alone*, I'll make a few calls?"

She could have melted right there on the spot. Told herself a lesser woman would have. No man had ever offered to draw her a bath before. And when, after they'd eaten and he'd tidied up her kitchen—another first—he made good on his offer. He filled the tub with fragrant bubble bath and helped her into it after making sure the water was just right. Then he kissed her senseless and walked out of the room.

She was drifting on a fantasy of him love-slave, her slave-master when he popped his head back in the bathroom, his cell phone at his ear. "How much of your time can you give me," he asked, tipping the receiver away from his mouth.

She blinked. "Until Monday morning?"

"Can you make it Monday noon?"

She blinked again, aware of the bubbles dissipating all around her and mentally reviewed her schedule and her sanity. She had two early appointments on Monday. Sylvie could handle both of them. "Sure," she said before she could second-guess the wisdom of her decision.

He grinned that killer grin and talking to what appeared to be his pilot, left the room.

An hour later, while she was still catching her breath and feeling caught up in some Alice-in-Wonderland fantasy, they were airborne in Nate's Challenger, jetting their way to Key West.

The weekend flew by like a dream. From the flight in Nate's sumptuous private jet, to the indescribably beautiful sunset on Mallory Square where street performers delighted the gathered crowd and luxury liners and frigates with sails furled glided in breathtaking silhouette against an apricot and purple horizon, it was a romantic fantasy come true.

They ate cheeseburgers in paradise at Jimmy Buffett's Margaritaville on Duval Street and ate stone crab with their fingers upstairs at Crabby Dicks'. On Sunday they spent hours at Hemingway House then walked the colorful streets packed with shops before renting a convertible and driving back up Highway 1 across the seven-mile bridge to Matecumbe and Islamorada. It was late afternoon before they returned to Key West again.

They lazed in their swimsuits on the sand-covered jetty of the McGrory's private residence until sunset, drinking rum punch and sharing long, languorous kisses. And at night...at night they made incredible love.

It was perfect. The sun. The surf. The man.

And then, like all good things, it was over.

On the flight back to West Palm Monday morning, while Nate went up front and chatted with the pilot, Rachael thumbed through a magazine and grounded herself in some very important facts. It didn't matter that he'd been gentle and fun and kind and attentive and looked at her sometimes as though she was the only woman in the world. It didn't matter that he made love to her as if the act they shared went far beyond the physical to something that had always eluded her.

What mattered was that their weekend together was all about stolen moments in time and that in time, those moments would be over and he would be gone. What she had to keep in mind was that she was most likely one of a long line of women he'd wined and dined and taken on a ticket to paradise.

*Paradise.*

Everyone—especially Rachael—knew that paradise wasn't real. Paradise was an adventure theme park with wild rides and adrenaline highs. Paradise was an illusion. And Rachael saw through all the smoke and mirrors to reality.

The reality was, Nate would leave or she would push him away. The reality was, when that time came, she was not going to let him take her heart with him.

"So..." Tony said, a speculative grin on his face as he and Nate sat at a corner table at the Surf Club bar on Miami Beach Monday night, "I've narrowed this down to cars, money or women."

Nate lowered a brow and considered his brother. Where Nate took after his mother, Tony was the spitting image of the old man. Fair skin, black hair and built like a linebacker—in fact, he'd played linebacker at Florida State. "What? I can't call my brother for a friendly nightcap without an ulterior motive?"

"Well, yeah, you could, but the fact is, you haven't. Not for a long time now."

Nate stared at his tumbler of Scotch on the rocks while rubbing his thumb along the condensation on the glass. A jazz riff, from the piano in the corner of the members-only bar floated on air lightly scented with pricey Cuban cigars. "Yeah," he finally agreed, meeting his brother's solemn face. "It's been too long."

Tony only nodded, lifted his own Scotch to his lips. "So, what's up, little bro?"

Nate rolled his head on his neck, stared past Tony toward the mirrored wall of liquor bottles behind the ornate bar. "How did you know it was love with Tia?"

Tony was quiet for a moment. He slumped back in his chair and pinned Nate with a look. "Are you asking how did I know when I fell in love with Tia or how did I know when *you* fell in love with her?"

Nate felt his jaw drop.

Tony shook his head, laughed.

"You knew? You've *known?*"

"Knew you thought you were in love with my wife? Oh yeah."

Nate sucked in a deep breath. Let it out. "And you didn't punch my lights out. *Why?*"

Tony, in a motion that neither brother realized exactly mirrored Nate's, rolled a shoulder. "Because you were so earnest in your determination to be honorable and not to let it show. Because Tia would have had my head on a platter if I had. And—"

"Wait. Tia knew, too?" Nate felt as though he'd just had a chair pulled out from under him.

Tony's shrug said, 'fraid so. He leaned forward and finished his thought. "And I didn't say anything because I knew you'd eventually figure out you weren't really in love with her."

Nate stared at his brother long and hard. "So why the hell didn't you let me in on this little pearl of wisdom?"

"Why didn't I let you know you weren't really in love with her? Would it have done any good?" Tony snorted affably. "Hell no. One, you wouldn't have believed me. Two, you'd have gone off half-cocked and made yourself even more scarce than you do now and three, I knew you'd figure it out for yourself one day. I'm thinking, by the look on your face, today's the day or something damn close to it."

*Or something damn close to it,* Nate thought, thrown completely off kilter by the way his mind had wrapped around thoughts of Rachael and would not uncoil. And now his brother was telling him he'd known all along about his feelings for his wife. And that those feelings weren't real.

He drained his Scotch in one long deep swallow then raised the glass, ice clinking, to indicate he wanted a refill. He'd barely set the empty back on the table when another appeared in front of him.

"It's damn confusing," he confessed, nodding his thanks to the waiter before catching his brother's amused expression. "Sure. Go ahead. Laugh. I'm a clown. Big whoop."

Tony just shook his head and grinned. "Oh, how the mighty fall. It's entertaining as hell to see the Don Juan of the debutante set twisted up this way."

"So glad to be of service." Nate scrubbed a hand across his jaw. "I think I'll get drunk."

Tony's scowl held little sympathy. "Might do you some good. Nothing like a hangover to make a man humble. And nothing like a woman to drive a man to drink. So, this would be about the elusive Rachael?"

Nate frowned into his glass. "How can I love Tia all this time...and then just...just...hell. What the hell am I *just?*"

The huge sigh Tony let out said Oh for Pete's sake, this schmuck really needs my help and I'm loving it. "At the risk of sounding way too analytical, let me number it off for you again. One, you didn't really love Tia, you were in love with the *idea* of loving her. Two, it was only a matter of time until some sweet little thing made you realize what you'd been missing. And three, you've never really been in lo—"

"Don't say it," Nate cut his brother off with a dark look. "I'm not ready to go there yet."

"So where are you ready to go?"

Nate stared into space, completely baffled. "I don't know. I can't figure it out. I can't figure *Rachael* out. I like her. A lot. I respect her. She's funny and bright and so damn stubborn she makes my teeth ache."

"I'm thinking she makes something else ache, too."

Nate tipped back his head, stared at the ceiling. *Oh yeah.* She turned him inside out with her uninhibited passion.

"So you've got the hots for a spicy little number. It'll pass."

Nate whipped his head to his brother, ice in his eyes.

The jerk laughed. "Whoa-ho. I'm loving this. So, those were fightin' words, huh? Thought they might be."

"I may just have to clean your clock," Nate said, knowing his grin took all the heat out of his threat. "You baited me."

"Yeah, I did. You're so easy. This woman. She's special to you. You just haven't figured out how to deal with it yet."

"What I haven't figured out is how to deal with *her.* She doesn't want a relationship. Works damn hard at keeping her emotional distance—it's like she's determined to prove to herself that what we've got going is based only on physical attraction."

"And you react to this how?"

"I'm afraid to scare her off so I just go with it. Play along with her cavalier attitude, since that's the way she wants it." Unaware, he tapped his index finger in time to the piano music. "Some sonofabitch hurt her," he said decisively. "And she's not about to open up to anyone—me included—and get hurt again."

"Are you going to hurt her?" Tony asked after a long pause.

God, Nate thought and drained his second Scotch, I hope not. "What I'm going to do is give her a little room."

"You're going to quit seeing her?"

"Hell no. I'm just going to play it her way and not crowd her. And maybe, if we take it slow enough we can both figure it out."

He hoped.

Just as he hoped to hell he figured out where this was going.

# Ten

Gusty clouds played a sassy game of peek-a-boo with the midnight moon. Soft light and fragrant scents drifted in through Rachael's open bedroom window from the lanai and splayed in dancing shadows across wildly tangled sheets.

"You...weren't...kidding."

Rachael could hardly catch her breath. A tropical breeze cooled her heated skin as Nate rolled off her with a satisfied groan.

"Kidding about what?"

"Strong—like bull."

Spread-eagled on his back beside her, he laughed tiredly, sounding pleased and smug and not nearly as exhausted as he ought to be. "I wasn't kidding about the other part, either. The part where I promised I'd make you scream."

Oh, yeah. That part. She'd loved that part. And every little part in between since he'd shown up at ten for a late-Friday-night date. He'd brought takeout Chinese and a hunger for something—in his words—a little more filling. Her.

She stretched and sighed and with lazy interest, watched the blades of the Panama fan spin shades of gray across her pearl-white ceiling. "Now you're just bragging, McGrory."

"And you're just…beautiful."

She turned her head on the pillow and met his gaze. The look in his eyes—so tender and so involved…with her…with the moment—said things he couldn't possibly mean. *I missed you. I love you.*

She pushed the idiotic thought away.

This was sex. Just sex. *Great sex.* That was the arrangement. That was the expectation.

But he'd been elevating her expectations with his unselfish attention to her every need over the past few weeks. He raised them again five minutes later and made her forget to remember to be cautious when he spread his fingers across her bare abdomen. Hiking himself up on an elbow, he leaned over her, pressed a lingering kiss to the soft curls covering her pubic bone.

She lifted her head, met the heat in his eyes as he looked up the length of her body while his mouth moved over her, sensual, stirring and slow.

Stunned and aroused and amazed, she blinked at him. "Again?"

His lips curved into a smile as he cruised over her skin then lightly nipped her hip point. "Again."

She threw her arms above her head, pushed out an exhausted, delighted laugh. "You *can't* be human."

He crawled up the bed, poised over her on all fours, a sleek, powerful cat on the prowl. Lowering his head to her breast, he rimmed her nipple with the tip of his tongue. "So, now you know my secret."

"Your…oh…um…secret?"

"I come from the planet Lexor," he murmured as he moved his attention to her other breast where he played and licked and drove her to a fever pitch of longing, "a star far, far beyond your galaxy, where I was trained from the cradle in the art of pleasuring green-eyed, redheaded women."

A laugh bubbled out, followed by a gasp…then a groan as he suckled her breast and slipped a finger inside her, softly swirling, expertly arousing. "They got any more back home like you?"

He bit her gently then soothed with a languid caress of his mouth. "You couldn't handle any more like me."

She wasn't even sure if she could handle *him*. At the moment, she didn't want to. She was more than content to have him handle her. And…oh…*oh*…he was doing a fine job of it. His mouth teased and caressed and his fingers, long and lean and so deftly skilled, found her most sensitive places.

She watched through passion-glazed eyes as he moved down her body again, shamelessly dug her heels into the mattress and lifted her hips as he made room for his broad shoulders between her thighs. With his gaze heavy-lidded and hot on her face, he tilted her to his mouth, dipped his head, and nuzzled her damp curls.

Her breath caught as he slowly closed his eyes. He was so beautiful it was almost painful to watch as his dark lashes lay heavy on his cheekbones. The picture of hedonistic indulgence, he found the center of her with his tongue—and drove her in long, torturous degrees over yet another edge she'd never been on before.

"Nate," she whispered. He was all she could think about, all she could feel. All she wanted as he gave her pleasure. Unselfish. Uninhibited. And so perfect it hovered just this side of pain.

He drew out sensations so lush and consuming she lost herself to the wonder of it and to his dark beauty finessing her back up that peak again with delicious and dedicated abandon.

His eyes were dark as his face appeared above hers. She cupped his cheeks in her palms, pulled him down to her mouth where she tasted him and herself and everything that was right in the night.

And when he pressed himself deep inside her, in this suspended moment in time, everything—*everything*—was also right in her world.

It wasn't a place Rachael trusted to last. And as she drifted off to sleep that night, she had to remind herself that anything that seemed to be too good to be real, probably was.


"Mrs. Buckley," Rachael said into her headset Monday morning, trying not to panic as Gweneth demanded yet more changes—and these were getting down to the last minute—to her daughter's wedding. It was slated for Saturday, only six days away. "We really must have things firmed up by tomorrow.

"Yes. That's *tomorrow,* tomorrow, but there's no need to panic. Truly. Everything's under control. I would like to suggest something, though, if I may. Why don't you give me a time that's convenient for you to come by my office this afternoon. I'll clear an hour or so and we can review everything in detail. I think you'll feel much more comfortable about your decisions when you see it all laid out with the changes you've made since we began planning." All five hundred changes, she added in a soundless grumble as she propped her elbow on her desk and pressed her fingertips to her temple.

"Yes, two-thirty will be perfect." She made a quick note to have Sylvie reschedule the Lundstrums for Wednesday afternoon and to do something about the thoughts of Nate that kept creeping into her mind. Random thoughts. Nate naked. Nate laughing. Nate feeding her mangos in bed then lapping the juice off her bare breasts, sucking it out of her navel, licking it from her thighs.

"We'll do a complete walk-through," she said, dragging herself back to the moment. "You're going to be surprised how neatly everything dovetails."

The moment the word *dove* was out, she regretted it. She slumped back in her chair, cursed herself silently and listened as Gweneth Buckley requested just one more teensy-weensy change.

"Two hundred doves as opposed to two is an option, certainly," she hedged through gritted teeth. "No doubt, they'd make a spectacular statement, and while traditionally the release of two doves is a metaphor representing the bridal couple's union, it's not a hard-and-fast rule. I wonder, though," she added, praying she could tactfully steer Mrs. Buckley away from certain disaster, "considering we're also releasing butterflies, while it certainly wouldn't be excessive," try *over the top*, she mouthed silently, "it might subtract from the drama of their flight.

"One other thing you might want to think about," she pressed on, praying she was getting through, "is the issue of…how do I put this delicately? Well, to be frank, two hundred birds have the potential to soil a number of designer gowns."

She blinked, then blinked again when Mrs. Buckley crisply advised her she'd simply have to ensure that that didn't become a problem. What? Like there were plugs for these types of things and she, personally, had to install them in two hundred birds?

The customer is always right. The customer is always right. She repeated the mantra for the next ten minutes until she was finally able to get off the phone. She'd pray for a miracle. Like that Gweneth Buckley would get a clue and have a change of heart about the squadron of doves.

She was massaging her temples, working on a dinger of a headache when Sylvie walked into her office, closed the door behind her and looked at her expectantly.

"What?" Rachael asked.

"I've been good, Rachael. I really have. I haven't asked questions. I haven't pried. But I'm popping a seam here, wondering how things are going with God's gift. Are you ever going to give up the details on Nate McGrory, or am I going to have to resort to groveling?"

"You're coming pretty close to it now," Rachael said with a slight arch of her brow.

"Details, Rachael. Please. I need details. Give 'em up before I slip into an info underload stupor."

The devil was in the details. Rachael knew that. And if she let herself think about them, she'd get that achy, empty feeling in her chest and she wouldn't be able to deal with everything on her slate today.

"There's not that much to tell," she lied. Not much but a great guy, great times, great sex worthy of the Book of World Records.

"Didn't your mother ever tell you your nose would grow if you told too many lies?"

If she lost sight of the fact that there was no future with Nate, the mention of her mother brought it back into focus again. She'd never called her mom back. Somehow a month had slipped by and she hadn't found the time to call and reschedule their canceled dinner.

All in all, she was pretty pathetic—she couldn't even extend her trust to her own mother. To her own family. She couldn't trust them to want to be a part of her life. Nate wasn't family. He was just a man. Just a man she could spend time with without falling in love. On that point, she remained rigid. He was just a man whose smile and gentleness and sense of humor she could love without loving him. She could love the way he touched her, love the way he moved inside her. What she couldn't love, wouldn't let herself love, was him. Just as he could never love her if he really got to know her for the coward she really was.

"You're making too much of it, Sylvie," she insisted, looking her assistant straight in the eye. "It'll run its course and that will be the end of it."

And her heart ached, just a little bit, at the thought of that day looming.

She mentally put on the skids. She wasn't going there. Had already worked it out in her head. And she had everything under control. When their fling was over, she would be ready for it.

She didn't need Nate McGrory. She didn't need anybody. She had her job. She'd made it enough before him. She'd make it enough after.

"So, how did the big Buckley event go last night?" Nate asked as he leaned back from Rachael's table the Sunday evening immediately following the Buckley wedding. He lifted his wine to his lips.

"Hitchless," she said with a relieved look on her face. Laughingly, she'd told him about the doves and the potential for disaster. "At least it appeared to go that way. I stayed until after the band played the first few numbers and then left my staff in charge. What a relief to have that one behind me."

"You love the pressure."

"Yeah," she said with a considering smile. "I do. And while I'm not changing history or shaping the global economy, I'm good at what I do. Can't think of anything I'd rather do, in fact—or what I'd do if it wasn't an option for me."

She worked too hard, Nate thought watching her. He'd figured that out over the past several weeks. But she thrived on it, just as he thrived on his packed schedule. He'd never begrudged it until lately. Lately, he'd wanted more time for Rachael. This was the first chance they'd had to get together in a week. He'd been quietly pleased when instead of going out tonight she'd prepared a delicious vegetable couscous and grilled mahimahi. She'd served it, along with a romaine salad, on her lanai.

Relaxed in a gauzy pale-yellow sundress with her bare feet tucked up under her bottom, she looked young and fragile and so much more vulnerable than she'd ever admit to being.

After spending two incredible weekends with her— and before that, as much time as they'd been able to eke out of those busy schedules—Nate knew now just how vulnerable she really was. Not because she showed that side of herself but because she took such pains not to. And because she went to great efforts to avoid letting him too close. She knew damn well everything about his family and he still knew very little about hers.

It didn't take a nuclear biologist to figure out she was intentionally shutting him out of that equation to make sure he couldn't get too close. And that was the rub. He wanted close. After his heart-to-heart with Tony and some serious think time, he'd realized Tony was right. He'd never really loved Tia. He'd loved the idea of being in love with her. The idea of one woman to commit to. Of a home and family to come home to. He hated like hell to admit that big brother had been right, but he was. Nate had never been in love.

Until now.

He watched the woman he loved with quiet eyes as she tipped her wineglass to her lips. He was in love with Rachael Matthews. Over the moon, take the big walk, tell it to the world, in love.

He was pretty sure she was falling or already in love with him, too. Just as he knew she was fighting it with the tenacity of an army Ranger defending his country. Because of her resistance, he knew he had to take this slow and easy or he'd scare her away before she had time to figure out he wasn't going anywhere.

"What?" she asked, and he realized he'd been staring. The quiet, cornered look on her face reinforced just how skittish she was. She'd sensed that his thoughts had turned serious, and she didn't want any part of it.

He let out a deep breath. Smiled. "I was just thinking…" What would you do if I told you I loved you?

Run like a rabbit, that's what she'd do.

"About?" She tipped her head, suddenly looking a little edgy.

"About…" He almost said it then chickened out. "Dessert."

The slight relaxation of her shoulders showed her relief. "Opps. Sorry. Didn't make any."

So, they wouldn't talk. At least not tonight. There was time. And he had something else in mind for now.

Her gaze tracked him warily as he rose and lifted her out of her chair in one smooth motion. "You *are* dessert, *mi corazón*," he whispered against her mouth. Then, carrying her inside, he walked straight toward the bedroom. "And I think I'm going to need at least two helpings."

"Oh," she said, looping her arms around his neck. "Goodie."

* * *

*Mi corazón.*

Rachael woke up from a dead sleep in the middle of the night. Her heart pounded like a sledgehammer. Her hands trembled. And Nate's words whispered around in her head like a taunt.

*Mi corazón.* My heart.

Sucking in a serrated breath, she sat straight up in bed, dragged her hair away from her face then pressed her palms to her heated cheeks. Felt them cool as the blood drained away.

She'd never had an anxiety attack. That didn't mean she didn't recognize one when she was in middle of it. Her heart fluttered like hummingbird wings. Her hands trembled. She couldn't draw a deep breath. And she was wide, wide awake. And scared.

*Mi corazón.*

His casually spoken words should have drifted away like smoke. They'd meant nothing. It had just been an expression. Yet, hours after he'd spoken them, hours diluted by sleep, they echoed in her head with the same tenacity that had roused her like a fire alarm.

She fought for another breath, willed herself to settle down. This was stupid. It wasn't that he hadn't spoken to her in Spanish before. In the heat of passion, in the middle of a sultry night, his mind as muzzy as hers in the blinding spiral of shared heat and tangled limbs. But that…that had been passion. That had been letting go.

He'd never said such words in the light of day. And just because he had, it hadn't meant anything. She couldn't take them to heart. She was not his heart. She knew that.

*Mi corazón.*

Tears welled. She blinked them back. No, she was not his heart—but somewhere between gentle smiles and sultry kisses, she'd let down her guard so much that she wanted to be.

Her shoulders sagged with the admission. Oh God, oh God, oh God. She was not his heart. But he was hers. She'd let him become hers. The anxiety that had awakened her transgressed to a heartache so powerful it made her chest tight.

Through a glaze of tears, she looked down at him, sound asleep, his dark head on her pillow. He was so beautiful. And she'd let herself fall in love with him.

Her knees were wobbly when she eased quietly out of bed, shut herself in the bathroom and leaned back against the door.

She was in love with Nate McGrory.

For a long time, she stood there in the dark, aware of her pulse pounding in her ears and the breath catching roughly in her throat. She smelled the clean scent of her melon shampoo and the sharp edge of her panic.

Caught up on that unsteady edge, her defenses collapsed. Pressing a fist to her mouth, she willed back tears and latched on to anger instead.

"Damn you," she cursed herself on a tortured whisper. "Damn you, damn you for being so stupid."

How had she let this happen? And what was it going to take to make her quit wanting the things she could never have? A man who could accept what she had to give him. A man who loved her in spite of her inability to open up to him. A man who needed her. A home that felt full instead of empty. A heart that didn't live in fear of being bruised.

She slid down the door to the floor, wrapped her arms around her updrawn legs and dropped her forehead to her knees. For long, lonely moments, she sat there, dry-eyed, the tile cold against her bottom, the door hard against her back, until numbness finally set in. Her armor. Her insulation. She'd fallen into that unfeeling state to protect her for as long as she'd had memories.

Yes, she knew she wasn't a child anymore, shying from the pain her father had inflicted with both his fists and his denial of the love a child was entitled to receive. She knew she wasn't that lost little girl wondering why her mother had turned her back on her, too.

She was a woman. She was stronger now. But she still felt that overwhelming, knee-jerk need to protect herself. And she knew what she had to do.

It was going to be hard to watch him go.

She sat in a chair by the bed the rest of the night, watching him sleep, waiting for daylight, feeling as though a ten-story building had crashed on top of her. Knowing she had to end it now because she wouldn't have it in her to recover if she let it go on any further.

The coffee was brewing when, fresh from a shower and dressed to attend a meeting at the Breakers at 9:00 a.m., Nate walked into the kitchen.

He smiled when he saw Rachael standing with her back to him at the kitchen sink. A punch of tenderness

154 TEMPTING THE TYCOON

hit him as hard as the fist of lust. Ms. Prim in her royal blue skirt and blazer. He didn't have to wonder what she wore beneath that sedate business suit any longer. He knew. Just as he knew—intimately—all of her soft, tender places, and that if he went to her now and said the right thing, touched her just so, he might be able to convince her he had time to mess her up again before they headed to their respective meetings.

"Good morning," he said, walking up behind her.

She jumped and pressed a hand to her heart.

"Sorry. Didn't mean to startle you. Hey. Hey," he repeated softly when he realized how tense she was. He cupped her shoulders in his hands and turned her to face him. "You okay?"

Her eyes were sober when she glanced at him, then quickly looked away. Her hands were cold as ice when he took them in his. She pulled them away and fussed with filling her coffee mug.

And while he told himself he was overreacting, suddenly he had a really bad feeling about the closed-off look in her eyes, about the way she refused to look at him.

Determined not to leap to conclusions, he crossed his arms over his chest and leaned a hip against the counter. "What's going on, Rachael?"

Her hands were shaking—although she was doing her damnedest to hide it—when she wrapped her fingers around the pastel-yellow mug he'd come to know was her favorite.

"We need to talk," she said and avoiding his gaze, lifted the coffee to her mouth.

"Okay," he said slowly, surprised at how calm he

sounded considering everything about her behavior was setting off warning bells. "Let's talk."

"I think…" she began, still not looking at him as she abandoned her coffee to hug her arms tightly around her midriff, "I think we need to consider cooling things off between us a little."

He stared at her—at the top of her head actually, because she wouldn't, absolutely wouldn't, look at him. "Cooling things off," he repeated, hearing the steel in his voice but not able to curb it as tension knotted in his gut.

Something in his voice must have warned her that if she didn't face him head-on with this, he was going to make her look at him. And that would involve touching and Rachael clearly did not want to be touched by him right now.

She lifted her head, met his eyes. He saw barely veiled panic and stoic determination.

She tried for a tight smile. Failed. "This has been happening a little fast for me so I'm thinking maybe…maybe we should just not see each other…for a while."

He clenched his jaw to keep an expletive from bursting out and fought to hold on to his patience. She's just experiencing a case of cold feet, McGrory. Nothing to panic about. "It's been pretty fast, yeah," he agreed softly. "And pretty good. Damn good," he stated for emphasis. "I'm not sure I see the problem here."

"The problem is, it's been…a little too intense for me. I'm feeling…crowded." She met his cold silence by looking away, her shoulders rigid. "We agreed,

Nate. We agreed going into this that when the time
came to end it—''

''Whoa, wait. End it?'' He wasn't calm anymore.
Every muscle in his body vibrated with the effort of
keeping his temper in check. Every muscle in hers
was wrapped as tight as the leash he had around his
anger. It took everything—everything—he had to settle himself down. ''Rachael…why don't you tell me
what this is really about.''

''It's about what we agreed to,'' she said, her eyes
just shy of pleading. ''We both agreed that when one
of us was ready to walk away the other would let
them go.''

''You agreed. I didn't. And I'm not ready to walk
away. Damn it, neither are you.

''No,'' he cut her off abruptly when she opened
her mouth to remind him about her terms. ''I don't
think this has anything to do with what's going on
between us. I don't even think it's about our so-called
agreement. I think it's about what you're afraid of.''

She closed her eyes, her fingers tightened on the
arms she'd wrapped around herself. ''Please don't let
this get ugly.''

''Ugly?'' He lifted a hand, laughed grimly. ''I'm
not making it ugly. You are. This is stupid. Rachael,
come on. Don't let a case of cold feet keep us—''

''I don't have cold feet. And there is no us. Look.
I have an agenda. I have my career and that doesn't
allow for relationship-building. I'm sorry. But that's
the way it is. We had a fun few weeks, right? It was
great. And now it's over.''

''Over. Just like that? Just because you're too

scared to see where it's going?'' he demanded, trying to figure out a way to break through to her.

"Because it's over," she insisted, her voice rising, her cheeks flaming pink beyond the pale. "I know this is a news flash for you, but you don't make all the rules. You don't call all the shots. You're the one who started this. And I'm sorry if it upsets you, but I'm the one finishing it."

Anger and, damn it, panic made his voice harsh. "And what if I said, I'm not going anywhere?"

"I'd remind you that we made a bargain."

"Screw the bargain." Nothing had worked so far. Maybe this would. He went for broke. "Rachael…I love you."

She flinched as if he'd hit her. She stared at him for several long, aching seconds before tearing her gaze away. "I think you'd better leave."

Silence shredded the air.

"That's it?" Dumbfounded, he followed her to her front door then watched, disbelieving when she opened it, a blatant invitation for him to go. "I tell you I love you and you open the damn door?"

"Goodbye, Nate."

He scrubbed a hand over his face, settled himself when what he wanted was to shove his fist through the nearest wall. "Rachael. What the hell happened between midnight and now that made you so afraid of me?"

"I am not afraid."

"The hell you aren't. You're scared to death to accept what a good thing we've got going. So scared you aren't thinking straight." He swore softly when she just stood there, resolute in the face of anything he had to say. "You're a lot of things, Rachael, but I never figured you for a coward. And I'm tired of talking to the top of your head, damn it! Look at me. Look at me and tell me you don't want me in your life."

Slowly, she raised her head. Her green eyes looked as fragile as blown glass when they met his. "You need to leave now."

Hopeless. It was hopeless to talk with her when she was in this mindset. She'd closed off completely. He let out a deep breath.

"Fine." He wasn't going to win this round. Not today. "I'm gone. But I want you to think about something. And I want you to admit the truth. This isn't about us. There is nothing wrong with *us*. This isn't even about me. It's about *you*. Someone hurt you. Hurt you bad and you're feeling scared and vulnerable.

"We're all vulnerable, Rachael," he added, feeling such a complex mixture of love and hurt and anger he didn't dare touch her. "You think you've got the corner on that particular emotion? Think again. We are all vulnerable," he repeated, never realizing until this moment exactly how vulnerable he was when it came to her. "Some of us just carry it differently than others."

Her hand clutched the doorknob in a white-knuckle grip as he walked through the threshold then stopped, one hand on the doorframe. He turned back to her. "Who hurt you? Can you at least tell me that?"

"Please…go."

"I can't fight this. I can't fight something that happened before I met you if you're not willing to fight

it with me. I can't fix what's wrong in your life if
you won't give me the chance to make it right.''

She looked past him to someplace…someplace
where he couldn't reach her.

''You know how to get hold of me,'' he said, and
after a long, searching look, walked out the door.

# Eleven

***

"**Y**ou okay?" Sylvie asked gently when Rachael walked into her office at nine that same morning.

So much for hiding her feelings. Sylvie saw right through her. But then, Rachael didn't have the strength to manufacture even a fake smile. Neither did she have the power to handle Sylvie's mothering. "I need to get right on the Buckley invoices, okay? Can you pull the file for me?"

"Honey." Sylvie followed her into her office. "What's wrong?"

Rachael shook her head, felt the tears gather and stubbornly blinked them back. "I'm fine. I just need to work, okay?"

"Okay," Sylvie said carefully. "Just…just let me know…if you need to talk or anything, I'm here."

Rachael swallowed, nodded and tried to show Sylvie with a quick look that she was sorry for being so abrupt, but that she needed some space right now.

She felt as if she'd been gutted. Ripped from one end to the other with a dull, rusty knife. And it was her own damn fault. And Nate's. For making her love him.

*I love you.*

Why had he said that? She stared blankly at the open folder Sylvie laid on her desk. Why did he have to plant the seed, make her wish, make her yearn for something he couldn't possibly mean? People said those words all the time. No one ever meant them. She thought of her mother, of her father who was supposed to love her and had never done anything but hurt her. Yeah. People said "I love you" all the time. It didn't mean anything. Not when they said it to her.

But God, it hurt. She couldn't imagine anything hurting any worse than this.

Steeling herself to believe she'd severed the artery before the cut got too close to her heart, she dug into the file, determined to lose herself in her work.

"Rachael."

She looked up to see Sylvie standing in open doorway.

"Mr. Iverson wants to see you in his office ASAP."

Iverson, as the head of hotel events, was her direct supervisor. "Did I forget a meeting or something?"

"Not that I'm aware of. He probably wants to congratulate you on the Buckley wedding. It was a huge coup for the hotel—could mean lots of future referrals."

"Not to mention the potential for charity functions

and conventions if Gweneth spreads the word to her
old-guard friends,'' Rachael added as she rose and
headed for the door, back in control. This is what she
understood. This is what would always be there for
her. Her work. "I don't have any appointments until
this afternoon so take messages and I'll be back when
I get back."

She felt grounded again suddenly. Her work was
the one thing she could hang on to. She'd given it
one hundred and fifty percent for as long as she could
remember. And in the long run, it was the one and
only thing she could count on. It was what was going
to get her through losing Nate.

"I'm sorry…did you say suspended?" Rachael
stared across Iverson's lacquered desk in disbelief.

The man had the good grace to squirm. "It's only
temporary. Just until we can get to the bottom of
this."

"The bottom of what? I do not understand. Not
any of it."

William Iverson was in his late fifties, slightly bald-
ing and in excellent physical shape. He paled beneath
his Florida tan and shook his head. "It's a bitch," he
agreed in an uncharacteristic lapse of professionalism.
"And I promise we'll get you reinstated…or possibly
reassigned to a different position if it comes to
that…in a matter of weeks. A month at most."

"I don't want a reassignment, nor should a rein-
statement be an issue. I haven't done anything
wrong." She rose, paced to the window, her arms
tight around her midriff, then spun and faced him
again as anger started to outdistance the shock.

"Okay. Let me see if I've got this straight. The Buckley wedding—which I'd thought had gone off without a hitch—had a problem after all. The doves—the number of which Gweneth insisted on using against my advice—did exactly what doves are wont to do and dropped a little unexpected gift on one of Gweneth's fellow Angels of Charity matrons who were in attendance."

"In her hair," Iverson qualified morosely. "And not just a fellow angel, the head angel."

Rachael went on as if she hadn't heard him. "And Gweneth laid the blame for this little faux pas directly on me. And *this* is reason for suspension? Why?"

"Because Gweneth Buckley cannot afford to have egg on her face with her fellow society matrons. And to save face with them—it's worse than death to become a fallen angel—Gweneth has decided to make you the scapegoat. She called not only our manager but several stockholders and demanded that you be let go."

"This is too ridiculous even to consider, let alone act on."

"Rachael—you do understand, don't you, that these women run the Palm Beach economy?"

"Oh, I understand perfectly. And no one has played the society game better than I have to land the Buckley account and give the woman exactly what she wanted. I gave her the perfect wedding—with the exception of her insistence on those damn doves— and what I now understand is that I'm getting drop-kicked out of sight to save her face. I repeat—this is too ridiculous for words."

"I agree, but I'm still under orders to initiate the suspension."

She shot past stunned and raced straight into outrage. "You do realize you're talking lawsuit here?"

"Now, Rachael. It doesn't have to come to that. We can work something out for you."

"Oh, you bet you can. I'll give you a week and then you'll hear from my lawyer."

"Don't do anything rash. Just think for a minute. See it from the hotel's perspective. Do you happen to know how many dollars in revenue Pettibone Pharmaceuticals generates for the Royal Palms annually? Between their seminars and conventions, it amounts to millions. It's possibly as high as fifty percent of the events' take. Do you happen to know Mrs. Buckley's maiden name?"

"Wild guess?" she said sarcastically. "I'm going for Pettibone."

"Exactly. We can't afford to lose their account—and our stockholders know it. Try to understand. I'd give anything if we could make this go away."

"Anything but giving me my job back," she stated flatly.

"Hang in there with us."

"Right. Just like you've hung in there with me."

"So...promotion *and* pay raise?" Sylvie asked anxiously when Rachael returned to her office fifteen minutes later.

She passed Sylvie by, sank down behind her desk and lowered her head to her hands. She felt ill. Physically, mortally wounded.

"Rachael?"

Slowly, she raised her head and with a shaking hand reached into her desk drawer for her purse. "I've been suspended," she said hearing the hollow ring to her voice. "Indefinitely."

"Say what?"

In clipped, precise words, Rachael told her.

"Oh, God, Rachael. This...this is so unfair. Are you saying they rolled over on this—just like that?"

Rachael rubbed her temple with her thumb. "Like a pack of dogs begging for bones."

She rose and shoved her desk drawer shut. She looked around the office, then walked over to the bookshelf. Tucking the picture of her family under her arm, she headed toward the door.

"Rachael?"

She stopped, turned and let Sylvie enfold her into a hug. "Don't let them get away with this."

"I don't intend to. But I've got to get out of here before I do something stupid." Like let them see her cry. It made her angry all over again that a company she'd given her all to could turn their back on her like this.

Beyond devastated, Rachael drove home in a fog. She shut herself inside her town house. The adrenaline rush of shock lasted about fifteen more minutes. Once she was alone, she didn't have to pretend anymore. She didn't have to show the world her strong side.

She cried. She raged. She threw things and cried some more. She sat alone with the shades pulled and her door locked for days. And sank into the deepest, darkest despair of her life.

She missed Nate. Wanted his arms around her. Wanted him to hold her and make the pain go away.

But Nate wasn't the answer. Nate was gone. And he wouldn't be coming back. Just like her job was gone. Everything that she'd worked for. Everything that was important. Gone.

When the phone rang, she ignored it. When Sylvie came to her door, she refused to let her in.

She couldn't. She just couldn't deal with it.

She didn't eat. She didn't sleep. She couldn't stop thinking that the one thing she'd thought she could count on—the job she'd invested her life in—wasn't even safe for her, no matter that she was blameless in this ridiculous turn of events. She'd run Brides Unlimited better than anyone could have.

And what had it gotten her? Beaten and demoralized and completely alone. As she'd always been alone.

It was on the fourth day, when she'd hit rock-bottom, that she finally found the backbone Gweneth Buckley had stolen from her along with her job. She looked at the pathetic lump of humanity staring back at her in her bathroom mirror and made a decision. Grief wasn't going to drive her actions any longer.

She'd needed this time, yes. To mourn. To wallow around in self-pity. But that time was over. She needed to get on with her life—and she needed retribution.

Righteous anger was calling the shots when she picked up the phone and dialed the one person she wanted to believe in above all others.

Nate slumped back in his chair, his suit jacket tossed aside, the sleeves of his white shirt rolled to his elbows, his tie loose. At his left was his chief litigator, Bryan Morgan, at his right, his executive secretary, Clarice Fox. Facing him at the far end of the conference table were the Borlin brothers, his newest clients, who were counting on him to make right the wrong done to them by a patent infringement.

When the intercom light on the phone at his elbow lit up, every muscle in his body tensed. He'd left word with the switchboard that there was only one person whose call was important enough to interrupt him with.

"Excuse me," he said to the group at large. His hand hovered over the receiver for a long second before he snatched it up. "Yes."

"Rachael Matthews on line one, sir."

He let out a breath he'd probably been holding since she'd shown him her door four days ago. "Transfer the call to my office, please. I'll take it there.

"I'm sorry," he said, standing, "I have to take this call. You're in good hands with Bryan," he assured the Borlins and, without another word of explanation, walked out of the meeting.

"Rachael," he said as he dropped into the chair behind his desk. "Hi."

Silence. He could almost see her gripping the phone with white knuckles. And yet he waited. This was her call. This was her move and he needed to let her make it.

"I'm...I'm sorry to bother you at work."

"It's not a bother," he assured her, concerned about the tension in her voice.

"I hope I didn't interrupt anything too important."

Only the potential for a cool half mill in billable hours and a certain court victory. "It's not a problem. How are you?" he asked, missing her so damn much he didn't care if she knew it.

"Honestly? Not so good."

No, she wasn't good. He heard it in her voice along with the tension, and he waited the length of a long breath before she spoke again.

"Nate...I need a lawyer."

Her statement took a moment to assimilate. It wasn't what he'd wanted or expected to hear. Not, I need you, not, please come back to me, but, I need a lawyer. "A lawyer?"

"Other than you, I don't know any. Have never had a need for one. I was hoping you could suggest someone in West Palm I could count on."

He stared beyond the office window to the view of Miami Beach in the distance and tamped down his disappointment. Okay. So she wasn't calling to profess her undying love. But she had called. He'd take what he could get and worry about the rest later. He'd been dying here. By long, slow hours. He missed her. He needed her. He wanted her on any terms, and if he hadn't heard from her by the end of the week he'd planned a trip to West Palm to confront her.

"Tell me what happened."

She did. Concisely, with little emotion in her voice. He listened, taking notes, shaking his head over the inequity, aching for the pain this had caused her and that she tried so valiantly to conceal. He knew what her job meant to her. He knew that they'd taken more than a position and a paycheck away from her. They'd taken her pride. And he was just the man to get it all back.

"I'll fix it," he said simply.

"No. Oh, no, I didn't mean for you to—"

"I'll fix it," he repeated firmly. "I want to do this for you, Rachael. You can trust me to make this right for you."

"Nate—"

But he'd already hung up the phone.

"So that's where that dress went," Rachael muttered to herself as she dug into her guest-bedroom closet. She'd been cleaning for three days straight—three days since she'd called Nate. Four years since she'd seen this particular dress.

It was gray. Tasteful. Understated. *Dull.* She dragged it off the hanger and tossed it toward the bed and the pile of clothes destined for charity. She'd found too many dull drab things in her closets. Had never realized how few bright, flirty, fun things she owned. And she didn't need gray dresses anymore.

She didn't need a lot of things, she told herself staunchly. Dressed in grubby cutoff jean shorts and a baggy tank top, she ambled out into the kitchen to pour another cup of coffee, but then thought twice when she realized it was getting dark. Mostly, what she didn't need was the victim mentality she'd been unconsciously grooming for as long as she could remember. That was all about to change, too. Several days of wallowing around in self-pity then pulling herself out of the muck had been grueling and painful—but they'd also been the best thing that had ever happened to her. It had forced her to deal with her feelings—feelings she'd been sweeping under the rug or ignoring for too many years now.

And it felt good. It felt—great. Freeing. Like the ultimate makeover of her spirit.

Her decor was also due for a makeover, she decided, after taking a quick shower. She dried her hair then slathered on lotion…remembering the night Nate had taken care of that job for her. An arc of pure longing eddied through her body and cut straight to the heart as she slipped into her robe, determined to think ahead from now on, not back.

Tomorrow she would paint. Something bright and fun and very Florida. She was tired of white walls and of sneaking her penchant for color into her life with carefully chosen accessories. Yeah—some of her art was bold. But not enough of her life was. Not nearly enough. Especially now that Nate was no longer in it.

And there was the rub. She'd been careful all of her life. Careful and cowardly. Where had it gotten her? She was alone. She was unemployed. Basically, she was pretty damn pathetic.

Since she'd forced Nate out of her life and she'd lost her job, she'd learned some things about herself—and most of it wasn't pretty. She'd learned even more when she'd faced her oldest demon and called her mother, insisting on a heart-to-heart chat.

That had been three days ago, right after she'd called Nate requesting the name of a good lawyer. Well, she'd gotten one, she thought, then allowed herself a smile when she thought of how quickly he'd jumped to her aid, no questions asked.

She sat down on the sofa with her nail polish and went to work on her toenails and, switching gears, mulled over the revelations of the conversation with her mother. She understood so much about their relationship now. Could kick herself for not pressing her mom about it sooner. But now she knew. Now she understood and she was going to do something to correct some of the mistakes she'd made that were directly related to those misconceptions.

Starting with Nate. She missed him so much. And she wanted him back. She'd just needed a little time to figure out how she was going to accomplish that.

First, though, she'd had to figure out what she was going to do with the rest of her life. Financially, she was all right for a while. She'd set money aside. She leaned back, extended her legs and admired the Valentine-red color of her toes. She could hold out for a few months until she had to generate some income.

It wasn't that she didn't have any confidence in Nate's ability to help her with the Royal Palms situation, but she'd already decided that on the remote chance they offered to take her back, she wasn't going. If that was the best they could do for her after all she'd given them, it just wasn't good enough.

But *she* was. "I'm good enough, and I'm strong enough and doggone it, I like me," she said with a laugh, paraphrasing lines from an old *Saturday Night Live* skit.

It amazed her, this feeling of euphoria that had grown since she'd worked everything out in her head. She was stronger now. She understood now. And when her security buzzer sounded and the voice on the other end was Nate's, she knew she was ready to face both him and her feelings.

Her heart did a little hopscotch at the sound of his voice. At the prospect of seeing him again. She'd known he was coming—Sylvie had called and warned her. Good thing, too. If he hadn't come to her by today, she was going to him tomorrow.

She buzzed him past security then raced for her bedroom and threw on a pair of white short shorts and a bright-red halter-top. Both new. Both constructed to dazzle. Then she went to work on her hair. It would take him approximately five minutes to drive from the security gate to her front door. She had to work fast.

The old Rachael Matthews would have lobbied for another few days to brace for this meeting and then she would have waded into the water one slow step at a time. The new one wouldn't. The new Rachael planned to dive straight in, the heck with the threat of the undertow. The new Rachael was no longer afraid she'd sink instead of swim.

She knew what she wanted now. Knew what she needed and what she deserved. And she was going to do everything in her power to get it. Starting with tonight.

She ran a quick check of herself in the mirror as her doorbell rang. "You'll do," she told herself with a grin. "You'll do just fine."

Nate had been preparing himself for what he'd find when he finally saw Rachael. He'd talked with Sylvie. He knew how broken Rachael had been when Iverson had suspended her. He remembered the look in her eyes when she'd told him it was over between them. Remembered the defeat in her voice when she called him looking for a lawyer.

She'd been hurting and scared and so vulnerable it made him ache at night. Ache to hold her. Ache to heal her. Ache to love her until all the pain went away.

So he was ready for just about anything when her door swung open—anything but the woman standing there.

"Hi," she said, a smile playing at the corners of her mouth.

"Umm.... Hi."

This woman didn't look beaten. She didn't look bruised. She looked breathless and sassy and as sexy as a siren on an uptown Saturday night.

"Were you planning to come in?" she asked with a playful light in her eye.

*Playful?*

"Are you okay?" he asked cautiously. Something wasn't right here. "Rachael...have you been drinking?"

She actually laughed. "Not a drop. Come in. Please. We need to talk."

"Yeah. That's why I came over. We need to talk about your job."

She shook her head, waved a hand in front of her. "No. I don't want to talk about that. Not yet. I want to talk about us."

"Us?" He felt as if he'd just turtled a Sunfish. The look of her, her mood, her confidence was a total departure from what he expected. And that one little two-letter word buoyed his hopes so high, he had to bring himself back to earth. "Us?" he repeated cautiously. "I thought there *was* no us."

She sobered, took his hand and led him to the sofa where she sat and crossed her bare silky legs beneath her.

"Sit. Please."

"Rachael—"

"No. Wait. I know I don't deserve to have you listen to me. I've been horrible to you and I'm so, so sorry. I need to explain. Can you give that to me? Can you give me the chance to explain a few things?"

He'd give her anything. But he couldn't tell her that just yet. He hadn't been lying the last time he'd seen her and he'd told her everyone was vulnerable. He still felt raw from the way she shoved him out of her town house and out of her life. He wasn't quite ready to lay himself open for her and have her shut him down again.

So he sat back, waited. And he prayed that what she had to tell him was something he wanted to hear.

# Twelve

Rachael watched Nate with her heart in her throat. He was so edgy in his silence, his own heart all but hanging on his sleeve…and she fell a little deeper in love. She wanted to tell him she loved him. But she owed him something else first. An explanation.

"Well," she said, tucking her hair back behind her ear as a second ticked to ten, then ten to twenty. "This is a little harder than I thought it would be."

"What's hard, Rachael?" he asked carefully, and she saw in his eyes that this sudden threat of cold feet on her part was hurting him. And she didn't want to hurt him. Ever.

"Admitting to mistakes. No one likes to make them—especially me—and it's been a real eye-opener to realize I've made more than my fair share. And now I need to own up to them." She stopped, drew a bracing breath. "Bear with me...I'm just going to lay it all out, okay?"

He nodded, his face a mask that suddenly covered his emotions. It was his lawyer face, she realized, about the same time she understood he was still unsure about her feelings for him. And why wouldn't he be? She'd given him nothing to hold on to.

"You...you scared the living daylights out of me." She stopped, smiled. "The first time I saw you...you just made me feel things I told myself I had no business feeling. You are so...so everything I've ever wanted. Everything I was afraid to believe I could have. That's why I tried everything in my power to force you away. But then, you already know that, don't you?"

He took her hand in his, held it tightly and waited.

"What you don't know is why. This is the hard part. This is where I tell you how pathetic I am. Correction. Was. How pathetic I was." She drew another deep breath, let it out. "Okay, just do it, right?"

He squeezed her hands. "Yeah. Just do it."

"I...I've got to go back a ways. Things were tough when I was a kid. My...my dad was...well, let's just say he'd never get father of the year award. My most vivid memories of him were of his fists. And his face...all red, veins bulging as he screamed at my mother. Once...once, he put her in the hospital."

"Rachael—"

She shook her head, clutched his hands tighter. "No. I've got to get this out. Long story short, though, we made a lot of midnight runs to women's shelters before Mom finally got the courage to break out of the cycle and leave him for good. I was nine.

And I still remember the antiseptic smell of those places, the kind, pitying eyes of the volunteers, the wild, vacant stares of the other kids and their moms who had fled for their lives the same way we had.''

She drew in another settling breath and, encouraged by the patience in his eyes and the stroke of his thumbs over the back of her hands, continued. ''Anyway, we left Ohio and moved here to West Palm. Everything was pretty good for a while and then it got better. Mom met John and fell in love. They got married and I had a real home—a safe home—for the first time in my life. It was perfect.''

''So why doesn't it sound so perfect?'' he asked gently.

She smiled. Shrugged. ''Because it wasn't.'' She gathered her thoughts and explained. ''Mom and John were happy. They started their own family shortly after they got married, and as much as I love the girls, I suddenly became a fifth wheel. Or so I thought at the time.

''This...this is hard,'' she confessed. ''What I have to keep reminding myself is that I was twelve then and I couldn't be expected to understand. All I saw was that after the girls were born, I suddenly wasn't important to her anymore. It was apparent that I was a part of a past she wanted to forget and I didn't have any place in her present or her future.''

''But that wasn't really the case, was it?''

She smiled sadly. ''What was really happening was that Mom had fallen into a depression. It wasn't just me she turned away from. She turned away from all of us. Poor John. It was all he could do to take care of her and of those babies. I just happened to be old enough to take care of myself. What I wasn't old enough to comprehend was that it wasn't me. This wasn't just happening to me."

"But it *was* happening to you. And it made you feel unlovable, unwanted and alone."

She looked up at him, smiled. "Thank you for that. Yes. That's exactly what I felt."

She thought back to those years when she'd only seen her mom turning her back on her. She was a child. She was twelve, struggling with self-esteem, and all she could feel was the rejection. Her father hadn't loved her. Now her mother didn't love her anymore, either.

"I was so miserable, so certain I wasn't worth loving, that I didn't understand my mother was struggling, too. Cause and effect, I guess, you'd call it. Anyway, I withdrew from her further and further over the years. Even after Mom had her depression under control, the only person I let her see was this self-reliant woman who didn't need her anymore."

"Because if you didn't need her, she couldn't hurt you, right?"

She compressed her lips, nodded. "So both of us …we just sort of let the distance between us breed and grow, both thinking that was exactly the way we wanted it—when, in truth, we've both been bruised by it."

She paused again, looked at their joined hands, took heart in the fact that not only had he not pulled away, he held her tighter. "And that leads me to you."

"I think I've got this part. Your knee-jerk reaction

was that since you were so unlovable, how could I possibly love you? How could anyone love you?''

Feeling sheepish, she nodded. ''Well, I'd racked up a fairly concrete track record to support that theory. Any guy who ever got remotely close—I pushed away when they started making noises about long-term commitment.''

''I could almost feel sorry for them,'' he said.

''Well, don't. I didn't love them. I don't think I ever loved any of them.''

''And now? Now what do you think?''

His eyes were so dark and so full of compassion and longing and love, she thought she'd burst from all the love she felt for him.

''Now I know what love is,'' she said without hesitation. ''Now I know I'd never even been close to it before.''

His eyes warmed to that smile she'd missed every waking and sleeping hour since she'd driven him away. ''How close are you now, Rachael?''

''So close,'' she said, lifting her hand to his chest, where his heart beat steady and true, ''so close I can feel it.''

He covered her hand with his. ''But are you ever going to say it?''

She laughed and fell into his arms. ''I think I just did—when I told you about my childhood. About my problem with trust. It was a big step for me, Mc-Grory.''

''I know.''

''I can't promise that I'll be up front with you all the time. With how I'm feeling. With what I need.''

''I know what you need. You need me. I'm the

man who understands you. I'm the guy who's going to be there, waiting you out when you fold up like a clam. I love you, Rachael. And I'm not going to let you push me away.''

She pulled back so she could see his beautiful face. ''That's what I love about you, McGrory. You don't know when to give up.''

''Not when it comes to you.''

''I love you,'' she whispered, pressing a kiss to his brow. ''I love your smile.'' Another to his lips. ''And your laughter and your strong mind and giving heart.'' She couldn't stop kissing him. ''I love that you're here, in spite of everything I did to drive you away. I love that you haven't walked back out that door and that you let me drone on and on about my dramatic and melodramatic youth—''

He stopped her with a kiss so full of tenderness and caring it brought tears to her eyes. ''Don't minimize what happened to you. Your childhood was traumatic and the fact that you've overcome it to become this strong, stubborn, self-reliant woman only makes me love you more.''

She pressed her forehead to his. ''Thank you. Thank you for not giving up on me.''

''You mean, when you shot me down time and again even after I blew a small fortune on flowers and Mara Lago?''

She smiled and buried her fingers in his hair. ''Yeah, then.''

''When you blackened my eye and bloodied my lip?''

''Umm. Yeah.'' She touched her fingertips lovingly

to the corner of his mouth. "You're not going to let go of that anytime soon, are you?"

"What I'm not going to let go of, is you."

"Promise?"

"Promise. You may have been unlucky in love in the past Ms. Matthews, but from this point on consider yourself the luckiest woman alive in that department."

"Does this mean I'm going to get lucky tonight?"

He laughed and, pressing her down into the sofa cushions, started tugging the strap of her halter top down her shoulder. "I'd say," he whispered against the breast he'd bared and sent a shiver sluicing through her, "you're about to get very, very lucky."

"So…maybe it was all supposed to happen like this," Rachael said later, rousing Nate from a hazy half sleep as they lay in the soft darkness of her bedroom. She lifted her head and propped it on her hands, which she'd stacked on his chest.

She felt so good sprawled on top of him. Her softness to his hard angles. Her sensitive breasts to his chest. "Could be," he agreed, running his hands up and down the length of her body, loving the feel of her bare skin beneath his hands, lingering at the curve of her bottom to press her against him.

They'd made love and talked and made love again. He'd told her about Tia and how it had taken meeting her to make him realize he had never really loved Tia.

"Oh…almost forgot," he said lazily. "I got your job back."

She reared back, bracing her palms on his chest.

"You got my job back?" she asked, incredulous, then laughed. "How?"

He drew her back against him, nipped at her shoulder. "The same way everything works in Palm Beach society. I made some calls to some key people and sang your praises, and they in turn sang your praises to some of Mrs. Buckley's Angels of Charity cohorts who put the screws to Mrs. B and voilà—to save face, she made some of her own calls and asked that you be reinstated."

She cupped his face in her hands. "Amazing. Thank you. Thank you for doing that for me. Now, how upset are you going to be when I tell you I don't want to go back to Royal Palms?"

"Because you deserved better from them than they gave you?"

"Damn straight."

He laughed and hugged her hard. "Somehow, I figured that stubborn streak might come into play, so I made sure the hotel offered up a contingency settlement to make up for the defamation of character, loss of salary, pain and suffering, and whatever else I could think of to throw in there."

She laughed. "Pain and suffering. I like that part."

"You're going to like this part even better." He named the figure the hotel had coughed up in an effort to avoid the lawsuit he had assured them he'd be filing on Rachael's behalf.

"Holy cow!" She sat straight up this time, straddling him in all her naked glory. She looked so pretty and pink and so damn sexy he had to wrestle her to her back again and take advantage of all the gratitude she felt compelled to bestow on him.

"I want what Tony has," he whispered an hour or so later.

She snuggled against his side and yawning, threw a bare leg over his thighs. "I think that's called sibling rivalry."

He loved it that she was secure in his love for her. "It's called I want it all, Rachael. I want to marry you."

She hiked herself up on an elbow, her eyes shining like emeralds in the night. "Doesn't that work out well...I just happen to know where you can get a really great wedding planner. And for you, I think she'd work out a real sweet deal."

"I've already got a sweet deal." As sweet as the lips that met his.

"And I'm the luckiest woman in the world."

"I'm going to take that as a yes. Yes?"

"You are definitely going to take that as a yes." She kissed him again. "Yes." And again. "Yes." And again before she settled back against his side with a contented sigh and punctuated her final affirmation with a jubilant raised fist. "Yes!"

# Epilogue

**W**ell, Rachael thought as Sylvie made final adjustments to her train in preparation for her walk down the aisle—*this* wasn't supposed to happen. She was *not* supposed to be worrying over details. Sylvie, her partner in Miami's newest bridal-consulting business, Miami Brides, had been planning this wedding for six months, step by meticulous step to make sure it was perfect.

And so far, it was.

It was as perfect as the man waiting for her at the altar with the smile that had stolen her heart the first time he'd flashed it her way.

Love. For her. It shone in Nate's flashing brown eyes as he stood in his black cutaway tux with his brother and Sam by his side.

Love. For him. It filled Rachael to bursting as she

clutched her bridal bouquet and walked on her stepfather's arm to her destiny. Love. For her mom who,
during the past several months, had laughed with her
and cried with her and in the process they had found
their way back to each other.

*You're beautiful,* Nate McGrory's speaking eyes
told her with a tenderness that made her heart sing.
*Come, mi corazón. Let's get these vows over with so
I can officially say you're mine.*

She hoped her eyes did a little speaking, too. *I have
always been yours. I will always be yours.*

She would remember every moment of this day.
Her mother's pride. Karen and Kimmie in lavender-
rose, smiling through their own tears that told her how
happy they were for. Her sisters and Nate's family
embracing their special day.

But what she would remember most of all was the
look in her husband's eyes as he held her in his arms
that night and filled her with a tender passion that
made her heart sing.

"I love you, Rachael. Now. Always. Forever."

Lucky, she thought as she lost herself in his love.
How did I ever get so lucky in love?

\*     \*     \*     \*     \*

# Having the Tycoon's Baby

## ANNA DePALO

## *ANNA DePALO*

A lifelong book lover, Anna discovered that she was a writer at heart when she realised that not everyone travels around with a full cast of characters in their head. She has lived in Italy and England, learned to speak French, graduated from Harvard, earned graduate degrees in political science and law, forgotten how to speak French and married her own dashing hero.

When not writing, Anna is an intellectual-property lawyer in New York City. She loves travelling, reading, writing, old movies, chocolate and Italian (which she hasn't forgotten how to speak, thanks to her extended Italian family).

Readers can visit her at www.annadepalo.com.

To my family and friends,
particularly my parents, Enza and Frank,
and my husband, Colby,
for encouraging me to
pursue every dream.

# One

"**I**'m calling a sperm bank and getting artificially inseminated."

Liz Donovan's pronouncement was met with a mixture of surprise and disbelief. Allison Whittaker, her best friend of more than ten years, was the person exhibiting the emotions in question.

They were sitting in the book-lined study of Allison's parents' house, an impressive redbrick colonial on the outskirts of the town of Carlyle, just northeast of Boston. Each year the Whittaker family hosted a Memorial Day Weekend barbecue and this year was no exception, even though Allison's parents, Ava and James, were traveling in Europe.

"But, Lizzie, the baby will never know its father. Doesn't that bother you?"

"Yes, but a sperm bank seems like my best choice

right now. Besides, I'll be able to pick eye color, height, everything I want.''

Allison was the person who had accompanied her to the hospital a few weeks ago when she'd had the outpatient laparoscopic surgery that had confirmed her gynecologist's diagnosis—and Liz's worst fear: endometriosis.

Fortunately, hers was a mild case, discovered early, and the short surgery had removed most of the offending implants around her uterus. But, there was no telling what the future would hold. Which meant, of course, that she'd be spinning the gaming wheel each year she waited to have a child—if it wasn't too late already.

Allison frowned. ''Wouldn't you rather use someone you know?'' she argued. ''Knowing who the father is has got to be a big advantage.''

Liz sighed. A part of her still couldn't believe that her time for having a baby might be running out. She wouldn't even turn thirty for another six months!

Having a family of her own had always been important to her: her mother had died when she was eight and she'd been an only child. Frankly, if she hadn't had such a burning desire to prove to herself and her overprotective father that she could and would succeed in the business world, she might have paid less attention to her career and more to the state of her basically nonexistent social life.

In fact, work was partly why she was at the Whittaker mansion today, despite the upheaval of the last couple of weeks. She was hoping to have a chance to discuss a big account for her interior design business,

Precious Bundles, which specialized in children's rooms and play areas.

Allison had suggested that she do the design for the new day care planned for Whittaker Enterprises' headquarters. If she got the contract, it would be Precious Bundles' biggest account to date and would bring her one step closer—one big step closer, she corrected herself—to getting her business on a sound financial footing.

With any luck, Allison's brother Quentin, the CEO of Whittaker Enterprises, would show up soon and she'd have a chance to seal the deal.

Liz determinedly pushed away the twinge of nervousness that usually accompanied any thoughts of Quentin and reached for the glass of lemonade that she'd set down on the coffee table. "Of course there are advantages to knowing the father, but who would I use? I'm not seeing anyone, and I don't have any close male friends."

Allison seemed pensive for a moment, then offered, "Well, I've got three brothers."

Liz's hand stilled, half to the glass, and she looked at Allison with a mixture of horror and amusement. "You're giving me nightmare visions of some teenaged schemes you got me involved in."

"You loved every minute of them!" Allison pretended to look offended.

Liz sat back against the cushions of the couch, the glass forgotten, and heaved another sigh. Allison could be tenacious. It was a trait that served her well as a hotshot Assistant District Attorney in Boston, but it also made her tough to argue with. "Even you have

to admit that volunteering one of your brothers for
sperm donor duty is a little on the wild side.''

"Why?'' Allison got up and started pacing. "It
makes perfect sense. My mother has been pushing for
a grandchild, but none of my brothers shows any signs
of delivering the goods, so to speak. And I'm not
about to marry any boring 'so-and-so the Third' to
make her happy!'' Allison stopped and gave her a
winning smile. "Besides, I know you'll make a wonderful mother. The best, in fact.''

"The best what?'' asked a deep voice from the
doorway.

Liz tensed and gave Allison a warning look.

Even after eleven years, Quentin Whittaker, the
oldest of Allison's three older brothers, hadn't lost the
power to make her nervous and skittish. Tall, at least
six-two by Liz's estimate, with raven-black hair cut
conservatively short, he had strong and even features
marred only by a small scar at the corner of his right
brow—the result of a hockey accident in college.

His eyes connected with hers across the study.
"Hello, Elizabeth.''

He never called her Liz, like most people did, or
Lizzie, which was what family and close friends
sometimes used.

It occurred to her that they'd first met in this room,
in this house: she'd been eighteen and on the verge
of graduating from high school and he'd been a
twenty-five-year-old on the verge of graduating from
Harvard Business School.

One look into his bottomless light-gray eyes and
she'd been flying through the heavens, borne on the

wings of teenaged lust and longing. Quentin, on the other hand, had seemed immune, then and in later meetings, treating her with polite reserve.

He moved into the room, heading for the huge mahogany desk sitting in front of picture windows at the side of the room. "The best what?" he repeated, addressing his question to Allison.

"Quent, Liz needs to have a baby. Fast."

"Allison!" Liz gaped at her friend. She'd forgotten how Ally could be like a dog with a bone when it came to one of her "ideas."

Quentin halted and frowned. *"What?"*

"The doctor told her today that she has endometriosis. The longer she waits to have a baby, the more likely it is that she'll never have one."

Quentin eyes pinned Liz to her seat. "Is that true?"

"Yes," she heard herself say in a strangled voice.

Allison ignored the quelling look that Liz threw her way. "She needs a sperm donor."

Quentin's eyes narrowed. "My hunch is that the reason you're telling me this is you're looking for a sperm donor?"

Allison rushed on, seemingly oblivious to Quentin's ominous tone. "Quentin, you've been getting a lot of pressure from Mom and Dad to settle down and produce a grandchild. And, you've said yourself you have no intention of getting close to the altar again. The way I see it, this is a solution to both your problems."

"Allison, please!" Liz could feel her face turning redder. She was mortified that her friend would suggest that Quentin, of all men, father her baby. And from the looks of it, Quentin looked equally horrified at the prospect.

"You don't know what you're asking," Quentin said to his sister. The expression on his face spoke volumes, including, clearly, that he thought that his sister had lost her mind.

Liz let out the breath she'd been holding. She'd been insane to think for an instant that Quentin would jump at the chance to father her baby.

"I don't know what I'm asking?" Allison asked, surveying her brother's charcoal-gray suit and blue tie with clear disapproval. "It's Saturday, Quent—Memorial Day Weekend—and where have you been? Working as usual, it seems. And if I know you, you came in to the study looking to do more work. I'd say I know exactly what I'm saying."

Liz stifled her rising panic. "Quentin, I want you to know I didn't ask Allison to bring this up." She shook her head when Allison opened her mouth. "In fact, I told Allison that I'd be making an appointment with a sperm bank."

Quentin swung to face her. "Have you both gone crazy?" He stuffed his hands in his front pants pockets. "I thought Allison's idea was a little off the wall, but—" he growled "—now I realize she's the more rational of the two of you."

Liz felt heat rise into her face. "A sperm bank is a perfectly reasonable idea. Many women choose it."

"You're not many women," he retorted.

Since when had he become an expert on what type of woman she was or wasn't? As far as she could tell, he'd acted for years as if he didn't know she was a woman!

She rose from her seat. She'd always found Quentin a bit intimidating, but her temper was getting the best of her. "I'll be the judge of that. After all, it's my problem!"

"What have you got to say to that, huh, Quent?" Allison piped in.

Quentin threw his sister a warning look before zeroing in on Liz again. "Why don't you just get married? What's wrong with that? Just find yourself a nice guy, and go make babies."

Liz sighed with exasperation. "Just like that, hmm?" She snapped her fingers. "And where do you suggest I find Mr. Nice?"

"Pick a guy," he bit out. "We're all easy prey."

"Oh, really? Well, perhaps that's the way you see it, but the view from over here is a lot different." She started counting on her fingers. "Let's see. It'll take a few months to meet someone suitable. Then a couple of weeks for dating."

She took a breath. "Third or fourth date, I let him have his wicked way with me."

A muscle started to tick in Quentin's jaw.

"That's about right, wouldn't you say, Quentin? After all, you guys are always complaining about how long the chase is."

"Elizabeth—" he said warningly.

She knew she was baiting him in a way she'd never dared do. It was reckless, but she didn't care. Maybe it was her medical diagnosis, but something had been unleashed within her. "Okay, now we're at about one month into the relationship. No time to waste, so I propose to him.''

She was on the verge of losing control, but all the despair she'd tried to keep carefully hidden was welling to the surface. ''Let's say I'm lucky and the first man I propose to actually likes me enough to marry me. Well, we'll need a few weeks to plan a quickie ceremony in front of a judge.''

''Elizabeth—''

She held up her hand to stop him. ''At this point, four or five months at least have gone by. But he's so taken with me, he agrees to have a baby right away! Well, that's going to take a few months of trying.''

She paused for breath. She was starting to sound hysterical. ''So, I'd say, six to seven months if everything goes *perfectly*.''

Quentin's fists bunched and he looked tight-lipped and grim. She knew she'd pushed him, but she was beyond caring.

''Listen, Elizabeth, I don't know what Allison told you, but I'm not in the market for fatherhood. I'm sure my mother would love to become a grandmother, but she has three others who can help her there.''

Allison coughed, and they both turned to glare at her. ''Oh, come on, Quentin. You know Mom and Dad have been pressuring you for ages. And it's not just because they want a grandkid. They're worried about you. Ever since—''

Quentin cut her off. ''My private life is healthy enough, thanks for asking.''

*Healthy?* Well, that was one way to put it. Quentin's private life had been prime grist for the Boston papers for years. If past record was anything to judge by, he preferred statuesque and glamorous career women with sleek pageboy do's, and model-perfect size-eight figures.

She, on the other hand, was so far from being his "type" that it was laughable. Her unruly chestnut hair fell below her shoulders, the thick, curling locks tending to frizziness. And her figure…well, she'd made repeated vows to shed those stubborn five pounds, but they seemed to have found a permanent home on her hips.

"Look, this isn't just a matter of a sperm donation. I'd want to be a father, not just some stud, to my kid," Quentin continued.

"Exactly." Liz shot a quelling look at Allison. "That's why a sperm bank is such a good idea."

"No!" Quentin and Allison shot out.

"Look, there's got to be another solution," Quentin said in exasperation.

"Another solution for what?" Matthew Whittaker, the middle Whittaker brother, asked as he sauntered into the room from the doorway leading to the front hall.

His question was greeted with stony silence.

Matthew's gaze swung from a frowning Quentin to an excited Allison, before coming to rest on Liz. He held up his hands. "Hey, don't everybody answer at once!"

"Lizzie's got a problem," Allison finally volunteered.

Matthew cocked a brow. "Oh, really? What sort of problem?"

"Yeah, what sort of problem?" Noah Whittaker, the third Whittaker brother, appeared in the doorway behind Matthew. He winked at Liz. "Hey, beautiful."

"Lizzie needs to get pregnant fast or she may never have a baby."

"Allison," Liz said sternly.

"Damn." Matthew shot Liz a sympathetic look. "What're the options?"

Allison gave her brother a level look. "Funny you should ask—"

"Well, if everyone in this family must know," Liz jumped in before Allison had a chance to speak, "I was asking for advice about a reputable sperm bank."

"Gonna go it alone, are you?"

Liz sighed in relief. Finally, an ally. "Yes."

"Congratulations."

"You'll make a great mama," Noah added.

Liz saw Allison throw her brothers a reproachful look.

Matthew looked perplexed. "What?"

"You just picked showcase number wrong," Allison quipped.

"At least we agree on that," Quentin said in a sardonic tone.

"Matt," Allison continued, "wouldn't it be great if Liz could use someone she knew instead? Say a family friend?"

Liz saw Matthew hold his sister's gaze for an instant, then lounge back against the door frame and fold his arms as if he were contemplating Allison's question. "Well, I'd say that would be a good idea."

"Right," Quentin said tightly. "I have an even better one. How about using a husband?"

"Liz doesn't have one, Quent," Noah pointed out with his typical lazy humor.

"Well, then she can damn well get one pronto."

"Tsk. Tsk." Matthew shook his head. "Don't you know women have choices these days, Neanderthal man?"

Liz could see that didn't go over well with Quentin. He gave Matthew a hard stare. "If you've got something to say, Matt," he said coolly, "I suggest you just spit it out."

Matthew regarded all the occupants of the room before saying, "Well, I'd say it's obvious. Lizzie needs a male friend she can trust, and I'm hands-down the best guy she knows." He winked encouragingly at Liz. "Honey, as long as I don't have to fill the whole turkey baster, I'm your man."

Quentin recovered with amazing speed. It was something he was known for. He'd been a star hockey player at prep school, and then at Harvard, due in no small measure to his quick reflexes. They also made him a formidable adversary in the boardroom. Always look prepared. Never be seen with your guard down.

He turned on his brother. "Are you nuts?"

"Not at all. Are you?" Matt returned mildly.

Noah swallowed a chuckle.

"You can't father Elizabeth's baby."

"Last time I checked all the parts were in working order."

Quentin's fists tightened. He couldn't remember the

last time he'd wanted to rearrange Matt's face. "You know what I mean, dammit."

"I don't know why you're annoyed, Quent," Allison piped up from the sofa. "After all, you're not interested."

Elizabeth saved him from a scathing reply. "I appreciate that you're all trying to—" she hesitated as her gaze met his "—help." She turned to Matt. "Thanks for the offer. But I've always thought of you as a brother. Let's not complicate the great friendship we have, okay?"

Matt smiled, admiration lighting his eyes. "Okay, but if you ever reconsider—"

"Thanks," Elizabeth said softly, then cleared her throat.

Quentin frowned. Why didn't she ever give him those soft looks? They'd known each other—what?— more than ten years.

Maybe it was him. He'd been annoyed as all hell the first time he'd caught himself having a physical reaction to her. She'd been just barely eighteen at the time and still a kid in his book.

Of course, that was ages ago. Before Vanessa had taught him no woman could be trusted.

His lips twisted at the thought of his ex-fiancée. At least she'd taught him a valuable lesson. To single women, he was just a big ol' pot of gold with a wedding band sitting on top of it.

Unfortunately, his brother hadn't wised up yet. Poor guy probably thought it was his charm that had all those women in hot pursuit.

"Matt, Elizabeth won't be changing her mind." He ignored Allison's frown. "She'll find a solution."

"I'm sure I will," said Elizabeth a bit stiffly. "Excuse me, will you?" she asked of no one in particular as she left the room.

"How could you!"

His gaze shifted from the doorway to his irate sister. "How could I what?"

"You could have shown a little sympathy."

He pushed aside the twinge of guilt. "I did." Then added, "But I'd say asking for a sperm donation is more than just a little sympathy." He then turned to Matt, who was still looking at him obliquely. "We need to discuss Project Topaz as soon as this shindig is over."

Matt gave a sardonic salute. "Yes, sir."

"Wisea—"

"Thanks," Matt interrupted, a laughing glimmer in his eye, then jerked his thumb at their brother, "but you have me confused with Noah."

Noah raised his hands and took a step back. "Keep me out of this one."

Quentin arched a brow—in his opinion, Matt could give Noah a run for the money in the smart aleck department. Wisely, though, he decided not to offer up his opinion. Instead, he strode from the room before Allison could start the argument she was obviously itching to have with him.

By tacit agreement, he and Elizabeth avoided each other for the rest of the afternoon. She bore up well under the stress, he noted. She oohed and aahed over Mrs. Cassidy's knitting. She pushed their neighbor's five-year-old daughter Millicent on the tree swing, and relieved Noah in a game of catch with Millicent's twin brother Tommy. She blushed as praise was heaped on her apple pies.

She ignored him.

He didn't know why the idea of Elizabeth using a sperm bank should bother him so much, he thought while he watched her chat with Noah. Maybe it was because the damn things made him—and all men, for that matter—seem so unnecessary.

But it wasn't as if he had a personal stake in the matter—other than the fact that she'd been a friend of the family for years, and everyone seemed to adore her.

The sane thing for him to do was to avoid getting involved. The best way to do that, of course, was to avoid her. Unfortunately, he'd already committed to working with her on the planned site for the day care.

# Two

Quentin always thought his office was immense, but it was starting to feel about as large as a broom closet. Elizabeth had arrived to discuss the details of the day-care construction.

His gaze swept over her again. A conservative blue suit clung to generous curves. Black pumps showed off a shapely set of legs, which, at the moment, were crossed at the ankle and tucked to the side of her as she sat, pad in hand and jotting notes.

He suspected wryly that she'd be disappointed to discover the overall effect was of a poorly disguised siren.

He was glad she'd shown up and appeared ready to put Saturday behind them. In fact, they seemed to be back to their old polite but distant relationship.

And that's just the way he wanted it, he told himself.

"May I tour the site for the day care now?" she asked politely.

"Of course." He rose from his seat and could have sworn she looked alarmed.

"Are you going to show me around?"

He arched a brow. "Yes, is that a problem?"

"No, no," she said quickly, depositing her writing pad and pen in her leather purse. "It's just I know you're busy, and I'm sure there's someone else you could ask."

"Well, the day care is an important project, isn't it?"

She darted him a quick look, but before he could interpret it, she'd started out of his office.

A mixture of curiosity and the need to fill the silence made him ask, "How long have you been on your own? You used to be with one of those big design firms in Boston."

"It's been two or three years."

"Things didn't go well in Boston?"

He silently berated himself for the obvious negative assumption behind that question, but she didn't seem to take offense. "No, not that," she replied. "I just always knew I wanted to run my own business."

Now that, he could identify with. He'd spent the past several years expanding Whittaker Enterprises and multiplying his net worth. He guessed he shouldn't be surprised that, while he'd been occupied with his career and hadn't seen much of Elizabeth, she'd been moving forward with her life as well.

The elevator opened on the ground floor and he led the way to the northeastern-most section of the building.

The room was large, sunlight streaming through the floor-length windows that faced the lawn at the back of the building.

"This is wonderful!" Elizabeth exclaimed, her voice proclaiming that she was pleasantly surprised.

Quentin supposed that comment reflected badly on the level of interest he'd shown in the construction of the day-care center, but aloud he just said, "I'm glad you approve." He leaned against the door frame, crossed his arms and watched her as she moved gracefully across the room.

Two paint-stained ladders sat on a tarpaulin at one end of the room. The painters he'd hired had been covering and smoothing over holes in the walls. The room had housed dozens of cubicles, and computer wire and cable had run everywhere.

She glanced back over her shoulder at him, her face alight with possibilities. "My initial idea is to create a door where one of the floor-length windows is now and create a small outdoor play area. Enclosed by a fence, of course." She paused, then added, "Do you think that'll work?"

"I don't think it'll be a problem to give up a little lawn."

"And it gives the kids a direct exit in case of fire. So that will be another advantage."

"Good."

"We'll need to set up cubbyholes against one wall."

"Cubbyholes?"

"Yes," she said patiently, "so parents can store things for their kids. You know, like diapers, bibs."

"Right." She could have told him they needed space suits and a couple of rocket ships, and he'd have taken her word for it.

He wracked his brain. Preschool was a vague and hazy memory. Had they had—what did she call them—cubbyholes?

"—kitchen?" Elizabeth finished.

"What?" He pushed away from the door frame.

"I said," she repeated, "you know we'll have to put in a small kitchen or pantry. And bathrooms."

He nodded. "I guess we can't have little Johnny standing in line behind some business executive to use the facilities."

A smile touched her lips. "Exactly. You know more than you think you do."

He brought his finger to his lips. "Shh. Don't let the word get out."

She laughed then, her eyes merry, the light glinting off her hair as she turned back to him.

She was gorgeous. Time—when he hadn't been paying attention—had been good to her. How hadn't he noticed? And *why* hadn't he?

It seemed impossible that Elizabeth was facing infertility. She exuded the Earth Mother. Her lush curves bordered on voluptuous.

The white blouse she wore under her open suit jacket clearly defined her large breasts and just hinted at the lacy bra that supported them. While her straight blue skirt ended, appropriately enough, just above her knees, it also allowed a display of shapely legs, show-cased in clear hose and high-heeled black pumps.

His only disagreement was with her hairstyle: she had hidden her thick, long auburn hair in a business-like knot. He wondered what she would say if he asked her to take it down, then felt his blood heat at the thought.

She started walking back to where he was standing. "Is that all?" he asked, keeping his voice even, al-though his body felt tight and all too aware of her.

"Oh, yes-s!"

Her exclamation ended in a gasp as she stumbled. Instinctively, he reached out to break her fall, catching her against him. He almost groaned aloud as her soft breasts collided with his chest.

Her face jerked up to his, her eyes wide, her face flushing with embarrassment. "I think my heel caught on something!"

He forced himself to look past her to the floor. "Definitely a crack. Must have been caused by the repair work. Looks like the floor will need a touch-up job." His eyes came back to hers.

She gave a weak laugh. "I'll have to be more care-ful. Otherwise *I'll* need a touch-up job."

She must have read something in his gaze, because suddenly all attempts at amusement faded and a stiff-ness came back to her shoulders. Her eyes widened—a fascinating shade of green flecked with bits of gold, one slightly more than the other—and her lips parted, drawing his gaze down to them.

They looked full, wet and infinitely kissable. In-stinctively, he bent his head.

A look of alarm came into her eyes and she quickly braced her hands on his chest. "I-I'll have some design plans in the next week or so," she said a bit breathlessly.

Abruptly, his head cleared and he dropped his arms so she could take a step back. "Right."

She straightened her handbag on her shoulder. "I—I'll call as soon as I have some plans done."

She couldn't escape fast enough after that.

Quentin swore silently as he watched her go.

Damn, damn. What had gotten into him? He'd been about to kiss her in the middle of his office building, in the middle of the day! Was he nuts? He hadn't seen her in a long while before the barbecue at his parents' place, but he'd known her for ages.

Of course, this was the first time she'd literally fallen into his arms! Still, he wasn't the seize-the-opportunity type. And Elizabeth had enough problems without having him add a lecherous employer to the mix.

He was still trying to come up with a good rationalization for what had almost happened when he sat down to his lunch meeting with Noah later that day.

"How did it go this morning?" Noah asked, reaching for the breadbasket lying on the conference room table.

"Everything's under control," he said nonchalantly without looking up from a memo the research and development department had sent him. "But I don't have time for it, so count on the day care being your project from now on."

"A real babe, isn't she?"

He didn't even pretend to not understand his brother's meaning. He gave Noah a hard look. "Elizabeth is soon going to be under contract. She's a business associate. And a friend of the family."

"Oh, come on, Quentin. You can't tell me you didn't notice those big green eyes and that sexy wa—"

"And I told you to keep your hands—and everything else for that matter—off of her." Not that he'd set a sterling example that morning, he reminded himself ruefully.

"Okay, you're the boss," Noah responded with an easygoing grin.

"Yeah, try to remember that for more than fifteen seconds."

After his encounter with Elizabeth that morning he'd decided the safest course was to get someone else to handle the day-care center. Not hiring Elizabeth wasn't an option—Allison would give him hell.

The obvious solution was to make sure Noah got this whole project finished ASAP. Much as his brother was making him regret that decision at the moment.

"You know," Noah was saying, "I was just kidding. Allison explained Liz's medical condition to me. Rotten luck."

Quentin knew his brother well enough not to dance around what was obviously on Noah's mind. "Of course Allison's harebrained solution would be creating a new subsidiary, Whittaker Spermbanks R Us."

Noah grinned. "Yeah." He poured himself some

water from the pitcher on the conference table. "Started off with the wrong brother though."

"Not you, too."

Noah shrugged. "You've walked the straight and narrow too long. Your idea of radical is wearing a tie with broad stripes."

"This from the guy who pestered me for weeks for an introduction to Samantha the Sweater Girl?" Quentin asked, pretending to look incredulous.

"That was high school, maybe college. You missed the turn to the uber-cool thirties a long time ago and just kept on going."

Quentin shook his head. "Great, I'm square, or whatever they're calling uncool these days."

"Look, all I'm saying is that donating sperm is not such an off-the-wall idea. We've known Liz for a long time. Helping her out—"

"For cripes' sake, you talk about it like it's offering to fix her leaky faucet!"

"Okay, it's different. And I'm not saying you should do it."

"Matt—"

Noah shook his head. "He hasn't said anything. Ally told me what he said at the barbecue, but he hasn't mentioned it since then that I know of."

Quentin felt himself releasing the tension he hadn't even known he had.

Noah gave him a quizzical look. "You should have gone for her when she was younger and visiting Allison all the time. I could have sworn she had a crush on you."

Ignoring Quentin's dark look, Noah continued irrepressibly, "God knows why though. There were far better specimens of male prowess hanging around the house. Women, go figure!"

"She was a kid!"

Noah eyed him speculatively. "Well, she's not anymore."

"Well, she's a business associate now."

"Yeah, but that won't last forever. And you do seem to be acting uncharacteristically passionate on the topic of Lizzie and insemination, Quent."

"You're barking up the wrong tree. I just don't want her to do something she'll regret. Call me old-fashioned, but I believe in making babies the traditional way."

If Noah was skeptical about that, he kept his thoughts to himself. "Allison's idea isn't so crazy, Quent. Mom has been after you for little Whittakers."

Quentin rolled his eyes. "Don't go there."

"All right, bro," Noah wiggled his eyebrows, "but you wouldn't have to donate sperm if you can convince Liz to do it the old-fashioned way."

Quentin nearly lost control of the cup of coffee he'd picked up. He set it down on its saucer with a clatter. "Oh, great, seduce my kid sister's best friend. I see that working out."

"All I'm saying is, why don't you take a closer look. This might be a long-term investment that's worth making."

Try as she might to concentrate on work, Liz found her mind replaying the events in Quentin's office.

Quentin had been about to kiss her. That much was

clear. And she, like a ninny, had reacted like a deer caught in headlights: wide-eyed and then bolting as fast as she could.

She sighed. It figured that, after all these years, when finally presented with the opportunity she used to fantasize about, she'd completely blow it. She just wasn't the cool and collected sophisticated type.

What remained a mystery was just why Quentin had almost kissed her. Was he curious about whether he'd be able to feel any attraction for her at all?

What would have happened if he had kissed her? She shivered, the thought sending prickles of awareness through her.

Then she stopped abruptly. What was she doing? She'd gotten over her infatuation with Quentin years ago, she told herself firmly. And nothing good could come of unlocking that door again, particularly now that she was working for him.

She should just be glad Quentin had decided to let her have the day-care project despite her totally unprofessional behavior at the barbecue on Saturday. The Whittaker account was really going to help her cash flow situation.

Her eyes strayed for the umpteenth time to the brochures at the corner of her wide Victorian desk, parked near the bay windows at the front of the first story of her house. The brochures had started to arrive from various fertility clinics in Boston.

Her initial panic and shock at the doctor's news had faded, but her bravado was also deserting her. How was she ever going to manage all by herself? A fledgling business, a new baby and a mortgage on a rambling old Victorian house that still needed lots of work.

Even the artificial insemination was going to cost money. She'd received a small inheritance from her Aunt Kathleen that she'd intended to squirrel away as a nest egg. As painful as the thought was, however, she'd probably need to use that money for the sperm bank.

Her thoughts were interrupted by the ringing phone. "Hello?"

"Hey beautiful, your prince has come."

Her lips quirked. "Well hello, prince. How are you?"

"Trying to keep five balls in the air as one of Quentin's loyal deputies." Noah gave a dramatic groan. "Got to reschedule our meeting for Monday. Looks like I'm going to have to be out of town again. If you're available, how about a working dinner tomorrow night instead?"

She couldn't resist teasing, "That would be Friday night. I'd have thought you'd have plans."

"I do, sweetness, I do," Noah drawled in a parody of seductiveness. "And that's to take a beautiful green-eyed brunette to the best French restaurant in Boston."

Since she'd always had an easy relationship with Noah, she wondered if one of his motives wasn't to cheer her up. Their meeting wasn't urgent and could wait until he returned to town. Aloud she said, "Who told you I love French food?"

"I have my sources. I'll pick you up at nine."

"Wonderful."

The next night Noah had her smiling the minute she opened her door, as he staggered back a step, clutching his chest. "Be still my heart. My dreams have been answered."

"Oh, you clown." She was wearing a short-sleeved blue cocktail dress, one she'd had at the back of her closet. Still, it was nice to be appreciated.

The maitre d' at Beauchamp greeted Noah like an old friend. Obviously, the upscale restaurant was a favorite. They were seated at a candlelit table near windows affording a view of the Charles River.

"I'm on strict orders to discuss costs and contracts tonight, but," Noah said, winking, "let's leave the boring stuff for after dinner."

"That's the way of it, is it?" Liz returned playfully. "Wine-and-dine me, and soften me up."

"You wound me."

"Au contraire. I just don't want you to waste your time."

Noah grinned. "Dinner with a lovely woman is never a waste of time."

She laughed despite herself until she looked into Quentin's eyes across the restaurant and froze. Allison had entered at his side.

Noah turned to follow her gaze and rose as his brother and sister approached, Allison leading the way, followed by the maitre d' and a forbidding-looking Quentin.

"What a pleasant surprise!" Allison exclaimed. Turning to Quentin, she prompted, "Isn't it?"

"Quite," he said dryly.

"Do you mind if we join you?"

"Not at all," Liz murmured. Quentin looked impressive and forbidding in a dark gray suit. She experienced the little flutter in her stomach and quivery tension that she'd always felt whenever he was near.

"Actually, I do mind," Noah spoke up and Liz threw him a startled look. "You're going to cramp my style. So beat it, kid."

Allison laughed and swatted her brother.

Liz felt her face heat. She stole a look at Quentin, who looked even more grim if that were possible. She cringed at the thought of how this must appear, and what he was thinking.

They were moved to a table for four by the deft and efficient maitre d'. Quentin sat himself across from Elizabeth, who seemed to be reading the menu with the fascination one would accord to the climactic scene of a potboiler bestseller. Uncomfortable, was she?

His eyes traveled to her lips, which were looking *only* slightly pouty this evening, he decided. The dress she was wearing revealed a creamy expanse which sloped gently down before leveling off at two perfect globes that strained against the confining fabric of her bodice.

His hands itched to release them from their confinement and weigh them in his palms, stroking his thumbs over nipples that would harden and darken at his touch....

Realizing the direction his mind was heading, he mentally braked.

Was he crazy?

He had no business speculating about her breasts—even if his overactive imagination insisted on supplying details to his fevered mind.

The woman had to be stopped.

He had to hand it to her though, she was a fast worker. Last week she was propositioning him, this week she was already moving on to fairer game. Maybe she preferred Noah—they'd always had a flirtatious banter. Maybe that's really why she'd found it so easy to say no to Matt. She already knew who her target was, and the sperm bank idea was a smokescreen.

Or maybe he'd convinced her with his arguments about finding a husband. The problem was he hadn't meant his brother.

He looked at Noah. His brother was susceptible to beautiful women. He'd be a sucker for one in need. He might not mind obliging....

"Don't you think so, Quentin?"

"What?"

Allison's eyes met his, amusement in their depths, as if she had been reading his mind. "I was saying we should order some of the vintage Chardonnay. That's a weakness you share with Liz." She turned to Liz. "Any suggestions?"

"I'm sure Quentin will make an excellent choice." Liz glanced at Quentin then and he gave the barest dip of his head in acknowledgment of what she'd said.

She wondered if Noah and Allison were as aware of the tension in the air as she was. As she passed the butter, her fingers accidentally brushed Quentin's, and she snatched her hand back, as if singed, nearly upsetting the small plate in the process. Quentin merely raised a brow questioningly.

During dinner, Noah asked her a few softball questions about the details of the day care. Once or twice her eyes connected with Quentin's, but he declined to add anything.

"How is Patrick liking the fly-fishing down in Florida?" Allison asked, changing the subject.

Liz smiled at the thought of her father. "He's loving it. I think Florida is doing wonders for his health in retirement."

Noah grinned. "Not to mention the merry widows."

Allison laughed and Quentin managed to quirk a lip.

Liz feigned annoyance. Her father had been alone way too long. If he did meet someone down in Florida, she'd be more than happy for him. "Not Dad. He'd rather kiss a fish."

"I bet he had a great time fishing over Memorial Day weekend," Allison said.

Liz smiled. "You're probably right. He had a big trip planned, but I haven't spoken to him in a week."

She felt three pairs of interested eyes and could have bitten off her tongue. She'd all but admitted she hadn't had the courage to tell her father about her medical diagnosis.

The rest of dinner passed in a haze for her. They discussed the latest headline cases that Allison's office was working on. And Noah and Quentin got into a discussion of the best way to promote their newest software.

When they emerged from the restaurant after dinner, Allison piped up, "Why don't I ride with Noah? His condo is mere blocks from mine in Downtown." Turning to Quentin, she asked, "You're heading back to Carlyle, aren't you, Quent? You wouldn't mind dropping Liz off, would you?"

Liz expected to hear an immediate protest from Quentin, but was nonplussed to hear him concur. "Sure, no problem." He gave her a sardonic smile.

Oh, my. She was in trouble. Noah bent over to give her a peck on the cheek. "I'll catch up with you when I get back." To his brother, he added, "Can I trust you with sweetness here?"

Quentin gave his brother a bland look. Something significant and unidentifiable passed between them and led Noah to chuckle before turning away.

All too soon she was alone with Quentin, whose sure and capable hand at the small of her back led her to a black BMW the valet had just driven up. "Buckle up" was all he said before they pulled away.

They drove in silence. Ominous silence, in Liz's opinion. Like the calm before the storm.

The inside of the car seemed too intimate a space, with the dark pressing around them and Quentin in the driver's seat.

She glanced at him from the corner of her eye. He was looking straight ahead, apparently focused on the road. She wondered what he was thinking.

Of course tonight must have looked exactly like what it wasn't, but she had a logical explanation. Unfortunately, she didn't have the courage to give it without prompting, and he wasn't giving her any encouragement at all.

As they neared Carlyle, she gave him directions to her house. He parked in her drive, helped her out and escorted her to the door.

She fumbled in her clutch for the key and managed to get the door open. "W-well, thank you for din—"

"Invite me in."

It wasn't a request, it was a demand. She nodded and he followed her in, closing the door with a click of the lock.

# Three

————

**H**er house, Quentin took mental note, suited Elizabeth. The first floor, or the front part of it at least, obviously functioned as her office. Victorian furniture with brocade cushions adorned the room. Vintage teddy bears perched on a small corner table and a quilt covered a mahogany rocking chair in another corner.

Feminine. Maternal. Elizabeth.

She started walking toward the back of the house. "Coffee or tea?"

No, just you, please.

Now where the hell had that unbidden thought come from? He was here to make sure she understood that Noah was off-limits to her. And the sooner she understood that, the better. "What the heck were you doing with my brother?"

She halted and turned to face him. "We were having a business meeting." Her tone was cool, but her heightened color betrayed her.

He moved toward her. "Stay away from Noah. He's not potential daddy material."

She belatedly recognized the threat that his approach posed and feinted to the left. He was faster, however, and moved to the right and caught her, his hands gripping her upper arms. "Last week you were setting your sights on me."

"A mere momentary lapse, I assure you," she bit back, trying to shrug him off.

"Am I passé already?" She smelled of lavender and felt even more fragile in his arms than that purple flower. Her movements were also bringing the tips of her breasts in contact with his chest. How horrified would she be to discover that her actions were having the unintended effect of arousing him? "What if I said I was too hasty in turning you down?"

"Too late."

"Don't you think you're being a little rash? I'm a much better catch than Noah."

"Y-you…" she spluttered.

"But I like to do a little research before closing a deal." One kiss. That's all, he promised himself, bending his head.

"You promised Noah you could be trusted," she gasped, her heart beginning to race.

"Did I?" he murmured. "I don't think one little kiss is a problem, do you?"

She tried to focus on why one little kiss would be a problem, but she drew a blank, her mind turning to mush.

His lips as they settled on hers felt firm, smooth, soft. They teased her lips, rubbing and coaxing, focused on eliciting a response.

She breathed in his warm male scent, felt the gentle scrape against her skin of the evening shadow covering his jaw. His lips moved over hers, urging her to respond, not with a command but with a sweet persuasion that had a languorous warmth seeping through her bones.

How many times had she fantasized about kissing Quentin? About him kissing her? About how he would be? About how they would be together?

And with that thought, she realized that she didn't want to think. She wanted to feel, to savor the moment.

She broke his loose hold on her arms and twined them around his neck and, this time, when he asked for a response, she parted her lips and allowed him to penetrate her mouth, kissing him back with all the pent-up ardor that she thought she'd locked away forever years ago.

She sensed him hesitate for a moment, as if her response caught him by surprise, and then he made a satisfied sound deep in his throat and brought her closer, so that she was flush against him, his arms molding her to him.

Her nipples puckered against his chest, where she could feel the steady beat of his heart. But instead of flushing with embarrassment, as she normally would have, she moaned and sought to get even closer to his warmth, his strength.

His mouth was hot on hers, their kissing taking on a greater urgency.

The reality of him was so much more overwhelming than anything she'd been able to imagine.

She was so lost in their kiss that the ringing sound didn't immediately penetrate to her clouded mind. Only when he groaned and set her away from him did she realize that the phone was ringing.

Her gaze connected with his and she read the blatant desire there. He looked ready to devour her whole!

Flustered, she looked around for her purse. Spotting it on a chair where she'd deposited it on the way in, she pulled out her cell phone.

"H-h-hello?" She cursed her wobbly voice.

"Hey, Lizzie." Allison's voice sounded from her compact folding phone. "I think I forgot my sweater in the back seat of Quentin's car. Can you check for me?"

Darn. How was she supposed to answer? "Er, hold on." She placed her hand over the receiver, and turned to Quentin, who had his hands shoved in his pockets, and looked like a lurking tiger. "Ally thinks she left her sweater in the back seat."

Quentin muttered something unintelligible. "I'll call her from my phone." He headed for the door, turning back when he reached it. "We'll finish this conversation later."

Taking her hand from the phone, she said, "Ally—"

"Can't find it? I could've sworn—"

"Quentin says he'll call you from his phone. He's looking now."

"What?" Allison's voice rose suspiciously. "Where are you guys?"

"Home. I mean, I am. Quentin just left."

There was a definite pause. "I'll catch up with you soon," Allison said quickly. "I think that's Quentin calling now."

Liz slumped into a chair. There was no way she and Quentin were going to finish what they started.

Thank God Allison had called!

After all these years of treating her like a pesky kid, it would figure the darn man would start paying attention just when she was facing her greatest crisis.

Not that he was truly interested in her, she reminded herself. He just didn't want her near his brothers. Because he didn't approve of sperm donations. And beyond that, he might have been curious enough to kiss her.

But that was all.

She bit her lip. She needed the Whittaker account, particularly now, when she might have to take a maternity leave and temporarily shut down Precious Bundles. On the other hand, dealing with Quentin was like handling a lighted stick of dynamite.

Her only choice was to avoid him as much as possible. On Tuesday she had an appointment at a reputable fertility clinic and sperm bank in Boston. The sooner she got pregnant, the sooner Quentin would know how ridiculous it was for him to think she'd seduce Matt or Noah.

\* \* \*

Quentin swirled the Merlot in his glass for the umpteenth time and tried to focus on the conversation happening around him.

Usually he was a natural at these charitable social
events. BookSmart was holding its annual black-tie
dinner—a fund-raiser for adult literacy—in the ballroom of the Stoneridge Hotel.

He should have been in his element. His eyes
drifted again to the woman across the room. He
guessed he shouldn't be surprised that the enterprising
Elizabeth Donovan was donating her time to raising
literacy. And it figured she'd be shimmering in a sat-
iny green strapless dress and matching heels.

As if the woman didn't glow already. Long waves
of chestnut locks caught the light as she bent her head
toward Eric Lazarus.

Quentin's eyes narrowed. Lazarus. They were about
the same age and height but he liked to think the
similarities ended there. If anyone deserved the reputation of a womanizing playboy, it was the young
stockbroker.

The guy had had the federal Securities and
Exchange Commission sniffing around him a while
back. Too bad, they hadn't come up with anything.
Rumors of Lazarus skating at the edge of the law had
swirled for years.

The lights blinked in the lobby where the crowd
stood, and the doors to the large ballroom opened,
revealing dozens of elaborately set tables.

Lazarus was helping Elizabeth into her seat when
Quentin arrived at the table he'd also been designated
to be seated at for dinner.

"Lazarus," he acknowledged with the barest dip of his head.

The man's eyes flickered before a practiced smile reached his lips. "Quentin. Good to see you."

Lazarus would pant and roll over for a chance to invest for Whittaker Enterprises. Quentin wondered which would hold the greater appeal this evening: Elizabeth's beauty or his money. His lips twisted as he settled into the chair on Elizabeth's left, Lazarus having already staked a claim to the one on the right.

Up close, he noticed that her strapless gown showcased a large expanse of flawless skin, her collarbone defining her bare neck, which was framed by thick, curling auburn locks that cascaded down her back. He wondered what it would feel like to bury his hands in that thick mass....

"I didn't realize you'd be here," he said, breaking the silence.

She turned to face him, her face impassive. "There are lots of empty seats left." She nodded to the other side of the table, and the room in general.

He refused to take the bait and ignored her uncharacteristic rudeness. "This one suits me fine."

He figured it was at least understandable that she'd be miffed at him. Not that he'd been unreasonable at her house on Friday night. When it came to potential fortune hunters, particularly those with strong reasons to need a financial bailout, he'd learned the hard way you couldn't be too careful.

Of course, he'd interrogated Noah, who'd set the record straight about his "date" with Elizabeth. His brother had exhibited no small amount of amusement at the questioning, but he'd found out enough to know the dinner had come about at Noah's instigation.

On the other hand, despite Noah's persistence, he'd refused to disclose what had happened after he'd driven off with Elizabeth. It was bad enough that Allison knew he'd been in Elizabeth's house that night. There was no point in letting them know just how badly he'd acted.

Which meant, he supposed, that he owed Elizabeth an apology. Given that she was pointedly turned away from him and conversing with Lazarus, he knew it wasn't going to be an easy one to give.

Elizabeth smoothed her napkin in her lap. "No, I haven't been to that new Italian restaurant. I've heard it's wonderful."

"Well, I'll just have to see about changing that," Lazarus said smoothly.

Quentin muttered a curse. If he had to jump in, there was no time like the present. "Business doing well these days, I gather."

Lazarus homed in, a gleam in his eyes. "Never better. I've got a little pre-IPO pharmaceutical company that's just a gem. I can't sell enough shares, if you know what I mean."

"Oh, I do," Quentin murmured. Sounded just like the type of super-speculative investment that a slick salesman like Lazarus would be peddling. "Sounds interesting."

Next to him Elizabeth nibbled at her dinner salad and focused her gaze on the animated stockbroker.

"Interesting isn't the word." Eric warmed to his subject. "We're talking major medical breakthrough for Alzheimer's here. As soon as the FDA approves this drug, this baby is going to go through the roof."

Eric reached inside his tux jacket and pulled out a business card. "You know, Quent, you and I go way back. That's why I want you to get on the ground floor of the next best thing."

Quentin took the proffered card. Of course he'd have to burn it the second he got near a match.

By the time the main course of filet mignon was served, he knew Elizabeth had to make conversation with him. The head of the charity was sitting at their table, and it wouldn't do for the newest board member—as he'd recently discovered—to be rude to one of the major benefactors. Whittaker Enterprises had given well into the seven figures to BookSmart.

From the corner of his eye, he watched her first grimace and then paste a determined smile on her face before turning to him. "I didn't realize you were so involved with BookSmart."

He forced himself to hide his amusement. "Philanthropy is a hobby of mine."

"Charity is a labor of mine."

"Touché," he murmured. "And how do you devote your time, Elizabeth?"

"I tutor people in English." She sipped from her water, and then returned sweetly, "And how do you spend your money, Quentin?"

The corners of his lips lifted. "I write a check with lots of zeroes so these people," he nodded to those around him, "can fund libraries and buy books."

If she was surprised at his forthrightness, she didn't show it.

"I hope our newest board member is doing her best to persuade you that we do great work here, Quentin," boomed Lloyd Manning, the President of BookSmart, from the other side of the table. "We want you to know how much we appreciate and need your help."

"Elizabeth's made it clear I play a key role." He shot a look at her embarrassed face. "She'll be a charming and effective fund-raiser."

Lazarus took that opportunity to ask Elizabeth to dance. As he watched them move together across the floor, he acknowledged that she'd grown up from the shy teenager she'd been when they'd met.

His mind went back to that day and the demure eighteen-year-old with a shy and winsome smile. At least that's how she'd looked when he'd come trotting down the stairs of his parents' house and had stopped in the foyer where his mother was greeting what he took to be another of Allison's friends.

Allison made the introductions. "Liz, my brother Quentin. Back oh-so-briefly from making waves at Harvard Business School to torture his kid sister over Christmas break. He had nothing better to do."

He looked for the first time into green eyes set in a perfect oval face. Five-seven or -eight, he guessed, with legs that went on forever beneath beige khaki shorts. She'd already been curvy then.

For sure, she would be breaking hearts among the high school boys.

That thought brought him up short. High school. This was his little sister's playmate. Annoyed with himself, he asked, "Liz? Is that short for something?"

"My name is Elizabeth. Liz is a nickname that my father gave me, and it's stuck," she answered.

It figured she'd have a seductive voice, too. He nodded toward his sister. "Are you Allison's play date for the afternoon?"

"I think they've made it out of the playroom, Quentin," Ava Whittaker interjected reprovingly.

"Nice to meet you, Elizabeth," he'd said before heading out the door. Because the more formal-sounding name had seemed to provide a little protection from her attractions, he'd grasped it like a life-saver.

He watched Elizabeth dance with Eric. Years had passed since their first meeting, but she was still wrong for him in every way. She wanted a father for her baby, and he wanted a no-strings affair. She'd been hired by Whittaker Enterprises, and he was the boss with a don't-mix-business-with-pleasure policy. She was his baby sister's best friend, while he said goodbye to lovers and moved on.

Eric's hand moved lower, dangerously close to covering Elizabeth's rear as they danced. Quentin unbent his six-foot-two frame from his chair and strode toward the couple. He could rationalize later.

Quentin clamped a hand on the shorter man's shoulder. "Sorry to cut in, Lazarus." He steered Elizabeth away before Eric could recover. Looking down into her lovely face, he knew that sorry was the last emotion he was feeling. "You can thank me later."

"Thank you?" Color rose to her face. "Why in the world would I thank you?"

"He was pawing you."

"So you saved me so I could be pawed by you instead?"

He laughed. "You seemed to enjoy it last time."

She pursed her lips. "You flatter yourself."

He sobered a little. "Lazarus is a snake. I wouldn't take what he was offering even if he was giving it away."

"Oh, I don't know. A freebie is hard to resist."

His brows drew together. "Don't tell me Lazarus is a potential candidate."

Green eyes met gray. "Okay, I won't."

Her cool attitude irked him, but he refused to be drawn in. "Listen, Elizabeth, I don't know what your current plans are, but Lazarus is bad news."

She sighed. "Eric's an acquaintance. I've made an appointment with a fertility clinic that also has a sperm bank."

He should have been mollified by that, but the mention of a sperm bank set his teeth on edge again. He needed to steer the conversation to safer territory and figured now was as good a time to apologize as any.

He cleared his throat. "I apologize for what I said on Friday night. I jumped to conclusions. Noah set me straight." He was *not* going to apologize for the kiss. It wouldn't have rung true anyway.

She'd been looking over his shoulder, but now her eyes jumped back to his. She looked startled, but then seemed to collect herself. "I—"

He cocked his head to the side. "—accept my apology?" he finished for her, when she seemed at a loss.

She nodded and a small smile played at her lips. "Yes."

He felt relief wash over him, and wondered why her response had been so important to him. "Let's start over."

She nodded, seeming to accept his offer to wipe the slate clean. "I'm sorry I was so rude earlier."

He shrugged. "No offense taken. You had a right to be ticked off at me. Anyway, money is my contribution. I'm too busy to volunteer much time. The fact that you're able to is impressive."

They lapsed into silence then, swaying to some Big Band tune as he guided her across the floor. She felt good in his arms, just relaxed enough to be guided by the subtle pressure of his hand on her lower back.

He enjoyed holding her like this, her body lightly brushing his as they danced. She was close enough that he could breathe in the soft, flowery scent of her. Close enough that he could, if he wanted to, brush his lips across her temple and the curling wisps of hair lying there.

"You dance well," he commented.

"You're surprised."

He thought for a second. "No," he said slowly. "It was just an observation. I knew you'd dance well. It fits with the overall package."

"Oh? And what might that be?"

His lips itched. "You're magnolias and cream with afternoon tea on the verandah." His voice dipped. "Lace and white roses. Incense with delicate spice. A Victorian lady in a rock 'n' roll age."

Liz told herself she should be careful. Quentin's

voice was having a lulling effect on her. "What tipped you off?" she asked lightly, teasingly. "The Victorian rocking chair? Or the brocade furniture?"

He smiled. "That helped. Your house says a lot about you."

"You have me at a disadvantage there."

His eyes gleamed. "That's easy enough to correct."

Liz realized he was teasing her, but still her heart jumped. "No, thank you. I have other plans."

She felt hot all over, not really sure how to handle this "new" Quentin, and said breathlessly, "The music's stopped."

Quentin reluctantly let Elizabeth go and followed her back to their table, where Lazarus had zeroed in on Lloyd Manning. When Elizabeth excused herself, Quentin settled back into his seat.

There were things about Elizabeth that touched him deeply. Always had. On some level, he mused, he'd known and refused to acknowledge it. That's why he'd avoided her all those years ago.

Now she'd grown, matured, and if anything her siren song was even more seductive for him. Her movements, her voice, her lovely face, they all called to him. But even more than that, he recognized her cool reserve for what it was. A front, nothing more. Just like his own professional demeanor.

If their similarities held true, underneath the cool reserve, Elizabeth was a passionate, giving woman. He'd already seen glimpses of it in her uncharacteristic sarcasm at the barbecue, and, God knew, in her response to his kiss.

His experience with women told him that he and Elizabeth were a combustible mix. One that he'd enjoy exploring and testing—if there weren't strings attached.

She'd turned down his offer, as he knew she would. He'd been joking—or told himself he was—when he'd invited her to his house. He'd wanted to establish some of the lightheartedness she had in his relationships with his brothers. But he'd also been disappointed.

Because the bottom line was he wanted her. That's why he'd reacted so strongly to her news about the sperm bank. That's why he'd growled at his brothers.

He took a sip of his wine. Yep. That was it. But just how far was he willing to go to have her? Disturbingly, right now he didn't have an answer.

# Four

Returning from the fertility clinic on Tuesday afternoon, Liz pulled up in front of her home on a tree-shaded block in the northeastern section of Carlyle and immediately noticed the black BMW.

Could it be—?

Before she could finish the thought, Quentin came striding around the corner of the house.

Her mind ran through the day-care project. She still had two days to get a more detailed plan to Noah.

Her eyes connected with Quentin's, and he stopped for a split second before striding toward her car. She accepted the hand he offered to assist her out of the car, steeling herself for the usual tingle along her nerve endings.

"I've been waiting for you."

"I see." She concentrated on keeping her voice even. "What can I do for you?"

She'd started for her front door and he'd fallen into step beside her.

"Allison asked me to stop off and pick up the decorations that you have for her cocktail party tomorrow night."

She'd designed small candle and dried flower arrangements for Allison's party tomorrow night for her coworkers. Her usual florist had dropped them off that morning. "I thought Allison was swinging by tonight for those."

He followed her into the house and loosened his tie. "Nope. She had an emergency court appearance this morning. She'll be burning the midnight oil tonight."

"Poor Ally."

"She called me a little while ago, knew I was in Carlyle and heading to Boston later. Asked if I could bring her the stuff."

He loomed in her office, making the space seem small. She tried not to think about the last time he was here. "I'll get the boxes for you," she said quickly.

"So where were you this morning?" he asked while she went through the boxes lying beside her desk.

She felt her face heat and cursed her Irish complexion for the umpteenth time. Too many years of Girl Scout training got the best of her however, and she heard herself say, "If you must know, since everybody seems to know my business these days, I had my appointment at the fertility clinic.''

"How'd it go?''

"Fine.''

"Think it's going to work for you?''

"Yes.'' She straightened and smiled brightly at him. He had his hands shoved in his trouser pockets and an inscrutable look on his face.

She nodded at the five white boxes she'd separated from the rest and stacked beside her desk. "Well, here they are. I'll help you put them in the car.''

"Right.'' He strode toward her, and she took a step back, feeling the edge of her desk at her backside. Any hope that he hadn't noticed her involuntary reaction was quickly dashed however.

Stopping so close she had to tilt her head back, he asked, "What's the matter, Elizabeth? Have you been thinking about what I said the other night?''

"About donating money to BookSmart?'' She shook her head. "I don't collect the money personally. Contact the public relations office.''

He smiled. "No, the other night when we got back here to your house. You know what I mean.''

"No, I don't have any idea what you mean.''

"Liar.''

"Are we going to engage in name-calling again?'' The air between them was heavy and charged.

He bent towards her. "Why don't we kiss and make up instead?''

His arms came around her and his lips captured her mouth. She knew she should stop him, but somehow that thought quickly became lost in the swirl of feelings rising inside her.

He rubbed gently, softly, against her mouth, then caught her bottom lip between his lips and sucked. Whereas his first kiss had been all deliberate seduction, this was a more subtle assailing of her senses, a more quiet awakening of her needs.

She felt hot and aroused, sensations curling through her, urging her to cast off inhibitions. When his tongue entered the warmth of her mouth, she met him, stroke for stroke, fueling the heat.

She'd never experienced these heady feelings with another man. And certainly not with a mere kiss!

She felt a pulsating warmth that coursed through her with a slow, deep, mounting intensity. His hands roamed up and down her back, caressing and molding, and she moaned, her hand coming up to the back of his head, urging him closer.

Abruptly, Quentin pulled back. Breathing deeply, he shot her a penetrating look. ''Don't tell me you haven't thought about that. We were on fire there.''

She looked at him uncomprehendingly for a moment, before she came back to reality with a thump. She shivered in automatic reaction to the loss of contact with the warmth radiating from him, and wrapped her arms around herself.

Well, of course she'd thought about it! For years she'd thought about it. Imagined it. But it was useless. Right now they could offer each other nothing—except the truce they'd called the other night at the charity event. Just as it had always been, their timing was off.

Her chin came up. "What if I did think about it? It doesn't mean anything. We want different things, Quentin."

His jaw tightened. "Not really."

"What?"

He raked his hand through his hair. "I've been thinking about what you said. You know, about needing to find someone fast and that being impractical, so artificial insemination being the next best thing."

"Yes?"

He slanted her a look she couldn't read. "You said four dates, one month, was the minimum amount of time before you'd consider marriage." He paused. "I can deal with that time frame."

Her breath caught. "What do you mean?"

"Surprised that you don't have a lock on shock value, Elizabeth?"

"No, it's just...I mean..." She gave up on trying to form a complete sentence and wrung out a strangled "I don't understand."

"Let's just say I think Allison may have hit on something."

"That may be a first. You and Allison agreeing."

He gave her a surprised look, nodded and then grinned for a second. "Just don't ever let her know. She'll never let me live it down." He sobered and his gray eyes connected with hers. "I want kids. You want kids. We're both prepared to do some unorthodox things to get them."

"But..."

He took a few steps away from her and then turned

back to face her. His charcoal suit, obviously custom-made, did nothing to disguise the male power beneath.

"I know what I said the day of the barbecue. What I meant was I had no intention of producing grandkids just so my mother can play grandma. I haven't been looking to become a father." His gaze raked her. "But I'm a businessman and I'd be a fool to turn down a good deal."

A good deal. That's what she'd been reduced to. A little flame died inside of her. She hated herself when she heard herself say, "What sort of deal?"

He shoved his hands in his trouser pockets again. "Have you thought about how you're going to manage with this baby? You've got a new business that needs all of your attention. That's a full-time job in itself."

"I'll manage. This is the twenty-first century."

"Precious Bundles has been in business, what? Two or three years? My guess is that your balance sheet is still not looking rosy—" he paused "—or rather, that it is."

Liz flushed. "That's about to change." Precious Bundles was still operating in the red. Most new businesses, she knew, failed within two years, unable to make the critical leap to ongoing profitability.

"What? With the construction of the day-care center at Whittaker Enterprises? Then what? The baby'll be due right around the time you'll need to land another big project. And who is going to hire a business whose sole creative power will be about to give birth, and will be out of commission for a while?"

Much as she hated to admit it, even to herself, he

was right. She was so close to making the business a success, and paying off her small business loan. She just needed a little more time—time she didn't have now.

Quentin was regarding her intently, seemingly able to read the flitting emotions on her face.

He walked over to her rose print couch and sat on the back of it, his legs stretched out ahead of him. "Look, I don't want to depress or scare you."

She gave him a skeptical look. "Really?" she said with a sarcasm that would have made Allison proud.

"Yes, Elizabeth," he said quietly.

Why did he have to call her Elizabeth in that quiet way just when she was building defenses against him?

"We're two adults who are attracted to each other. You want a baby." He blew out a breath. "And I eventually want kids, too."

"Eventually?"

"Yeah, it's not something that's been on my mind a whole lot. I haven't been planning on getting married. At least, not the traditional love-and-happily-ever-after variety."

"Because of Vanessa?"

His eyes narrowed at the mention of his ex-fiancée. "You could say that."

Quentin's engagement had been called off seven years ago just before the wedding. Quentin had remained closemouthed about it all. Not even Allison knew what really had happened.

Liz had been guiltily relieved when the wedding was cancelled. Although she'd met Vanessa at several social occasions, she hadn't really known her.

She forced herself to point out the obvious. "You don't have to be married to have kids."

"In my book you do."

He was making her insides clench nervously. "What are you saying, Quentin?"

"I'm saying, let's give it a shot. Four dates. At the end of it, we decide whether we like each other enough to get married and have a kid together. Right away."

The suggestion was shocking. Clinical, business-like, devoid of emotion, but shocking nonetheless. "Don't you want to marry someone you love?" she blurted.

"I told you, I'm done with that. Elizabeth, I'm a very wealthy man. I don't have any illusions about how the vast majority of women see me."

She looked at him sitting on the back of her sofa, six-foot-two of prime manhood with looks that would make even her oldest clients swoon. Was the man crazy? "And how do you think the vast majority of women see you?"

"As a checkbook," he said curtly, then went on, "what I'm offering here is not the love-and-romance stuff, but something better."

"Better?" she echoed.

He pushed away from the sofa and started pacing. "Yes, better. You get peace of mind and the baby you want. Financial support to make sure the baby is always well cared for and to make sure Precious Bun-dles stays afloat until you can focus on it again. As for me, my parents will get the grandchild they've been pining for, and which they think it's my duty to produce. Legitimately.''

"What happens after the baby is born?''

"That'll be up to us. We could stay married.'' He shrugged. ''Our arrangement wouldn't be so different from those of lots of other couples at the country club.''

His cynicism ran deep, Liz realized and wondered yet again what had happened with Vanessa. ''Would that be part of the bargain? I'd entertain your clients and executives and dine with the other trophy wives at the country club?''

"No.'' He shook his head in disgust. ''I don't even belong to the Carlyle Country Club. I hate that crowd. But the type of marriage we're thinking about wouldn't be unusual for them.'' He gave her a sardonic look. ''And no, I wouldn't expect you to entertain for me. Just don't expect me to like changing diapers.''

She gave him a droll look. ''What about the fact that I'm still employed by you? Won't people start talking?''

He shrugged. ''The day-care center will be finished soon. And as long as we're discreet, it's nobody's business. I'll admit I have a rule of not mixing business and pleasure—'' he paused ''—but rules are meant to be broken in the right circumstances.''

As crazy as it sounded, the whole scheme was starting to make sense to her. ''And we'd—'' she searched for a delicate word even as her face heated ''—have a baby the old-fashioned way?''

He gave her a sudden lopsided grin. "Or die trying."

She nearly choked. Just how much trying was he planning on doing?

His eyes caught hers, and he asked provocatively, "What's the matter? Do you want me to demonstrate again that we're a combustible mix?"

Automatically she raised her hand to ward him off. "No!" She collected herself and said less stridently, "No, another demonstration isn't necessary."

His eyes gleamed. "I'll pick you up Saturday at eight."

"Where are we going?"

"Leave that to me. I'll call."

And with that he was out the door with the boxes and Liz felt the oxygen in the room again.

By late Saturday afternoon, Liz was running out of things to do to quell her nerves and keep her mind off her looming date with Quentin that night.

When the phone rang, it was a welcome relief. "Hello."

"Hello, sweet pea."

Her face bloomed into a wide smile. "Dad!"

"So! You haven't forgotten the voice of your dear ol' Dad? Thanks be for small favors!" Her father answered in his booming Irish brogue.

"Now, Dad, I just spoke with you."

"And when might that have been, I ask you? Why, a week from Wednesday last, if it isn't a day!"

Wisely deciding to change the topic of conversation, she inquired, "How's the fishing down in the Florida Keys? Still good?"

"Aye, couldn't be better. Caught a bass as big as anything you've ever seen." Her father sighed contentedly. They chatted about his trip a bit and then he asked, as she knew he would, "How's my little girl?"

"Working hard."

"Not too hard I hope. How's about looking to give your dear ol' Dad some pitter-patter of little feet to chase after?"

"Dad!" Her mind drifted to Quentin and she yanked it back.

"Don't 'Dad' me. I worry about you."

Liz sighed in exasperation. Quentin wasn't the only one getting parental pressure. Unfortunately, her father didn't know what a painful topic babies had become. She tried for a lighthearted approach. "If and when I decide to give you 'little feet' to chase, I'll let you know."

"Ah, you're a hard one, lass."

*"Goodbye, Dad."*

Liz sighed. Ever since her mother had died when she was eight, it had been just her and her Dad. He'd loved her mother Siobhan and had been devastated by her loss. He had had to be both mother and father to her.

And there was the source of the one complaint she could have about her father. He was too overprotective, treating her still as "his little girl."

Naturally, he had tried to convince her to move to Florida when he had retired down there. But she had already started her professional career in Carlyle and had been reluctant to move. She'd also been quietly chagrined that he'd sold his construction business at retirement without even asking if she'd been interested in taking over the company. Sometimes she wondered if things would have been different if her father had had a son.

Elizabeth's house was quiet when Quentin pulled up on Saturday night. He'd dressed in black trousers and an open-collar gray shirt with matching blazer. Reservations at Casa Vittoria in nearby Prescott, the new restaurant Lazarus had mentioned the other night. He derived grim satisfaction from knowing he'd outmaneuvered the stockbroker.

He'd been pumping Allison for information about Elizabeth when his sister had suggested in exasperation that he find out for himself by picking up some party decorations that Elizabeth had done for her.

The more he thought it over, the more he realized that Allison might have had a brilliant idea after all. Frankly, life had started to bore him. The endless procession of Vanessas, each of whom saw him as Mr. Moneybags.

His mouth twisted in memory. Seven years had passed since he'd been a lovesick twenty-nine-year-old entrepreneur on the fast track. So taken in by a pair of wide blue eyes that he'd been deaf to the discreet warnings that family and friends had tried to send his way until it was almost too late.

There'd been an engagement party of course. An expensive dinner affair that Vanessa had insisted on holding at the poshest country club in town. ''But

darling, everyone makes their engagement announce-
ment at the Bridgewater,'' she had pouted when he'd
voiced some doubts about the necessity of the whole
thing.

Towards the end of the evening, he'd ducked outside to one of the many terraces to nurse a drink of
scotch. Vanessa and her close friend Mara had
stopped to chat in the hall inside.

''Vanessa dear, I'm so happy for you!'' Mara had
said in her cultured but squeaky voice.

''Thank you, darling.''

''The Whittakers, my goodness!'' Mara had fanned
herself with her napkin. It was clear she'd had more
than a couple of drinks. ''Why, many are predicting
Quentin will be worth over half a billion by the time
he's thirty-five! How ever will you manage to spend
all that money?''

Vanessa's tinkling laugh had sounded then. ''Oh,
Mar, how can you ask that? Have you ever known
me to live below my budget?''

Mara had pretended to consider that question.
''Well, *no.*''

They had both laughed like two conspirators sharing an inside joke.

''And just in the nick of time, too,'' Mara had gone
on. ''You're so lucky to have reeled in Quentin just
as the last money in your trust fund disappeared.''

''Not luck darling,'' Vanessa had said, winking.
''Just playing my cards right.''

''Is poor André brokenhearted?'' Mara asked with
a giggle.

''But that's the best part, darling. Quentin is a

workaholic *bore,* but that leaves me plenty of time to continue to recreate with darling André.''

His face had drained of color. The portals to his heart had slammed shut at that instant, and he'd padlocked them for good measure.

The ironic thing was, now even work had ceased to matter as much. And wouldn't Vanessa get a kick out of knowing that?

Sure he still worked damn hard. He just wasn't as driven as he used to be. That fire-in-the-belly, ruthless, single-minded determination to succeed had started to fail him. If ambition were a fire, he'd gone from being a coal-burning furnace to a gas fireplace: all the blaze, but no real heat.

At thirty-six, he realized he wasn't getting any younger. A few months back, one of his chief competitors had up and died at the office from a heart attack. The guy had burned out at the ripe old age of thirty-nine. Since then, he'd caught himself being pensive at odd moments.

So maybe it was time for new challenges. And Elizabeth was that, he thought. She'd demanded a lot, more than he was willing to give. But he'd hit on a plan that would suit them both. A brief period of dating and if all went well, a marriage built on practical considerations.

He'd have her, and the kid he'd almost given up on after Vanessa had cured him of that love-and-marriage garbage. Elizabeth would get her baby and peace of mind.

It was perfect. Brilliant. And he was going to make

damn sure he wrung every second of satisfaction out of it.

Starting right now.

The minute she opened her door, he saw red. Deep, rich wine red. On a dress that hugged her curves in a warm embrace. With a halter-top that exposed her creamy shoulders and graceful neck.

He cleared his throat. "Here." He handed the flowers to her. "For you."

"Th-thank you." She bent her head to sniff the fragrance of roses mixed with lilies.

He followed her into the house. "You're welcome."

"Lilies are my favorite."

"They match the color of your dress." Great line, Whittaker.

"Make yourself comfortable. I'm just going to put these in water before we go," she called over her shoulder.

He'd watched her sashay to the kitchen. If anything, the back view of her in that slinky dress was even more arresting than the front one.

She came back with the flowers arranged in a glass vase that she set on an end table. "Would you like something to drink?"

"No. Let's get going." He sounded more brusque than he'd intended, and she looked taken aback.

The truth was he didn't trust himself in the house with her. Her toenails, he'd noticed, were painted a deep red and peeked out from strappy, high-heeled sandals. The effect was unbelievably erotic.

After she'd gathered a black sequined purse that he

swore could hold no more than a set of keys, and a fringed shawl, he followed her out the door.

Casa Vittoria was a quarter of an hour away on a road he knew well, so they reached the restaurant in what seemed like record time.

They were seated at one of the best tables in the house and Quentin made a mental note to thank his secretary Celine for seeing to it. Immediately a waiter appeared to offer them menus and the wine list, while another filled their water glasses. The first waiter recited the specials of the day in accented English.

Quentin looked up in surprise from the wine list when he heard Elizabeth ask a few questions in seemingly flawless Italian. When the waiters had departed, he asked, "Where did you learn Italian?"

A smile touched Elizabeth's lips. "College. I minored in Romance languages. After my mother died, Dad and I vacationed abroad a lot. I guess it was his way of trying to compensate for my mother being gone. By the time I got to college, I loved French, Italian, Spanish." She'd been turning the stem of her water glass as she spoke and now groped to steady it as it almost tipped over.

Ah, Quentin thought with satisfaction, at least she felt a little of the tension he'd been feeling since he'd first laid eyes on her this evening. Emboldened, he reached out and removed her hand from the glass to trace slow circles on the back of her palm. "Careful," he murmured.

The soothing motion of his index finger on her hand sent a languid warmth through Liz, even as she felt caught and trapped by Quentin's intense gaze. His eyes had turned a deep slate-gray and she wondered idly if she'd ever seen that shade before.

Only the arrival of the waiter to inquire about their wine selection saved her. She quickly withdrew her hand and tried to steady her breath, thankful that Quentin had been distracted.

"I thought I'd order a Chardonnay," Quentin said with a telltale twinkle in his eye, and Liz realized he was teasing her about her partiality to the wine.

"Mmm, that would be wonderful." She took a sip from her water glass as Quentin ordered an old vintage. Seeking a neutral topic, she said, "Allison says you've been very busy lately."

She hadn't said a word to Allison about her "dates" with Quentin. It would get Ally's hopes up prematurely.

Quentin sighed and leaned back in his chair. "Yup. I'll be traveling most of next week."

"You don't seem happy."

He gave her a tired grin and for the first time she noticed he looked a little peaked. "Living out of a suitcase is never fun."

"But you have to do a lot of it."

He nodded. "More than I'd like. The computer world is a mile a minute. And a lot of our business partners are based in California. What about you?"

"Most of my clients are based in Massachusetts. There's a fair amount of travel, but it's local."

The waiter returned to take their order and when he departed again, Quentin asked, "Have you thought about how you're going to handle that when you've got a kid?"

The directness of the question threw her, and she looked at him startled. He shrugged. "It's come up at work. We have part-time, flex-time and work-at-home arrangements for our employees."

"That's admirable."

His lips quirked in that telltale way she associated with his sardonic half smiles. "The truth is that if I hadn't thought it was good company policy, my mother and Allison would have had my hide."

She tried not to laugh. "I'm sure your employees thank you."

He arched a brow. "Actually the biggest dividend was getting on the cover of Parent-Child magazine over the caption 'Trailblazing Cutey-Pie CEO Is Big Hit with Both Wall Street and Sesame Street Crowds.'"

She laughed delightedly and he joined in.

"Worse things have been said about you," she offered.

He nodded. "Yeah, that's true. Expect the worst and get pleasantly surprised."

"Oh, is that your motto?"

"One of many," he parried.

"And the others would be—?"

"Today's dreams are built on yesterday's reality."

She cocked her head. "Hmm, never heard that one before."

He motioned away with the glass in his hand. "Made it up."

"Ah," she sighed, "a closet philosopher."

He raised an eyebrow. "The Victorian lady meets Machiavelli?"

"Is that who you are? The realist philosopher who thinks the worst of human nature?"

He leaned forward. "Every entrepreneur is partly Machiavellian. Comes with the territory. Don't let anyone tell you differently."

"Meaning I'm just masquerading as a demure and proper Victorian lady?" she asked, guessing that Precious Bundles qualified her as an entrepreneur.

His gaze perused her and then he grinned unexpectedly. "No," he rejoined, "that's just one side of you. Another is the bottom-line businesswoman. Otherwise, when I offered you my deal, you'd have slapped my face and cut me dead."

He was dissecting her unerringly. "Perhaps I've just decided to play along."

He shook his head. "Nope. You play for keeps."

A shiver went down her back. Playing for keeps was exactly what they were doing, and the stakes were never greater.

# Five

When they arrived back at her place, she invited him in for tea, and, after a brief pause, he made a sound that seemed like a yes and followed her in.

Inviting him in was the most nonchalant move. She was desperate to have him think she was able to handle their dates with cool aplomb.

She thought of his past dates. How had she compared? She'd done her best tonight to fit his type. She looked down at her dress as she poured water into her floral tea kettle. The dress had been an impulse buy yesterday. Afterwards, she'd stopped in at Louise's Spa and Salon for a matching naughty red pedicure.

Yes, she looked a little vampy. And it had required every inch of nerve she possessed to try to pull off that look tonight.

She'd wanted to attract Quentin of course. But another part of her had also wanted to shock him—make him see her as a bold, daring woman who was comfortable with her sex appeal. She'd been pleased when she'd opened her front door to him tonight and seen his eyes widen.

She set the kettle to boil and started arranging some of her homemade pecan chocolate chip cookies on a platter. She always baked when she was nervous, as she had been before their date this afternoon.

Now if only she could pull off the rest of the evening without making a cake of herself. She looked down at the platter. Too bad she hadn't thought of baking a cake instead to guard against that urge.

When she came back into the living room with her laden tea tray, Quentin was fingering the lace tablecloth covering one of her end tables. "Antique?"

"My mother's," she said as she set down her tray on the coffee table. "It's a McConnell family heirloom. Just like most of the antiques I own."

He sat down on the hump-backed sofa beside her. Liz was grateful the sofa was firm and straight-backed, in the Victorian style. Anything else would have made sitting within a hair's breadth of Quentin unbelievably intimate.

"Tell me about your mother."

"There's not much to tell." She sighed. "She died when I was eight. She had an inoperable tumor."

"I'm sorry," he said deeply.

The look in his eyes was one she'd never received before: sympathy mixed with respect. "I have some memories of her. Sometimes when I see gardenias I'll remember her flower arrangements, or when I smell split pea soup, I'll remember her cooking dinner.''

"How old was she when she died?"

"Only twenty-nine."

"The same age you are now."

He'd obviously drawn conclusions about the connection between her mother's death and her own need and desire to have a child as soon as possible. "Yes, but I'm going to win my battle."

He nodded. "Growing up without a mother can't have been any fun, but you succeeded anyway."

She cleared her throat and looked away quickly. Compliments were not something she accepted comfortably. "Th-thank you," she managed.

She was, Quentin thought, a delicate flower with a strong stem. Her straight back and thrust-back shoulders would have impressed the finest etiquette teacher. The clean lines of her oval face were full of delicacy and strength at the same time.

When she'd invited him in, he'd hesitated. The two of them alone in her house would present a temptation that was hard to resist.

But he'd figured she'd just misinterpret him if he declined her polite offer of tea, just as she'd obviously misinterpreted his abruptness when he'd picked her up at the beginning of the evening.

When the truth was the woman was bringing him to a slow boil. All that fire covered by a cool veneer was enough to drive any guy crazy. Especially one with a newly discovered taste for a chestnut-haired interior designer with a honeyed voice and a peaches-and-cream complexion.

A heaviness settled beneath his belt. Damn. He cleared his throat. "Tea looks good. Going to pour us some?"

"Oh, yes." She was embarrassed to discover she'd forgotten to serve the tea.

Great, Liz. She chalked up another strike against the cool and sophisticated image she'd wanted to project tonight.

She brushed his knee as she poured tea, and tried to ignore the quiver that went through her. She determinedly picked up a cookie. If she was going to be sinful, better that it be with food.

She went still as Quentin picked up a strand of her hair, eyed it idly, and then proceeded to twist the end of it around his finger.

"Cookie?" she offered.

He chuckled. "Sure." He paused. "I seem to have my hands full—" he nodded at the hand that still had hold of her long hair "—so why don't you feed it to me?"

"I, umm...."

"Here, I'll give you a hand," he said, then bent forward to take a healthy bite out of the cookie still in her paralyzed hand.

Oh, my. She felt nervous and languorous at once. How was that possible?

He bent forward for another bite and took the remainder of the cookie out of her hand.

"I hope you like pecan chocolate chip," she said inanely.

He swallowed. "I do. I hope you do, too."

"Oh, they're my favorite."

He nodded thoughtfully. "That's good. Very good."

"Why?"

"Because I'm going to kiss you and it will be a whole lot more enjoyable if you like the taste of pecan chocolate chip."

"Oh!"

And that was the last she got to say before he let go of her strand of hair, turned her toward him, and took possession of her mouth.

The first time he'd kissed her had been a masterful seduction. The second had been gentle persuasion.

This was sheer bliss. He seemed familiar now with how to touch her. Seamlessly, they moved together from gentle nibble to the deep, soul-searching quest of mouth on mouth.

Liz shuddered. Her hands moved through his hair, bringing him closer, seeking more of the pleasure he gave, the sexual knowledge he possessed, the comforting familiarity he harbored.

Quentin's brain clouded. He'd intended to give her only a light, teasing kiss tonight, to ease their way into a more intimate relationship. He'd underestimated their need, their desperate desire for each other. The one or two kisses they'd shared up till now had done nothing to dampen that.

The sweet lavender scent of her seduced his senses. Her skin was so soft and smooth, he had an uncontrollable desire to touch it, expose more of it.

His hand propped up her chin to deepen the kiss, then touched the side of her face before wandering to stroke her arm, her midriff, the line of her hip.

He urged her backward until she felt the arm of the sofa under her head. Her mind clouded as his lips left hers to run a line of moist kisses across her soft cheek, nibble at her earlobe, and then trail down her neck.

She shifted restlessly.

"Shh," he coaxed. "Easy. Nice and slow and easy."

He sounded more in control than he felt. His hand shook slightly as he unclasped the back of her halter-top dress.

Lord, but she had a powerful effect on him. He wondered now how he'd been able to keep his hands off her for so long. Frankly, if he'd had any idea of how easily she'd be able to get under his skin, he didn't think he'd have had a hope in hell of staying away from her.

Her eyes flew open when he eased the dress and its built-in support from her, exposing her breasts.

He looked into her incredible golden green eyes. "Beautiful." His voice sounded hoarse with desire. Reverently, he reached out and caressed her breasts.

Liz closed her eyes again. The feel of his hands—strong and slightly callused against her nipples—was incredible.

When his mouth replaced his hands, she jerked at the unexpectedness of it and then shuddered with pleasure. She tangled her fingers in his hair, holding him to her. The steady, rhythmic pressure of his mouth sent waves of electric sensation through her.

Just when she thought she couldn't bear it any longer, however, he moved to the other breast, replacing his hand at the first, where the nipple was now wet and distended from his attention.

Again he brought her to the brink. When she thought she couldn't bear his attention any longer, his lips finally came back to hers. Mouths met, hands roamed, bodies shifted. She wanted him so much. Why wait?

And with that thought, she pushed until his jacket came off his shoulders and down his arms and then set to work on the buttons of his shirt.

He lifted his mouth from hers and gave a husky chuckle, looking down at his suit jacket bunched around his wrists.

''Please...'' She felt as if she'd only been dreaming of the possibilities up till now and he'd awakened her to real emotion, real sensation, real desire.

Leaning back, he finished off his jacket and shirt with a couple of quick, efficient movements. He was lean with strong shoulders and fine ebony hair on his chest. She trailed her fingertips over him and his eyes closed, seeming to savor the moment. Then he raised her hands above her head and leaned back down toward her.

Cold replaced by hot. Lips replacing air. His hands and mouth played over her body.

She felt the evidence of his need for her and instinctively reached down between their bodies to touch him.

Groaning, he pressed himself into her palm for a moment and then tore his mouth from hers and sat back.

His eyes were hot, his breathing a bit labored.

Her first instinct was to sit up and press her mouth to his and move his hands back to her breasts, where they could continue to do wonderful, wicked things to her. But then she read the look in his eyes. The look that said, stop me now or I won't be able to stop at all.

As he reached out to pull up her dress to cover her, realization dawned about how far they'd gone—and how fast.

She felt herself redden, embarrassed because he'd been the one to stop. She moved to get her dress back on without revealing her breasts again, refusing to look at Quentin—which was ridiculous really, since he was sitting on the sofa, right next to her, half dressed.

"Do you need a hand?" he asked, his voice deep and still a little thick from the effects of their love-making.

"I believe your hands are what, ahh, caused this predicament to begin with," she muttered half to herself, still refusing to meet his gaze.

He held his offending hands out in front of him. "Okay, guys, now cut it out." He knitted his brows. "How many times do I have to tell you not to wander off?"

She looked up, having hooked the halter-top back into place. "What? Oh." She planted her hands on her hips and decided to play along. Anything, anything to diffuse the situation. "The old the-hands-did-it routine."

He gave her a serious look. "Hanky and Panky apologize."

She tried desperately and unsuccessfully to school her face.

"I'd suggest handcuffs, but they'd just consider that kinky."

A chuckle escaped her.

He gave her an amused look, then picked his shirt up off the floor and stood to shrug into it before grabbing his jacket. Bending, he gave her a firm peck on the lips and filched another cookie. "Thanks for a wonderful evening." He shoved his hands in his pockets and cocked his head toward the door. "Come lock me out, so I'll know you're safe."

The flowers arrived the next day. A dozen, long-stemmed white roses with reddish tips interspersed with lilacs. The note said simply, "Thanks for a special night. Will call soon. Quentin."

The next week passed quickly for Liz.

On Tuesday, she was at Whittaker headquarters to speak with potential contractors for the day care and was almost limp with relief, knowing Quentin was traveling and not in the building.

The brochures from the fertility clinic continued to lie in her desk drawer where she had placed them. They beckoned to her, telling her she was crazy to have even entertained Quentin's scheme.

Allison called on Wednesday. If Quentin had divulged any information, she couldn't tell from Allison's responses.

"We won!" Allison exclaimed over the phone.

"Won?" Had Quentin said something to Ally about their date?

"The trial. The jury came back with a verdict in our favor. Those crooks are going to pay through the nose!"

Liz sighed in relief. The last thing she needed was for Allison to jump the gun and start broadcasting to all-and-sundry that she and Quentin were becoming parents—together. "That's great!"

Allison seemed to come back to earth. "So how have things been in Quentinland?"

"You mean the epicenter of the Whittaker quest to take over the computer world?"

Allison snickered. "You know, Liz, that's why I always thought you and Quentin would be a fantastic match. You'd be the magical antidote to his outsized ego."

"Oh, I don't know. Quentin isn't that bad."

"What? We're talking about the guy who honked and hollered when he picked me up from the prom. The guy who suggested my first boyfriend was one French fry short of a full pack."

Liz chuckled. "You mean, Lenny? Wasn't he the one who accidentally bonded his fingers together with glue?"

"That's beside the point," Allison retorted. "The point is that my brother has been the bane of my existence. And he's so obtuse, he doesn't even know it."

She couldn't resist asking, "Why would you want to pass him off to me then?"

Allison sighed. "I know. It's diabolical of me. But it's the only way I could think of to get rid of him finally." Then added in exasperation, "Now it seems not even you want him."

Liz rolled her eyes. Heaven help her, they were skating on thin ice. She was able to end the call, however, before Allison got any further down that dangerous road.

Allison's call broke some of the restless tension of the week, but by Thursday morning Liz was eyeing the telephone like it could sprout legs and walk away.

With some determination, however, she finally got enough concentration to focus on Mrs. Elfinger's playroom. So when the phone rang, she answered with a distracted, "Hello, Precious Bundles."

"Which one am I talking to?"

She fumbled with the receiver and nearly dropped it. "Which—uh, what?"

"Which precious bundle am I talking to?" Quentin repeated. "You know, that's a very suggestive line. Another guy might not understand."

She colored. "I haven't had any problems so far." Trust Quentin to be able to fluster her even when he was hundreds of miles away.

His chuckle sounded over the line.

"How—how have you been?" she asked, striving for polite conversation.

"Working my butt off. We should have this deal sewn up soon though. We're acquiring a Web site to provide phone-book-type information through Whittaker's portal site."

"Sounds like you're making inroads into the market." Allison had told her when the portal site had been launched three years ago.

"Yeah," Quentin was saying, "but we're just one step ahead of our competitors. We need to stay on it."

She eyed the arrangement of flowers at the edge of the desk. "Thank you for the flowers. The roses and lilacs are still blooming beautifully."

"You're welcome." Was it her imagination, or did his voice drop a notch? "Sorry I didn't call earlier, but we've been on almost a 24/7 schedule here. I've been thinking about you."

She tried for a lighthearted laugh. "Thinking about how many other ways I might try to insult you?"

"Nope, not by a long shot."

A tingly warmth went through her. She didn't want to dwell on what he had been thinking about.

After a pause, he continued, "I'll be back in the office on Monday. Meet me there. We'll have lunch."

"I—I'll be at your offices on Monday anyway to look over the day-care site. The contractor I hired has been tearing down walls."

"Great. Come to my office when you're done. We'll go to lunch from there."

When Liz walked into Quentin's private reception area at noon on Monday, a sprightly sixty-ish woman looked up at her inquiringly.

"I'm here to—"

"—see Quentin," the gray-haired woman finished with a smile, rising and coming around her desk. Liz felt interested eyes sweep her from head to toe. "He's just finishing up a call. Can I get you something to drink, dear?"

"Oh, no, I'm fine, really."

The door on the far wall opened suddenly and Quentin appeared, his suit jacket missing and his hair tousled where he'd obviously been raking his fingers through it.

When he noticed her standing in front of Celine's desk, he stopped abruptly and smiled. "Elizabeth."

She felt foolishly happy at his sudden smile. "Hello, Quentin." She was acutely aware of Celine absorbing everything with great interest.

"I see you've met the incomparable Celine O'Sullivan," he said, amusement in his eyes.

Celine shot him a reproving look. "Now, Quentin, you know I'm just a little ol' secretary trying to put up with you until I can retire and collect that pension you've been promising me."

Quentin just chuckled as if that had been a long-standing joke between them.

Liz wracked her brain. The last time she'd been in Quentin's office, another woman, a temp obviously, had sat behind Celine's desk. "I don't think I've met Ms. O'Sullivan before."

Celine gave her a bright smile. "Just Celine, dear. And no, we haven't met before, though I believe we've spoken by phone."

Celine threw Quentin an amused look that he returned blandly, and Liz realized Celine must have been the woman who had called her to set up that first meeting in Quentin's offices—the one that had ended with the clinch and near kiss downstairs at the site for the day care. Feeling her face heat, she wondered what Celine knew about that initial encounter.

"I've heard so much about you," Celine went on. "You're Ally's friend, aren't you?"

"Yes, I'm Liz."

The phone rang then and Quentin strode back to his office, leaving the door ajar, and calling over his shoulder, "I'll be back in a minute."

Celine's eyes twinkled. "He really is a good man but don't ever tell him I said that."

"The newspapers love him."

"Oh, phooey!" Celine waved a hand. "Quentin would rather pore over business reports than spend time at social functions, which he sees as a necessary evil of his job. The papers love him just because he's young, handsome, rich and eligible."

Celine gave her an encouraging look that nearly made Liz blush. Obviously Quentin's secretary had formed her own opinions and one of them was that Quentin should settle down.

She hated to think of Quentin leading some solitary existence however, so she asked, hoping to change the subject, "But he doesn't just work?"

"Oh, my dear, Quentin was always very intense— and I've known him for years, worked for his father since Quentin was a baby."

Celine looked away, reminiscing. "Everyone knew he was going to do great things. And I don't just mean in business, although goodness knows he's been successful there. I mean, the kindness, too. He's very loyal to those around him." Celine's eyes came back to hers. "Why, the stock that man has gifted to me...well let's just say, I'm not still in this job because I need it."

Liz absorbed the information. If his secretary was to be believed, there was a whole other side of Quentin that a privileged few were allowed to see.

Liz glanced up as Quentin reappeared in the doorway. "Sorry," he said ruefully, "minor emergency with our European operations, so this is going to be a long call."

Liz nodded. "That's no problem at all. It'll just give me a chance to go back down to the day-care site and make some more progress."

"I'll call the restaurant and move back that lunch reservation for you, Quentin."

"Thanks Celine." To Liz, he said, "I'll come find you when I'm done."

When Liz got downstairs, the day-care center was a scene in suspended chaos. The workmen were all on their lunch break. Tools lay scattered amid ladders and buckets on the tarpaulin covering the wood floor.

Liz had been down here during the morning to talk to the contractor, but now she had a chance to take measurements without getting in the way of the construction crew. She pulled a retractable tape measure from her bag along with a pad and pencil and set to work.

After almost an hour she'd taken some measurements, jotted down some notes, and drawn a couple of rough sketches of some details she was considering.

She looked around the open space again. Yes, it was coming along just as she'd envisioned. They'd have an office to one side for the administrators, some child-size tables and chairs for the kids set up in the open area in the middle, and play stations to the left for building with blocks or playing with dolls.

She was still uncertain where to put the cubbyholes for the kids though. The far wall looked good. But so did the one on the left. She bit down on the edge of her pencil, contemplating the options. The wooden, paint-stained ladder near the far wall caught her eye.

With the ladder, she'd be able to mark off where the cubbyholes and cabinets would be placed and get an idea of how it would look.

She decided to try the right wall and walked over to the ladder. When she set the ladder against the wall, it was just high enough for her to mark off where the tops of the cubbyholes and cabinets would be.

Starting at one corner, she climbed up the ladder and marked off where the cubbyholes would start, then got down, moved the ladder over, climbed up again, and marked off some space for cabinets. She'd set those a little higher, she decided, and break up the architectural lines a little bit. Given how many kids there'd be, they might have to have two rows of cubbyholes, one on top of the other.

She moved the ladder over again and made some additional markings, then took a step down before realizing the end of the wall was within reach.

Taking a step up again and balancing on her beige sandals, she reached over and marked a spot on the lower corner of the wall before reaching to do the upper corner near the ceiling. She was just a couple of inches short, so she took a step to the side and leaned over a bit further.

Suddenly the rung of the ladder under her feet gave way and she lost her balance. "Ohh!!"

Rather than hit the floor with a thud, however, she was surprised to find herself caught in a pair of strong arms. The ladder went crashing to the ground, the sound reverberating in the large, empty space.

"Dammit! What the hell were you doing?" Quentin demanded.

She brushed back loose strands of hair from her face. "My job."

"Balanced on top of a ladder with—" he looked disdainfully at her strappy sandals "—Barbie doll footwear?"

"The ladder gave way!"

He nodded grimly toward the ladder with the broken rung now lying sideways on the floor. "Yeah, but that still doesn't explain what in the blazes you were doing on top of it."

If he'd simply been concerned, she'd have reacted differently. Instead, his anger fueled her own temper. "What I was thinking was that I should do my job." She thought a second. "You're paying me to get this day-care center done, and if you're satisfied with the end result, you can keep your opinions to yourself."

It was ridiculous to be having an argument when he still held her in his arms, but she hated being scolded like a child. "Put me down," she said. Then added, "Please."

He hesitated for a second, seeming reluctant, and then lowered her to the floor. The second her right foot hit the ground, she winced.

"What's wrong?" he demanded.

Even if she'd wanted to hide her reaction from him, she couldn't have. The pain shooting out from her foot was strong and sharp. "I think I strained something."

# Six

**O**h, heck. He picked her up despite her halfhearted protests.

"Be quiet and stop squirming," he grumbled. "You're going to a doctor."

"Well, of course I am—"

He looked down at her and the look in his eyes was enough to silence her. He bent with her and let her pick up her purse.

Damn.

His heart had risen to his throat when he'd seen her teetering on that ladder with those ridiculous sandals and his alarm had made him sound sharp.

Even now his pulse was galloping, except, if he was willing to admit it to himself, it wasn't only because of what had nearly happened. The side of her breast pressed against his chest, her rounded backside within inches of his hand under her legs. He gritted his teeth to tap down the welling of lust.

He strode with her past some gawking messengers and the receptionist, whose look of surprise turned into one of amusement at the sight of her boss carrying a woman in his arms.

"Suzy, call Dr. Grover and tell him I'll be there in fifteen minutes."

"Right away!" The receptionist placed the call, and Quentin could hear her talking to Dr. Grover's office assistant even as he strode through the automatic front doors of the building.

"Put me down! I'm capable of getting myself to the car—"

"How?"

Color rose to her face. "And anyway, I have my own doctor."

"Glad to hear it," he said pleasantly, "but today we're seeing mine."

"You're used to calling the shots, aren't you?" The question was accusatory. "Don't you ever take commands?"

He slanted her a look. "Under the right circumstances…" he murmured, letting the sentence trail off—and was rewarded with another blush.

"Where are we going?" Liz glanced out the car window at the highway exit they were passing, then jerked her head around to Quentin. "You just passed my house."

The doctor they'd seen had told her that her ankle had been badly sprained. While she wouldn't need a cast, she'd have to use crutches for the next couple of weeks.

"We're heading to my place."

"What?" Panic roiled her stomach.

He took his eyes off the road for a second. "Don't worry. I don't have any nefarious schemes in mind."

"Of course not." So what if she'd been thinking just that? "I simply meant, to what do I owe the pleasure of your unexpected and unsolicited invitation to your place of abode?"

He chuckled, then cleared his throat. "You're going to need someone to look after you for a while. I have a great housekeeper. You'll love her."

"Oh, no—"

He tossed her a penetrating look. "Don't even try to argue."

She raised her chin. "I'll be able to manage just fine."

He looked back out at the road. "How? You're supposed to keep off that foot. Do you have anyone at your place to help with cooking meals? Running errands? Getting around the house?"

"I can stay with Allison."

"Forget it." He took his eyes off the road long enough to shoot her a droll look. "You know as well as I do that Allison works late regularly, particularly when she has a trial going on. And, except for the occasional cat-sitter, she doesn't have any household help at her apartment."

He was right, much as she didn't want to admit it.

"Look on the bright side. This will give us a chance to see if we're really compatible."

She felt a little flutter of panic. "What about my things?"

"Not a problem. I'll swing by your place and pick up anything you need." He paused, then added, "Does this mean you accept my invitation?"

She studied his profile until he turned and looked at her blandly. She sighed. "Yes."

She'd seen Quentin's house from the outside of course. She often passed it on trips to meet clients in the most exclusive section of Carlyle. He'd bought it shortly after his engagement.

The wood frame house dated from the mid-1800s. White shingles and a white picket fence set off by black shutters and doors. The two-story structure was partially obscured from the road by two large oaks in the front yard.

She'd often thought it was the sort of house she'd have bought if she could have afforded it. And, she'd often itched to have a look inside, wanting to know if it would be as she'd imagined. But her enthusiasm had been tempered by the knowledge that Quentin had bought it for another woman.

"I'll show you around a little so you have your bearings," he said as soon as they were inside. "I don't keep a big staff here because I'm often traveling. Just a weekly cleaning service and gardener. Fred O'Donnelly and his wife Muriel fill in as the part-time butler and housekeeper."

She admired the alabaster banister on the stairs leading from the foyer, where they were standing, to the level above. The wood shone with a dark-red

glow. "Is this the original woodwork in the house?"
she asked as she turned to look at the nearby doors
and their equally dark wood frames.

"Yes." He opened the door on their left and she
used her crutches to hobble into the living room after
him. "The fireplaces have also been carefully main-
tained."

A spectacular marble mantel dominated the room.
A couple of mauve couches faced each other across
a small coffee table set on a cream mohair rug. "The
stuff in this room, and in most of the rest of the house,
I moved in from my bachelor pad. I started some of
the essential restoration and renovation, and thought
I'd leave the decorating to Vanessa—"

He cut himself off and his jaw tightened. "The engagement was over before we got to that point, but
then you probably know that, don't you?" He slanted
her a look.

"Allison did mention the engagement, yes." She
had been living in Carlyle but working for a design
firm in Boston at the time. She had dreaded perhaps
being hired by the future Mrs. Quentin Whittaker to
do the interior decorating for the house. When the
engagement had been called off, all the local gossip
columns had carried the news. Speculation had run
rampant over the cancelled engagement of the scion
of the Whittaker clan to the Boston Brahmin society
belle.

She used her crutches to maneuver over to the mantel. "It's lovely."

"I'm glad you like it." His voice held a note of
quiet pride.

"Who did you hire for the restoration and reno-vation?"

He mentioned a name she was accustomed to deal-ing with. "Yes, I know them well. They do great work."

He glanced at her crutches doubtfully. "If you can manage, I'll show you the rest of the house."

"I'd love to see more."

The downstairs was completed by a study, dining room, kitchen and family room. All contained the same lovely woodwork. The spacious kitchen con-tained all the modern amenities, though its traditional style made it harmonious with the rest of the house.

"The kitchen had just been redone when I bought the house," Quentin offered as they moved to the stairs.

"Mmm." She was distracted by her surroundings, or she would have noticed his pause as they reached the bottom of the stairs.

"I'd better carry you."

"Oh, that's not necessary...." So far, being held in his arms hadn't failed to send her pulse racing. "I can manage these steps just fine—"

"Yeah," he took the crutches from her suddenly nerveless fingers, "but I can't manage to just stand back and watch you," he replied in a smooth voice.

Before she knew it, she was swung up into strong arms and held close to a broad muscled chest. If she'd forgotten anything from her encounter earlier that day with certain parts of Quentin's anatomy, this was a great reminder! "Put me—"

"—down," he finished for her. "No. Now stop fidgeting."

His warm breath disturbed some tendrils of hair at her temples. With her arm around his neck and her hand holding his far shoulder, she felt his muscles flex and move as he effortlessly carried her up the stairs.

She focused her gaze at his collarbone and bit her lip. The temptation to kiss along his jawline, just shadowed with stubble, was disturbing.

When they mercifully reached the second floor, he put her down, being careful to support her with one hand until she'd had a chance to plant the crutches he handed back to her.

She cleared her throat. "Thanks."

"You're welcome."

The second floor had five bedrooms, and two were not furnished at all, she soon discovered.

"I haven't had a chance to do anything about those," he said almost apologetically. "It's been years since I bought the place, but I've let the decorating sort of languish."

They paused outside the third door. "This is the master bedroom," he said as he opened the door.

She wasn't sure what she'd been expecting, but it wasn't the sight that greeted her. Antique furniture in a rich rosewood filled the room, which was dominated by a king-sized bed. Cream-colored bedding, upholstery, and drapes offered a sharp contrast to the wood finish. The result was breathtaking.

Quentin liked antiques? And if looks were anything to judge by, he was fairly knowledgeable. She was impressed. She was, no, stunned. "This was in your apartment?"

He grinned at her shocked tone. "Hey, don't sound so surprised. The word 'taste' and I are not completely incompatible."

"Sorry, it's just I pictured something…er…."

"—with leather and lots of mirrors?" he supplied with a chuckle.

An involuntary smile rose to her lips. Embarrassed that he'd been able to guess her thoughts, she changed the subject. "I had no idea you liked antiques."

"At Harvard, I'd sometimes go for a drive to take a break from cramming for exams. Occasionally I'd come across an antique show, or just someone's yard sale."

"I'm just surprised because you didn't seem to give any thought to the decor in your office," she offered.

"True. But that's not personal space, it's work space. I figured those guys at the architectural firm knew what they were doing. I sure paid them enough."

She picked up the clock on the bureau. Its elaborate woodwork marked it as a Victorian-era piece. "This is just charming."

"I have a great collection of clocks and time-pieces," he said as he came up to stand next to her.

"I suppose the watch museum in Geneva is your favorite museum?" she teased.

"You've been there?" He looked surprised. "I've visited several times, when I can spare time on a business trip."

"Yes, I visited it on a trip to Europe during college."

"This furniture I picked up through an antiques dealer. Except for the bed frame. That I bid on anonymously at an auction."

"Yes, it's impressive." She went over to the bed and gave it an obligatory pat. "Do you know the age?"

"Dates from the 1890s."

"Did you need to restore it?" He had walked up behind her as she skimmed her fingertips over the headboard.

"No, it had been kept in great shape."

"That's good." She was very aware of him and the tension coiling within her. Trying to keep the conversation going, she went on, "Intricately hand carved, I see."

"Yup." Was it her overly-sensitized senses, or had the timbre of his voice deepened a notch? She kept her gaze focused on the headboard.

"Must have been expensive." He was very close now, his breath disturbing her hair, and blocking her means of escape.

"Yeah, but I liked the intricate carving."

His hand settled over hers on the headboard, guiding the tip of her index finger over the swirling indentations and protrusions of the smooth wood.

Oh, boy. She was melting like butter in the sun with the heat emanating from him. Her gaze fixed on his hand covering hers, unable to look away or slip her hand from his as he continued to move their hands over the headboard.

"You can tell he took his time," he said huskily. "Everything needed to be perfect, and so he created something astoundingly beautiful."

Just when she thought she couldn't stand any more, he dropped his hand from where it covered hers. Before she could exhale however, his hands settled on her shoulders and he nuzzled her neck.

She struggled to keep her voice even. "Perhaps the craftsman didn't work alone."

He turned her to face him. He was smiling, his eyes crinkling in amusement. "You think?"

"As an expert on antiques, I can assure you, he didn't."

"How can you be sure?"

"Great work is often revealed to be the result of a great collaboration," she managed to say before his head dipped for a kiss.

"Maybe he was a hermit."

"And creating a beautiful headboard big enough for a king-sized bed?" she asked skeptically.

He chuckled. "Hmm, good point." His lips trailed kisses from her brow down to her jaw. He removed one of her crutches and dropped it on the bed, replacing its support with his arm around her waist. "Maybe he just liked big beds."

It was getting harder and harder to concentrate on their conversation. "He must have had someone to inspire him."

His fingers fumbled at the zipper of her sleeveless top. "Honey, you're inspiring me right now."

Only when cool air greeted her back did she realize he must have lowered the zipper on her top to allow himself better access. His hand came up to cup her breast over her sagging top and he allowed his thumb to trace around the outer edge of the nipple before peeling the top away from her.

She heard his swift intake of breath and met his hooded gaze. "Do you have any idea what you do to me?" he asked huskily. He lowered his eyes again to her breasts, which strained against the wisp of fabric that was now their only protection against his heated gaze.

Then all coherent thought was lost as he bent his head and his mouth closed over one tight nipple through the lacy fabric of her bra. He began to suck, his tongue moving over the peak again and again.

Liz moaned and distantly heard her remaining crutch hit the carpet with a thud. Her hands moved to hold his bent head to her breast. His arms now were her only support as he transferred his ministrations to her other breast.

She thought she would die from the pleasure of it. The gentle sucking was causing a myriad of exquisite sensations to course through her and settle at the juncture of her thighs.

"Quentin, oh, please…"

Only the two of them and their overpowering need for each other seemed to matter.

He deposited her on the bed and came down on top of her. His kiss was all hot and hungry male passion.

His hands were everywhere, caressing, stroking, smoothing, stoking her passion. Her bra was disposed of and her breasts lay against his hair-roughened chest. The friction, coupled with the feel of his erection at the juncture of her thighs, caused the tension to coil ever tighter within her.

He sat up quickly, and though she felt momentarily bereft, she was glad to see him shrug out of his suit jacket and then divest himself of his shirt and tie.

His chest was covered in a T of curly hair that tapered down and disappeared into the waistband of his pants, which could not hide his erection.

Her gaze lingered for a second before rising up to meet his eyes. The passion reflected there caused her breath to catch.

She'd wanted him, wanted this, seemingly forever. She raised her arms to him but he shook his head.

"No, not yet," he murmured. "First let's get you out of these." He unbuttoned her pants and peeled them from her, panties and all, careful not to jolt her injured ankle.

She felt vulnerable, exposed, lying there before him, without an item of clothing to hide any of her flaws. She lay still, waiting for his reaction and was surprised by his slightly crooked grin.

Trailing his eyes from her hips up to her face, he explained, "Your hair is the same color *all over.* I was curious about that."

She felt the heat rise to her face even as he chuckled and came down beside her, his leg urging hers apart. His hand cupped her intimately before he used two fingers to begin a swirling motion against her hot center. Slowly and deliberately he built an ache of pleasure until she squirmed on the bed for release.

"Quentin!" she gasped.

"I want to hear you say 'yes,'" he reproached on

a laughing groan. "Can you say it for me, sweetheart? I want to hear you say it."

Coherent thought was impossible. Never had she felt so sensual.

"Give yourself to me," he rasped.

His supplication was Liz's undoing. She went spinning into oblivion. "Oh, yes! Yes! Please, Quentin!" He made a guttural sound of satisfaction at her climax.

After her gaze refocused, he came up over her. "We're not finished yet, honey. Not by a long shot."

Just as he bent his head and positioned himself to enter her, they both heard it. The unmistakable sound of the front door opening, followed by a called-out "Hallo-o? Quentin?"

The breath hissed out of Quentin as he slumped on top of her, collapsing in seeming defeat. "Damn, damn, damn."

Liz tried to clear her head. "Who—?"

"Muriel. The housekeeper," Quentin's muffled voice announced grimly from the pillow next to her.

"Oh. Ohh!!" Liz struggled to sit up. "Oh, my."

Quentin lifted his head and gripped Elizabeth's arms to stop her from struggling. "I'm upstairs, Muriel," he shouted. "I'll be down in a minute." Then he levered himself off of her, generously giving her a hand so she could sit up.

Her gaze took in his muscled, still aroused body. The man was flat-out gorgeous.

"Stop giving me those looks, sweetheart. Otherwise, we'll finish what we started, Muriel or no Muriel."

She felt the stain of a blush and quickly looked

about the bed for any item of clothing within her reach.

"Here." He held her bra and panties in his fist. "They were on the floor."

"Thank you." Then with as much dignity as she could muster, she took her underwear from him.

"Victoria's Secret black satin. I would never have pegged you," he said, pulling on his trousers.

She felt her blush deepen. "Stop it," she muttered. She envied the way he'd rapidly collected himself when they'd been interrupted.

He sat down on the bed next to her, his still unbuttoned shirt gaping open, and lifted her chin so that she was forced to meet his gaze. "You have the most fascinating blush." He glanced down. "It starts amazingly far down."

She pulled her chin away. "Irish blood. Some of us aren't blessed with a poker face."

He grinned. "Thank God for that."

She jumped when he bent and placed a moist kiss at the center of her cleavage.

He winked, looking devilish. "Just wanted to see if it feels as hot as it looks."

She grabbed a pillow and aimed for his laughing face, but he grabbed it before it could reach its mark. "Get dressed. I'll stall Muriel and be back in a minute to help you downstairs."

As soon as he was gone, Liz tried to make herself as presentable as possible. She ran a brush through her hair and applied some lipstick. Her clothes were a little mussed, but they'd have to do.

She mulled over what had just happened—or

rather, what hadn't, thanks to Muriel's fortuitous interruption. She'd been angry with Quentin's high-handedness when they'd left the doctor's office. Yet, a short time later, she'd been rolling on his bed with him.

She had to be careful and guard her emotions. Quentin had made it clear that theirs would be a union based on practicalities and that's just the way he wanted it. If she didn't remember that, she'd be in trouble.

Muriel turned out to be a pleasant, plump-faced woman around sixty with steel-gray hair and glasses hanging from a chain around her neck.

"Allison sent you over," Quentin repeated slowly.

"Why, yes, dear," Muriel said. "She called me about an hour ago. Said she'd heard Liz had had a fall and you'd taken her to your doctor. When the doctor told her you'd mentioned on the way out that you were taking Liz home to keep an eye on her, she called me straight off."

Liz caught Quentin's droll look and bit her inner cheek to keep from laughing.

"Yes, indeed," Muriel continued. "She suggested I might want to come on over to see if someone was needed to look after Liz." Muriel placed her hand over her heart. "In a bit of a muddle, aren't we?"

Quentin had his suspicions about his sister, but decided to keep quiet about them for now. "A muddle all right." And he knew exactly which of his siblings was responsible. He scratched the back of his head.

Muriel gave him a beatific smile. Celine's bridge

partner knew how to play it fast and sly. He'd bet against the house that Muriel was in cahoots with his sister. "I'm going to go back to work. On the way home, I'll pick up some things for Elizabeth from her house."

Muriel clasped her hands. "Splendid idea." She walked over to Elizabeth, balanced on crutches, and began to lead her to a kitchen chair. "Why don't I fix us some cool iced tea, hmm? Then we can set you up with a phone and fax and anything else you need in Quentin's study."

# Seven

"**I** have Mother Teresa at the house, her bridge partner at the office, and the Whittaker Women's Patrol every place else," Quentin said morosely.

Matt snickered.

"At least Fred's not spying on you through the bushes," Noah offered.

They were at Earl's having a couple of beers at the bar, as they sometimes did on those rare days when all three brothers had no plans and weren't busy at work.

It was welcome relief for Quentin. Elizabeth had been camped out at his house for over a week. During that time, his mother, his sister Celine and Muriel had conspired to make sure he wasn't able to have a free moment alone in Elizabeth's company.

"Frankly, I'm surprised," Matt said quietly. He

nursed his beer, arms resting on the bar, gray eyes surveying the bottles lined up in front of the mirror on the back counter. "Is it just the weather that's got you all hot and bothered, Quent, or something else?"

Quentin nudged Noah on his other side. "You think he speaks in tongues?"

Noah gave a lopsided grin. "Naw. We probably knocked loose a few too many marbles when we used to kick his butt."

"Selective memory, little brother," Matt retorted. He took a good gulp of his beer. "Let me spell it out for you two clowns. Muriel, Celine, Allison and Mom all existed in your life last week, Quent. And the week before that, and the week before that. Why are you so worked up about it now? What's different about this week?"

"Matt," Quentin said slowly, as if talking to a child, "Muriel is camped out at my house."

"Mmm-hmm." Matt cracked open a peanut. "So I hear."

"She's up in the morning making fluffy pancakes when I get down to the kitchen, and downstairs watching *Murder, She Wrote* reruns when I go to bed at night. The woman never sleeps!"

"She naps in the afternoon when you're at the office," Noah offered helpfully.

"Damn straight." Quentin signaled for another beer. "Allison calls every night." Just when he thought he'd have a few moments alone with Elizabeth, his sister would call. He'd be treated to peals of laughter and snatches of a one-sided conversation that would go on and on.

"Oh, man," Noah commiserated.

Quentin thought he'd had them last Saturday, Muriel's bridge night, but then Allison had shown up with pizza.

He'd practically wrung his hands with glee on Monday when Muriel had reluctantly announced she and Fred needed to attend a church meeting. But then his mother had called and asked him to stop by on the way home from work to pick up some books that she wanted to give Elizabeth. Of course, the whole thing had turned into a two-hour detour and by the time he'd gotten home, Elizabeth had been asleep.

He didn't kid himself that he understood women, but after nearly thirty years with Allison, he'd started to understand some of the devious paths her mind ran down. She and his mother—along with Muriel—were running interference for Elizabeth. Their suspicions had been awakened about his current relationship with Elizabeth, and although they couldn't know about the "deal" that had been struck, they suspected enough about his motives to believe that Elizabeth needed some protecting. And he wouldn't put it past Allison to have decided that having Elizabeth so close yet so unattainable was exactly the sort of lure he needed.

"Keeping Liz under lock and key, huh?" Noah asked, pulling him back from his thoughts.

"It's unbelievable," Quentin said, then caught himself and shrugged. "It's all the same to me." Except it wasn't.

"Your bad mood wouldn't have anything to do with Lizzie, would it, bro?" Matt arched a brow.

Quentin hadn't told his brothers about his "arrangement'' with Elizabeth. They knew something was going on, they'd just uncharacteristically avoided probing. Anyway, how did he explain that he might father Elizabeth's baby after the negative reaction he'd had to the possibility they'd do the same?

Quentin shook his head. "She hasn't bothered me."

Like hell. Sure she hadn't intruded on him, but her mere presence in his house was driving him crazy. Knowing she was down the hall—maybe in that lacy negligee he'd retrieved from her house for her—was enough to make it hard to get to sleep.

"Great." Noah exchanged a look with Matt. "Then you won't mind her puttering around the house all weekend under the same roof."

"Shut up." Quentin sighed. He wasn't fooling anybody.

"Monday is the Fourth of July," Matt said matter-of-factly.

Quentin took another swig of beer. "Think she'd like to sit on the grass, listen to the Boston Pops and watch the fireworks?" he asked morosely.

"Women love that kind of stuff," Matt said.

"Can't go wrong," Noah seconded. "Pack a picnic basket. And don't forget the Chardonnay."

"Great." Quentin felt some of the tension ease from his neck and rolled his shoulders. He thought his instincts were right, but it was good to know that Matt and Noah agreed.

Noah tossed some bills on the counter. "Gotta run."

"Noah," Quentin stopped his brother.

"Yeah?"

"If you or Allison 'coincidentally' shows up at the concert on Monday, I'd have to kill you."

Noah grinned. "I'll pass that warning along."

Saturday night. Unbelievably Muriel had left around eight, saying Fred needed her help installing some shelves.

Right, thought Quentin. As if he'd fall for that ruse. He wondered what the "plan" was now. Had the dogs been called off? Had Noah relayed his message of the night before to Allison, and had his sister finally seen fit to give him some breathing space?

Well, he wasn't falling for it.

Think they could make him dance like a puppet on a string, did they? So, he was alone in the house with Elizabeth. That didn't mean he'd start pawing her at the first opportunity.

She was holed up in his study, doing work. Fine. He'd cede his work space to her for the evening.

He'd just make himself comfortable on the couch, get a cold beer and watch the Boston Red Sox play while he looked at the latest status reports from various departments at work.

It was the bottom of the fourth and still no runs when the phone rang. Dropping the report he was reading, he reached for the cordless on the end table. "Hello?"

"Oh, Quentin,…hi."

"Don't sound so surprised, Allison. This is still my house."

"Of course I wasn't surprised, Quent. Don't be

silly." Allison paused. "It's just that I thought Lizzie would pick up. I've gotten used to calling her over there."

Quentin crossed his legs on the coffee table. It was payback time. "Your timing's off."

"What do you mean? Is Liz there? Pass her along, hmm?"

"I mean, you're too early to interrupt us *in flagrante delicto.*" He glanced at his watch. "Call back in an hour or so."

"Quentin!" Allison exclaimed.

"Bye, Ally."

"Quentin, wait! Quentin?"

"You've got five seconds."

"Okay, you're onto me." Allison sighed dramatically. "What do you want? Should I engage in self-castigation? Promise I'll never hatch another devious scheme?"

"Don't make promises you can't keep."

"All right, all right. But remember, big brother, you're there alone with Liz and I'll expect my trust to be repaid."

"Contrary to popular belief, I'm neither a depraved animal nor an ogre," Quentin said dryly. "I've even heard some women have confessed to liking me. 'Charming' and 'gentlemanly,' I believe, were the words used." He paused. "On the other hand, that could just be a vicious rumor."

Allison laughed. "You of all people shouldn't believe gossip!"

"Yeah," he conceded.

"Just remember what I said," Allison replied before hanging up.

Quentin replaced the receiver, shaking his head. He got up to get himself some chips to go with the beer.

It was ironic. Here he was, parked in front of the television on a Saturday night, alone with his beer and chips. He shook his head. He led a far more boring life than most people—including his family, it seemed, and not to mention, Elizabeth—believed.

He picked up the discarded report from the couch and scanned it. Settling back he began to read.

Half an hour later, he'd digested most of the report and searched for last month's report from the same manager. The only way to get a good picture was to put things in historical context.

He searched his briefcase with no luck. It was probably on top of his desk. In the study.

He paused in the doorway to the room where he usually worked at his desk. The yellow light cast by the lamp failed to reach the shadows at the edges of the room.

Elizabeth sat in the easy chair, reading. Unobserved, he studied her. Her hair was up, pinned in a loose knot, some tendrils escaping and caressing her face. Tortoise-rimmed glasses perched on the edge of her nose, a slight frown betraying her concentration.

She looked adorable and Quentin was unprepared for the tenderness he felt. He stuffed his hands in his pockets. "Don't you know that frowning causes lines?"

She glanced up. "You startled me!"

"Sorry." He made his way into the room. "I just came to find the report I'm missing."

Remembering the glasses, Liz quickly took them off. She hardly ever got caught wearing them. It helped that she was only slightly farsighted.

"Don't take them off on my account," Quentin said in an amused voice.

She reached for her eyeglass case, embarrassed he'd read her actions. "I guess you've discovered my dark secret. Are you going to tell your brothers that Liz Donovan is the mousy librarian sort that you took her for all along?"

He glanced back at her and stopped rifling through the papers on his desk. "It's a good thing you took them off—"

She knew how she looked, but did he have to spell it out for her?

"—because I think women in glasses are very sexy."

Her eyes shot to his face.

"I see I've surprised you. Again."

She thought about what her reaction had been to seeing his bedroom for the first time and felt heat rise on her face.

He removed a stapled-together set of papers from a pile. "Finally."

"I'm glad you found the report."

He walked over and sat himself in an armchair nearby. "Aren't you going to ask me why?"

She pretended to pick a piece of lint off her khaki shorts. "Why what?"

"Why I think women in glasses are sexy."

"I'm sure you have your reasons," she said politely. She waved a hand. "After all, ah, men seem to discover their 'type' early on."

He leaned forward and braced his arms on his haunches. "I've given this some thought." He turned his head toward her and Liz raised her brows inquiringly. "It's the intelligence that glasses signal."

"Hmm."

"Also, they kind of make a man itch to peel away the layers. What's she hiding? Can she be wild and uninhibited as well as prim and proper? That's the mystery."

She folded her arms. "I see."

"The library was one of my favorite hangouts." He grinned. "All those sexy librarian types hitting the books."

"Sort of like the fox in the henhouse, hmm?"

He sat back and laughed. "Sort of," he said, still grinning.

"What about those women you're always pictured with in the papers? Bambi or whatever?"

"Bambi?" he spluttered, laughing again.

She nodded seriously.

"All right." He held up his hands in mock defeat. "I'll admit I haven't been picky when it comes to my Friday night dates." He shrugged. "I've taken out whoever is around and willing to go to these boring social functions I always seem obligated to attend."

"And 'whoever is around' is the sleek high-society type."

He sighed. "Whether the woman is my type or not

is often beside the point.'' He nodded to the papers she'd set aside. ''Work?''

She felt herself smile. ''Yes. We bespectacled librarian types spend a lot of Saturday nights alone working.''

The corner of his mouth curled up. ''So do we dashing playboy types,'' he admitted. ''I'm camped out with my files in front of the TV in the other room.''

''Oh!''

''Why don't you join me?'' He looked around the study. ''Work someplace else for a change.''

The offer was tempting, Liz thought. She didn't have a good reason to refuse, so she let him move her things to the other room, hobbling behind on her crutches.

When they had her settled in an armchair, Quentin put the television on mute so that he could keep tabs on the game while he and Elizabeth worked.

''By the way,'' he said, ''Monday is the Fourth of July. I thought I'd go to the Boston Pops concert. Care to come?''

He'd sounded so casual, it took Liz a moment to digest what he was saying. She'd wondered in the past few days whether her accident had derailed their four dates and now felt ridiculously pleased that he wasn't abandoning their original plan. Aloud she said simply, ''That sounds wonderful.''

They worked in companionable silence for over an hour. It was closing in on nine o'clock when Liz caught herself staring off into space. She removed the glasses she'd put back on in order to work.

"Problems?" Quentin asked.

Liz shook her head. "No, just envisioning what the Lorimers' kitchen would look like in yellows and blues." Her lips curved. "And how to fit in Mrs. Lorimer's request for an island, two sinks, and a built-in cupboard."

Quentin quirked a brow. "Here's my solution—hit Mr. Lorimer up for a bigger house."

Liz laughed. "His wife has already tried that. He doesn't even understand why she wants to do away with the avocado-green appliances."

"A sink is a sink." Quentin sat back on the couch. "Anyway, what's the problem? Didn't bell-bottoms come back into fashion? In a couple of years, the neighbors will be falling over themselves to copy her."

Liz tilted her head to one side. "Ah, I see. Retro-chic."

"Exactly."

She pursed her lips. "Kitchen appliances don't come back into fashion the way clothes do. When was the last time you saw someone trade in their washing machine for a washboard?"

"Yeah, all right, I'll give you that." Quentin eyed the television. Bottom of the ninth and the score was tied.

"Thank you."

"So what about giving her two kitchens. His and hers, maybe."

"That's ridiculous."

Quentin folded his hands behind his head. "Oh, I

don't know. The guy might want to mess around on his own sometime."

She rolled her eyes. "I don't think—"

Not taking his eyes from the television, Quentin interrupted, "Okay, then add onto the house. Does the kitchen share an outer wall?"

"I already thought about that." She shook her head. "They've got a patio in the back and a driveway along the side of the house. I can't expand."

Quentin took his eyes off the television. "Get rid of a closet or two. Knock down a couple of walls. Give her a pantry instead of closets. The hubby won't care, he thinks she has too many clothes anyway. And she'll be so taken with the idea of expanding the kitchen, she'll forget about the closets she's losing."

Liz tapped the eraser-end of a pencil against her lips. "Hmm, that might work. She does have a couple of closets next to the kitchen."

"Next year, she can get the husband to go along with the idea of expanding another part of the house to add a walk-in closet. And ta-da," Quentin snapped his fingers, "another project for you!"

To say she was surprised at his insight was an understatement. She supposed she shouldn't be. After all, he'd risen high and fast in the business world. And he really did have a good idea. She started to tell him so when she was caught by the action on the television screen. "Quick! Raise the volume. I think the Red Sox have scored!"

Quentin scooted forward and grabbed the remote.

"A home run, folks!" the announcer exclaimed.

"And that's the ball game. Red Sox 4, Orioles 2. We'll be right back after these messages!"

Quentin looked at her. "I didn't know you were paying attention."

"I guess I was doing a better job of hiding it than you were," she shot back.

Quentin grinned. "Sorry. I swear I was paying attention to Mrs. Lorimer's kitchen—too."

Liz folded her arms. "And I was about to tell you that you had a great idea—about the closets, I mean." She paused. "Thanks."

"You're welcome."

They smiled at each other for one inane instant.

They were so comfortable together, Liz thought. Why had it taken them years to reach this point?

And yet, he hadn't confided in her. Not about Vanessa. If they were going to have a baby together, she'd want to know that much about him. He could play his cards close to his chest, but sometimes he'd need to throw one on the table.

"Quentin?"

"Hmm?" he answered, not tearing his eyes from the screen.

He must have figured that if she was onto him, there was no reason for him to hide his divided attention anymore, Liz thought ruefully. She took a deep breath, "What happened between you and Vanessa?"

His eyes shot back to hers. "Pardon?"

"Why did you break off the engagement?"

Quentin looked back at the screen and sighed. "Game over." He flicked off the television with the remote in his hand.

Liz shifted a little in her chair. She would not regret asking him. The worst he could do was tell her it was none of her business.

She hoped he wouldn't. She didn't want the evening—and their newfound camaraderie—to end on a sour note. She didn't want to remember that it was her fault by blurting out the question that had been gnawing at her since…well, since longer than she cared to remember.

He was quiet for an instant. "I found out she didn't love me so much as my money—and the status of being Mrs. Quentin Whittaker."

There, he'd gotten it out. He hadn't told anyone before about the end with Vanessa. Not even his brothers.

He waited for the humiliation to burn. Leave a bitter taste in his mouth. But saying the words, the emotions were a distant echo of what he'd once felt. He figured he'd finally reached the point where he could look back with disappointment and not bitterness.

She nodded. "How are you so sure about Vanessa's motivation? Surely, she didn't come right out and say she was marrying you for your money."

"Don't be too sure," he muttered.

"What?"

"I overheard her and a friend of hers talking. On the balcony, at one of those black-tie affairs that Vanessa loved." He shrugged. "They didn't know I was there."

"I see."

"No, you don't see." He ran his fingers through his hair. "Apparently, I was the fish she managed to reel in before her trust fund money ran out.'' He laughed mirthlessly. ''Vanessa always had expensive tastes.''

''I'm sorry.''

He shook his head. ''There were family and friends who tried to give me a heads-up. But I ignored them.'' He paused and then said reflectively, ''I guess I should consider myself damn lucky it all came out before the wedding.''

Elizabeth bit her lip. ''Surely she must have had some feelings for you.''

Now that he'd started, he figured he might as well tell all. ''She was planning to take up with an old lover of hers after the wedding. Conveniently, my work schedule gave her lots of free time.''

Liz looked at Quentin—all six feet two inches of pure male sprawled on a bottle-green sofa. She couldn't imagine wanting anything—or anybody— else if she had him.

What a horrible blow to his pride it must have been. How humiliating, too, to know that others had known—or at least suspected—even when he hadn't.

''A workaholic bore, she said.'' He grinned unexpectedly. ''Not too far off the mark—'' he cast her a sidelong look ''—even if some people insist on seeing me as a playboy.''

Liz felt herself flush. She could hardly explain her view was due both to finding him very attractive and needing a defense against that attraction.

''Now you know the details.''

''Yes.'' She felt ashamed at her nosiness, but something compelled her to ask, ''How is what we're doing any different? It seems to me that, by the terms of our, ah, agreement, I get to use you for your money.''

''Nothing wrong with that *if* both parties are up-front about it.'' He regarded her levelly. ''Let's just say that, after Vanessa, I've started to think that it's not such a bad deal…*if* the ground rules are established at the beginning.''

''Rather cynical, wouldn't you say?''

He shrugged. ''Look, even if the romance-love thing exists, a lot of us aren't that lucky. A sizable chunk of the world would probably be better off approaching the whole thing like a business deal.''

''I see.'' So that's where his brilliant idea of having a baby together had come from. It was all part-and-parcel of his post-Vanessa philosophy about love and marriage. It had just taken him time to realize she'd presented him with exactly the sort of proposition that he'd come to see as ideal. Except for speeding up the baby stage, it all fit very nicely.

''By the way,'' he said quietly, bringing her back from her thoughts, ''you were wrong when you said you're no different than Vanessa.'' He paused. ''You won't have any lovers on the side. That's part of the deal.''

His steely look nearly took her breath away. Even though she knew it wasn't possessive in the way a man normally felt for a woman, it made her quivery inside.

# Eight

They were settled on the Esplanade next to the Charles River in Boston on Monday evening waiting for the Boston Pops to play at their annual Fourth of July concert.

A rectangular red-checked sheet that Muriel had found was set out beneath them. With some help from Muriel in retrieving things, Liz had prepared tarragon chicken salad sandwiches on French baguettes, mesclun and tomato salad with vinaigrette, and apple cobbler for dessert.

Quentin had good-naturedly teased her about the pretentiousness of the mesclun in her salad, and she'd retaliated by poking fun at the age of the Chardonnay that he'd picked out.

Ever since her discovery a couple of nights ago about the deep-seated roots of Quentin's cynicism about women, Liz had been troubled about having bitten off more than she could chew. On the other hand, she figured things were in some ways simpler than she'd thought. There was little chance that Quentin would fall in love and want to marry someone and regret the "deal" he'd entered into with her.

Even if he did, she decided she'd cross that river when she came to it. After all, she and Quentin had yet to agree whether he would try to father her baby. Tonight she was going to enjoy this concert.

A slight breeze teased her hair, but otherwise the evening was balmy and clear. She tugged down the hem of her knee-length, blue cotton dress. "It's wonderful out here."

He looked up at her from behind wire-rimmed sunglasses. He was sprawled on the blanket, his hands behind his head, looking up at the dark evening sky. He radiated relaxation in navy T-shirt and gray khakis. "Haven't you ever come to listen to the Pops on the Fourth?"

She shook her head. "Actually, never. When Dad and I moved to Carlyle, he'd send me back to spend summers with Aunt Kathleen on the Jersey shore. After that, I'd always have the types of summer jobs that got busy on holidays."

"Like what?"

"Oh, you know, baby-sitting, serving ice cream, working at the bike rental shop."

His eyebrows rose. "You worked behind the counter at an ice-cream parlor?"

"Candy-cane-striped apron and all."

His lips quirked. "I can't picture it."

"In college, I was known for the homemade variety," she informed him, pretending to look down her nose.

His smile widened. "Do tell."

He reached for her hand on the blanket and began drawing small circles on the back of her palm, sending a delicious tingle through her. "It's not that complicated to make ice cream. You just mix eggs, sugar, milk and cream. The hardest part is getting the right consistency."

"You learned to cook—"

"Aunt Kathleen. Dad's okay, but I took over most of the cooking by my teens."

He was silent for a moment, his fingers stilling on her hand, and she could feel his gaze through the sunglasses. "You and your father are close." He made it a statement, not a question.

"Yes, but it's a complicated relationship."

He angled his head even as his hand crept up and began stroking her arm. "Is there any other type?" he drawled.

She smiled, momentarily forgetting about that wicked hand. "I tried to be the son that never arrived."

"Ahh." Quentin thought back to what he knew about Patrick Donovan. Big Irishman, owned a small construction company before retiring. They'd had a few business dealings, enough for Quentin to know the man was a shrewd operator.

Liz scanned the crowd, which had thickened in the last half hour. "The silly thing is that my father loved having a daughter." She put her arms behind her and braced herself on her hands, lifting her face to the small breeze. "I was all pink frills and baby dolls. The little girl he needed to protect."

She gazed back down at him. "The only problem was that I felt too protected. I wanted Dad to see me as independent, capable."

Ah, Quentin thought, so that's what made Elizabeth Donovan click. Fascinating. He sat up and removed his sunglasses. "Kind of hard to ask a guy who's lost his wife not to be protective of his little girl."

She sighed and nodded, looking away. "Yes. I've come to understand that."

"Is that where starting your own business came from? Sort of a strike for independence?" he asked, though he already knew the answer.

His perceptiveness surprised her, but she merely nodded in agreement. "Some of it was that. But I was also ready to move on from the big architectural firm. I had my own ideas, and I wasn't getting the chance to realize them."

Why had she revealed so much to him? One minute they were talking about ice cream, the next she was baring her soul.

He raised a finger and traced a line between her brows. "Don't look so worried."

She tried for a game smile. It had been years since she'd taken out these feelings and examined them. It was one thing to think about these things privately, it was another to give voice to them.

As if reading her turbulent thoughts, Quentin stroked her hair and said, "It's all right. All kids have some fears."

She looked at him, so strong, so solid, so seemingly cool and invincible. "Really? What were yours?"

He chuckled. "I guess I opened myself up to that one. Mine was that I wasn't sure I'd be able to fill Dad's shoes with the company." His gentle stroking was soothing her and she nearly purred when he started to massage her scalp. "Even us sons have our worries."

"Hmm."

"I remember your father had a small construction company. Sold it as I recall," he said casually.

She blinked, trying to keep her mind focused on the conversation. "Yes, mmm, he sold it when he retired."

To a larger conglomerate which had subsequently been sold to a holding company that Quentin had formed with some more minor business partners. Quentin realized she didn't know about the relationship between him and the company that her father's old business had eventually been folded into.

Knowing what he knew now, he doubted the information would be welcome to her. And, frankly, he didn't need another strike against him. No doubt, on some level, Elizabeth questioned whether her father would have sold the company if there'd been a son around.

The concert started then—the Pops launching into a rendition of Sousa's "The Stars and Stripes Forever"—and they lapsed into silence.

They had a new connection between them, Liz thought. Forged of newly discovered shared experiences. She hadn't thought it would be so easy to talk to him, tell him things that she hadn't even revealed to Allison.

She stole a look at him. They were more alike than she'd ever imagined. Although, she mused, maybe she'd always intuitively known about his power to read her like a book and that had been part of the tension between them.

There was only one word for a man who made her feel like he could glimpse her soul: Dangerous.

When they arrived at Quentin's empty house, he carried her back from the car. She didn't protest as much as she had in the beginning, though the tingle of awareness was there every time. It ran through her from the thousand points where their bodies touched.

He deposited her in the living room. "Coffee," he suggested.

"Please, let me do it," she said, grabbing her crutches, which he'd carted in with her. "You can finish unloading the car."

He hesitated for a second, then nodded and strode out.

When his back was turned, Liz gave a little smile. Maybe it was his recent knowledge of how important her independence was to her, but he'd just stopped himself from giving orders instead of taking them.

She hummed a little as she reached the coffeepot. The crutches slowed her down a bit, but the doctor had said she might be able to get rid of them within the week.

When Quentin materialized, she let him take the coffee cups and followed him back into the living room. He sat right beside her on the couch, the arm of the sofa preventing her from shifting away even if she'd wanted to.

"I enjoyed the concert," she said, suddenly a bit shy. "Thanks for taking me."

"You're welcome." It had been hard keeping his hands off her on the lawn. Now that they were alone, his self-control slipped down another notch.

He searched his brain for suitable conversation. "I've always liked concerts. My mother forced all of us kids to take up an instrument. Mine was the sax." He looked around. "Wonder where Muriel hid the damn thing."

She chuckled. "Hall closet, second door on the right, behind your hockey trophy from high school and an old basketball."

He should have known. "Gave you the grand tour, did she?"

"I'm afraid so." She tried to hide a smile by taking a sip of her coffee. "It happened one day when you were at work."

"Figures."

Elizabeth stifled a yawn with her hand, then rubbed her eyes.

"Tired?" he asked. He moved his hand to rub the nape of her neck, which, he'd come to realize, was an erogenous zone. He looked forward to replacing his hand with his lips soon.

"Mmm." She arched her neck to give him better access. "Quentin?"

"Yes?" Her eyes were closed and he leaned toward

her, intent on trailing his lips along the curve of her long and graceful neck.

"Why do you call me Elizabeth?"

The question caught him off guard and he reversed his forward motion. Heck of a time for her to ask *that*. "Are you sure you want to know?"

She opened her eyes to gaze at him. "Is it really terrible?"

He pretended to contemplate that for a second. "Depends on how you look at it." She looked irresistibly sweet sitting there on his couch. He nearly groaned aloud when she wet her lips.

"I really want to know."

His cover was about to be blown, but there was no help for it. He took a deep breath. "Calling you Elizabeth helped me mentally keep you at a distance." He blew out the breath. "Elizabeth is a lot more formal-sounding than Liz or Lizzie. It reminded me to keep our relationship on a strictly 'hello-goodbye' basis no matter how lovely you were and how attracted I was to you."

Reading the mixture of doubt and surprise on her face, he added ruefully, "You were a threat. I was a twenty-five-year-old guy who found himself in the uncomfortable position of lusting after his little sister's best friend, who wasn't even out of high school." His eyes connected with hers. "Of course I was going to cut you out."

Her brows had drawn together in puzzlement. "I thought you didn't like me. Matt and Noah were friendly, you were—"

"—a jerk. Purposely."

"You weren't impolite," she demurred, her forehead clearing. "Just...aloof."

"Right. I was going to make damn sure you stayed Allison's little friend and that's all." There, he'd said it. All of it. He itched to push her back against the sofa pillows, but he restrained himself so she had time to absorb what he'd just sprung on her.

Liz thought back to the times she'd sporadically seen Quentin during high school and college. "Once we got into that kind of relationship, it was hard to break out of it," she mused. "I got used to making polite chitchat with you."

"Yeah, once we fell into a pattern, it was hard to break it. Anyway, I figured you didn't like me too much anyway. I was distant and cool to you from the beginning."

She felt giddy. He'd desired her. He'd had to push her away. A wonderful shiver ran through her at the same time that she became aware of the intense look on his face and recognized the leashed desire there.

She let him take the coffee cup from her suddenly nervous fingers and deliberately place it on the coffee table next to his own. He picked up her hand then and kissed her wrist, her palm, his eyes never leaving hers. "I want you," he said, his voice smoky.

He searched her face and seemingly satisfied with the expression that he read there, he cupped the back of her neck and inexorably drew her toward him.

Her eyes drifted closed as his lips whispered over her eyes, her nose, her cheeks before, finally, settling on hers.

Liz melted into the kiss. His lips were smooth,

warm, enticing, and she nearly moaned in protest when they finally left hers to trail across her jaw, then down along the side of her neck. "Elizabeth," he said huskily.

She thrilled to the word, recognizing it now as a verbal caress. Would she ever be able to hear it again without being reminded of hot looks and smoldering desire?

"I hope to God we're not interrupted this time," he breathed against her neck, then pulled back to look at her. "Are you sure? Because I won't want to stop."

Any twinges of doubt she had were drowned in the overpowering desire coursing through her. "Yes. I'm sure," she heard herself say.

He must have heard the aching need in her voice, because he eased her back onto the pillows of the couch, careful to straighten her bad leg, and tugged on the zipper at the back of her dress until it rasped downward.

It seemed that she'd been waiting half a lifetime for this moment and in a way it was true. She'd felt an immediate physical attraction the first time she'd met him at eighteen.

His mouth latched onto a nipple through the thin, semi-transparent material of her bra and she gasped. He began a firm and rhythmic sucking that steadily increased the tension coiling within her.

She pulled at his T-shirt until she freed it from his waistband. "Help me," she pleaded.

He quickly sat up and his eyes burned into hers. He removed her bra and tossed it aside, then yanked his T-shirt over his head. When she moved to touch the well-sculpted muscles, thrown into relief by the lamplight, his hands closed on her wrists. ''No,'' he said thickly, urgently, ''need a bed. Now.'' Then he scooped her up and strode with her out of the room, up the stairs, and to his bedroom.

It was heavenly being carried by him, yet she tested his control by trailing her hands and lips over those parts of him that she could reach. He had a wonderful, corded neck, she decided. Strong and powerful and yet infinitely inviting to nibble on, especially near the pulse she found beating strong and quick. When she briefly lifted her head and noticed the tick working in his clenched jaw, she grew bolder, drawing his head down to hers.

''Holy Mary,'' he ground out, as he managed to get to the side of the bed and deposit her carefully on it.

Her dress was bunched at her waist. One sandal dangled precariously from her foot, the other having been lost somewhere on the way up the stairs. She kicked off the remaining shoe while he pulled off her dress and underpants.

He paused for a moment and grinned. ''Red silk panties from Frederick's of Hollywood.'' He arched a brow. ''You definitely have a thing for underwear,'' he murmured.

''They do mail order,'' she said unnecessarily, then added, ''Muriel stopped by my house for some more of my things. She seems to have picked out my raciest underwear. There wasn't a plain cotton pair among them.''

Quentin laughed huskily. ''Remind me to give her a raise. Although,'' he paused, ''it was unholy for her to bring back that stuff and then help deny me the pleasure of it for so long.''

He threw her clothes onto the nearby night table, and then she watched him divest himself of the remainder of his clothes. He was aroused, and when he came down beside her, she breathed in his musky male scent.

''You on top,'' he said. ''We don't want to hurt your ankle.'' Before she could protest, he'd carefully rolled her on top of him.

His hands intertwined with hers and he raised her arms above her head, leaving her vulnerable and exposed to his mouth, which took and plundered hers.

Liz felt the world shrink till nothing existed but the two of them and this moment. Her tongue dueled with his, her breasts pressed against his chest, his hair teasing her already sensitized nipples.

He gave a low groan, his erection hard against her, as his lips slid to her throat. ''That's right, yes,'' he whispered roughly. His hands pulled her even more firmly against him.

Her legs opened, slid around him, until he was there pushing up against the most secret aroused part of her. She'd wanted this for so long. Wanted him. One downward movement of her hips now and he'd be inside her, filling her in ways she'd only dreamed of.

''Quentin....'' She turned her head and met his hooded, smoky gaze.

''Say it,'' he muttered.

For a moment, she didn't understand. Then her heart leapt.

''Say you want me.''

Even as her heart cried out, she gave him the words he asked for. "I want you," she gasped and moved her hips, taking him in, feeling him stretch her, fill her. *I love you.*

Then he began to move inside her and her hips moved in counterpoint to his thrusts, undulating in a rhythm that matched the pace he set.

"That's it, honey. Yes," he coaxed. "Reach for it, baby."

She clenched around him spasmodically. "Quentin!!! Oh, please. Oh—yes!" Waves of sensation mixed with feeling and emotion wracked her.

He quickened his pace then, thrusting hard and fast. Her climax seemed to trigger his own. He threw back his head, gave a hoarse shout and surged into her one last time.

"Damn, sweetheart, you nearly killed me there." Quentin propped himself up on an elbow and caressed her thigh with his other hand. A thin sheen of sweat glistened on his skin.

It had been the most intense and satisfying sexual experience of his life. All he could think was: they should have done that a long time ago.

Liz hugged the sheet to her and waited for her racing heart to slow its pace. All she could think was: they should never have done that.

How could she ever have thought that going to bed with Quentin wouldn't cause a seismic shift in her world? And, oh God, they'd been so carried away, they hadn't even used protection! Although it was unlikely, there was a possibility that she might even now become pregnant.

The last thing she needed was for him to know just

how much she was affected, however, so she tried for sophisticated nonchalance. "You do know how to move fast," she said with a laugh that sounded forced to her own ears.

He chuckled. "You call eleven years of suppressed desire 'fast'?"

"Well, we're officially only on our—" she thought for a second "—second date. Although," she conceded, "things have been complicated by the fact that I've been living in your house."

He smiled wolfishly. "Yeah, that means you owe me at least two more dates." He paused. "By the terms of our agreement," he reminded her.

Liz quaked inwardly. Two more? Heaven help her, how was she going to survive two more dates with Quentin? He wanted a nice, uncomplicated business arrangement. And she…in the midst of their passion, she'd admitted to herself that she loved him.

There it was. She forced herself to examine the admission unflinchingly. What was she going to do?

He gave a quizzical half smile. "I'm different from the other men you've been with."

*Yes, you're the only one I've been in love with.* Yet, she could hardly answer with the truth.

She had, in fact, slept with only one other man. Soon after she'd learned of Quentin's engagement, she'd told herself to stop being silly and deluded. At twenty-three, it was time to give up hope Quentin would miraculously discover one day soon that he couldn't live without her.

So she'd finally accepted a date with Kevin Delaney, a nice, somewhat staid accountant who'd been hounding her for a date for at least six months. That Kevin's coloring and height gave him a more than passing resemblance to Quentin, she hadn't wanted to examine too closely.

Fireworks hadn't gone off, the world hadn't tilted on its axis, and she'd been forced to admit she'd made a terrible mistake.

There'd been men since then, of course, but nothing had gone beyond a few dates. The men had all been safe choices—as Allison uncannily liked to point out—unlikely to press her for more, content to let her set the pace.

Quentin broke into her thoughts with a teasing, "Am I supposed to take silence as an admission that I'm that good?"

If only he knew the truth! "Yes, well, everybody's unique," she managed in a strained voice.

Quentin frowned. He didn't like thinking about Elizabeth with other men. "Speaking from your wealth of experience?"

She was hugging the sheet to her if it were a lifeline, unaware that the effect was to outline her ample chest—a chest he was intimately acquainted with now. "No, just one or two experiences."

One or two experiences? She'd gone to bed with him like a fall leaf hitting the ground at the first breeze. He couldn't resist asking, "So I compare favorably?"

"Yes." He had to bend his head to catch her monosyllabic response.

Troubled green eyes looked up into his. "I don't think this is going to work."

He tensed and stilled the hand caressing her thigh. "Meaning?"

She bit her lip and glanced away from him. "This is more complicated than I thought it would be."

He experienced an emotion suspiciously akin to panic at the thought that she might be trying to back out of their plan. Yet a part of him acknowledged that she was right. Going to bed with her had rocked his world.

Aloud he tried, "There's nothing complicated about two people who are attracted to each other acting on that attraction. I'd say this is as simple as it gets." His voice sounded hard to his own ears.

She turned back to him. "You know, it's more than that. We're talking about having a baby. Bringing a baby into this world through a business arrangement, instead of because two people love each other enough to get married and have a baby together."

He frowned. "You make it sound like most marriages are flawless relationships. The fact is they're usually far from that." Panic made him perversely willing to argue with her instead of pushing her back against the pillows and using more primitive ways to persuade her.

"How can you be so cynical when your parents have a marriage that anyone would envy?" she asked with a troubled look on her face.

He sighed. After the debacle with Vanessa, he himself had pondered what made his parents' relationship work. "My parents are the exception. They didn't see each other for two years when Dad was in the military. They almost eloped because my grandparents objected to my mother getting married before she finished college. They had lots of time to paint rosy pictures of each other, and, believe me, even then, their marriage hasn't been a walk in the park. Dad was so busy building his company that my mother basically raised us on her own."

Liz sat up in bed, careful to keep the sheet from falling and exposing her breasts. "The exception is what I've been looking for." She twisted the sheet nervously in her fists. "What I'm willing to wait for."

Quentin's face was devoid of expression, giving her no clue as to what he was thinking. "This was a m-mistake." She took a deep breath to steady her voice. "I'm sorry."

"You want out of our agreement," he said flatly, his hooded gaze revealing nothing.

"Y-yes," she whispered.

He sat up and swung himself out of bed. Her gaze raked down his muscled back, tight buttocks, and strong legs. She drank in the sight before he started to dress.

When he turned back to her, he wore a cool and remote expression. "This was what we agreed on, nothing more and nothing less," he said smoothly. "One of us could have stopped the whole thing at any time during our four dates."

She willed herself not to cry. She bit her lip and looked away. "Well, I wouldn't worry about anything. With my condition, it will be difficult to get pregnant even at the right time—which this isn't."

# Nine

Thirty-eight, thirty-nine, forty. She finished counting the days on the calendar in her hand.

She was late. No question. How was that possible? With her condition, getting pregnant should have been difficult. Yet one night, one unforgettable night, in Quentin's arms, had been enough.

Panic assaulted her. She'd have to visit her doctor to confirm. But she already knew the diagnosis. She was never this late.

She'd done a good job of avoiding Quentin since that fateful night. He'd reluctantly agreed to drive her home after she'd agreed to allow Muriel to come over and help her for the next few days—until she could walk without the crutches.

In fact, since that night she hadn't seen Quentin and had dealt only with Noah about the day-care project.

If Noah had thought it strange that she and Quentin didn't deal directly with each other, he kept his thoughts to himself.

She'd been miserable, of course. She'd lost weight in the past month, which made the pregnancy a double surprise. She'd have to force herself to eat more now for the sake of the baby.

If only she could deal with her problem sleeping through the night as easily. Since leaving Quentin's house, she'd lain awake many a night thinking about what to do.

Yet, she hadn't been able to work up any interest in the literature she'd collected at the sperm bank.

She thought back to the night she'd lain in Quentin's arms. Their mutual desire, once unleashed, had been a force greater than either of them, demanding satisfaction. Afterward, she'd become frightened by the emotions he'd aroused in her and what she'd allowed herself to admit in a moment of passion: she loved him.

She'd reacted by retreating, doubting whether she could go on with their plan without incredible heartache. And Quentin had exited her life, a tacit understanding between them that they'd both ''forget'' their night of shared passion and go on with their lives.

The trouble was, in less than nine months, they'd have a very real and constant reminder of that night!

Liz's visit to the doctor's office the next Friday confirmed what she already knew. If the doctor was surprised at the rapid turn of events, he didn't show it.

After receiving instructions from the doctor about appropriate supplements, collecting what seemed like three dozen pamphlets on childbirth, and scheduling her next visit, she left the doctor's office and drove home.

What was she going to do? She might be able to convince everyone she'd been artificially inseminated in such a short time, but what would she do when the baby arrived? What if it was a little boy with the Whittaker trademark gray eyes? How long before her secret would become known?

Of course, she could move to another town. Maybe even join her father down in Florida. But that would mean folding up Precious Bundles and starting again from scratch.

No, she had to face reality, which was bearing Quentin's child right here in Carlyle, which was Whittaker family home turf.

Sooner or later she'd have to tell Quentin, of course. But, please God, not now.

She needed time to marshal her forces. Time to think. And, Lord knew she didn't want Quentin to think she was going to him for money. That would only confirm his opinion of women and their motives.

Ordinarily, she'd turn to Allison in moments like these. Ally was at her best in crises. But she knew what Allison's reaction would be. She'd be overjoyed that the plot she'd originally set in motion had come to fruition. She'd insist on telling Quentin right away and having him assume his responsibilities—financial or otherwise—or else.

Arriving home, she dropped her purse on a side

table and headed toward her desk. The only other person she could trust was her father. And he wouldn't be happy.

She chewed on her lower lip and eyed the phone on the desk as if it had been possessed by evil spirits.

How her father would react to the news that his only child—his unmarried daughter—was pregnant, heaven only knew.

Well, best to get the inevitable over with, she decided. Grimly, she picked up the receiver and dialed her father's number. His greeting a second later made her stomach twist in knots.

Patrick Donovan immediately started in on his favorite topic: his only child's recalcitrance about calling and visiting. "Lizzie, if you're too busy to come down here, I'll come to you instead. It'll do me some good to see the lads."

By lads, of course, her Dad meant his sixty-ish buddies, business associates, and fishing companions, many of whom had yet to be lured to sunny Florida, despite, she was sure, Patrick Donovan's formidable sales pitch.

Her father having given her an opening, she took a deep breath and plunged in. "I'm glad you're planning to come up here. How about Labor Day Weekend, Christmas, and, let's say, the middle of next April?"

Her father laughed. "Ah, it warms my heart, it does, that you're so anxious to see me. And what would next April be, if you don't mind my askin'?"

She closed her eyes. "Having a baby. No due date

yet. But if we're lucky, you'll be here for the blessed event.''

There was a pause at the other end.

''Dad?'' she asked uncertainly, opening her eyes.

''What!'' She heard him mutter under his breath. ''When I said I was lookin' forward to the pitter-patter of li'l feet, sweet pea, I thought it was clear I preferred for you to be married at the time. Seems like I was right to worry about you up there all alone.''

She winced. She'd known he would be disappointed in her. Still, it didn't make things any easier to hear him give voice to it.

''Next you'll be tellin' me who the father is, no doubt,'' her father grumbled.

She steeled herself for what was to come. ''Quentin Whittaker.''

''Saints alive!'' Then, ''Whittaker, is it?''

''Now, Dad, don't be angry—''

''Angry?'' Her father gave a hearty laugh. ''I'm delight-ed!''

''What?'' He couldn't have shocked her more if he'd just announced plans to give up fishing and join an order of Franciscan monks.

Her father chuckled. ''Well, I'm going to be a granddaddy. Now, mind you, that's enough to warm my heart. But, sweet pea, you've also managed to bring the family business back into the family!''

''What are you talking about?'' For a moment, she wondered about the onset of senility, then dismissed the thought. Her father was as sharp as a tack.

''Quentin owns most of what was Donovan Construction, Lizzie.''

"Wha—? How?" Her world tilted on its axis. It wasn't possible!

"Oh, he didn't buy it outright," her father continued chattily. "No, he bought it from Scudder Brothers about a year after I sold out to them. Quentin is the major shareholder in a holding company called Samtech Enterprises that now owns what used to be Donovan Construction."

Liz's head began to pound. The enormity of her predicament hit her like a ton of bricks. It was even worse than she'd realized...for she'd unwittingly played into her father's hands.

Her father thought she'd just provided him with the keys to a business it had taken him a lifetime to build. A company she'd always wondered if he would have sold if he'd had a son to enter the still testosterone-dominated construction business. Now, with any luck and with Quentin's help, he had the chance to pass the business along to a grandson.

Her father suddenly asked suspiciously, "He asked you to marry him, hasn't he, sweet pea?"

Liz felt her temper begin to rise. Why, her father already had her at the altar! "I haven't told him."

"You have'n— In the name of all the saints, why not?" her father boomed. "At least have him own up to his responsibility."

A responsibility, was she? "Maybe I don't want to marry him, have you thought about that?" Let him chew on that for a while! "I'll tell him about the baby in my own time," she warned, "and don't even try to interfere!"

"Now don't get your back up, sweet pea—"

"Don't sweet pea me. I don't need another man trying to tell me what to do!" She sounded shrill but she was beyond caring.

Her father's rumbling laugh sounded over the phone. "Tried to tell you what to do, did he? He'll learn. Donovan temper's one to be reckoned with."

"Goodbye, Dad." She dropped the receiver back in its cradle.

How could Quentin own Donovan Construction and she not know it? Because he didn't own it directly...and because he hadn't mentioned it to her!

Suddenly she had a more ominous thought. What if Quentin had purposely kept the information from her? She thought back to the Fourth of July concert and their conversation about her father. Surely he must have known then, if not before, that she would have considered that tidbit of information very important.

While she'd been spilling her most private thoughts and fears about proving herself to her father, he'd known—known!—that he held Donovan Construction! When had he planned to share that information with her, she wondered?

She drummed her fingers on the desk and narrowed her eyes. Maybe in the delivery room? Yes, she could see it now. Quentin and her father having a nice little chuckle over her prone and exhausted body, which had just brought forth the much anticipated little Whittaker-Donovan heir.

She could just throttle Quentin! After what she'd told him, he must have known she would be unwittingly playing into her father's hands. And, yet, he hadn't warned her. Hadn't said anything at all but had made mad, passionate love to her.

Hurt intruded where the anger was. She'd trusted him! Shared feelings with him that she'd never voiced to anyone else.

Well, she'd show him. She wasn't some little thing that needed to be protected from the truth, manipulated, or told what to do. She'd have her baby on her own and she'd manage just fine!

"She's what?"

"Liz is pregnant."

Quentin stared at his sister. All his life she'd been the bearer of news designed to bring upheaval to his life, but she'd just surpassed herself, whether she knew it or not.

Elizabeth pregnant. He was going to be a father. "How pregnant is she?"

Allison's lips quirked and she quipped, "Oh, you know, just a little bit."

Quentin prayed for patience. "How far along is she?" He already knew, but he wanted the confirmation his instincts were right.

Allison gave him a quizzical look. "I don't know. She didn't say."

"Did she tell you who the father is?" Quentin demanded.

"She went to a fertility clinic—"

Quentin's hands bunched into fists. Was that possible? Had Elizabeth followed through on her plans for artificial insemination soon after their night together? Was this baby not a Whittaker after all? His jaw tightened. There was one way to find out.

He strode out of his office and Allison hurried after him. "Quentin, where are you—"

"I'll be out this afternoon," he informed his secretary as he aimed for the elevators beyond the reception area. "I'm not reachable."

"You're always reachable," Allison piped up as she tried to keep pace with him. "Where are you headed?"

Quentin ignored the question. The elevator arrived and he stepped in, turning to face Allison, who was insisting on answers.

"Just what's happened between you and Liz?"

"I'll let you know as soon as I find out," he told her before the doors closed.

His mind worked furiously as he drove to Elizabeth's house, keeping just the wrong side of the speed limit. What if the baby was his? Had she been planning to keep it from him? Or had she really gone from his arms to the cold and clinical ones of a fertility doctor? He felt a nerve begin to twitch at his temple.

One thing was for sure. If this baby was a Whittaker, he was going to make damn sure Elizabeth acknowledged the kid's paternity.

He pulled up in front of Precious Bundles, and strode to the door, taking the porch steps two at a time. An OPEN sign showed through the paneled glass. As he let himself in, he turned to give it a flick.

Elizabeth sat at her antique desk, cradling the phone between her shoulder and one ear and jotting notes on a pad in front of her. Her eyes widened the minute he entered. "Y-y-yes, Mrs. Bradford, the wallpaper should be delivered Tuesday."

He walked to the desk and leaned over, planting his hands on the smooth mahogany finish. She scribbled something and the pencil point broke from the pressure.

As she reached for something else to write with from the pencil holder, he caught hold of her hand, forcing her to look up. Get off the phone, he mouthed and then let go of her hand.

"O-o-okay," she stammered and he was unsure who she was addressing. Maybe it was for both his benefit and Mrs. Bradford's. "Yes, right. Speak with you on Tuesday."

Liz set the phone in its cradle and looked up at Quentin. He looked like a tiger ready to pounce.

"One question." His voice was deceptively soft. "Is it mine?"

His slate-gray eyes caught and held hers. Magnetic, intense, relentless in their scrutiny.

"Yes."

His shoulders relaxed and a little bit of tension seemed to roll out of him. "You told Allison that you'd used a sperm donor," he accused.

"No, she just assumed and I let her think that. Anyway, it's not a lie. You were one of the first donors she suggested."

"When were you going to tell me?" he demanded.

That did it. Anger was the last thing she was willing to take from him! "About the time you decided to tell me that you own my father's company!" She rose from her seat. He still towered over her, of course, but at least she no longer felt like a criminal being interrogated under a strobe light.

She unflinchingly met his stormy gray eyes until he turned away and began to pace in front of her desk. "I didn't think it was important. At first, I wasn't even sure if you knew or not."

"After the Boston Pops concert, you knew it would matter to me but you said nothing!"

He stopped to face her again. "All right, I should have told you. But right now, we have a bigger problem. You're pregnant and we need to figure out what to do."

His cavalier dismissal of her concerns about Donovan Construction fueled her temper. "We? I thought we agreed there would be no 'we.'"

He smiled grimly. "That was before I knew I was going to be a father."

"Well, don't worry then. You're not," she snapped.

"I fathered the child you're carrying!" His eyes narrowed. "Or were you lying?"

"I admit you made a small contribution. That's a far cry from saying you're going to be a father."

"A small contribution?" he snarled as he advanced. "I'd say it was a major contribution to our mutual enjoyment."

"I was raised by a single parent, and the baby and I will be just fine on our own."

He halted, seemingly arrested by her words, and then stuffed his hands in his pockets. "So you know that a single parent can do just fine, but having two helps."

She'd made him furious, and surprisingly she didn't get nearly as much satisfaction from that as she thought she would.

A muscle twitched in his jaw. "Your baby is a Whittaker. Are you sure you want to deny your child all the advantages that entails?"

She met his gaze steadily. "I wouldn't deny you access to the baby, if that's what you really want. But," she added, "despite whatever you may believe about women, money isn't what I want. For myself or this baby."

He frowned and seemed to choose his words carefully. "All things considered, whatever I believe about your motives isn't relevant anymore."

*"It's very relevant."* She shook her head. "Listen to yourself! You're talking about all the material things you could provide for this baby."

He looked grim. "That's the customary male role. Breadwinner. Provider. Are you going to deny me that?"

"I'm not going to deny you anything important, Quentin. I'm not going to stop you from seeing your son or daughter. But I don't need anything else." Except you, always you.

He looked like he was about to say something and then changed his mind. He nodded curtly, turned on his heel and stalked out.

Liz sagged into her chair and finally allowed herself to give in to the tears. She'd accomplished what she'd set out to do, which was tell him off and take a stand about being able to raise the baby on her own. So why did she feel so miserable?

* * *

That night Allison dropped by unannounced. In her typical no-nonsense style, her friend wasted no time in cutting to the chase. "Lizzie, when I mentioned you were pregnant, Quentin left his office like he had the devil nipping at his heels."

"Allison, I—" Liz swallowed. It was going to be hard to broach this subject with her friend, no matter how long they'd known each other, no matter how many secrets they'd shared. They were in her living room, Allison having just dropped into an armchair while Liz took the couch.

"Have you talked to him?" Allison demanded. "I swear, if he's insulted you, I'll, I'll—" Allison paused for breath. "Well, I don't know what I'll do exactly, but it will be really painful for him."

"Ally—"

"He can be overprotective, but that doesn't mean he needs to pull his boorish older brother routine with you." Allison fumed. "I mean, he already has me for that! And besides, he has to respect you for deciding—"

"Ally, I'm having Quentin's baby."

"What?" For once Allison looked flummoxed. "How...? Why...?"

"You missed 'where' and 'when,'" Liz said dryly.

"Now's not the time to joke around!" Allison's brows knitted. She tossed the cushion she'd been toying with on the coffee table and walked over the fireplace.

Liz had known this was going to be difficult. She just hoped Allison wouldn't be mad at her forever.

Right now, Allison looked a lot like her courtroom self.

"Okay, I think I just ran through several emotions there." Allison blew a breath. "You're in luck because angry and hurt passed in about two seconds, and now I'm just happy."

"Oh, Ally." She should have known Allison would be loyal.

"How could you not have spilled the beans?" Ally held her hands out in exasperation. "You let me think…well, you know."

Liz cleared her throat. She and Ally had had very few secrets from each other, but this one was a doozy. "You're Quentin's sister. You would have felt compelled to tell him about the baby, and knowing you, you would have browbeat him, too." She gave a weak smile, then added, "Anyway, we had a terrible argument."

Allison's eyes widened. "Ooh, I would have loved to see that! Quentin never gets out of control. Ruins the cool CEO persona."

"I provoked him," she admitted.

Allison chuckled and folded her arms across her chest. "Even better. Was he furious that you hadn't told him right away about the baby?"

"Not only that. *I was angry.* Did you know that Quentin owns Donovan Construction through a holding company?"

Allison's mouth dropped open, then she strode over to plop herself back down in the armchair, seeming to need the support. "Oh, my."

"Oh, yes. A crucial fact he failed to mention even after he…we…." She felt her face heat.

"I see."

"My father's ecstatic. I'm not only going to produce the long-awaited grandbaby, but I'll be bringing the family business back into the family. Quentin will carefully manage it, of course, until—" she crossed her fingers and let her voice drip with sarcasm "—with any luck, it passes to the wee grandson."

"Agh."

She nodded grimly. "Exactly."

"What was Quentin's reaction?"

If only he'd had one! "He figures he should have told me about the company, but he didn't think it was important enough to mention at first."

Allison rolled her eyes.

"He insists on accepting financial responsibility for the baby."

"Naturally. Quentin's been accepting responsibility since he was in the cradle."

Liz nodded. It was part of why she loved him. But she couldn't—wouldn't—let him act out of responsibility here. "Right. Well, I won't let him do it."

"What?" Allison looked alarmed, then leaned forward in the armchair. "What do you mean?"

"I mean," Liz said firmly, "we made a mistake. Since I was the one who wanted to get pregnant, I'm prepared to raise the baby on my own."

"Mistake? Are you nuts?" Allison jumped up and planted her hands on her hips. "Do you think my brother goes around impregnating women like that?" Allison snapped her fingers, then shook her head. "Of course not. Quentin never does anything impetuous. He wants you. Otherwise you'd never be having his baby."

Of course Allison wanted everything to be wrapped up tidily. After all, she was the one who early on had come up with the scheme of using Quentin as a sperm donor. Liz sighed inwardly. "Want is different from love."

"No, want is the road to love."

"He doesn't even like me."

Allison quirked a brow in a way that reminded Liz of Quentin. "Oh, come now." She folded her hands behind her back and started to pace. "Let's examine the evidence, shall we? My brother has avoided entanglements for the last seven years. Within weeks of meeting you again and hiring you for the day care, he breaks one of his own golden rules by mixing business with pleasure."

Allison stopped and threw her a piercing look. "Not only that, but he does this knowing he's playing with fire. After all, you're a woman who's desperate to have a baby. Inexplicably though, he gets angry when you talk about artificial insemination and tells you to get a husband instead!" Allison rested her hands on the back of the armchair and leaned over it. "Then he all but volunteers for the job himself!"

Liz nearly smiled. Allison making a case was a sight to behold, even when it was at her expense. And although Allison couldn't have known about Quentin's idea that they consider a marriage of convenience to have a baby, she'd come remarkably close to the truth.

"I'm dying of curiosity, but I'm not going to ask exactly how this happened—" Allison paused and gave her a knowing look "—though I'd make a good listener if anybody needed one. Let's just say I know one thing and that is that you and Quentin have more chemistry than I've seen since high school."

Liz sighed.

"You love him, don't you?"

The unexpected question and Allison's understanding look caused unexpected tears to well in Liz's eyes.

Darn. She didn't want to cry in front of Allison, but there was little she could do to hide the wetness of her eyes.

"Oh, Lizzie!" Allison sat down next to her, and gave her a quick hug. "It's okay."

"N-n-no, it's not," Liz choked out. "I've made a complete mess of things."

Allison frowned. "You? I'd say Quentin's at least equally responsible if you want to call this a mess."

Liz stifled a sob. "All I wanted to do was have a baby."

"And you are! And I'm going to be an aunt!" Allison laughed. "And my mother—oh my gosh, Mom is going to be ecstatic!"

"About my trapping her son?" she warbled.

"No, silly, about you and a grandbaby! This has been near the top of her wish list for a while."

"What do you mean?" Liz looked at her friend's suddenly sheepish face.

"Well, er—"

Realization dawned. "I've been an open book, haven't I?" She'd gone out of her way for years not to show any particular interest when Quentin's name was mentioned. She could have saved herself the effort, it seemed.

Allison grinned. "It was hard to miss your hero worship."

"I'd gotten over that," Liz protested. At the very least, she liked to think her teenage crush had developed into more mature feelings.

Allison rolled her eyes. "Thank goodness. Quentin's my brother, and I think he's pretty terrific, but the stuff of fairy tales he's not."

Liz gave a choked laugh.

"See, you agree with me!" Allison gave her a quick, reassuring squeeze, then said briskly, "So, don't even try to give me any nonsense about Quentin. He deserves to get all the diaper-changing misery one man can get. And as for you and him, everything will work out, you'll see."

# Ten

Liz felt under siege. Her father was threatening to come up from Florida and "set things to rights." As Allison had predicted, Quentin's mother was over the moon about the baby, and had called to say that if there was anything Liz needed, she and James would be there before Liz finished asking.

In her typical tactful way, Ava had acted as if there was nothing in the least bit shocking about her thirty-six-year-old unmarried eldest son having suddenly impregnated her daughter's long-standing best friend.

But if Liz thought Quentin had inherited his mother's tact, she was wrong. Dead wrong.

One minute she was speaking with the construction contractor for the day care, the next she felt the hair on the nape of her neck rise and stir.

"I want to talk to you."

She eyed him warily. He was looking every inch the corporate executive today, a black, custom-tailored suit set off with a power-yellow tie. "I'm speaking with Mr. Higgins."

He ignored the frigidity in her voice and took her arm. "I'm sure this can wait while I discuss some urgent business with you." She found herself led away as the contractor readily took the hint and went back to his work.

The minute they were alone in the hall, she turned on him, incensed. "That was rude."

He shrugged. "He works for me. Don't worry about it."

"Oh, is that the way of it?" she answered in an icy voice fit to do Patrick Donovan proud. "People are just supposed to defer to your desires? No one would dare defy the mighty Quentin Whittaker, hmm?"

He ran a hand through his hair in a gesture she was coming to recognize as a sign of his frustration. "Have you been thinking about how you're going to manage with this baby? And keep Precious Bundles afloat?"

So that's why he was here. "I'll manage. I will not accept money from you," she responded firmly and, she hoped, repressively.

"You're already accepting money from me, re-member? The day-care project for Whittaker Enter-prises," he said coolly.

Uneasiness stirred in her stomach. "That's different."

"Is it? What would happen if I decided the day care was something the company no longer needed?"

Her eyes widened at the implied threat. "That would be breach of contract—"

"Even if you could afford to sue, which we both know you can't," he continued, his voice holding a touch of steel, "I could afford a settlement. But it might take a while to negotiate."

He didn't need to add what they both knew. She couldn't afford to wait for a settlement. Suddenly she understood why Quentin had the business reputation he had—he had earned it. And now she was the target of his ruthless business methods.

But something about the set, closed look he wore made her check her temper and, instead, study him, tensed for her answer.

He'd been hurt in the past, she knew, and he was clearly going to protect himself from being that vulnerable to a woman again. That had obviously led him to the conclusion that he ought to bargain with her as he would deal with a business rival. Just as he'd originally tried to strike a deal with her for a baby and a marriage of convenience. A deal that had gone hopelessly awry and landed them...here.

Armed with that realization, she found herself asking, "What are you suggesting?"

"Marry me."

Her heart leapt, but she forced her voice to remain level. "Why?"

"You're having my baby, that's why."

"That doesn't mean you have to marry me."

He frowned. "In my book it does." He regarded her intently. "I've thought about this from all the angles, and this is the best solution. We'll get married—at least until after the baby is born.''

When she started to protest, he held up his hand. ''Hear me out. It's best for you, me, and the baby. We'll go through with the original plan but this time we'll do it for the short haul. I want the baby to be born a Whittaker. And my parents will get the grandchild they've been pining for, and which they think it's my duty to produce *legitimately*.''

She couldn't resist asking, ''What do I get?''

He paused for a second, as if the question had caught him off guard. ''You get peace of mind. Financial support to make sure the baby is always well cared for. Financial support to make sure Precious Bundles stays afloat until you can focus on it again.''

Liz repressed a twinge of hurt. She'd known he was treating this like a financial bargain. What had she expected? she silently scolded herself. A declaration of undying love?

Aloud, she said coolly, ''I'll think about it.''

When he didn't respond—didn't even move a muscle, actually—she started feeling uncomfortable. ''Have you finished?''

His eyes narrowed. ''No, dammit! I haven't.'' Before she could register what he was about, he grabbed her arms and his mouth came down on hers in a hard kiss. He made sure she felt all of his frustration before setting her roughly back away from him.

''Let me know when you've thought about it,'' he bit out before turning and striding away.

\*   \*   \*

I'll think about it?

Quentin thought he'd never dealt with a more contrary female in his life. And that was saying something, considering who he was related to!

He ached just looking at her, wanting to strip her naked and make love to her thoroughly, and all she could do was look at him with those amazing green-gold eyes and say coolly, *I'll think about it?*

Okay, yeah, maybe he should have told her about owning Donovan Construction. At first he hadn't thought it was important and then he'd delayed telling her until it was too late.

He gazed out of the windows of his office, his hands shoved deep into his trouser pockets. He could see the office towers across the highway, part of the hi-tech corridor outside Carlyle, and, more distantly, the green of verdant hills. He often liked to chew on a problem this way, contemplating the distant Massachusetts landscape.

He'd bungled the plan, of course. He'd meant to approach Elizabeth with infallible logic. Persuade her that getting married was the best option.

But instead of making her see how much she needed him to keep Precious Bundles going while she had their baby, he'd used—he winced as his mind flirted with the dirty word—blackmail.

Once she'd started again on not needing his money, his response had been driven by pure male need for dominance and control.

Except was that really it? No, it was his need for her, he realized, that had made him lose his head. Her and the baby, of course. For he realized, he wanted this baby—his baby and Elizabeth's—with an intensity that surprised him.

If only the darn woman would cooperate with his plan to set things right.

To add insult to injury, his whole family seemed to have taken sides and they weren't flying the Whittaker colors.

His thoughts drifted back to that morning when his sister had stalked into his office unannounced. She'd been angry and had let him have a piece of her mind. It was her parting shot that had stayed with him all day however.

Allison had jabbed a finger into his chest and had accused, "You tried to bully her into accepting your terms! You threw money at her because you think she's just like Vanessa and that's all she's interested in. Isn't that right?"

"Are you nuts?" he'd growled back, still sensitive about his admittedly deplorable behavior and quasi-blackmail of Elizabeth. "I wouldn't use their names in the same sentence."

"Why should I believe you?"

When he failed to respond, Allison had stalked out, leaving him to chew over her question.

He gazed at the landscape in front of him now. And thought about Allison's question again.

Why?

Because it was ridiculous, that's why. Vanessa represented everything he abhorred. She was greedy and manipulative. And she'd taught him a tough lesson in life and love.

He paused and puzzled over that.

Love? Had he really loved Vanessa?

The feelings he'd had for her paled in comparison to those he felt for Elizabeth. In fact, he'd spent the past three days in purgatory waiting for Elizabeth to decide either to open the gates of paradise to him or…well, the alternative didn't bear contemplating.

So why did he persist in believing Vanessa had betrayed his love, while believing he didn't love Elizabeth?

Realization dawned like the sun spreading its rays across a new morning sky.

He was afraid of the power Elizabeth would have over him if he admitted anything he felt for her came close to being spelled l-o-v-e. If Vanessa had hurt him, Elizabeth's ability to wound him would be enough to send him to his knees.

But dammit. He did love Elizabeth. And it was because she was the antithesis of Vanessa. She was caring, sweet, vulnerable.

His family thought he was the bad guy, but the truth was, he hadn't been able to put Elizabeth out of his mind. His thoughts had an alarming tendency to drift off during conference calls at work, meetings with clients—in fact, just about anywhere.

He supposed he had no choice now but to wait for her response to his proposal. It was her move.

He could think of only one way to tip the odds in his favor. One way to obliterate what he'd said and make it her decision to marry him and have the baby be born a Whittaker…unpressured by his ownership of Donovan Construction and by his money.

He reached for the phone and dialed his lawyer.

He'd just finished the call when a booming voice from the reception area caught his attention.

Just what he needed. Another unexpected visitor. He was still recovering from Allison's "visit" that morning. When he got to the reception area, however, he came to a dead halt.

It had been a few years, but he still recognized the burly Irishman.

Elizabeth's father. Great timing.

"Mr. Donovan." He made his tone respectful.

Patrick Donovan turned from Celine and raised bushy eyebrows. Although Quentin had the height advantage by a good two inches in his estimate, the older man was still able to look him in the eyes.

"Now, now, lad. We're practically family. I'll have none of that Mr. Donovan stuff. It's Patrick."

"Er—Patrick then."

Elizabeth's father nodded toward Celine, who'd risen from her desk chair. "I was just tellin' this beautiful lady that I was here to see you but I didn't have an appointment."

At the word "beautiful," Quentin watched in fascination as a shade of pink stained Celine's cheeks.

Well, well. Looked like his longtime secretary might have met her match in the charm department.

Quentin gestured behind him to his office. "You don't need an appointment," he said smoothly. "Come on in."

"Don't mind if I do."

"Celine, hold my calls."

She nodded. "Of course."

Patrick preceded him into his office and Quentin

walked to the minibar set up in an alcove. "It's early, but can I get you anything?" He felt like a scotch himself.

Patrick settled himself in a leather chair at right angles to the couch. "Scotch. On the rocks. It's early but not early enough."

Quentin poured scotch into two glasses and handed one to Patrick. "I'm going to guess that Elizabeth doesn't know you've come to see me."

"And you'd be right." They both downed some scotch. "Always knew you were a quick study."

Quentin leaned forward and rested his elbows on his knees, nursing his glass between two hands. "What did she tell you?" he asked, testing.

"Just that she'd finally broken the news about the baby to you."

So his marriage proposal hadn't reached Patrick's ears. He figured she wouldn't tell her father until her mind was made up. No use raising false hopes.

"Can't say I was happy to hear my daughter was pregnant out of wedlock."

Quentin nodded, wondering if Elizabeth had ever told her father about her medical condition. The answer appeared to be no, so he just kept silent. Heck, even her medical condition didn't explain why *he* was the one who'd impregnated her.

"What's done is done, however." A smile suddenly creased Patrick's face. "And a grandbaby is a grandbaby."

Quentin sipped the scotch. Well, at least he had Patrick's approval in one direction.

"Mind you, I won't see Liz hurt. But I've got a feeling that you two will work out your problems."

Quentin wished he were that optimistic. He cleared his throat. "Has she said anything to you about Donovan Construction?"

Patrick's brows snapped together. "Yes, breathing fire and brimstone last time I talked to her about it."

Quentin grimaced.

"'Course I was pleased as punch about that part at least." Patrick's brows lifted. "Bringing the company back into the family, so to speak." The older man leaned forward suddenly. "You would pass on Donovan Construction to the baby, wouldn't you?"

"It's part of the baby's heritage as far as I'm concerned. I wouldn't sell it." He paused. "Whether Elizabeth accepts my marriage proposal or not."

Patrick sat back, satisfied. "Glad we see eye to eye."

And Quentin was beginning to see even more. And to understand just why Elizabeth had been so angry about the whole Donovan Construction business. Her father obviously saw the company as an added little dividend to becoming a grandfather.

He cleared his throat. He had to tread carefully here. "She wants to be respected for her accomplishments, not for whom she married." If she agreed to marry him, that was, he added silently.

"'Course she wants to be respected for her accomplishments," Patrick said, calling him back from his thoughts. "Worked damned hard to start that business of hers." Patrick swirled the golden liquid in his glass.

Quentin thought about the question he wanted to

ask, then decided to go ahead and ask it. "Why did you sell Donovan Construction, if I can ask?"

Patrick sighed and settled back in the chair. "Construction's a tough business and it's gotten harder for the little guys to stay afloat. When I retired, selling seemed like the right move. The business had a better chance of surviving as part of a bigger company. Figured I was making the right decision for most of the employees, saving their jobs in the long haul."

"You never considered having Elizabeth run the company?"

Patrick's frowned. "Good God, no!" The fingers of one hand drummed on the arm of his chair. "Why in the world would she have wanted to get involved in a down-and-dirty business like construction? 'Sides, she was building a nice career for herself in architecture."

"Maybe because there was a little company with the name 'Donovan' stuck on it." Quentin took a sip of his scotch and regarded the older man steadily over the rim of the glass. He was treading on dangerous territory, but he knew he needed some answers if he was ever going to build a lasting relationship with Elizabeth.

Patrick was silent for a minute, digesting the information he'd been given. "Would have been a fool's errand, in any case. As I said, the company wasn't viable on its own in the long run. Not the way the construction business was going."

Quentin nodded in agreement. "Did you ever talk to Elizabeth about your motivation for selling?"

Patrick sighed. "No, I don't think I ever did. I

guess I should have." Gazing out the window, he added, "Wouldn't have wanted her to get any silly notion that I was selling because I didn't trust her."

Quentin gazed out the window, too, relieved that he'd gotten his point across. "The thing is, Elizabeth does have a head for business, she's driven and she's got a vision of what she wants."

"That she does," Patrick concurred, a note of pride in his voice.

"Why don't you tell her that sometime?" Quentin met Patrick's eyes, green like Elizabeth's only without the golden touches. "Even the best of us need to hear the words occasionally."

Patrick paused a moment, considering, then nodded slowly. "I will. That I will," he said gruffly.

Attempting to lighten the mood, Quentin chuckled and rubbed his chin. "You think the world is ready for Donovan-Whittaker offspring?"

Patrick slapped him on the back, tacitly acknowledging the newfound understanding between them. "I've wondered myself."

Liz spent a sleepless night tossing and turning. As soon as she seemed to drift off, her dreams were of Quentin. Quentin asking her to marry him. Quentin making love to her. Quentin amused, irritated, annoyed.

She got out of bed at seven, and noted that her face showed her sleeplessness. She looked bleary-eyed, and worse.

She padded around in her robe and nightie, fixing herself eggs, toast and juice. God, she missed her morning cup of coffee. But she'd sworn off caffeine the minute she'd discovered she was pregnant.

Once she had a food-laden tray, she moved to the living room. She placed the tray on the coffee table and eased herself onto the couch to watch the morning news.

Quentin had not called. It had been three days. Isn't that what she wanted though? Still some small part of her, she guessed, had wanted him to continue pursuing her, refusing to take no for an answer.

At noon, the phone rang when she was going through some antique auction catalogs.

Her first thought was: Quentin! Then she felt irritated for the way her pulse raced. Even if it was him, she needed to remain calm and collected.

In fact, it wasn't Quentin, but his lawyer.

"Ms. Donovan," the attorney intoned, "I spoke with Mr. Whittaker this morning and he requested I call you regarding the terms of your, ah, financial agreement."

Her hand tightened on the receiver. "Yes."

"Mr. Whittaker has authorized me to transfer all of his shares in Samtech Industries to your name. Are you agreeable to such an arrangement, Ms. Donovan?"

Her world spun around and her hands felt clammy. "Yes," she managed, fighting to keep her composure. What had Quentin done?

"Good. I'll finalize all the paperwork for the transfer of shares and I'll contact you at the end of the week when the documents are ready to sign." The lawyer ended the call with a final word about information he'd need from her.

Liz replaced the receiver in a daze. Quentin had decided to hand Donovan Construction over to her. And in the process, she realized, he'd gotten rid of her fear that by accepting his marriage proposal she'd be playing into her father's hands.

But why?

Even for a man intent on taking financial responsibility for fathering a baby, it was a generous gesture.

Unless he didn't do it just for the baby, her heart whispered. There was no stipulation that she'd hold the company shares in trust for their child.

It almost sounded like one of those grand gestures only a man blinded by love would make. A man intent on proving to the woman he loved that he trusted her, that she had nothing to prove except to herself.

Could it be?

She realized how big a leap it was for him to trust a woman after having been treated so shabbily by Vanessa. She pressed shaky fingers to her lips.

He'd confessed to wanting her. Feeling an unwanted attraction from the time he'd first met her. She desperately wanted to believe....

Yet, if she loved him, wasn't he worth fighting for? He might not love her. But at least she was sure he wanted her, and if Allison was right, they were on to something that could become deeper and more lasting...with her help.

She looked at the clock and then picked up the phone. For her plan to work, she'd need Allison's help. This time, she had her own proposition to offer Quentin.

# Eleven

**S**hortly before seven o'clock the next night, the scene was set for seduction. Mouth-watering aromas wafted from Liz's kitchen to where she stood in the living room. The roast was in the oven, along with baked new potatoes lightly seasoned. Squash, fresh rolls and, her specialty, chocolate cake with mocha icing, rounded out the meal.

She held a match to the last candle, the one on the mantle. Candlelight always set the right romantic mood.

Blowing out the match, she turned to survey the scene. She'd moved her grandmother's antique table, just large enough for two, into the center of the room. An heirloom lace tablecloth graced the table, which was also set with heirloom china, crystal, and silverware.

Fortunately, her father had announced yesterday afternoon that he was going to pay an overnight visit to a friend of his in nearby New Hampshire and wouldn't be returning until tomorrow night.

He'd returned yesterday from his morning errands in an unexpectedly jovial mood, answering her questions with "that's wonderful, sweet pea" or "whatever you like, Lizzie, honey." Her suspicions had been raised, of course, but she hadn't gotten anything out of him.

Well, if tonight went as she'd hoped, her father would have something to be happy about. Somehow that thought didn't bother her. So what if her father unexpectedly got what he wanted? She'd have Quentin.

She passed over to the mirror above the side table to check her appearance one last time. She'd bought the black lace negligee and matching filmy robe with Quentin's reaction in mind. If his past reactions to her lingerie were anything to judge by, she was right on target with the armor she'd chosen for battle.

She stared critically at the face that looked back at her. Her hair curled past her shoulders and framed a face currently dominated by wide, anxious green eyes. At least her lips still appeared perfectly lined in a shade of wine.

All in all not bad, she decided, but she'd better cut the anxious look. If Allison had done what she said she would, Quentin would be here any minute.

Right on time, the doorbell rang. Liz sent up a silent prayer as she walked to the door on unsteady legs.

Quentin looked dumbfounded for a second when

she opened the door. Then his gaze flicked over her, a hot intense look in eyes that seemed to heat wherever they landed. Finally, he extinguished the twin flames, and his mouth set into a hard, thin line.

"Allison wanted me to stop by on the way home from the office. Said you had some books for her." His eyes narrowed. "But I see this is a bad time."

Bad time?

One second she was flustered and feeling the flush to the roots of her hair, the next she was confused. Then it dawned on her that he didn't realize she was waiting for...him!

Quentin continued to glower at her belligerently, yet words of explanation wouldn't come and she found herself moving aside and saying simply, "Come in. I'll get the books for you."

Once she closed the door, the little entryway seemed dominated by his presence. She was also mortified to discover that the cool evening air had caused her nipples to pucker and jut through the thin silk she was wearing. She felt his gaze like a brand.

"Lead the way," he said, his voice sounding a little strained.

She turned and went toward the living room, her mind racing, all the while aware of his deliberate tread directly behind her. Why did she feel like he was ready to pounce?

When he spotted the cozy little table illuminated by candlelight, he said coolly, "You're expecting someone."

"Er—yes. Yes, I am." Her voice sounded breathless to her own ears.

"Not Lazarus." He made the words nearly a challenge.

She almost laughed. That the thought would even enter his head gave a little boost to her confidence. He showed all signs of being jealous. "No, not him."

"Not that it's any of my business," he said, seemingly biting out the words with effort, "but is it anyone I know?"

"Yes, you know him. Quite well in fact."

A muscle worked in his jaw. "Can't be Matt or Noah. They know I'd kill them," he muttered, almost musing out loud.

Really, she'd have to thank Allison later. Whatever Allison had said, it was clear she'd led Quentin to believe he wasn't the man Liz was expecting to ring her doorbell. In the process, Allison had given her a much needed boost of confidence. "I can't believe you'd do bodily harm to either of them."

"You're evading the question."

"Who do you think it is, Quentin?" she said softly, her heart flipping over.

Their eyes met and she knew the love she felt was shining through her eyes.

"I know who I want it to be, dammit." In two strides, he reached her, enveloping her in his arms as his mouth descended.

She kissed him back, putting her soul into it, even as the tears slipped from beneath her lashes.

"God, sweetheart, don't." He cupped her face and caught the tears with his lips. "Don't cry. I'm not worth it."

His tenderness just made the tears flow faster. He

kissed her cheeks, her eyes, and made forays back to her mouth in between. "Elizabeth."

"You g-gave me the s-stock," she sobbed.

He cupped her face. "That's why you're crying?" He gave her a lopsided smile. "Honey, I'll give you whatever you want. Name your terms."

He looked so sweet and endearing, she blurted, "I want you. I want you to love me. To love our baby."

He stood stock-still as if she'd hit him over the head.

"I love you," she whispered.

He grinned suddenly and then leaned his forehead against hers. "You've got me. All of me. Heart, stock and barrel." He drew back and wiggled his eyebrows suggestively.

Her laugh came out as a hiccup. "That's an awful pun."

He gave her a soft kiss. "I love you."

Now it was her turn to look shocked. "You— No, that's not possible."

He chuckled. "Why not?"

"You said you were done with that romantic love stuff, that it was much better to treat the whole thing like a business proposition."

He tucked a loose strand of hair behind her ear. "So I did. I was an idiot. You broadsided me, sweetheart. I had it all figured out, and you came along and scrambled the whole puzzle again. By the time I'd sorted it all out, the pieces were in different places and the picture looked a lot different."

He looked suddenly sheepish. "And maybe I was

just feeding you a line that sounded good because I was desperate.''

''Desperate?'' she echoed.

''Yeah, desperate to stop you from going ahead with the whole sperm bank idea while I had time to figure out why it kept mattering more and more to me what you did.''

His words sent a thrill through her, but she couldn't help asking, ''What about Vanessa?''

''What about her?'' His brows drew together. ''She bruised my ego, and, yeah, I got very cynical about women for a while. But I realized that what I felt for her wasn't nearly as strong as the feelings I had for you.''

''You so much as talked with that idiot Lazarus—'' Liz tried hard to hide a smile ''—and I got jealous. Not to mention hitting the roof when I found you having dinner with Noah—'' He broke off at her smile and shook his head ruefully.

''You really thought Noah and I...''

''Yeah, I was really far gone.'' He sobered then and said, ''I should have told you about Donovan Construction—''

She placed a finger on his lips to silence him. ''I don't want the stock. I realized after your lawyer called that the company wasn't nearly as important to me as you are.''

He nodded. ''I didn't want you to think you couldn't marry me because I owned the damned company.''

''Yes,'' she said softly, ''I know and that meant the

world to me. You also made me realize that I had nothing to prove."

His eyes glittered and then he smiled. "I'm glad you recognize that. You're an entrepreneur, Elizabeth. Don't ever doubt it."

"I cried when your attorney told me about the stock."

He frowned and shook his head. "I didn't think the reaction would be tears. I guess I'll never understand women."

He really was a sweetheart! Not to mention being devastatingly attractive and the father of her unborn child. How lucky could one woman get? "Don't worry. I intend to spend a lifetime giving you lessons."

She was rewarded with a quick grin. "Oh, yeah?" he said, his voice dropping an octave. "I think I'm ready for the first one." He swept her up in his arms and she had no choice but to link her arms around his neck as he headed for the stairs to the bedroom upstairs.

"The roast—" she protested.

"—can wait."

A wave of heat swept through her. He was carrying her up the stairs and she made one last attempt to explain. "I cried when your lawyer called because your giving the company stock to me made me hope that you cared and not just about the baby. Then I realized I loved you so much, the company didn't matter. What I wanted was you. That's when I decided to seduce you tonight."

"Thank God for that!" He looked down at her appreciatively as they entered her bedroom. "I promise to be willing and eager prey," he add huskily.

He took off his suit jacket and tie and then came down on top of her on the bed, nuzzling her neck, his hand stroking up her thigh.

"Who's supposed to be seducing whom?" she asked breathlessly.

"Ah, Elizabeth. I can't keep my hands off you."

She laughed helplessly. "That's what got us into this situation to begin with, if I recall. The fact that we both couldn't keep our hands off each other."

He moved her filmy robe aside so he could kiss a shoulder. "Mmm." His lips trailed up the side of her neck and she turned her head to give him better access. "Let's take it slow and make it last this time."

His lips moved to her mouth and gave her little nibbling kisses. When his hand moved up to cup her breast intimately, her eyes fluttered shut as she let herself delight in the feel of his hand kneading her soft flesh. "Ah—" she swallowed a gasp as his thumb traced over her nipple "—I'm a little more sensitive now."

He lifted his head, and his eyes, already smoky gray with arousal, met hers. "Yes, I can tell." He paused. "Could you take my mouth on you?"

The question and the image it evoked was so erotic, she shivered and her already distended nipples jutted even more prominently beneath her negligee, as if asking for him to do what he had only voiced till now.

"Oh, please, yes."

He smiled, seemingly pleased at her enthusiasm, and slowly moved his hand over her shoulder and down her forearm, taking the thin negligee strap with him and exposing her breast to his hot gaze. "You're getting more assertive. I just hope that I can keep up with you—both in bed and out."

"Or die trying," she teased, echoing his words when he proposed that they enter into a business arrangement to get her pregnant.

"Or die trying," he murmured, his eyes never leaving hers as his head descended and his lips closed over one nipple. His tongue swirled around the peak and then began a steady sucking motion that had her hips rising off the bed as delicious sensations rippled through her.

His hand moved up her thigh to inch the bottom of her negligee farther up. She felt his erection pressing against her and moaned softly. When he lifted his mouth from her, she lowered the strap of the negligee that had remained in place so his lips could find her other breast.

His hand sought the spot between her thighs and she moved her legs apart to afford him access, sighing when he cupped her and began moving his palm in slow circular motions against her warmth.

She pulled his shirt from the waistband of his trousers and moved her hands beneath it to caress his back. His hand against her moist heat was fanning the flames inside her.

It was time, she decided, to give as good as she got.

And with that thought, she moved her leg against the bulge in his trousers, stroking him through the fabric until he lifted his mouth from her and groaned.

"You know, for someone with only a couple of sexual experiences, you really know how to pack a punch!"

She looked down at herself and then at him. "You're wearing too many clothes," she teased.

"That's easily remedied." Standing up next to the bed, he undid the buttons of his shirt and took it off, then raised his arms and lifted his undershirt over his head, tossing it on the floor to meet his shirt.

When he started on his belt, she stopped him. "Let me." She wanted to undress him, to peel away the layers, as she'd spent years longing to do.

He let her undo the belt and lower the zipper of his suit pants before he stepped out of the trousers, kicking off his shoes and socks in the process. When he pulled her up against him and gave her a soul-searing kiss, she twined her arms around his neck and gave herself up to it, glorying in a dream come true.

When they finally came up for air, he groaned, "God, sweetheart, I've got to have you."

The words sent tingles along her nerve endings. They both had the power to affect each other deeply, but, she realized, she trusted him in a bone-deep, instinctive way.

Lifting her negligee over her head, she tossed it on the floor to meet his shirt. "I love you, Quentin," she said throatily. She skimmed her fingers over his chest and down his forearms, emboldened by the power he had infused her with. "And I'm going to show you how much."

Her hand rubbed against his erection, stroking him through his boxer shorts, before she divested him of his last piece of clothing and caressed him with her bare hand.

His eyes closed and his breath hissed between his teeth. "I don't know how much more 'showing' I can take...." he warned.

She laughed softly. Would she ever have imagined even a few months ago that she'd literally have Quentin in the palm of her hand?

His eyes opened. "What's so funny?" he said roughly.

When she shared with him what she'd been thinking, he pretended annoyance. "Oh, yeah?"

"I was just teas—oh!" Her sentence ended in a gasp as he tumbled her to the bed.

His hands made short work of the black silk panties she wore, and then he was trailing kisses down her body, between her breasts, and lower.

When he rose over her again, he muttered, "I can't wait, Elizabeth."

"Then don't," she whispered and drew him down to her, her legs opening so that his erection was hard against her. "Make love to me, Quentin."

"Lord, yes."

Quentin probed against her until he found her opening. Slowly he eased himself inside her, gritting his teeth against the urge to go faster. She was so tight and warm, he was having trouble not losing his mind.

Elizabeth's legs came around him and took him in the rest of the way, until he was buried in her warm wetness. "Oh, Quentin!"

Her sigh of pleasure was nearly his undoing, but he

forced himself to go slowly, sliding in and out of her steadily and deliberately.

She was everything he ever wanted, everything he ever needed, and he groaned with the effort to hold off his climax.

Liz rubbed her hands over the sheen of sweat that glistened on Quentin's skin. She breathed in his musky male scent, kissed his shoulder, and rubbed her breasts against his chest. He was making her almost mindless with need.

His eyes were shut, his jaw clenched, his breathing labored. She gripped his hips, sinking her fingers into his flanks, and urged him to go faster, her hips rising to meet his thrusts. The tension coiling within her was almost unbearable.

"Elizabeth, sweetheart, let me—"

Before he could finish, she found her release, unwinding against him and crying out.

Quentin felt his mind shutting down. Instinct took over as he drove himself into her until the world exploded. He collapsed against her, spent but replete.

"I love you," she whispered.

"Let's never stop saying it, sweetheart."

# Epilogue

"**H**ow the mighty have fallen." Noah Whittaker shook his head at the sight of Quentin pacing back and forth in the living room of his house, three-week-old Nicholas Patrick Whittaker snuggled on his shoulder, emitting periodic burps as if on cue from his father's gentle pats on the back.

Quentin troubled him with one quirked eyebrow and a sardonic smile. "You don't know what you're missing."

Noah grinned and nodded when the baby burped. "Right. Fortunately, I don't."

Quentin was getting used to his brother's teasing. These days nothing could puncture his sense of blissful contentment. Opening his heart to Elizabeth had been the best thing he'd ever done. And the birth of Nicholas had just cemented that happiness.

"Fortunately you don't what?" Allison asked as she entered the room followed by Elizabeth.

Noah lounged back on the sofa and pasted a beatific look on his face. "Er—fortunately I don't have a thing to do besides watch Quentin burp my fantastic brand-new nephew."

Allison looked skeptical, causing Quentin to hide a grin. He turned as Elizabeth reached for the baby, and they exchanged loving looks. Motherhood had left her glowing from within—helped along by a healthy dose of love from him, he liked to think. He gave her a quick kiss as he handed the baby over.

"Ugh," Noah grunted in good-natured disgust. "The resident love bunnies at it again. Don't you guys ever give it a rest? You'll be giving Junior here a brother or sister before he's crawl—"

Allison interrupted, "Watch it, pal. You never know when you'll be next."

Noah pretended to look offended. "You'd wish that—" he jerked a thumb at the picture of connubial bliss created by his brother, sister-in-law, and nephew "—on me?"

"I have the most *da-arling* friend," Allison said sweetly. "You'll love her, really you will."

Noah raked fingers through his hair. "I should have never become an accomplice to your plotting," he grumbled. "I should have known once you knocked off ol' Quent here, it would be just a matter of time before you got around to me."

Liz turned to her friend. "Well, I guess I do have to thank you for originally suggesting Quentin as a sperm donor, as crazy as the idea sounded at the time.''

Noah guffawed. ''That was the tip of the iceberg.''

Liz saw Allison's guilty look even as the suspicions started to creep in from the edges of her mind. ''What does Noah mean, Ally? Tip of the iceberg?''

Noah smirked from his position on the sofa, and started counting off on his fingers. ''Well, let's see. First, there was the plot to lure Quentin to the French bistro and make it seem like you and I were on a date.''

Allison glared at her brother, and Liz's jaw dropped open. ''You planned that?'' she asked Ally.

''Then there was the plan to throw you and Quentin together with weak excuses like having Quentin pick up cocktail party decorations for Allison from you,'' Noah went on with equanimity, obviously enjoying himself.

''Noah, you know you're going to pay for this, don't you?'' Ally asked in a voice coated with artificial sugar.

Liz swung to her husband. ''Did you know about all this?''

Quentin shrugged. ''I suspected some of it.'' Then added dryly, ''But I'm sure there are details of the master plan that I'll be finding out years from now.''

''Yeah,'' Noah agreed, ''and then there are details that not even Allison could have foreseen. I mean, who knew that Elizabeth's father and Celine would hit it off? Patrick's moving back to Carlyle and I doubt it's only to be closer to the baby. Those two will probably be heading off to the land of wedded bliss soon, and, Ally wasn't even trying to get *them* married!''

Allison finally threw up her hands. "Okay, okay. I'm guilty as sin. I admit it." She shrugged. "What are you going to do? Sue me?" With a sly glance from Liz to her brother, she added, "As far as I can tell there would be no damages awarded anyway." She glanced at little Nicholas dozing in Liz's arms. "Unless you think my darling pint-sized nephew is a bad outcome?"

Liz looked down at her now sleeping son and her heart swelled. She and Quentin had created this miracle together, a product of their love for each other, which continued to grow every day. She glanced up as Quentin slid his arm around her and knew he could read her answer—identical to his own—in the love in her eyes.

"No, Allison, this isn't a bad outcome at all. Thanks for helping us along a little," she said before raising her face for her husband's kiss.

\* \* \* \* \*

# *Celebrate 100 years of pure reading pleasure with Mills & Boon®*

To mark our centenary, each month we're publishing a special 100th Birthday Edition. These celebratory editions are packed with extra features and include a FREE bonus story.

Plus, you have the chance to enter a fabulous monthly prize draw. See 100th Birthday Edition books for details.

*Now that's worth celebrating!*

### September 2008

**Crazy about her Spanish Boss by Rebecca Winters**
Includes FREE bonus story
*Rafael's Convenient Proposal*

### November 2008

**The Rancher's Christmas Baby
by Cathy Gillen Thacker**
Includes FREE bonus story *Baby's First Christmas*

### December 2008

**One Magical Christmas by Carol Marinelli**
Includes FREE bonus story *Emergency at Bayside*

Look for Mills & Boon® 100th Birthday Editions at your favourite bookseller or visit
www.millsandboon.co.uk